WHOM THE GODS WOULD DESTROY . . .

GLAUCUS—His looks, wealth, and lineage made him welcome in the centers of power . . . in the beds of Pompeii's most desirable women. But the one woman he wanted could cost him his life.

IONE—Beautiful, sheltered, and pledged to the goddess Isis. Passion made her question if she was truly priestess or prisoner.

LYDON—Gladiator, champion of a thousand combats, he hid the secret that could doom him to certain death.

CLODIUS—Poet, master of words, love made him speechless and jealousy would make him a traitor.

JULIA—Raised in luxury, yet she would deny her father, her gods, her heritage, to embrace an outcast love.

ARBACES—High priest of Isis. His goddess had made him wealthy, powerful, and a master of deceit. Now he'd make himself master of Pompeii . . . even at the cost of a thousand lives!

DRIVEN BY BLIND AMBITION, GRASPING AT FORBIDDEN PLEASURES, THEY DANCED AT THE VOLCANO'S EDGE.

THE LAST DAYS OF POMPEII

THE
LAST DAYS
OF POMPEII

---

based upon
the television script
written by
Carmen Culver

novelization by
David Wind

A Dell Book

Published by
Dell Publishing Co., Inc.
1 Dag Hammarskjold Plaza
New York, New York 10017

This book is based on a David Gerber Production in association with Co-
lumbia Pictures Television and Centerpoint Productions, Inc. co-produced
by RAI-Radiotelevisione Italiana; David Gerber, Executive Producer;
Peter Hunt, Director.

Dell ® TM 681510, Dell Publishing Co., Inc.

ISBN: 0-440-14666-6

Printed in the United States of America

First printing—May 1984

PART
I

Chapter One

Only a trace of the moon remained as the first faint bands of dawn slowly chased the darkness from the sky above the port city of Pompeii. It was that time of special quiet, those moments before the golden sun rose to reveal the magnificent azure sky that joined together the sea, the city, and the mountain which towered over all.

Far beneath the surface of both sea and land, beneath the peacefulness of this new dawn, thousands of feet below, an ancient and restless force had begun to stir. There the peaceful glow of the sun was mocked by the fiery brilliance of rivers of molten lava, as they forged new pathways within the maze of ancient caverns. Steam and gases forged in this subterranean furnace occasionally broke free, their wispy, cloudlike vapors giving no hint of the power of the forces that shaped them, no indication, no warning of the danger they foretold.

The streets of Pompeii were silent, as if the stone and dirt were recovering from the revels of the previous night, dreading the day to come. Slowly the city's slaves began to open their eyes and raise themselves from their pallets.

The sky lightened further, as the silence was broken by the sound of wood against stone. The tattoo created a steady rhythm that rose above the bubbling sound of the waters that ran along the narrow gutters within the streets and carried the refuse of the city to the sea.

As the first pale colors of the dawn streaked the heavens, a young woman turned onto Mercury Street, her staff held in front of her, moving steadily from side to side, never silent as it told her where next to place her feet. Suspended from her left forearm was a basket filled with fresh flowers, picked while the moon still lit the sky, and still covered with glistening drops of dew. Towering behind her, its presence growing more powerful with the coming of day, was the magnificent mountain of Vesuvius, at whose base lay the flower beds from which the girl had just returned.

It was a scene of exquisite beauty, almost equaled by the beauty of the young flower girl, only now sixteen years old. Her blue-green eyes were sweet and innocent, and her golden hair was streaked with platinum—a loving gift of the sun. Yet what called attention to her was something far different. There was a look of sad pensiveness etched across her features, and a strange tilt to her head, sign to any who cared to notice that it was her ears and her staff that guided her along the street.

For Nydia, the magnificence of the marble-columned forum she was approaching would only be a special sound. For Pompeii it was the center of life, but it was recognized by her only through the memory of how many steps it took to cross, and by the familiar sounds of the shopkeepers she knew within the macellum.

While the blind slave girl threaded her way through the market area and the dawn finally captured the sky, the macellum came to life. Greengrocers and fishmongers set up their stalls, calling back and forth to each other in greeting, barely noticing Nydia, although it had been she who for several years seemed to signal the start of each day.

Nydia continued through the long forum, moving confidently past the high-windowed jail, with its crude messages scrawled on the walls.

From around the far corner of the jail came a dwarf, dressed in the traditional robes of a Greek. He carried a roll of paper, a small pastepot and brush, and a wooden stool. When he saw the blind slave girl, he paused, and a smile softened his overabundant face. "Good morning, Nydia. Your flowers are beautiful this day."

Stopping, Nydia's head turned in the direction of the voice.

"Are you not early, Philos?" she asked, pleased to hear her friend's voice.

"I do what I must to earn a few coppers," he replied as he set down the stool and unraveled the paper. "Today my art takes yet another form." He laughed in self-derision.

"Are you painting another sign? Of what today?" Nydia asked.

"Fifteen pairs of gladiators—fifteen!" he read in a loud voice.

"Oh," Nydia whispered, having momentarily forgotten about the spring games. Sighing, she smiled at Philos, and then continued toward the waterfront where she would sell her flowers. Behind her she heard Philos pause in his work to read aloud one of the poems scrawled upon the jail's wall: "Nothing can last forever; though the sun shine gold, it must plunge into the sea."

Nydia steeled herself as she turned into the very heart of the forum and crossed the large open rectangle, being careful to stay away from the area of disrepair caused by the most recent earthquake. Reaching the center of the forum, she paused when she sensed a group of people running in her direction. She heard the heavy breathing of men, and as they came close to her a deep, coarse laugh rang out. Someone tugged at her basket, and she pulled it toward her, instinctively knowing that someone had taken a bunch of flowers.

"For you, Melior," yelled the thief, a large, well-muscled gladiator whose voice Nydia recognized instantly as that of Sporus. The sound of running feet stopped, and Nydia waited for something further to happen.

Another gladiator, his long hair framing a youthfully strong and handsome face, gripped the thief's shoulder in a vise of steel. "Hold, Sporus," he ordered. The voice belonged to Lydon, champion gladiator of Pompeii. Moving with the natural grace of an athlete, he took the flowers from his fellow gladiator and returned them to Nydia's basket. He stood for a moment, gazing at her face.

Moving her hands over the surface of the dewy flowers, Nydia smiled, nodding her thanks to Lydon, but she did not

speak. She sensed his stare and waited for him to say
something. Before he could speak, however, another voice
cut through the air—a deep, gravelly voice she recognized as
that of Gar, the new German gladiator. Lydon returned Gar's
call with a wave of his well-muscled arm; then, without
speaking, he cast Nydia one more longing gaze and rejoined
the other men on their morning run.

Continuing on her way toward the docks, Nydia passed the
statue of Vespasian, Rome's emperor; around the base of the
statue a multitude of vendors had already set up their stalls
for a day of selling foods, jewelry, and tools.

Just as she reached Marine Street, a loud blast of trumpets
shattered the peacefulness of the morning. Stopping, she used
her staff to edge her way to a wall and the security it
afforded. She knew that the sounding of the trumpets meant
that she would have to wait for a procession to pass. Nydia
was soon pressed closer to the wall, and well to the back of
the crowd of people straining to see the colorful parade. She
heard a familiar voice but realized it was too far away, so she
leaned back to await the passing of the procession while she
used her ears to learn everything she could.

Several feet away from Nydia stood the beautiful woman
whose voice Nydia had recognized. Chloe was still dressed in
the colorful and revealing blue robes she had worn through
the night. Her dark, glistening curls were piled high, accenting her large blue eyes and vibrantly sensual mouth. The
beauty of her face was not obscured by its overabundant
painting, and although her stance, clothing, and makeup were
marks of her trade, none found her offensive, because Chloe
was dressed only as her profession required, and in the streets
of Pompeii a prostitute was as common a sight as that of a
soldier.

Rising on the balls of her feet, Chloe tried to get a glimpse
of the oncoming show while one of the vendors she knew
slightly spoke to her.

"Isis, indeed! A lot of foreign nonsense! Our old Roman
gods are good enough for me!" declared the food vendor as
his eyes fanned across Chloe's ample breasts, and he winked

knowingly. "But the procession does bring the people out. Good business for us both—yes, Chloe?"

Rather than answer him she turned back to the parade, gasping at the splendor of what she saw. Indeed it was a fabulous show that the cult of Isis was giving the people. First came a troop of little girls dressed in flowing white robes, their only decoration the floral garlands in their hair. While the girls on the outside and in the front scattered herbs and flower petals, the girls in the center kept time with stringed sistras, dancing in rhythm to their own music.

Following them were the young neophytes, also dressed in white robes of Egyptian design. On the head of each rested a band of gold shaped in the likeness of a cobra poised to strike. In the center of the neophytes, carried by four of the priests, was a litter holding a caged bear, resplendent in a wide collar of gold shining against the wealth of its dark fur. The bear gazed out at the crowd, examining the people with bored disdain.

Behind that litter came yet another, carried by more white-robed men. In this one sat an ape, dressed in saffron silks and looking like nothing less than an emperor.

Chloe shook her head in wonder at what she saw. Following the ape was an old man with a long white beard leading a donkey adorned with golden wings. The sound of pipes and flutes stirred the air as a young girl led two Egyptian ibix on golden chains. As the birds passed, a cry rose from the people who lined the street. "Isis! Isis! Isis!" they shouted, their voices threatening to drown out the music itself as the center of the procession came into view.

Twenty priestesses, dressed in white, with cobra headbands holding flowing white veils, led an open litter.

"Ione," whispered the vendor into Chloe's ear when the beautiful young priestess came into view.

Ione sat regally, her long hair lifted by the breeze, unencumbered by the flowers woven through it, its darkness accented by a sheer, white veil. In the middle of her forehead was a small round mirror enclosed by serpents rising along both sides. Her robes of gold and crimson were partially

covered by a flowing black cloak embellished with silver
stars and crescents. When Ione passed the spot where Chloe
stood, a lance of sunlight was reflected from the golden sistra
Ione held aloft. The curved instrument cried out with a
strange sound when she shook it toward the crowd. In her
other hand she held a golden cup shaped like a boat. Her
patrician face was calm, distant and detached, yet in her
innocent beauty she radiated a power recognized by both men
and women within the crowd.

Chloe gazed at the noble-born priestess, suddenly sad that
fortune had treated her so differently. To have been born free,
to not be owned by someone, and to not have to let men paw
her body for a few coppers—these were things she could only
dream about.

As the litter bearing Ione passed by, music rang out again,
and more priests of Isis emerged onto the street, these dressed
in tight ceremonial robes that left one shoulder bare. In their
hands they cradled ceremonial bowls, again of Egyptian design.

Golden palm leaves waved, and peacock feathers of every
hue were illuminated by the sun as the priests of Isis walked
on. A white cow, crowned with a large garland, was led by a
priest holding a golden lead. Behind them came yet another
priest with a large, jeweled-skin snake slithering along his
arm, its tongue darting out at the crowd.

Then there was a break in the procession, a space of
several yards before the next man appeared: Calenus, wearing
the robes of a high priest; Calenus of the oily skin and small,
beady eyes. He carried a golden coffer. Next to the overweight priest strode Antonius, a young man of seventeen.
The crowd sensed in him a strangeness; he possessed the
powerful, intense carriage and the deep-questing eyes of an
idealist who has found what he has searched for. His hair,
like the priestess Ione's, was full and flowing, and his bearing,
like hers, was proud and noble. There could be no doubt that
they were brother and sister.

Behind Antonius and Calenus came another rank of priests
in white robes. The crowd fell silent as the high priest of Isis
appeared, walking in a slow, dignified manner. He was called

Arbaces, and his dark skin, short-cropped hair, and closely kept beard drew attention to his handsome, Egyptian face. Although more than forty years old, his body was still lithe and firm. He was bared to the waist, and his stomach muscles rippled smoothly when he walked. Golden armlets of serpents wound around his upper arms, and a striking golden cobra coiled about his neck. His only garment was a saffron skirt that clung tightly to his hips, again accenting the lithe power of his body.

Arbaces walked proudly, his head held straight, his dark eyes fixed before him, never wavering, never looking at the crowd that lined the street. Everything about him proclaimed his rank. As he passed, many in the crowd cheered and cried for the glory of Isis. Others shook their heads sadly and turned back to their work.

Sensing that the procession had ended, Nydia took a deep breath and with her staff sounding the way once again began her trek to the waterfront. She had many flowers to sell, for her mistress, Stratonice, wife of Burbo the tavern keeper, would expect the money before the morning was gone.

The waterfront was alive with people. Some ships were docking, while others sat heavy in the water, loaded with the goods of Pompeii, ready to cast off their lines and venture out.

Glaucus, a young Greek nobleman, stood in the prow of his small pleasure craft and watched the frantic scurrying before him. Once the scarlet sails of his ship had been reefed, twenty slaves rowed rhythmically toward the dock. He smiled at the sights before him, enjoying the play of the breeze as it tugged at the gold-embroidered robes he wore and swirled about his dark curly hair. His face, strong, handsome, and youthful, was complemented by the intensity of his pale blue eyes.

Pompeii held many memories for Glaucus—pleasant and passionate memories of summers past. Yet as he stood in the prow of his ship, he knew that this summer would be different. The restlessness which had been so much a part of him since leaving Rome could not be denied. A sense that his life was changing was strong within him, but how it would change he could not even venture to guess. His life had always been one of ease. His wealth allowed him the assurance that he would never have to do anything he chose not to do. But of late, Glaucus had become dissatisfied with everything.

Lifting his head, he gazed at the imposing vista of Vesuvius. Its high peak rose proudly toward the heavens, and Glaucus realized how much he had missed Pompeii, his summer home.

Behind him his captain shouted orders and the rowers heaved the oars into the ship, while other slaves secured the ropes cast to them from the dock.

Glaucus shifted to look at the merchant ship on the left, and saw its captain lean outward to speak to another person on the dock. Smiling, Glaucus saw Olinthus, the sailmaker, wave to him before he replied to the captain of the merchant ship. Returning the wave, he rested on the railing and continued to watch the activities on the waterfront.

"It's a fine sail you've made for us, Olinthus," yelled the merchant ship's captain.

Olinthus, large and big-boned, nodded and smiled, his teeth flashing white through a bushy beard. He gave the captain a light bow. "And it's a fine day for a sail," he replied gravely.

"Then why the long face? Do you itch to be on the sea again? Come with us, my friend."

Olinthus shook his head, a sad look crossing his features, yet a sadness denied by the sparkle in his eyes. "No, I'm landlocked for life, and content to be so."

The captain of the merchant ship straightened and looked past Olinthus. He shook his head and laughed, pointing to a group behind the sailmaker. "More contentment than those poor bastards, anyway," he offered.

Even as Olinthus turned, Glaucus' eyes followed the captain's pointing finger to a ragtag group of men, women, and children being herded by guards. Glaucus saw the prisoners huddling together as they walked, trying to take comfort from each other even as the guards whipped them along.

Glaucus glanced at Olinthus and saw a pained expression on the sailmaker's face as the captain continued talking.

"Christians! By the gods! They're everywhere I go, spreading through the empire like a pox," said the captain, shrugging his shoulders at the helplessness of it all. He turned back to his ship, ignoring what was happening on the dock.

But Glaucus could not turn away from the scene. He sensed a change in the air, a difference from last summer. There was a tinge of danger, and also an overpowering sadness. In that instant, Glaucus knew that his youth was about to end, that he would soon be facing the next step in his life. But those thoughts were wiped from his mind when the coarse voice of one of the guards—Drusus by name, he recalled from last summer—began to prod a fallen Christian. "On your feet, damn you!" he ordered. An old man tried to rise in obedience to the order, but the strength left his arms, and he fell again to the ground.

"Get up!" Drusus shouted. His heavily muscled arm, covered by brass armplates, rose threateningly, coiling the whip backward like a snake about to strike. Suddenly his arm was stopped by a large, strong hand.

"Let him be," Olinthus said in a low voice.

Still cowering on the cobblestones, the old man stared up at his benefactor, his eyes widening with a new fear. "Olinthus," he pleaded. "No . . . ."

Spinning, Drusus pulled free of Olinthus' grip and quickly unleashed the whip. The crack of leather striking flesh was loud on the dock, but Olinthus held himself straight, his arms now at his sides.

Drusus laughed sarcastically when he drew back the whip once again. "Turn the other cheek, Christian lover," he spat to the sailmaker. "Or perhaps you'd rather join this lot?"

Olinthus silently wiped the blood from his cheek as Drusus turned his attention again to the hapless Christians, prodding them along once more.

Glaucus had observed the whole episode with a strange sense of detachment. The same feeling had been a part of him for many months now, and he had hoped that here in Pompeii his apathy would leave him. But he had yet to put a foot upon the dock, and already he knew his wish was not to be fulfilled.

Then he heard the sailors on the merchant ship begin to shout out the name of Isis as they lined the railing. Glaucus turned and witnessed a strange procession wind toward the ship, past the Christian prisoners.

Following in the wake of the cult of Isis came three richly adorned litters, each borne by two slaves. In the lead was the merchant Diomed, the most important merchant in Pompeii. His wife Lucretia was in the second litter, and his daughter Julia in the third. Their progress was slow, impeded by the crowds, and Diomed, sitting on the uncomfortable litter seat, was growing impatient. *After all*, he thought, *is it not my ship that's being blessed by the high priest?*

Diomed shook his round, fleshy head impatiently as he stared at the people on the waterfront. He was the wealthiest man in Pompeii, and he cared not that he had made his fortune from fish sauce. It did not matter what people said of him, since he knew they were only envious. All that mattered were his coffers filled with gold. The only thing he cared about was his money. And the acceptance of his family by Pompeii's nobles—a feat he was forever trying to achieve.

"Faster!" he ordered the slaves bearing his ponderous weight. They were just a little short of their destination now and Diomed could see the tall masts of his ship.

The front slave, Medon, who was not a litter bearer but rather the household slave, had been drafted because of the sickness of another, and was unused to this heavy labor. Under the weight of his fat master, Medon's breathing was forced and he felt his legs becoming heavy like stone, but he willed himself to obedience and pushed onward. It was only when they passed the band of Christian prisoners being herded by Drusus that Medon lost his concentration and stumbled. A cry of pain tore from his throat as the handle of the litter landed across his calves, pinning him to the ground.

Diomed, thrown rudely about, landed on the ground in

much the same position he had ridden, squarely on his large buttocks. "You idiot!" he screamed, his face turning a mottled shade of red. "How dare you!"

Petrus, the slave who had supported the rear of the litter, bent over the older slave, trying to suppress his rage at his master. With one hand he lifted the litter's pole and with the other helped Medon to his feet. His hand tightened reassuringly on Medon's arm at the look of fear the older slave cast at his master.

"Come, Medon," Petrus whispered, but Medon stood still as he stared at Diomed.

"Forgive me, master," he pleaded.

Seeing the accident, the women in the following litters had gotten down and come forward. Lucretia, Diomed's wife, stopped next to Julia, their daughter. Both were dressed flamboyantly, each showing an equal lack of breeding and taste. Not until one looked at both their painted faces, and saw the twenty-year difference between mother and daughter would one know who had learned from whom. And on close inspection, ignoring the garishness of her dress, the gaudiness of her jewelry, the outrageousness of her orange-hennaed hair and overpainted face, one could also see a soft and true beauty lurking beneath the layers of cosmetics coating Julia's face.

After darting several embarrassed glances at the milling crowd, Julia turned to her father. "Oh, Daddy, get up! You look like a fool!"

"I will not be spoken to like that," Diomed declared as he forced his bulk up. Then he turned to Medon, staring at the slave with open anger. "And you! I . . ." But he stopped, unable to find the exact words he wanted—a problem he had always had. Then he shrugged resignedly. "Remind me to sell you," he finished.

"Yes, master," Medon replied. He knew he had been saved, for Diomed would not sell him. There was a very important reason for that. Very important.

With Julia on one side and Lucretia on the other, Diomed

walked toward his ship and the members of the cult who awaited. "Worthless old goat," he grumbled a moment later.

Petrus and Medon stared at their retreating backs; Petrus placed a calming hand on Medon's arm. "Are you all right?" he asked.

Before the older slave could reply, Olinthus, the sailmaker, approached them, blood still oozing from his torn cheek.

"Olinthus," called Petrus in a low voice as he saw the wound. "What happened? Are you all right?"

Olinthus nodded toward the Christian prisoners, watching grimly until they disappeared around a corner. "I fare better than our loved ones who will die today. Oh, Petrus, I would gladly take their place."

"It would be more uselessly wasted blood," said Medon who reached out to clasp Olinthus' shoulder.

Olinthus snapped his head up and stared at Medon. "Not wasted! For each of us they kill, two will rise up to take his place!"

The three men gazed at each other knowingly, their expressions stern and accepting of their fate. Then they too turned to watch the ceremony that was about to begin.

From another street leading onto the waterfront came three young men of noble birth, drawn there by the sounds of music, as well as by their own boredom. The leader of the group suddenly stopped, and the two others did the same, their gazes following their leader's, which was focused upon Ione, the beautiful priestess of Isis.

"Isis! Isis! Isis!" shouted the man called Sallust.

Clodius shook his head sadly at his friend. Although the poorest of the three, he was the group's leader by dint of his more noble ancestry. "Sallust, would you worship at her feet?" he asked with a derisive laugh curling his lip into a sneer. "My own aspiration rises higher," he added, his eyes sweeping upwards to caress the lush curves of her body.

"And higher . . ." added Lepidus, the third of the trio.

"But only as high as hers, surely," Sallust interjected lewdly.

"Not so high as that," Clodius corrected his friend, "for she means to remain a virgin."

"Or to become one," Lepidus injected.

"For shame, Lepidus. To cast aspirations on such aspirations," Sallust enjoined.

"Which should inspire admiration," added Clodius, now fully into their game of semantics.

"Or assignation," came Lepidus' quick wit.

"Or fornication!" Clodius declared. "But come, let us see what Isis is blessing today!"

"And how much gold fills the cult's coffers from this deed of godliness," added Sallust.

They went forward, and as they did, Clodius' gaze again shifted until it settled upon Julia's back. He stared at her, a strange feeling coursing through his veins, a feeling he struggled to suppress, to deny with all the powers he could summon.

Julia turned suddenly, and he saw her eyes widen when they met his. Slowly, Clodius bowed low, sweeping his arm in a wide mock-courtly gesture as he winked at her, allowing his leer to surface once again.

His reward came when her face turned crimson and she stiffly turned her back to him. Shrugging, Clodius caught up with his two companions and settled down to watch the spectacle.

Julia, her breathing suddenly forced, refused to turn again after being treated so humiliatingly. *Why could he not give her the respect she so badly wanted. Did he not see how she felt? Was he so unfeeling?* she wondered. But Julia knew the answer, one she wished vainly she could deny: Clodius was nobly born. She was a common woman born to a merchant of fish sauce. Therefore nothing could ever come of what she felt for him—nothing.

Willing herself not to think of Clodius, she concentrated on what was happening around her, trying not to shrink from her mother's shrill voice.

"How beautiful," Lucretia cried out. "Oh, Diomed, I wish you had allowed me to join the procession!"

"No wife of mine will parade in the streets of Pompeii

with a crowd of religious lunatics. You've already given that scoundrel Arbaces half my estate as it is!''

"But, dear," Lucretia purred in silly, sweet tones, "Arbaces is blessing your ship. I thought you'd be pleased . . ."

"Oh really, Mother," Julia whispered sarcastically.

"Julia, you will show your mother some respect! Now, where is that captain? One would think that when I came to see my ship off, the captain could at least—"

"Later, please, dear. Arbaces is about to begin," cautioned Lucretia, her eyes rapt and attentive as they feasted on the dark-skinned body of the high priest who was making his way through the ranks of his cult members toward the ship.

Now the only sounds heard on the docks were the plaintive wails of the music from the cult. The people watching had all fallen silent as they waited for the ceremony to begin.

Glaucus, still standing in the prow of his ship, was reluctant to move, for his position provided him a rare view. He could see everything. As he scanned the crowds on the waterfront, he saw his old friends Clodius, Sallust, and Lepidus. They were barely ten feet from the ship, and although they hadn't yet seen him he knew they soon would.

His attention was caught by the magnetic presence of the high priest and he watched and listened intently as the man began his prayers.

"Mighty Isis! Goddess of man, ruler of the world," chanted Arbaces, his arms held wide, his face directed upward to the heavens. "Thy name and thy divinity are adored throughout the universe. We come to offer in thy name this new ship, as a first fruit of the flowering spring."

"Poetical, this Egyptian priest. You might take lessons from him, Clodius," Sallust whispered.

Clodius glared, his face suffused with anger, but he held back his anger. He knew the value of his poetry well enough.

Arbaces solemnly accepted an urn from Antonius, the young priest, and lifted it high in the air. Sunlight reflected from the gold and the small Egyptian figures upon it glinted into life, even as he prayed on.

While Arbaces' hypnotic voice resounded, Diomed sighed

heavily, bored by the religious patter and wanting only for his ship to cast off, so that his profit would come back the sooner. Shifting his bulk, Diomed turned and for the first time saw the smaller pleasure ship behind him. He looked up to see a figure on the prow, draped in the Greek robes of a nobleman.

Squinting against the sun, Diomed saw the handsome face and dark curls of Glaucus. Even as he watched the young man, he saw Glaucus turn and walk to the lower railing. There, with the gracefulness of the young, he sprang from the ship and landed easily on the dock, where he began to order his men to their tasks of unloading his belongings.

"Ah, he's back again for the summer," Diomed said to himself.

"What?" asked Julia.

"Young Glaucus," Diomed explained.

"The Greek," Julia said, not particularly interested in him, as her eyes strayed toward the group of three young noblemen, with Clodius at its center.

"We must speak to him, invite him to the villa."

"Flowers. Pretty flowers. Won't you buy some flowers," called Nydia as she walked along the dock, trying to sell her basket of beauty. When she was within two feet of Diomed and Julia, she paused.

"Father, we hardly know Glaucus. And, he's a noble."

"I know what he is," Diomed snapped. "Do you think we are not good enough for him? What with the money I've made?"

Nydia had frozen when she'd heard Glaucus' name mentioned. Drawing up her courage, she turned toward Julia. "Please, mistress . . ."

Julia glanced at Nydia, recognizing the girl. "No flowers today, Nydia," she said before turning back to Diomed. "Daddy, I wish you would stop your matchmaking."

But Nydia was not interested in selling her flowers; there was something more important. "Please, mistress, is Glaucus here?" she asked.

Puzzled by the slave's strange insistence, but unwilling to

take her eyes from her father, Julia answered her. "He's just arrived, but Nydia . . ." she began, finally turning to look at the girl, only to find her gone. Sighing, Julia focused her attention on her father. "Daddy—"

"No more. I think the time is right for you and young Glaucus," he said in a faraway voice.

Sighing again, Julia returned her attention to the ceremony.

Having had his fill of the ceremony, and becoming impatient to set up his house, Glaucus had jumped to the dock and begun ordering his men about. Once things were organized, he turned again to gaze at the crowd. As he did, Clodius turned also, and their eyes met for the first time.

"Sallust, look! Can it be Glaucus returned to us?" Clodius asked with a warm smile on his face.

"Glaucus!" called Sallust, grabbing Lepidus' arms and spinning him around while Glaucus walked toward them.

"The terrible trio!" he declared as he was engulfed by their arms and touched by their bodies. A moment later he drew back to look at his three friends. "As drunk as when I left you last summer."

"You came by sea?" Lepidus asked, glancing at the ship. "A curious way to travel from Rome."

"No, I came from Rome to Naples yesterday. I saw this wonderful ship there, and . . ."

"You couldn't resist," Sallust finished for him.

"And they say that money is the root of all evil," Clodius sighed.

"Not money, Clodius," Lepidus cut in. "The love of money."

"Then I'm in love!" Clodius declared.

"Poetry still isn't paying?" Glaucus asked.

Clodius drew his shoulders straighter to show the offense he felt. "I beg you to remember—"

"That you're a Roman, an aristocrat," Glaucus finished for him. "You don't work for filthy lucre."

"Nor for any other reason," Sallust said with a good-natured laugh.

Clodius ignored Sallust as his eyes stayed locked with Glaucus'. "What would you have me do? Hang my poems outside the book stall, to be pawed at by the sweaty hands of the vulgar?"

Glaucus' face changed, his features becoming stoic and contemplative. "Crueler than war is the soft and corrupting hand of luxury that maintains its iron grip."

"Oh, to be so corrupted," cried Clodius, raising his eyes toward the heavens.

"Tell me," asked Lepidus, "how goes it in Rome?"

Glaucus, still laughing at Clodius' clowning, shook his head slowly. "This Vespasian is a decent enough emperor, for a change. Perhaps because he's not a nobleman. But when he goes, as he will soon, we'll be left with his son Titus, who cares for nothing but the games."

As the three listened to Glaucus, Nydia, following the sound of his voice, made her way slowly to where the four men stood. Sensing a lull in their conversation, she called his name.

Glaucus turned at the call, and saw the young woman standing near him. He gazed uncertainly at her, his mind working quickly until her name surfaced. "Nydia, my little friend. Look at you, how you've grown."

"You've come back," she whispered, her words self-conscious in her ears, her face scarlet with discomfort.

"I have indeed," Glaucus replied. "And you must visit me. I can only imagine the state my garden must be in after all this time."

Nydia smiled shyly. "You shall see," she said as she took a flower from her basket and handed it to him. The instant she felt it taken from her hand, she turned and walked away.

Glaucus stared at the flower for a moment, and when he lifted his head to speak to Nydia, she was gone. Shrugging, he turned back to his friends, who were once again watching the ceremony.

He stared at the newest scene unfolding before his eyes, and suddenly his breath seemed caught as he watched the most beautiful woman he had ever seen being escorted from a litter and led toward the merchant ship.

Although a wispy veil was on her head, her dark, glistening hair flowed freely on the breeze. Her features were perfect, patrician and strong, and the beauty etched on her porcelain skin was breathtaking. He saw immense depths within the sapphire blue of her eyes, and the subtle sensuality of her mouth seemed to cry out to him. Her brightly colored robes and her black and silver cape were not able to hide the perfection of her body from his eyes.

"Who is she?" he asked in a husky voice. Never in his life had he been so affected by a woman, so strongly attracted—never.

Clodius turned at the question and then followed Glaucus' gaze. "Which one? Oh, in the ceremony. That is Ione."

"The divine Ione," added Sallust.

"You've never seen Ione before?" asked Lepidus incredulously. "No, of course not. She was living in the country until recently."

Clodius laughed suddenly, and the other three stared at him. "Yes," he declared expansively, "Glaucus is definitely back. Not three minutes off the boat and he's spotted his quarry for the summer season. And naturally, he chooses the richest woman in Pompeii!"

"And sad, is it not," said Sallust in mock solemnity. "The stars are crossed this day, Glaucus, for Ione has been taken."

"No!" Glaucus almost shouted the word. "By whom?"

This time there was no smile on Clodius' face when he spoke. "The cult of Isis is becoming very popular here, with both the nobles and the mob, especially since Arbaces became the high priest."

"In Rome as well . . . so long as the cultists pay homage to the emperor and the old gods," Glaucus said.

"Or so long as they appear to," Lepidus added acidly.

"Then Ione is a priestess?" Glaucus asked, his eyes still fixed on the beautiful woman standing now at the bow of the ship.

"Not yet, but she will be soon. Her vows of chastity have already been spoken," Clodius said.

"What is the good of a Venus if she be made of marble?" Glaucus asked sadly.

"Patience," counseled Clodius. "In these days a pure woman is one who has yet to be asked."

"I'm afraid you'll just have to settle for one of your many other ladies," said Sallust with a smile. "Let's see, there was Lucinda and Melinda and . . ."

"Jocasta and Lucasta," added Lepidus

"And—what was her name? The one with the gold-tipped"— Clodius held his hands a foot out from his chest in an evident and time-honored gesture—"ah . . . fingernails?"

Laughter rang out from the small group, but although he laughed, Glaucus' eyes never strayed from Ione as she stood before the ship, reciting a litany for the sea.

> There are waves like chargers that meet and glow,
> There are graves ready wrought in the rocks below.
> On the brow of the future the dangers lour;
> But blest be this bark in the fearful hour.

When she finished and stepped back, the sailors applauded her loudly and the sails were unfurled. A gust of wind blew in as on command and filled the sheets, and a great shout escaped outward from the crowded dock as Arbaces lifted a golden sword and cut the mooring ropes. The ship seemed to pause uncertainly for a moment, but then it moved and slowly made its way out toward the sea.

Glaucus watched it all, but the instant the ship moved his eyes returned to Ione's figure as it was engulfed by the others from the cult and she led back to her litter. *I will see you again*, he promised her silently.

He heard his name called, and before he turned to greet whoever it was, he saw a strange look flash across Clodius' face. Turning, he saw Diomed approaching him.

"Welcome, noble Glaucus," Diomed said with a bow from his oversized waist.

"Good heavens, have I become so august in so short a time?" he asked the merchant.

"Well done, Diomed, to manage a greeting without once referring to your notes," Clodius said sarcastically.

Diomed glared with open hatred at the young nobleman, but forced himself to gaze at Glaucus. "I saw you admiring my new ship."

"It's yours?" Glaucus asked with evident surprise.

Diomed almost preened before Glaucus. "Indeed it is. I've expanded my interest to exporting—wine, cloth, all the best that Pompeii has to offer."

"The goddess of fortune smiles upon you," Glaucus said benignly.

"I believe less in the deities than in the virtues of hard work, whose profits you see before you." Diomed paused for a moment to point to the outgoing ship. "We celebrate the launching tonight. A few friends, a humble meal; we should be honored if you would consent to grace it with your presence."

"I shall!" Glaucus stated, and then made a subtle motion with his arms to include his three friends.

"And your friends, of course," Diomed conceded with only the slightest hesitation. But after he had spoken, he favored Clodius with a withering look.

"Most kind," Clodius said as he met the merchant's eyes openly.

"We will be dining late tonight—the games, you know," Diomed said airily. "Are you attending? You must share my box. They've matched our champion, Lydon, with the Roman contender!" Diomed shook his head and laughed as he went on. "These Romans, they make sport of us provincials. But Lydon will carve up their favorite and serve him to the mob!"

"Thank you, no," Glaucus said when Diomed finally took a breath. The games were not to his liking—too much blood and needless butchery—but he knew his views were not shared by the majority.

"Daddy," Julia called as she joined the men, "we must go."

"Oh, yes," he said, glancing from Julia to Glaucus. "Well, then, until this evening."

Glaucus nodded to Diomed and accepted the deferential smile the merchant bestowed upon him. When the merchant and his daughter walked away, he saw Julia turn her head quickly to glance back at them. He noticed also as Clodius, the object of her attention, returned her gaze with a cruelly mocking smile.

"Careful, Glaucus, the fair Julia has designs . . ." said Sallust.

None of the men saw the quickly hidden surge of anger that had flashed across Clodius' face, especially Glaucus, who was staring at the now fading procession of the Isis cult.

"So have I," Glaucus whispered.

Far beneath the mortals who played, talked, made love, and carried on their usual business, the bowels of the earth continued to seethe. Red-gold lava twisted within the cavernous passages below Pompeii, seeking an exit. The giant plates—the very basis of the earth—shifted slowly, moving toward their destiny as surely as did the humans who as yet were so unaware of what was soon to happen.

Chapter Two

Several hours after the ceremony of Isis and the departing of Diomed's ship, the slave Medon finished the last of his errands. Before returning to Diomed's villa he went to the sailmaker's shop.

Olinthus and his shop were the spiritual center of Christianity in Pompeii. Although Olinthus himself was not a known Christian, he was a devout soul and a man of deep spiritual strength. Regular meetings were held in a secret room within his shop, and the prayers and hopes of the Christians were heard frequently within its confines.

Entering through the front door, Medon saw Olinthus working at his forge, hammering a glowing piece of metal shaped like a cross. With sweat sparkling on his massive chest, Olinthus bent the outer lengths of the cross, slowly forming them into the shape of an anchor.

Medon, watching his friend work, went to a vacant spot on the bench to wait for him to pause. Olinthus took one more swing with his hammer and put the anchor back into the furnace. When he turned to face Medon, his face was carved into angry lines. "I do not understand what God intends," he said with fury and pain in his voice.

Medon sighed, but when he spoke, his voice held no hint of shared frustration; rather, it was calm and gentle: "You understand that we know that God will send his son again."

"When? We've waited almost fifty years! Fifty years since he was crucified. God makes it hard! Our fellow Christians die today, served up as amusement for the mob. A spectacle of blood!" Turning, Olinthus vented his rage, not upon

Medon but upon the fire, as he picked up the old wood and leather bellows and began to fan the coals.

While the flames rose, casting orange shadows upon the walls, Medon tried to find the words to ease his friend's mind. But before he could speak, Olinthus turned back to him, his anger still ripe and strong.

"And other spectacles will surely come. Oh, Medon, we await that last day of judgment, when this old world and its rotting generations are consumed in fire. How vast the spectacle will be then!" Within his impassioned tones, something more than anger could be heard.

The door opened again, and both men turned to see a boy of ten enter the shop. The boy paused when he saw the rage on Olinthus' face, but then he walked quickly to him. Medon watched as the anger left Olinthus' face and he caught the boy in his arms and gazed gently into his eyes.

"But we must have faith, eh, Catus?" Olinthus asked their young messenger.

Catus smiled at the softening of Olinthus' voice. "Do we meet tonight?" he asked.

"No," Olinthus said quickly. "It's too dangerous. You should not have come here either."

Catus shrugged, and then wound his arms more tightly around the large man's waist.

Medon stood and started toward the door. "I must go. Diomed is holding a banquet after the games. I'm sure he's already driven the kitchen slaves to their wits' end."

Olinthus looked out the window. "Not that way, Medon— you'll be seen. Go the other way."

Medon went to a solid wall. At its center he paused to run his fingers along one seam. He pressed at a certain spot and a panel slid open to reveal a hidden passage. "God be with you," Olinthus whispered as Medon disappeared.

On the other side of Pompeii, far from Olinthus' shop, sat the villa of Diomed. It was every bit as pretentious as its owner, who had built it with the mistaken belief that money automatically created beauty.

The triclinium, the huge dining room that was the focal point of the villa, was as beautiful as Diomed's misguided efforts could make it. The subdued tones of a nobleman's dining room would not suffice; this was Diomed's pride, and the gaudy, undulating colors that enclosed the room were the best that money could buy. The floor was a colorful mosaic showing Triton surrounded by dolphins, octupi, and myriad other sea creatures. The walls, washed a brilliant ochre, were divided into uniform sections by half-round columns of the finest pink marble.

Centered within each section were magnificent frescos, each one individual in style and execution. Several long marble tables were surrounded by couches, which were now being draped by the slaves in anticipation of the evening's festivities.

Medon, after arriving through the slaves' entrance, came into the dining room to make sure that the preparations were going as they should. Petrus, the slave who had been with him earlier at the waterfront, glanced up and caught the older slave's eye.

Medon nodded, signaling to the other that they would talk later. Just then Diomed stormed into the dining room. "Where have you been?" he demanded of Medon.

"Doing as you instructed, master," Medon said with eyes downcast.

"Well, do better than that. Those cooks are worthless. I'll be shamed tonight before my guests. Make sure I am not," he yelled irrationally, "or believe me, not even Zeus himself can save you!"

"All will be as you wish, master," Medon stated.

Diomed was about to speak again, but Lucretia rushed into the triclinium with Julia only a step behind. "Diomed," she cried, "we'll be late for the games."

"Mother, please calm down," Julia cautioned.

"And don't forget to count the silver!" Diomed ordered Medon.

"Diomed!" Lucretia yelled once again.

Diomed turned his anger on his wife: "Lucretia, why

didn't you tell me that Gaius will not be coming tonight?'' he demanded.

"Really," she said in exasperation. "You know that he and his high and mighty wife Fortunata never descend from their mountain retreat.''

"But that leaves only a few Roman nobles.''

"Really, Father. All this playing up to nobles," Julia said with a sigh. "They smile and eat your food, and then they laugh at you behind your back. What do you hope to gain?''

"Julia, you'll drive me mad yet! I am doing my best to see we take our rightful place in society. I want to see you marry well. Maybe we'll even be in Rome one day, and you—''

"What patrician is going to mix his precious blood with that of a merchant's daughter?" she asked acidly.

"Blood, foolish girl, runs precious thin in winter, without the warming cloak of riches. They may laugh at me, these Roman nobles, because I've made a fortune with my fish sauce. But all the while their eyes are on my purse, wondering just how much it outweighs their own!''

"Still," Lucretia cut in, "they are proud.''

Diomed smiled and gazed at his daughter. "Perhaps. But when they see our Julia courted by a Greek noble . . .''

"Young Glaucus is good-looking," Lucretia said in an almost dreamlike voice.

"The hell with looks! It's culture, it's breeding! Show me a Roman who can deny that a high-born son of Athens is his better!'' Diomed stated intensely.

"That's true too—even though Greece belongs to Rome.''

Julia stared at her parents in disbelief, listening while they talked as if she were not there. Finally, when she could stand it no longer, she spoke out. "Daddy, I hardly know Glaucus. Besides . . .''

But Diomed cut her off before she could finish. "You will!'' he stated. "Now come along or we'll be late for the games.''

Sighing wearily, Julia followed her parents from the room, struggling in vain to banish from her mind the handsome face of a nobleman, but not the nobleman her father had decided upon for her.

*   *   *

The temple of Isis shone proudly in the early afternoon sun, its roof supported by a multitude of columns, its interior open and inviting to all.

Behind the temple sat a larger building, known as the sacrarium. It was here that the priests and priestesses of Isis lived, and here that their most secret ceremonies were performed, concealed from the prying eyes of the curious.

But this day the open temple was filled with a variety of people, and at the front of the building, high upon an altar, stood a priest and priestess of Isis, mumbling inaudible incantations and passing their hands over an open fire. With each pass, the crowd gasped at the sudden surge of multicolored flames spewing forth.

Next to the altar, at the entrance to the temple, was a marble statue of the goddess Isis. Those who had seen the procession that morning recognized that the marble deity was dressed exactly as Ione had been earlier. The same cape of black and silver adorned her arm and back, and she wore the same golden headpiece of a coiling cobra.

Glaucus' thoughts were still fixed on Ione as he strolled nearer to the temple, accompanied by his friend Clodius.

"You look splendid, Clodius," he said absently, forcing his eyes from the temple.

"Do I not? Though my tailor is hinting that my poems make him a poor dinner. But I must look well; who knows when I might meet a rich widow, or even a pretty woman."

"Ah, pretty women—the solace for all ills."

"And who knows better than you, my noble Glaucus?"

Before he could answer, a sharp clap sounded and a litter stopped next to the two men. Glaucus turned just as the thin curtain was pulled aside and a voluptuous woman leaned out, her eyes sparkling mischievously.

"Glaucus, you've returned at last," she breathed.

Glaucus stared at the woman for a moment, and then bowed low, glancing quickly at Clodius, who was doing the same. "Who is she?" he whispered frantically.

"Lucinda," Clodius whispered back.

Raising his head, and favoring her with a full smile, Glaucus spoke. "Lucinda, what a delight."

"Wretched man. I haven't heard a word from you all winter," Lucinda pouted.

"But no winter's wind could chill my memories of our summer's idyll," Glaucus replied poetically.

Lucinda laughed gaily at this and stretched out her hand. When Glaucus took it, she fixed him with a deep stare. "A pretty speech, but there is much in Rome to warm a man in winter."

Ignoring this, Glaucus kissed the back of her hand lightly and started to release it, while behind him, Clodius cleared his throat meaningfully. "You do remember my noble friend Clodius," he said, attempting to pass her hand to his, as manners required, but the noblewoman refused to be put off and gripped his hand even tighter.

"You'll come to me, of course," she stated to him, her eyes now smoldering pinpoints of undisguised desire.

"I count the moments," he said in a low voice filled with as much sincerity as he could muster. The instant he felt her fingers loosen, he pulled his hand away and bowed low again before her. He waited a moment longer as Lucinda's eyes swept over his body, and when the curtain fell back into place, he breathed a sigh of relief.

"Now I remember why summers in Pompeii take so much out of one," he whispered to Clodius.

Then his eyes returned to the temple and to two figures standing by the statue of Isis. When he recognized who they were, he caught his breath, for one of them was the very reason he was there. He nudged Clodius gently and tilted his head toward the two people.

Clodius, always alert for whatever was happening, followed the direction of his friend's gaze, noting its intensity. He saw the two people standing near the base of the statue, absorbed in conversation, ignoring the people within the temple as well as those walking on the streets. Smiling, he guided Glaucus toward Ione and Antonius, neither any longer dressed in the robes they had worn in the morning's procession.

Both now wore garments of the costly material reserved for the very rich and the very noble.

As they drew closer, Glaucus could hear Ione's voice. "So much has happened," she said emotionally.

"True, but Father would approve of what we do. It is for the best, sister."

"So I pray daily. Oh, Antonius . . ." But Ione stopped when she gazed past her brother's shoulder and saw the two men who were approaching. One she recognized—Clodius, the penniless nobleman who lived off the goodness of others— but the other man was a stranger. She could not help but notice his dark curly hair, and his face, so very handsome. She noticed that he walked with an almost animallike grace, and that his eyes, so blue, seemed to pierce her to the very core. Within their depths she sensed a wistful yearning that seemed to call out to her.

"Ione?" Antonius asked, turning to see what had caught her attention.

"Ah, the lovely Ione and her brother, Antonius. Good day," Clodius said smoothly. "Please, meet my Greek friend, Glaucus."

Ione's eyes went to Glaucus' face, her gaze captured by his. She barely nodded her head in greeting.

Glaucus bowed with almost too much politeness, but when he stood again, his eyes never wavered from Ione's. "Good day, Lady Ione," he said in a husky voice. "It is indeed a privilege to be introduced to you."

Ione could not resist his eyes. She was suddenly conscious of the unusually loud beating of her heart. She wanted to reply, but her throat was dry, and her mind refused to allow any thoughts to form. She could do nothing but continue to gaze into the seemingly endless depths of Glaucus' eyes.

"A pleasure," said Antonius as he bowed slightly to the stranger who had such an obviously strong effect on his sister, but his greeting went unacknowledged.

"Excuse me," came a deep voice, breaking the silence that had fallen over them.

Everyone's eyes went to the newcomer, and Glaucus heard

Ione draw in her breath when the man grasped her arm. "Come, Ione, it is time," said Arbaces with a glare directed at Clodius and Glaucus.

Without a word, she turned and followed the high priest, while behind her, Antonius did the same. Glaucus looked at Clodius, his question apparent on his face.

For once, Clodius spoke seriously, stunning Glaucus, who was used to his friend's usual jocular banter. "Don't even think of Ione. For when you trifle with her, you trifle with Arbaces, and he is a man who does not like to lose—anything, ever!"

Glaucus nodded his head thoughtfully, but could not stop himself from gazing at Ione as she walked away. Ione turned, and for a brief instant their eyes met once more.

"Damn it, Glaucus, come along," Clodius said. "Now, will you change your mind and go to the games with me?"

"Not I, you bloodthirsty Roman," Glaucus said with a smile that softened the harshness of his words. "I'll see you later, at Diomed's."

Clodius struggled, then bid goodbye to his friend, who continued to stare at the sacrarium into which Ione had disappeared.

In the sacrarium, Arbaces, Ione, and Antonius entered the main gathering hall, finding it filled with the priests and priestesses of Isis. Pausing in the archway, Arbaces turned to Ione and her brother, a smile softening the harsh lines of his face.

"We must be off to the amphitheater. We'll escort you to your house as we go, my dear," he said to Ione.

"Thank you, Arbaces," she said with a shake of her head, "but I want to stay with Antonius for a while."

Arbaces was about to protest, but knew the wisdom of not being too severe, too soon. "Very well," he said, inclining his head to both of them before he signaled his followers on.

When they were alone at last, Ione gazed at Antonius, her features troubled and grave. He smiled softly at her and stroked her cheek. "Do not be sad."

Ione took a deep breath and forced a smile to her lips. "How could I be when my little brother is to be made a priest? But I shall be lonely when you are living here, instead of in our home."

"Isis will soon call you into the temple, too."

"I'll miss you, Antonius," she said in a voice choked with emotion as she suddenly embraced him.

"And I you," he whispered, holding her close. "You've always been more a mother to me than a sister."

"I wish you could have known her. Even my own memories are fleeting—warm arms, a smile, a loving face," she told him as her large eyes filled with tears.

"And it is all those things I think of when I think of Isis."

Ione nodded, willing her sadness away. "I know. It is as if we've found our mother again in her."

By mid-afternoon the streets of Pompeii were all but deserted, for the games were just getting under way. Those few who stayed away from the amphitheater were either Christians, slaves, or the business people who catered to anyone not attending the games. Of course there were a few other exceptions, such as Glaucus, for he despised the games and the bloodlust they seemed to inspire in the people. For him, sport was the thrill of seeing fleet men run a race, or watching two well-matched athletes wrestle until one was victorious. For when the winner was declared, he would always help the man he defeated from the ground, not leave him to lie there with his life's blood seeping into the dirt of the arena. No, for Glaucus there were better things than the games.

Restless, Glaucus walked through his house and toward the garden. He paused when he stepped outside, spying someone bent over the flower bed. Suddenly he realized it was the blind slave girl.

"Nydia?" he called.

Nydia's back tensed, and she quickly reached behind her for her staff. Rising, her face flushed, she turned toward

Glaucus. "I . . . I wanted it all to be perfect before you saw it," she said.

"But it is beautiful. You must have been keeping it up all these months." When Nydia nodded, he sensed her shyness. "But my dear, this was so much work. You must allow me to offer you something in payment."

Nydia stiffened at his words, drawing her shoulders back proudly. She wanted nothing for what she had done; she had done it for him, because she had wanted to. "No," she said, "it was meant as a token of . . . of friendship. If a slave may be allowed to speak of such things."

Glaucus stared at the woman/child, realizing his mistake. "Forgive me, Nydia. I am stupid sometimes. Of course you're my friend," he said as he reached out and touched her gently on the shoulder.

Nydia blushed again, this time with a warm rush of pleasure brought on by his words and his touch. His next words, however, abruptly sent her emotions reeling once more.

"Nydia, you know many things—do you know Ione?" he asked.

"I know of her, yes. They say she is beautiful."

"She is indeed!"

"She is from Rome itself, and very high born."

"Oh?" Glaucus said, his eyebrows rising at this piece of very pleasing news.

"And very pious," Nydia added.

"Oh," Glaucus whispered.

Nydia smiled a small, secret smile of triumph. "Yes, they say she sends away every man who even looks at her with desire."

Frowning, Glaucus pondered Nydia's words. "Perhaps not every man," he ventured. "Who knows . . . ?" His question was not directed at Nydia, but at himself. Shrugging, he gazed at the blind slave, and then patted her shoulder affectionately. "Again, thank you for tending my garden," he said.

Absorbed in thought, Glaucus left the garden and stepped

back into his house. A moment later he called to his house slave and instructed him to prepare his bath.

He then went into the large room he had built only last year. Looking around, he smiled. The gymnasium was his pride and joy, the perfect place to clear his mind of his troubled thoughts of Ione.

Stripping the rich robes from his body, Glaucus stepped naked into the center of the room. From the time he had been four, he had trained like a true Greek, tuning and honing his body into a perfectly running machine. From the age of eight he had competed in the games in Athens, a tradition centuries old, consisting of events which proved the worth of a man.

Carefully, slowly, Glaucus began the ritual he had learned as a child, stretching his muscles, working his way across the floor in smooth, rhythmic movements, losing himself within the patterns that the exercise required.

Deep in the heart of Pompeii, in the free section of town, there were still other people who did not go to the games. Many could be found in places like Burbo's tavern, left mostly empty after the regular customers had gone off to enjoy the gladiators and to drink their fill of spilled blood.

Those who remained behind were the slaves who worked in the tavern and the prostitutes who were recovering from their early customers, all the better to prepare themselves for those who would need their bodies after their blood was aroused to a fever by the deaths they witnessed.

Xenia, one of the aging prostitutes who worked at the tavern, had just returned from an errand and was slowly climbing the outside stairs. Inside, Chloe stood in her bedroom, staring at a mirror of polished steel. She held a brief costume before her, considering the effect it would have on the men who would watch her later.

She held the costume against her body and twirled, her feet moving gracefully. She stopped midway through her turn as something caught her attention. She stared at the wall and at the latest addition to the mural, a vulgar depiction of an endless orgy. Shrugging, she turned to the the artist who was adding yet another passionate love scene. "What do you think, Philos?" she asked.

Philos raised his tiny body and winked noncommitally. "I think you are very beautiful, and very unhappy, yes?"

"You know me so well. What can I do? Petrus will be watching me tonight, for I'll be dancing in his master's house. Oh, Philos, you know how hard it is for him."

Philos nodded his head sympathetically, but before he could reply, Xenia strutted boldly into the room.

Both Chloe and Philos stared at her, open-mouthed, startled by her overpainted face and blatantly flashing robes.

"Where is Nydia?" Xenia asked Chloe.

"Out selling her flowers."

"Oh," Xenia pouted. Then she turned and saw Philos, and stiffened for a moment.

"It's all right, he's not a customer."

Xenia stared at him, letting her eyes travel up and down his short length. "Pity," she said with a smile and arched eyebrow. "Shall we say . . . half price?"

Philos laughed pleasantly, and drew himself up to his full four-foot height. "My dear, you simply do not understand artistic . . . ah, proportions." He gazed at her with obvious meaning, but Xenia was a simple-minded soul, and not one to grasp subtle meanings. She shrugged her shoulders just as Philos and Chloe burst out laughing.

Xenia, suddenly defensive because she did not understand, turned to Chloe with a pout: "It's not fair, Chloe, you going out tonight. There'll be mobs of customers. You know how it gets here after the games."

"Nothing like a good day of killing to stir up the blood," Philos stated with a grin.

"What does Diomed want with you anyway?" she asked.

"He's having a banquet. I don't want to go, but Diomed's an important client. Stratonice will turn me out if I refuse. Plus, I need the money." A baby's cry cut through the room, giving added meaning to her words. Whirling, Chloe went to a curtain and pulled it aside. She picked up her child and drew him close, rocking him slowly, feeling the warmth of his body against hers.

"Don't I, my baby?" she cooed. "Don't I need that money for you?"

"I can't think why Diomed chose you, when I'm by far the more . . . professional," Xenia stated, unaffected by the tender scene before her.

Disregarding the bitter envy apparent in Xenia's voice, Chloe kissed her son before looking back at the other woman. "You're forever getting extra work from Calenus, and do I complain? But I can't help but wonder what a priest of Isis wants with a . . ."

Xenia smiled at the unfinished question, and gazed smugly at Chloe. "That is my secret. But I'll tell you this," she said haughtily, "I won't be stuck in this place forever!"

"You can't really believe they'll make you a priestess?"

"Calenus says that if I do my work well . . ."

"Xenia, you're a hopeless dreamer," Chloe said with a sigh.

Xenia's laugh was sharp and brittle. "And you're not? Always going on about the kingdom of heaven and such?"

"You're not a Christian?" asked Philos, alarmed by the dangerous words.

Chloe refused to meet the dwarf's eyes; instead she returned the baby to its cradle before speaking. "Of course not," she half-lied, "I only . . . wonder sometimes."

"You'd better stop wondering," Xenia warned, "or you'll end up feeding the lions, like those fools in the arena today."

Philos, who had gone back to his painting, shook his head slowly. "What a world of dreams is Pompeii, where each person strives to be what he is not." Then he turned to stare at the two women, pointing his brush at them. "And you're the same. When all the while you know you'll die as you have lived—in bed!"

As if in accent to his words, a knock echoed in the room. Xenia opened the door wide, arching her eyebrows at the slave standing there.

"Petrus!" Chloe cried in surprise.

"Well, Chloe," Xenia said as she looked from the slave to the other prostitute, "I see you have time for slaves, even slaves who don't pay."

Alarmed by the underlying threat in Xenia's voice, Chloe spoke in a low, pleading voice. "Please, Xenia, please don't tell Stratonice."

"We'll see," Xenia whispered airily as she started from the room.

Philos quickly got up and crossed the room, sensing the need for Chloe and Petrus to be alone. "Xenia," he called after the prostitute, "about that half-price offer . . ."

The door closed, and Chloe and Petrus were alone. Immediately they seemed to melt together in an embrace, their arms going around each other, their mouths crushing intensely in passion and love.

Chloe drew her lips from his, leaning back to stare into her lover's soft, deep eyes. "Oh, Petrus, I am so glad to see you. But how did you get away?"

Petrus let his eyes wander over the contours of her face before he answered. "Diomed is at the games. Medon is covering for me, but I can't stay too long, there's a banquet tonight."

Chloe's stomach lurched cruelly. Stepping back, she turned from him and began to speak in a hesitant voice. "I . . . I thought you knew. I'm . . . entertaining at the banquet."

She sensed without looking at him that his body had tensed, that his jaw had become firm and set as it always did in anger. "Petrus," she whispered as she turned back to him, her eyes moist and pleading.

"How can you do it?" he whispered in a cutting voice. "How can you 'entertain' those people who will cheer today while our loved ones die?"

"Do I ask how you can serve them?" she asked sadly. "What choice does either of us have? We own no free will, we are both slaves, of a kind."

"You don't know what it's like for me! To think of you, night after night, lying with any man who has the price!"

"But *I* know what it's like for me," she shot back, stung

by the selfishness of his words. "And I know that life can never be any different for us." Taking a deep breath, Chloe forced herself to soften her words. "But Petrus, with the help of God we can bear it, because we know our son may not have to live as we do."

Petrus stared at her, unable to move, denying his feelings, yet overcome by them at the same time. He watched her go to the cradle and lift up the boy. A burning streak of anger and pain shot through him, lending sharpness to his tongue.

" 'Our' son! How can I know he is mine, no matter how much it pleases you to think it so?"

Stung again by the brutality of his words, Chloe nonetheless stood proud under his glaring eyes. "I thought it pleased you also, to see this child as the symbol of our love. To see us—to think of us as a family."

Chloe walked to him and, with the baby in one arm, reached out to stroke his cheek.

Shaking his head in denial, Petrus pulled away, then turned and left the room.

"Petrus!" Chloe cried after him. But the man she loved did not turn back to her, and soon he was gone, leaving her alone with her child, while she cried softly at what might be her irretrievable loss.

Chapter Three

The population of Pompeii was twenty thousand, and today the great oval amphitheater, which could comfortably hold the entire number, was almost filled.

Level upon level of people were in the stands, talking, cheering, flirting, gambling, and buying their fill of foodstuff and drinks from the multitude of vendors hawking their wares. The open upper stands were filled with the poorest of the free citizens, while each of the lower levels held progressively wealthier ranks. The lowest seats and boxes were reserved for the very privileged—Roman vacationers, nobles, priests and priestesses of the various and sundry cults, along with the prominent locals, including the wealthy merchants like Diomed, and their families. The high-ranking civil officials, as well as the resident noblemen, whether rich or not, such as Clodius and his friends Sallust and Lepidus, were also seated in the large boxes, separated by mighty columns.

Seated in the center of the high ranks, in the place of honor, was the giver of these games, Quintus the lord magistrate. At the age of fifty, with his short-cropped silver hair, he looked as august as did any emperor of Rome. Seated at his side was Tibius, the second magistrate, his puppetlike assistant.

But none of the political and social machinations mattered today, especially not to those people who were seated above the privileged few. All they wanted was for the fights to commence, and for their bloodlust to be sated. Throughout the games they would look at Quintus, for he alone held the power of life and death over the men in the arena.

Boisterous shouts rang out from the crowd's throats when the gladiators entered the arena. An especially loud roar greeted one of them, the gladiator Sporus. He was dressed in highly polished brass and leather, his helmet gleamed in the sun, and his shortsword glinted with a silvery glow.

Behind Sporus and his opponent came three more pairs of combatants. This match would have four pairs fighting, enough to satisfy the simmering mob for a while.

The eight warriors faced the stands, their arms raised in the traditional salute while they waited for the magistrate to give his signal. When he did so, dramatically, the crowd tensed in anticipation.

The eight gladiators faced each other and saluted graciously. But the impatient crowd urged them on with stinging reminders that they were nothing more than warm-up entertainment.

Sporus gauged his opponent, a man he had never met before, and set himself. His adversary's trident could be used effectively, he knew, but just how well he would have to wait and find out.

From all around him came the sounds of fighting, yet he circled his opponent warily, waiting for the man to make the first move. His legs felt light, even though they were encased in heavy brass. His breastplate was secure against his chest, but he knew it would not be strong enough protection from a direct thrust of the trident.

Spinning, Sporus dodged the man's first lunge and, as he turned, struck the trident with his sword. Suddenly everything except the man he fought disappeared from his thoughts.

Sweat ran along the deep furrows in his cheek. His breathing was deep and strained. The sun was a burning ball above him, and beneath the helmet and armor, Sporus baked. *Get this over with quickly!* he ordered himself just as his opponent lunged again.

Sporus pivoted on his heels as the trident's tip grazed along his breastplate. He spun in a circle and his sword flashed in the air, catching his opponent just above the elbow.

A scream of pain tore from the gladiator's throat, accompanied by the spurting blood of an opened artery.

The man dropped the trident but quickly recovered, letting go of his shield and picking up the long three-tipped spear with his uninjured hand. Turning, his eyes wide and filled with pain, he charged madly at Sporus.

Sporus knew it was over, all but the last stroke. When the gladiator reached him, he sidestepped the charge and sank his sword deep into the man's throat. A moment later he pulled the blade free and moved aside as his opponent fell to the ground.

Turning, Sporus faced the magistrate and bowed low, while a slave appeared with a long grappling hook and began to drag the defeated gladiator away. Under the growing applause, he started toward the far side of the arena, smiling at the sound of his name issuing from the mob. But too soon, the cries faded, and a new call was sent up.

"Lydon!" "Bring on Lydon!" "Get on with the show!" the people shouted, souring Sporus' victory, if only for himself.

Fighting off the jealous thoughts, Sporus stepped down into the underground passageway and found Marcus, his manager, smiling at him as he always did at the time of victory.

"Well done, Sporus; no use wasting time, eh?" he said in his coarse voice, winking as he patted the gladiator on the shoulder. But then Marcus looked out at the arena and tensed.

"Break, Melior! Break, you jackass!" he shouted. "You killed a good man, Sporus," he said without looking at his gladiator.

"And saved a better," Sporus rejoined.

"Damn you, Melior," Marcus shouted to the arena. "Ahh, he's cut."

Sporus stared at his manager, but the man's attention was fixed in the arena. He shook his head sadly, knowing that he had served his purpose for the day and that Marcus was no longer interested in him. Glancing once more at the remaining gladiators, he saw that Melior had recovered from his wound and was facing his opponent bravely. Sporus watched the large German slave, Gar, circle his opponent. Shaking his

head again, Sporus turned away from the battle and continued
through the underground passage to the dressing room.

Entering the dimly lit room, alive with the mixed smells of
metal, leather, blood, sweat, and fear, Sporus looked at the
people within. Slaves were dressing the men, and the gladiators themselves inspected their weapons, sighting along the
lengths of swords, testing the points of tridents. He paused
for a moment to stare at a broad, naked back. His eyes
dropped lower, taking in the swell of the man's full buttocks,
barely hidden by the thin straps of a loincloth. The man's
body was magnificently proportioned, with every muscle flowing into the next. The smoothness of his skin glowed with
perfection and power.

Sighing regretfully, Sporus stepped next to Lydon as he
stared out the barred window. Sporus saw that only two
gladiators remained in the arena, the large, clumsy German
and his opponent.

Gar was dressed in thick, heavy armor, and in his hands
was the long two-handed sword of his people. He was flailing
away madly, trying to strike his quick-legged opponent before the man could penetrate his defense with his own sword.

"I'm afraid your young German shows little promise,"
Sporus said to Lydon.

Lydon favored Sporus with a sidelong glance. "Gar's raw.
But I was that raw once. He'll learn."

"If he lives long enough," Sporus replied with a short
laugh. Reaching out, he traced an old scar on Lydon's chest
with a strange familiarity.

Lydon jerked away from the man's touch and walked
toward the bench where a slave waited to help him dress.

"Gar's strong, of course," Sporus called to Lydon. "Perhaps
even stronger than you. But he lacks your speed. . . . Although he's not weighed down by too much brain!"

Lydon didn't bother to reply as he pointed out the armor he
would wear today and began to ready himself for his match.
A few moments later he again heard the cry of the crowd,
calling out his name.

The slave put on the arm shielding of thick leather and

brass, and adjusted its protection so that Lydon could move the arm freely. Then he held out the leather belt with the short skirtle on it. Lydon stood, and the man belted the single article of clothing around his waist.

Only after the slave had knelt and laced up the high sandals, and affixed the brass shin plates to it, was Lydon ready.

"Oh, oh!" cried Sporus, who was now half out of his armor. "Gar's been cut."

Lydon went to the window and saw Gar staring at the flow of brilliant scarlet blood on his upper arm. With a rage that rocked the very sands beneath his feet, Gar set himself again, and advanced on his opponent.

"Good," Lydon whispered in approval.

"But will he be good enough?" Sporus asked.

Lydon stared at Sporus for a moment. Again the calling of his name became chantlike, as the mob cried for their champion.

"They call," Sporus said.

"Let them," replied Lydon, sitting down again.

Sporus walked to him, smiling softly, no longer feeling any pangs of jealousy. In actuality, Lydon and Sporus were friends, bound as would be anyone who faced death so frequently together. But for Sporus, there was an unattainable something else that haunted him daily. Taking the oil from the slave, Sporus began to massage Lydon's tense shoulders. "But you're the hero."

Pulling away from Sporus' touch, Lydon stood and faced him. Before he could speak, however, Marcus stormed into the room.

"Lydon! Why aren't you ready!" he shouted darkly.

"There's time, Marcus," he said as he reached for the trident the slave held out. He inspected it, and then looked carefully at the array of nets before pointing to one. The slave picked up the net and handed it to him.

Another loud cheer sounded in the arena, and Marcus looked out the window. "Gar! Clumsy bull," he spat. "I'll never get my investment out of him."

"Take heart, Marcus, you'll make plenty out of me again," he said sarcastically.

"If you live!" Marcus retorted, his round face suddenly serious. "I've seen this Roman fight. Lydon, he's quick. And as to money, you have no complaints. . . ."

"If only he didn't throw away every coin he earns," Sporus cut in with a smile.

"Sporus . . ." Lydon growled in warning.

Suddenly Sporus' face turned serious as he stared at Lydon. "Be careful," he whispered earnestly.

Lydon returned Sporus' stare and slowly nodded. Then he turned and followed Marcus from the dressing room.

The passage from the dressing room to the arena was not long, but it was crowded. As Lydon and Marcus walked, they passed various dressing rooms and dungeons. Off to the left Lydon saw the pit holding the lions, and he heard the low growl of one of the hungry beasts. A few steps beyond that was the dungeon holding the Christians brought in that very morning. As the two men passed its barred door, Lydon heard an old man praying and he paused to look at the men, women, and children who were marked to die today.

"I don't like it," Lydon said as he tore his eyes from the scene.

"What? Sharing the bill with Christians? You're too proud," Marcus chided.

"I don't like whetting appetites for Christian blood."

"Why pity them?" Marcus asked with a laugh. "They think they're going to a better place. It's you and me I'm not certain about." But Marcus fell silent when he saw the tight cold look on Lydon's face and the dangerous narrowing of the gladiator's eyes. "Lydon," he continued, his voice softer, "blood is blood. Just make sure it's not your own that's spilled."

And then they were at the entrance to the arena. Lydon looked out at the crowd and at the two men still fighting. Both Gar and his opponent were still standing. Lydon saw the scarlet trail of blood on Gar's arm, and saw too the rage on the large man's face. He watched Gar charge, swinging the longsword mightily. Suddenly the other gladiator slipped, and Gar lunged, pushing the sword through the armored breastplate. A moment later a mixed chorus of cheers and boos followed Gar to the underground passage.

As Lydon faced Gar he smiled as the young fighter spoke: "I won! Lydon, I won!"

"Your first, and well done," he said encouragingly, noting the proud tilt of the man's head in response. "But," he cautioned, "you still need some work with your parry."

"Yes, Lydon," Gar said humbly, his smile no longer full.

Lydon clasped the German by his shoulder. "Got them all ready for me, have you?" he asked, and was rewarded by a look of hero worship at the compliment.

"Gar, get something on that arm!" Marcus ordered bruskly. Gar nodded and started toward the dressing room just as another lion roared out its cry.

Then Lydon stepped out into the arena. At first a hush descended on the crowd, but when he lifted high the trident and net, a roar of combined anticipation and delight shook the amphitheater. Slowly, calculatingly, Lydon walked along the circular arena, the powerful muscles of his oiled body glistening under the rays of the sun. Lydon no longer heard the crowd, the women who called out in open invitation to him; he now heard only his own thoughts.

He was Lydon, champion of Pompeii, the best gladiator in the world. But before he had become that, he had been born the son of a slave. His father was Medon, slave of Diomed. As a child, Lydon had been Diomed's slave too. When he had grown big and strong, Diomed had seen a profit in him and sent him to Marcus to be trained as a gladiator.

For Lydon, it was a new life. He learned, and grew, and became the best. Within his first two years, he had won enough money to buy his freedom—and almost anything else he might desire. He was the champion of Pompeii, and tonight, he realized, would be his crowning glory. Tonight he had been invited to the banquet of his former owner. He would sit with the nobles and he would claim his rightful place among them.

But first he must win his match, he told himself as he stopped before Quintus and saluted. Behind Quintus he saw Diomed, but did not acknowledge the man's presence.

Turning to go to the center of the arena, Lydon paused when he saw a beautiful noblewoman drop her silken veil over the barrier. He knew it had been done with obvious intent, as it had been done many times in the past by many women. Smiling, he walked to it, and picked it up. Gazing boldly at the woman, and at the open invitation in her eyes, he returned her veil.

"The gods be with you, Lydon . . . especially Venus."

Lydon held her gaze for a moment, although he cared nothing for her. He had retrieved the veil as a dramatic gesture, not as an indication of interest.

Finally, after making everyone wait, he gazed out at the arena, seeing his foe for the first time. The man was enormous, and heavily armored with a breastplate that Lydon knew had been dipped into molten gold. The gladiator's face plate was gilded also, and his shield was etched in the same metal, decorated the way only a Roman gladiator's would be. In his right hand the Roman carried the only unadorned piece of equipment he possessed, a heavy, sharp sword.

Reaching the center of the arena, Lydon stopped to face his opponent, calmly staring into the dark eyes barely visible from behind the faceplate. He gave the Roman a cynical smile as the procurator came between them. He looked at the magistrate; when Quintus gave the signal, the procurator touched both warriors on the shoulders and stepped back. A single trumpet sounded, and the fight was on.

"Charge and be gored, you ox!" Lydon shouted bravely, more for the benefit of the crowd than for himself. But even as he spoke, he watched his opponent's eyes and saw him about to move. The man charged quickly, faster than Lydon expected he would, and he barely stepped out of the way of the sword.

Backstepping, Lydon stared at his adversary, recalculating his first impression. The Roman was better than Lydon had at first thought.

Bait him, he told himself when their eyes met again. *Test him*, he commanded himself. He feinted with the trident, and as the man shifted, he feinted with the net. But the Roman read his move and attacked straight on.

Whirling, Lydon spun out of the blade's path, barely escaping its point. Again he stepped back, this time to let the crowd know he was uninjured.

The spectators let out a collective cheer, and then gasped in warning. Spinning, Lydon sensed what the man was doing and flicked his trident toward the Roman's faceplate. The gladiator stopped, weaved beneath the trident, then stood in a glaring challenge.

Lydon had never been defeated, and because of that he felt a confidence few could claim. Whether wielding sword, whip, ax, or trident and net, Lydon was sure of himself, and he had never been more confident than now.

He began to whirl the net while he circled the gladiator. His eyes never left the other's face, and his breathing was smooth and even. He flicked his wrist quickly, and the net flew into the air. He had anticipated the Roman's next step and was sure the net would trap him. Just as it reached the Roman's head, the man, using his incredible swiftness, rolled from beneath it and sprang to his feet a half second before the net hit the earth.

Lydon was unprepared for this maneuver and was caught short when the Roman lunged at him with the sword. Using the trident, Lydon parried quickly as he dove to retrieve the net. Before he'd fully regained his balance, the Roman attacked in a swift series of strokes.

Lydon warded off all but the last blows, and for those he sidestepped, whirled, and ran five feet from his opponent. The Roman, confused by the action, stumbled in his effort to reach Lydon and fell heavily to the ground.

The mob cheered wildly, crying Lydon's name over and over.

Seeing that his ploy had worked, Lydon stepped forward, the trident lifted and poised for the kill. He stared into the eyes behind the faceplate and, seeing the fear and defeat within them, let a slow smile spread across his face.

Lowering the trident in an expansive gesture, Lydon flicked the net at his opponent in an offer of assistance.

Again the mob lustily screamed out its approval.

The Roman eschewed his opponent's offer of help and quickly regained his feet as he carefully watched Lydon's face. Then, while Lydon once again bowed to him, he leaped forward, his sword flashing in the sun. The crowd screamed in fear. Lydon whirled, a laugh erupting from his throat, but against the sound of that laughter pain flashed through him from the burning touch of the sword's sharp tip, opening a long thin line across his ribs.

He was near the underground entrance, and saw the fear and concern on Marcus' face. "Damn!" he heard Marcus scream. "Attack him, Lydon! Now! Get on with it!"

But Lydon chose to ignore the advice; instead he turned his back to the Roman, and walked toward the cheering crowd. With his hand holding the net crossed in front of the wound, few were able to see that their champion was injured as he strutted proudly before them. Then he bowed to the cheering masses. As he straightened again, he let himself stumble.

With a grimace, he turned in yet another direction and bowed to more of the crowd. But this time he did not straighten up. His handsome face twisted in pain, and he dropped to one knee. As he did, the net fell away to reveal—for the first time—his bloodied chest.

A gasp rose among the people as they saw their champion wavering. Then another cry rang out, exhorting Lydon up. "The Roman!" they shouted in warning.

Lydon forced himself to stay calm and play his part to perfection. He knew the wound was not serious, but it was bad enough to hamper him in a long contest. He willed himself to remain in the helpless position while the thousands of bloodthirsty people waited for the end to come. Then he twisted his head just enough to see the Roman running toward him at full speed.

Tightening his hand on the net, Lydon tensed every muscle

in his body. As the Roman grew larger in his vision, his mind
sent its order: *Now!* In one lightning motion he rose to his
feet, whirling, the net arched in a perfect trajectory. Before
the Roman realized what was happening the net had settled
over him.

Using every ounce of his enormous strength, Lydon whipped
the net strings closed and pulled, spilling the Roman to the
ground. Still moving with the grace of a lion, Lydon drew
back the trident, its triple fangs gleaming in the air, and thrust
forward. The trident sank in at the very spot where the
Roman's faceplate and breastplate met. Lunging, Lydon used
his heavily armored shoulder to push home the trident, driving it completely through the man's neck, leaving him twisting helplessly on the ground, his thick blood spilling out.

With his chest rising and falling from the strain of his
deed, Lydon turned to the people in the stands, who were
already on their feet, shouting and screaming his name. But
his eyes were fixed on only one spot, the seat of Quintus, the
benefactor of the games.

Quintus scanned the mob quickly, taking their reaction to
this match. He saw that the majority were screaming and
stomping, unanimously giving the thumbs-down sign. Drawing himself up proudly, Quintus extended his arm and gave
the thumbs-down to Lydon.

Bowing, Lydon allowed himself to smile. "My thanks, my
lord magistrate, but he's already dead." With that, Lydon
stepped back and extended his arm to the crowd, accepting
their ovations. As the volume of their shouts built higher, he
turned and walked toward the exit and the men who waited
there for him.

Before he could say anything in response to their con-
gratulations, another cry rang out, and a chill raced along his
back. Lydon turned and saw the crowd, led by the priests and
priestesses of Isis, waving their arms and shouting in rhythm:
"Kill them! Kill them! Kill them!"

Soon the entire mob had joined in, and the thunder of their
voices was like the drums of the gods, beating a death knoll.

Then a gate opened, and the group of Christians were

pushed into the arena. Lydon stared at them, wanting to leave but unable to make his feet obey. He heard the same man who had been praying earlier call out in a calm voice and gather his people around him. ''Don't fear, my children. True life is just beginning. God is waiting for us. Let us meet him with glad hearts.''

Lydon saw a little boy, clutched in his mother's arms, go stiff as the roars of the lions grew loud. Another gate opened slowly, and the boy's mother pulled him still closer to her, burying his head against her breasts.

The old man moved again, urging his people to kneel in prayer while he took off his cape and covered the faces of two other children. The gate opened with a final clang, and the voices of the praying Christians were drowned out by the hungry roars of the lions and the bloodthirsty cries of the mob.

Turning away before the lions reached their victims, Lydon started quickly into the tunnel, refusing to stay and watch, caring nothing about what the others would say. He felt a strange relief that he was still able to walk, and to breathe, and to fight another day.

The sun had set, but the streets were still crowded with carousers who had spent the afternoon at the games, and who obviously had every intention of spending the night in celebration as well. This was especially the case in the poorer sections of Pompeii where the people had little to excite them except for the occasional games which allowed them to slake their bloodlusts. Taverns throughout the area overflowed with patrons, and drunken shouts filled the air while those already besotted slept on the ground.

At Burbo's tavern, the most notorious of all the watering holes in the heart of the city's slum district, the situation was no different. The rundown tavern was filled to capacity with raucous customers. Those at Burbo's were different in one aspect, however: it was there that most of the gladiators chose to drink.

This night was especially busy for Burbo's. Stratonice,

Burbo's broad-shouldered giant of a wife, stood as one on guard, protecting her property. Serving maids slithered between customers, fending off their hands while serving them and taking their money quickly and efficiently. The noise level was especially high, although it seemed not to bother anyone.

To Stratonice the sound was that of money, and a rare faint smile creased her face. But that smile disappeared when one of the customers grabbed the breasts of a serving girl. The girl turned quickly, slapping the offending hand and dashing a jug of wine in the poor fool's face.

The customer vented his rage by drawing back his fist to hit the serving girl, but he missed and instead hit the man next to him. Enraged, the man turned and punched the first man. In an instant, Stratonice was beside them. "Not in my house you don't!" she roared as she lifted the first man by his hair, holding him two inches off the ground and shaking him like a pup. When she put him back on his feet, the man tried to swing at her, but Stratonice punched him swiftly, knocking him to the floor. She picked him up again and, with everyone opening a path, marched him to the door and threw him into the street.

When she turned around, everyone cheered her through their laughter. But then the crowd's attention shifted, as they stared at the doorway. Another cheer resounded loudly and everyone rose to their feet to applaud the newcomers, for the champions of the games had arrived. Lydon entered, flanked by Sporus, Marcus, Gar, and several others.

"Well done, Stratonice. You should never have retired from the arena," Marcus said admirably.

"Is that a challenge, Marcus? There's many a man whose lost his head to me."

"But only in the ring," he countered.

Stratonice barked her laughter and slapped Lydon heartily on the back. "Cheated Proserpine again, have you!"

"Still champion, and that's worth a drink all around!" he said in a loud voice. He tossed some gold coins to the large woman before walking a bit stiffly to the bar.

"Didn't we fight today as well?" Sporus called out to the crowd who had already lost interest in all but Lydon.

At the serving bar, Marcus stood next to Lydon, while Gar stood on his other side. Looking out at the filled room, Marcus spoke in a loud voice: "Lydon's still only champion of Pompeii, but I'm going to make him champion of all Campania. And then . . . on to Rome!"

"The Flavian amphitheater will hold fifty thousand," Gar stated wisely.

"If it's ever finished," called Melior, another of the gladiators.

During this conversation one of the prostitutes came up to Lydon and pressed her ample charms against his body. Before Lydon could react, Sporus shoved her aside. "Don't crowd, my dear, the man's been wounded."

Turning, Sporus draped his arm around Lydon's shoulder, but Lydon, in no mood for Sporus' unending advances, shook him away brusquely. "Where's Nydia?" he asked one of the serving girls.

The girl nodded her head toward the door, and Lydon followed her direction and saw Nydia just closing the side door. He stared at her for a moment, noticing how pale and tired she looked.

"Nydia," Lydon called as he broke away from his friends and walked toward her.

Nydia, recognizing Lydon's voice, smiled at him. "I was worried," she said when he reached her side, "I heard you had been hurt."

"It was nothing," he replied as he gazed openly at her. He wished that she could see him, but he knew the hopelessness of that. Impulsively, he pulled out a small purse and put it in her hand, covering it with his own. "Here," he whispered.

"What . . . No, Lydon, you mustn't give away your money."

"I want you to have it," he whispered fiercely. "Take care that *she* doesn't see it," he cautioned as Stratonice approached them.

"Come, Lydon," Stratonice called, "have another drink."

"No, I must be off," he protested.

Then Sporus' sarcastic voice rang out loudly. "Our hero has been invited to Diomed's banquet! He's becoming quite the gentleman, you know."

Marcus, hearing of this for the first time, jerked up and walked stiffly to the gladiator. "No! I forbid it!" he commanded.

"You forbid? You forget yourself, Marcus," Lydon growled dangerously. "I'm not your slave any more, nor Diomed's either!"

Urgently, Marcus pulled Lydon aside, and when they were alone he spoke quickly and sincerely. "Please, Lydon, this banquet is not for you. The lords and the ladies don't mix with gladiators."

"Were they not with me today?" he asked while he stared into the manager's craggy face.

"In the arena, yes. There you're their hero—their God. But they are not like us. For you, winning means life. For them, winning or losing is a banal thing, too small to matter. It's all measured out in this day's petty triumph, that day's minor loss. But in you, they read a meaning to their existence. For them, you face and grapple with a fate they can see. When you win, sweet life is the prize. When you lose, your death is the proof. And the play they watch, from first to last, is clear and brief, all done in a moment's span. That they can understand."

Lydon stared at Marcus for a moment, and then let his laughter bubble out. "Such philosophy from the very merchant of death. What has all this to do with Diomed's banquet?"

"One thing. Safe in their arena seats, they worship you. But at their tables, you are too real. The blood that stains your fingers taints their meals. They'll taunt you out of fear."

"Taunt me? Marcus, I am their champion." With that he turned and walked proudly out the door.

The moment Lydon left the tavern, Stratonice swooped down on Nydia, grabbing her roughly and shaking her. "Let's have it!" she demanded.

Nydia pulled out a small purse and handed it to her mistress.
"This is all I made from my flowers," she said.

"I saw what Lydon gave you," she snapped, grabbing the
blind girl's free hand and forcing it open. She took Lydon's
gold, and flung Nydia's small purse at her. "Do you expect
me to keep you on that?"

Gar, who came over to see what was going on, laughed
sharply and grabbed Nydia to him, cupping one of her barely
budding breasts as he did. "Let me keep you, for tonight at
least. I promise you," he said in a seductive voice, "you'll
see nothing."

"Feel nothing either, I'll bet," Stratonice laughed derisively.

Gar, flushing at the insult and at the laughter of those who
had overheard, stood straighter as he glared at Stratonice.
"Take care, woman, Pompeii may have another champion
one day."

"So, our little Teuton has a temper."

"He has!" cried Sporus. "You should have seen his hot
blood flowing down his opponent's sword!"

"Did it now?" Stratonice asked. Then she tussled Gar's
hair in a friendly, almost flirtatious, gesture. "Let's see how
hot his blood runs in this game," she said, pushing Nydia
closer to him. "She's yours!"

"No! Let go of me," Nydia screamed.

Melior, standing with another of the tavern's whores, heard
Nydia's cry. Frowning at what he saw, he started toward her.

"Listen, bitch! You'll do what you're told, or I'll see you
back to that cheat of a slave dealer who palmed you off on
me without my even knowing you hadn't an eye in your
worthless head!" Stratonice whispered huskily.

"Do what you like!" Nydia spat back.

Stratonice's face turned purple and her hand lashed out,
striking Nydia's cheek. She drew back her hand again, but it
was caught in a viselike grip. Turning, she found herself eye
to eye with Melior.

"I wouldn't do that, Stratonice," he whispered. "Lydon
might not like it."

Stratonice glared at the gladiator, but fear replaced the

anger in her eyes, and after she moistened her lips with her tongue, she pulled her arm free and walked away.

"Marcus," called Gar, releasing Nydia, "please don't tell Lydon. I . . . I didn't understand about the girl."

Marcus shook his head disbelievingly, as did Melior. "Be grateful you've the body of a bull, lad. You'd never make your living with your brain," Marcus said.

Gar stared at him, not sure of what he meant; finally he shrugged and turned back to his wine. Behind all of them stood Chloe, watching what had happened. She feared for Nydia's safety, but knew she would be late for the banquet if she dallied. Sighing, she pulled the cloak more tightly about her costumed body, and left the tavern. As the sounds of laughter receded behind her, she hoped that this night might turn out better than these early events foretold.

Chapter Four

Diomed's triclinium was alive as it had rarely been before. A multitude of guests reclined on the couches lining the large marble tables. Slaves walked to and fro between them, their trays never empty, filling the guest's plates. Music floated through the air, and the sounds of conversation were like the low roar of the ocean itself.

Diomed was everywhere, making sure that his guests were happy and satisfied. Lucretia, the attentive hostess, tended to whatever little needs might arise among her guests. A sudden loud blast of music heralded yet more entertainers, playing their instruments so loudly that the guests had no choice but to cease conversation to watch a troop of jugglers who leaped madly about, twirling long knives over the heads of the startled guests.

Those who were able to contain their amazement continued to recline on their couches, probing daintily at the rich food, picking up succulent morsels with their jewel-bedecked fingers.

The music rose to a crescendo, and the jugglers ended their act, bowed, and withdrew amidst loud applause. The music picked up again, but at a more reasonable level, and the conversations interrupted moments ago were resumed as though without pause.

Glaucus shared a lounge with Clodius, and next to them were Sallust and Lepidus. As usual, Glaucus watched everything through amused eyes, and he barely managed to hold back his laughter when he overheard Lucretia talking with a noblewoman he knew.

"You've done wonders with this place. It was such a wreck after the last earthquake."

"Diomed bought it very cheap," Lucretia began, but was cut off by Clodius' darkly rasping voice.

"From my uncle," he said.

While Lucretia glared at Clodius, Glaucus forced himself to keep a straight face. "Just before Nero had him beheaded, poor man," she snipped back at Clodius, a moment before Medon came up behind her.

"My lady," said the slave.

Dismissing Clodius with a toss of her head, she turned to the slave and began walking with him while he whispered in her ear. Suddenly Lucretia stiffened and whirled to stare at the slave, a smile boldly etched on her face. She spoke quickly to Medon, and then left the room as the slave started away.

Medon went straight to Diomed and bent to whisper in his master's ear. Diomed sat straighter, a dark scowl suffusing his features. Sighing, Diomed rose from his seat.

Clodius, who along with Glaucus had observed this exchange, leaned closer to his companion and whispered conspiratorially: "A worthy lot, eh? Well, the secret of their success is simple, my friend. They value money beyond all else. Old Diomed, now . . . he'd pick a coin out of the gutter with his teeth."

Glaucus laughed uncomfortably at Clodius' opinion of Diomed, perhaps because he saw the truth in it, and also in the words aimed at wealth, any wealth. "You take the triumph of mere money as a personal affront," Glaucus stated.

"And as a moral catastrophe as well," Julia said, stepping next to the two men.

Both Glaucus and Clodius turned their startled faces to see Julia smiling icily down at them. Both nobles moved, making room for Julia to sit, just as Diomed passed them.

"Julia," he said, stopping to look at her as if this were the first time he had seen her this evening, "you look lovely. Doesn't she, Glaucus? Such a . . . noble-looking girl, isn't she?'' Diomed beamed at Glaucus, missing Julia's embarrassed, baleful glance.

"She is indeed," Glaucus responded to Diomed's retreating back.

"And that's no common achievement," Clodius said slyly.

Once again Julia glared at Clodius, but Glaucus, sensitive of his host's daughter, spoke softly. "Come, Julia, sit with us and forgive our crude manners."

Julia gazed first at Glaucus and then at Clodius; finally she nodded her head and sat between them.

While Julia made herself comfortable between the two noblemen, Diomed continued on his mission, meeting Lucretia just outside the dining room. He stopped, anger coloring his face as he hissed his words in a heated whisper.

"What's Arbaces doing here? Is he hoping to collect even more for the blessing of my ship?"

"You misjudge him, Diomed," Lucretia coaxed calmly as she laid a hand on his arm. "If you could only understand the joy he has brought me. How he has lightened my soul. . . ."

"And my purse," Diomed cut in.

Lucretia pulled her arm away, her lips petulant, her eyes scheming. "Very well. If you want it said that we give less than the Conjuctus family, or the Pompidii."

Defeated again by his own desires for social status, Diomed sighed. "Medon, fetch my strongbox."

"I'll invite Arbaces to join us," Lucretia said quickly, with a smile of victory settling on her lips.

"You'll get back to our guests, now!" he ordered. This time Lucretia heard the tone in his voice that warned her that she had pushed him far enough—for now at least.

After dismissing his wife imperiously, Diomed started toward the atrium.

Hearing footsteps on the stones, Arbaces turned from the impluvium's shallow waters, and the low sheen of the moon reflected in them, and raised his eyes at Diomed's approach. His eyebrows arched when he saw the bulging purse Diomed carried, and he quickly rearranged his countenance to disguise the contempt he felt for the fat merchant.

"I thank you, Diomed," he said when the man held out the purse to him. "But you mistake the purpose of my visit."

"Your purpose?" Diomed asked as he quickly lowered the purse.

"I have been thinking much of late on the republic."

Impatience at being taken from his guests almost made Diomed snap at the high priest, but his years as a merchant had taught him when to hold back his temper. "We'll not see the like of the republic again, I fear," he said hesitantly.

"We rule the world," Arbaces went on, "yet we cannot rule ourselves. Why? Because we have no moral leaders in whom the people can believe."

"Too true," Diomed agreed. "It's lamentable, and had I the leisure to discuss it . . ."

Refusing to be put off by Diomed's anxiety, Arbaces continued leisurely on. "Even our emperor, Vesparian, poor man—his legacy, a senate crippled and depleted by its own evil. He searches in vain for a few just men to bring to Rome, to fill the ranks," Arbaces said in a strangely melodic way while his eyes searched Diomed's face to see if he had yet gotten the true intent of his message.

But Diomed, still puzzled by the high priest's words, and impatient to return to his guests, merely shrugged. "So he does."

"He searches throughout the empire," Arbaces said in the voice he used as a priest, "and he would search even here, in Pompeii, for a man of moral ambition, could he be but found."

"There is Quintus, the lord magistrate," Diomed offered.

Arbaces turned from Diomed for a moment and took a deep, dramatic breath. "The magistrate," he said sarcastically, "offers us a few token Christians in the ring, hoping for reelection! But he does not understand the people as I do. And as you do." These last words were spoken in a lower voice, as Arbaces' dark eyes locked with Diomed's.

Again, Arbaces walked from Diomed, leaving the atrium

and entering the garden. Diomed followed after the priest, fascinated by what he thought he detected, yet afraid at the same time that one of his guests would see Arbaces and be embarrassed.

"The people, Diomed, are in despair. They pray to the vast array of Roman gods, yet they find no answers, no hope. That is why they flock to my temple. They know that if they will only give their hearts to Isis, she will grant them peace— and the prosperity which she has always granted her believers from the beginnings of time."

Although his interest had been piqued, the prospect of a sermon in the midst of his banquet spurred Diomed to interrupt. "Sir, I know little of religion. I am a man of commerce," he added as he again tried to give Arbaces the purse.

Having led Diomed to just the point where he wanted him, Arbaces held up a hand as a sign for him to stop. "And yet you are a man with all the qualities which I as a priest labor to engender in mankind. You are honest, intelligent, and generous to a fault. Those are the very qualities from which the republic sprang, when the word *noble* still had a meaning."

"Noble . . ." echoed Diomed, caught off guard by Arbaces' use of the word.

"And that is the very reason I turn to you," Arbaces declared.

Diomed tried to focus his thoughts, but all he could do was stare at the priest. "You mean to say I should run for public office?"

"Really, a man of your stature? You must surely have thought of this already, with the elections so close at hand. What better way to attract the Roman emperor than as the head magistrate of Pompeii?"

"Rome," Diomed whispered reverently. "Do you think . . . ?"

Arbaces smiled then, secure in his knowledge that his manipulation was taking hold, and waiting in silence for Diomed to take the bait fully.

"I suppose the people like me well enough, but . . .

The money. I have a good fortune, true, yet to mount a campaign . . ."

"Should not cost you much," Arbaces said benevolently. "I have but one true mission—to bring the word of Isis to mankind. The people have been good to Isis, and have enriched my temple with their offerings. The man who promises to stand behind its aims in office will be helped to gain that office."

"Who would not?" Diomed said eagerly, as his small eyes widened with greed. "Such *noble* aims. And you have gained great power in Pompeii."

"Not I, but Isis," Arbaces reminded him humbly.

"Of course."

"But Pompeii is only one of my missions. I mean to carry them on, city by city."

"And meantime, through me, and others like me, you'll seek Rome's favor," Diomed said thoughtfully. "An astounding plan!" he declared with a wily smile.

"Master, forgive me," called Medon as he stepped into the garden, "but your guests . . ."

"By Jupiter, I'd quite forgotten," he said honestly. "Arbaces, do stay and dine with us," he said suddenly, not caring what his guests thought.

Bowing slowly, Arbaces smiled. "You're very kind, but we in the service of Isis follow a simple life. But we must speak more of this matter soon."

"We shall," Diomed promised as the priest nodded once more and walked away, leaving Diomed to contemplate the possibility of a greatness to come.

Inside the gigantic dining room none seemed to have missed Diomed. The entertainment continued, and the many guests partook of the rich offerings. And Julia, still seated with Clodius and Glaucus, tried to make herself enjoy the banquet, and to not stare at Clodius so longingly.

"You seem rather sad," Glaucus observed after watching the overly made-up young woman for several moments.

Julia forced a smile. "I shall try to be gay, even though

I'm in mourning—for a world that's far too coarse for our Clodius.''

Glaucus laughed heartily and looked at Julia in a different light, falling in with her light and flirtatious banter. ''But surely a world with some fine things in it.''

Julia favored Glaucus with a smile, even as she observed Clodius from the corner of her eyes, gazing at them strangely. His eyes were clouded, and his face tightly drawn. He looked as if he were about to say something, when a sudden loud commotion disturbed the entire banquet.

A half-dozen yelping hunting dogs charged into the room, barely held back by a woman dressed as Diana, complete with bow and quiver. Following this came four glistening Nubians, carrying on their shoulders a wooden frame. Hanging within it was a boar, trussed as if it had just been killed, but in fact fully cooked.

The small parade circled the room, giving everyone ample opportunity to see the masterpiece. A carver danced at the rear of the strange procession, striking his two large knives together in time with the music. Suddenly the entourage stopped, and the carver whirled to the side of the boar, lunging dramatically and laying open one side.

A flock of multicolored birds emerged amidst a flurry of wings, to soar about the room, circling frantically above the heads of the startled guests. But the carver did not stop at that feat; rather, he continued to dance about, expertly cutting perfect slices of meat, and serving the boar to the guests on knifepoint, favoring Glaucus with the first piece.

''Well done,'' Glaucus cried when the carver set the meat on his platter.

''Oh, you must try it with honey,'' Julia advised. ''Daddy had the bees brought in from your native Athens.'' She reached across and picked up the jar.

Glaucus smiled at her as he took the jar and spooned the amber liquid on his platter. When he was done, he passed it to Clodius, who sat scowling at him strangely.

''Thank you, no. But a touch of fish sauce might go well,'' he said acerbically.

Glaucus saw again the cold flash of anger Julia directed at his friend. She quickly rose to her feet, her face flushed beneath the heavy rouge. "Thank you for the stimulating conversation," she said pointedly to Glaucus.

She was gone before he could reply. Clodius, the strange expression still on his face, watched her until she disappeared.

Then Glaucus heard a deep rumbling laugh and saw Diomed approaching. The host of the banquet seated himself across from the two young noblemen, smiling a secret smile, his eyes vague and distant while he nodded absently to Lucretia.

And when another course, complete with entertainment, came out, Glaucus drew his eyes from Clodius to watch the newest procession.

"I say these troubles we're having are all the fault of the mob. They've turned the gods against us with their impiety and arrogance," said one of the noblemen sitting near Diomed.

The last wave of entertainers had departed, and the feast had resumed its normal pace.

"It's true," stated an obese merchant next to Diomed. "Who among us keeps a fast these days? And no one gives a fig for Jove, or any of the gods for that matter. Why. . ." But his words were cut off as strangled, gurgling sounds issued from his mouth. A piece of meat was caught in his throat, and his face was rapidly turning a horrid shade of purple. Two slaves rushed to his aid, pounding him harshly on the back with perhaps more vigor than necessary.

Ignoring this scene, Glaucus entered the conversation, trying once again to rid himself of his apathy. "Yet Isis seems a favorite divinity here in Pompeii."

"And deservedly so," Diomed stated, seeing his chance to advance what he had been favored with earlier. "This Arbaces also, a more pious priest you couldn't find. He eats no meat, walks barefoot, and passes most nights in meditation."

"Why, Diomed, you amaze me," Lucretia said, surprised at this newly revealed knowledge of her husband's. "I didn't know you had any interest in religion."

"Did you not, indeed?" His words were like a slap in her face as he glared at her. "Now *you* amaze *me*."

"And me," Clodius cut in sardonically. "For what right-thinking man in these troubled times could deny that we depend on the gods for the prosperity of the state? Sorcery, augury, astrology, incantations, divinations . . ."

"Take a breath, man," Glaucus cautioned, seeing the worried glances with which the others favored the impoverished nobleman.

"Superstition, witchcraft, magic, charms, and portents!" Clodius continued. "What are these but payments in return for the protection of the gods?"

"No one can deny that the magistrate does his duty of maintaining public worship," said another, ignoring Clodius.

This was what Diomed was waiting for, and he pounced on it with much the same enthusiasm as shown by the lions when they had pounced upon the Christians that afternoon. "His duty, yes. As the law requires. But he does no more than that. Did you not see the way he acted at the games today?"

"With the Christians?"

Diomed nodded to the speaker. "I fear he misreads the people. He doesn't see the danger there."

"Danger, Diomed?" asked yet another man, drawn into the conversation by the obvious seriousness of the others.

"Surely you have felt the people's discontent."

The fat man, having recovered from his choking, rejoined the conversation as he hefted another piece of meat in his hand. "Diomed's quite right. In their hearts, the people have abandoned the gods of Rome. They're searching now, looking at Isis, Mithras, even at the Christians . . ."

"They need a leader who'll give them something to believe," Diomed asserted. "A leader who'll stand for something."

"Or one who can make them think he does!" Clodius added, smiling when the others laughed knowingly at his words.

Diomed frowned. "Your wit is short, Clodius, and has no point."

"Thank heavens it's only my wit."

A roar of laughter and approval greeted Clodius' words, and Diomed knew he'd lost his moment. But then the guests were all turning to stare at a new arrival, and Diomed rose quickly and started forward.

Standing in the entrance to the triclinium was Lydon, dressed in his finest, and gazing out at the crowded room. He stood awkwardly, refusing to look at Medon, who stood nearby, an anxious look on his face. The old slave hoped that his son was not hearing the low whispers of the guests who were shocked by his arrival.

"Lydon! I had given you up," Diomed declared as he neared the gladiator.

"I . . . I beg your pardon, Diomed. I was certain you said this was the proper hour," Lydon replied, flustered that he had been mistaken.

"Did I?" Diomed said, his tone as obviously mendacious as his words. "How clumsy of me. Well, never mind that. There's no doubt something left in the kitchen. Find yourself a place," he offered, gesturing toward the already overflowing couches. "You all know Lydon of course," he called out to the guests by way of introduction.

Lydon colored angrily under the realization that Diomed was making a fool of him. Finding himself uncertain as to what to do, he stared out at the sea of faces, until at last one man nodded toward him and extended his hand, offering him a seat at his couch.

It was Glaucus, embarrassed for the gladiator, who offered him a spot on the couch. When Lydon sat, a smile of thanks on his face, one of the women nearby whispered loudly enough for all to hear, "Ye gods, next that merchant will be inviting the slaves to sit with us!"

"Pay them no mind," Glaucus whispered to Lydon, but he knew his advice would not be easy to heed. He had been raised in nobility, and knew that for most of the people around him, graciousness was in short supply.

Suddenly a loud explosion sounded, and everyone turned in the direction from which it came. The door opened again, and a group of dancers emerged, waving flaming brands, which they swallowed as they danced among the guests. Then a group of slaves appeared carrying a large tray which held a replica of Vesuvius made of egg whites, and sending forth from its center wisps of white smoke. Everyone applauded when one of the fire dancers laid his brand to the top of the mountain, igniting the material, which flared quickly and then exploded. A moment later, golden honey ran like lava from the crater, coating the confection with a sparkling glaze.

"Our very own Vesuvius!" cried a guest, leading the others in applause. The revelry stopped abruptly, however, when—as though prearranged—a sudden deep rumbling filled the air and the triclinium began to vibrate. Women screamed, and men's faces blanched. Platters and goblets danced on the tables, and everyone seemed frozen to the spot. "Earthquake!" one woman screamed. Just as she spoke, the trembling within the room ceased.

"Quickly!" Sallust yelled, when color returned to his face. "Someone hurry! Throw another Christian on the fire. The gods are angry tonight!"

His words were the very thing that everyone needed to break the hypnotic tension gripping them. A moment later everyone began to laugh.

"Boy!" called Diomed. "The wine!"

As the slave Petrus left to fetch more wine, a noblewoman leaned across Glaucus, ignoring Lydon as she did, and spoke to Diomed. "The people say it's the Christians who cause the earthquakes."

"No doubt about it!" Diomed agreed.

"Nonsense," said Glaucus. "The tremors are caused by Vesuvius. None but a fool would believe otherwise."

"Of course," Diomed said quickly, flushing as he tried to recover from his mistake. "What I meant was that there's no doubt that the mob thinks it's the Christians."

The noblewoman drew back a little, but still leaning across Glaucus, she turned to smile at Clodius. "These tremors are so nerve-wracking. One's never sure when they'll stop. Why, in the last one, I was thrown right out of my bed!"

"Were you?" Clodius asked innocently.

"I was terrified. Where were you in the last quake?"

"With a lady," he said gravely.

"Was she terrified too?" the woman asked in a coy voice.

"No," Clodius said wih a grin, "but then, she wasn't thrown out of bed." His grin developed into a full smile as he reached for her hand and drew it to his lips, studying, at the same time, the size of her ring.

Her low, sagacious laugh rang in his ear, but her eyes told him that all he had to do was ask. As he released her hand, Clodius looked around the hall, stopping when his eyes met Julia's. What he saw there was real pain, and not a coy maiden's pretense. Suddenly he could not keep up his mocking front, and turned his eyes from her accusatory look.

"My friends," called Diomed, his voice theatrically loud. "They say it is Vesuvius who brings the quakes. So I say, away with Vesuvius." Diomed gestured to the slaves, who immediately started from the room, carrying the mountain of sweets with them. "The ladies shall have it to themselves," he declared. "Lucretia, take them to your chambers. . . . Show them that diamond I bought you," he ordered magisterially.

Lucretia rose obsequiously and nodded to the other women to follow her. Surprised at this sudden turn of events, the women walked from the triclinium, wondering what was happening.

"Our own treat will be quite as good, as you will see," Diomed declared to the men who stared at him. "Yes, quite as good," he repeated.

Just then a drum sounded. Glaucus leaned back, awaiting the next spectacle in Diomed's seemingly endless entertainment. Yet under the surface he felt the same detachment, the same aloofness that had been a constant companion for the past months. Only once had this strange sensation disappeared, and that had been when he had seen and spoken with Ione.

The drum rolled again, and a curtain parted at the far entrance to the room. Music started, a deep, driving beat that sent tremors of anticipation through the men. Then a dancer burst forth, her body barely concealed by her diaphanous costume.

Her long dark hair flailed the air, and she began to move with a graceful sensuality that flowed from every part of her luscious body. Long golden earrings dangled and spun when her head moved. Golden fibers within the veils shimmered with the reflected light of the torches. Even as she moved, her eyes were everywhere, seeming to caress each face, yet in fact searching for someone.

Then she saw him, and their eyes locked for the briefest second. Chloe almost lost her balance, but quickly she forced her trained muscles to obey and, in an effort not to falter, increased the sensuality of her dance. She knew from that one brief glance that Petrus was on the verge of breaking. She had seen his dark eyes flare with anger, jealousy, and hurt. Whirling, she took off the first of five thin veils, praying that somehow she would make it through this awful night.

Medon, watching Petrus, moved quickly to the younger slave's side. "Hold strong," he whispered as he thrust an empty wine jug into his hands. "Fill it!" he ordered in a strong whisper. "Bring it to the women."

Petrus started to argue, but his eyes fell on Chloe's flowing body, and his stomach churned threateningly. Turning, he stalked out of the triclinium, anger and humiliation weighing heavily upon him.

From the corner of her eye, Chloe saw Petrus leave the room; she breathed a sigh of relief. Looking at Diomed, she saw the signal he had arranged earlier, and stared at the recipient of his pointed gaze. Taking a deep breath, she fixed her eyes on Lydon's strong body. Then, with a seductive smile set on her lips, she undulated toward him. Slowly, gracefully, Chloe shed veil after veil, stopping near one man, then another, favoring each with the veil just removed, but escaping before the man's hands could capture her. She continued her erotic dance until only a thin strip of gossamer loincloth remained. By the time she reached Lydon, her body was coated with a fine sheen of perspiration that glowed under the flickering light of the torches.

Lydon watched Chloe closely, stiffening slightly when she started toward him. He was aware of the many glances directed at him, and of the envy in the eyes of the guests. Suddenly he found himself tensing, letting his muscles expand, and enjoying the attention the others were showing him.

He smiled wickedly at Chloe when she neared him, and widened his eyes when she removed the last veil to stand totally naked before him. She spun in a graceful circle, her arms snaking out quickly, her breasts bobbing enticingly. Then she was next to him, leaning over him, her long-nailed fingers tracing his muscles, her body still moving in time to the music.

Yet Lydon saw that except for the smile, her face was expressionless, blank—her eyes seemed almost dead. "Careful, Lydon," Clodius said from the gladiator's side. "She knows how to bite!"

Lydon laughed self-consciously at the nobleman's remark, even as Chloe moved her body closer. He could smell her now, the scent of various oils and her own heady female fragrance. Then her hand slipped inside his toga, her nails playing across his chest, stopping at his nipples to pinch and pull, as her eyes bored into his.

"You see, Lydon," shouted Diomed gaily, "you arrived just in time!"

But Lydon did not hear him, nor was he aware of the laughter that greeted the merchant's words as he held Chloe's gaze with his own.

"And can you blame her?" Diomed called out to the guests. "Our Lydon is known as the champion—and not just with his sword, you understand!"

Another loud round of laughter greeted this remark, as the guests grew aware of what the finale to Diomed's entertainment was really to be.

Glaucus, hearing the rude laughter, glanced at the victim of Diomed's words. He saw the pained, embarrassed expression on the gladiator's face, and forced his eyes away from the man.

"Show us how it's done, Lydon!" cried one of the guests.

Lydon tensed indignantly when Chloe's hand went lower and slid along his thigh. Anger and humiliation welled within him, until suddenly he pushed Chloe from him. Rising swiftly, Lydon glared furiously at Diomed.

"I see all too plainly why I have been invited. Do you take me for a slave?" he asked in a voice that was barely above a whisper. The thick cords of his neck muscles trembled with his anger, and a single vein throbbed powerfully.

Diomed purpled at his former slave's insolence, but controlled himself and even smiled. "How quickly we forget our past."

"Come, come, good Diomed," Glaucus called. He placed a restraining hand on Lydon's forearm, his apathy dispelled for the moment by his disgust of Diomed's treatment of this simple man. "I'm sure there's no man here who would embarrass any gentleman—no matter by how much his skill may exceed our own."

Lydon turned to Glaucus, his gratitude clearly reflected in his eyes. Then he looked at Chloe, and saw too the apology and sorrow on her face. Nodding to Glaucus, Lydon spun on his heels, his shoulders straight, his muscles rippling with tension as he walked from the room.

Diomed licked his abundant lips. Looking at Glaucus, he assessed the amount of damage his prank had done to one of his many plans. "My dear Glaucus, I do hope I've not offended you." But all he received in answer to his words was a cold stare from the handsome Greek's eyes. "Oh, dear," Diomed mumbled, almost to himself.

Clodius' laugh boomed out, followed by words that barely concealed his disdain of the merchant. "The lady is waiting, Diomed," he said, pointing to the naked dancer. "You must pay her, if only to insure she holds her tongue and does not tell all Pompeii about this failure."

Diomed glowered at Clodius, but forced himself to nod as the other men laughed in agreement at the young man's words.

But Glaucus watched only the young woman. She stood

proudly, even though he saw her trembling with fear and rage while she waited for her money.

Diomed disdainfully threw her a purse, and then focused his attention elsewhere. As she left, Chloe quietly gathered her garments to her. Glaucus stood when Chloe reached the exit, and with a nod to Clodius and his two other friends, readied himself to leave. He was tired from this long first day back in Pompeii, and more than a little disgusted by what he had witnessed at the banquet. But right now, all he wanted was a good night's sleep.

In the entry hall of Diomed's villa, Lydon put on his cape and angrily pulled open the front door. Just then Medon came rushing toward him.

"Lydon! Wait!" he called.

Lydon froze for a moment before he turned to face his father.

"My son," Medon said tenderly as he placed a hand on Lydon's shoulder.

"Please, Father, let me be," he pleaded.

Then Chloe came toward them, pausing when she saw him. "Lydon," she called.

Lydon pulled away from his father's hand and stared angrily at Chloe. Then he strode out the door, his name ringing in his ears as Chloe called out again.

Chloe stopped at the door and turned to Medon, her face sad, her eyes brimming with tears. "Forgive me, Medon. I didn't know it was Lydon who was to be made sport of."

"You're not to blame," the slave said. "My son is headstrong. I've prayed he would change and give up this life of killing, but he won't listen to me."

"Perhaps, like me, he sees no other way to live," Chloe said bitterly.

"You can't give up hope," Medon warned.

"No, Medon, but my hope lies where yours lies—in my son."

"And Petrus," Medon reminded her.

"Does it? Did you see his face tonight?"

Before Medon could console her, voices reached them as the guests began to walk into the entry hall. Chloe glanced at them, and then smiled at Medon. "I must catch up to Lydon and explain," she said, leaving quickly before the guests reached the doorway.

In the dark alleyway behind Burbo's tavern, two figures stood close together, whispering secretly. Calenus, the priest of Isis, second only to Arbaces, gestured toward the mouth of the alley while his beady eyes continually swept the area before him. He saw the side door open and he quickly ducked behind Burbo.

Stratonice stuck her head out. "Burbo! Get in here!" she screamed.

"In a moment," he called back. A second later the door closed. "Old cow," he spat.

"You could have joined the priesthood," Calenus whispered.

"And become a slave like you? No, thanks. I still remember when *you* were high priest of Isis. But now all I hear from you is 'Yes, Arbaces,' and 'No, Arbaces.' "

"You forget, my brother, that under me the temple was nothing. Arbaces has made it rich beyond imagination. He has all Pompeii at the feet of Isis, spilling golden coins like rain."

"While he holds out clean hands to catch them, and leaves the dirty work for you," Burbo chided.

"And you get your share, no?" Calenus said pointedly.

Burbo grunted. "Of the dirty work? Indeed. But . . ." He rubbed his thumb and forefinger together in accent to his unvoiced statement.

Calenus smiled his nasty smile and extended the bulging purse that had been in his hand. "For the Christians you gave us today."

Burbo hefted the purse and smiled at its weight. "Arbaces must be very anxious to rid us of the Christians."

"He intends to see that no one competes with Isis. A man like Arbaces has plans. His schemes are those I intend to be a part of. I study him, brother. I learn how he bends, I learn how he thinks. The day will come, I tell you, when he can make no move without me.'' Calenus froze at the sound of approaching voices, raised in apparent anger. Shrinking back against the wall, he leaned close to Burbo. ''I must not be seen here,'' he whispered urgently.

''It's only Lydon and Chloe,'' Burbo assured him. After the gladiator and the prostitute had mounted the stairs, Burbo ushered Calenus from the alley but stayed outside himself, trying to hear what the two new arrivals were arguing about. A moment later the tavern door closed, and their voices were gone.

''Burbo!'' came Stratonice's shrill cry.

''Coming,'' he replied. ''Bitch,'' he whispered.

Above the alley, inside Burbo's tavern, Lydon and Chloe continued to argue. ''I don't want to discuss it any more!'' he snapped at Chloe, refusing to accept her apology.

He walked away from her, and went to a door near the end of the hallway. He knocked gently.

''Yes?'' came the low voice.

''It's me,'' Lydon said. A moment later the door opened, and he stepped inside. Pausing, he gazed at Nydia's lovely face. He saw that she was holding Chloe's baby against her.

Nydia reached out with her free hand and touched his shoulder. She was instantly aware of the tremendous tension beneath her fingers. ''You are troubled,'' she whispered. ''Why? You won today, you should be happy.''

Lydon sighed, and then, as he looked at the young slave girl, he told her what had happened at the banquet. When he was finished he sat on her pallet, while she stood in the middle of the room.

''Lydon, you cannot blame Chloe. She needs the money. She wants to send her baby to be raised by a family in the country . . . if she can raise enough.''

''I don't blame Chloe, I blame myself—for forgetting who I am! And who I'll always be.''

''No, Lydon, you are the champion . . .'' she began, but he cut her off angrily.

He stood and began to pace within the confines of the

small room. "Champion, am I? I'm a slave, Nydia, as surely as my father is, as you are."

"But you bought your freedom," she protested.

"Didn't I, though—with the blood of others. And I was fool enough to think that that made me free. Yet outside the arena, who is the great Lydon? A nobody, with no money and no trade!"

"You can't believe that."

"I can. You don't see their faces, Nydia—I do. And when I kill in the arena, I look just like them. You have no idea how ugly a man can be."

He stopped pacing to look at her, and at the baby in her arms. His anger melted suddenly, and his gaze became soft and caressing. He went to her and raised one of his large hands. Gently, softly, he stroked her cheek, and then moved his fingers across her closed eyelids. He spoke quietly: "Maybe that is what saves you. You are forced to live in this cesspool, yet it never seems to touch you."

"That's not true," she whispered sadly.

"It is. You're so much finer than the others."

"Don't mock me!" Nydia exclaimed, hurt by his conde-scending tone.

"I would never mock you. You're the only thing that gives me any hope," he whispered as he stroked her cheek again.

Nydia drew away from his touch. Shaking her head, she edged away from him, unable to see both the hurt that suffused his features or the love that was in his eyes.

"Please, Lydon, I must sleep, and the baby too. I have to work in the morning." He sighed deeply as he turned, and moved slowly to the door.

"Good night, Nydia," he said.

"Good night, Lydon," she replied, troubled and unsure of why she felt guilty at her refusal to let him touch her.

Chapter Five

As the spring changed into summer and the sun brought more and more heat to the streets of Pompeii, Glaucus continued to rise early, as was his custom. Though his days were filled with numerous activities, he found himself looking forward to the only thing that made him feel a part of life. Only in the mornings, when he walked from his house to the temple of Isis to gaze at Ione's beauty, did he find relief from the listlessness that depressed him.

For too many weeks Glaucus had allowed his mind to dwell on the future. There were too many things that bothered him. Wherever he walked, he saw the poor and the wretched. Although his purse was full, he was conscious of the multitudes surrounding him, the people who had nothing. There were many speculations, questions about life, but when each day drew to a close, he had found no true answers. Yet each day he began his search anew, always starting with the one object most likely to prove unattainable.

He realized it was becoming an obsession, this need to at least see Ione each morning, to stand in her presence. At least for those few short minutes each day he felt alive.

Today as he reached the entrance of the open temple he saw that a large crowd of worshipers had gathered. Scanning their faces, he recognized many, including the merchant Diomed and his garishly attired wife, Lucretia. Then his attention was drawn to the altar where Ione stood, her beautiful face rapt with attention as she watched Arbaces and a writhing, screaming woman, dressed in rags, kneeling before the high priest.

"O mighty Isis," Arbaces called out, his hands reaching

toward the heavens, "mother of us all. Send down, we pray, thy healing rays to touch this afflicted woman, and make her whole again."

Spittle drooled in a thin line from the side of the woman's mouth. Her limbs jerked uncontrollably. Arbaces bent and grabbed her by her shoulders. She screamed, then stopped—her eyes wide, fixed on the priest's face.

"Woman! Hear Isis speaking through me and believe! Devils! Spirits! Monsters!" he cried. "Flee this woman's body! Let you be gone!"

The woman howled loudly, as if she had been struck. Then she sagged in Arbaces' arms, her head falling limply forward. Arbaces lowered her to the ground as a low moan issued from her throat.

The crowd edged closer, and a collective gasp issued up when the woman began to lift her head. Her eyes were open now, clear and focused. A smile softened her grizzled features, making her look much younger.

Then she bent her head low, her face almost touching the bare feet of the priest. "O great Arbaces," she called in a clear voice no longer tinged with insanity.

But Arbaces stopped her by pulling her to her feet and guiding her to the statue of Isis.

"Pray not to me, woman, for I am nothing. It is Isis, in her mercy, who has saved you."

The woman burst into tears and threw herself at the foot of the statue. "Isis," she cried, "mighty Isis, my goddess."

Again Arbaces faced the crowd, his naked chest glistening with sweat, his voice deep and powerful: "Heed well this woman's fate, and in it, read your own! She disobeyed her master, and for this Isis justly struck her!"

The poor and the slaves in the crowd stared fearfully at the priest, while the rich murmured their approval of his words. But for Glaucus, it was all a show. He watched the people surge forward, laying their donations at the feet of the statue. He noted how Diomed made a great show of tossing a thick purse at the deity's feet, all the while gazing up at Arbaces.

Then he saw Ione turn her head slightly to stare at her

brother, who stood silently at the rear of the altar, his face pale and drawn, his eyes glazed, unseeing, uncaring.

As Glaucus watched Ione move toward Antonius, he noticed also the movements of the crazed woman who had been cured so miraculously only moments before. Casting a glance over her shoulder, she eased her way from the crowd and toward the sacrarium, a place she, of all people, should not belong. Glaucus smiled at the sudden swiftness of her movements, and realized that she was far younger than she had appeared to be.

"Cured," he said mockingly and turned to look back at Ione. He saw her talking to her brother, and noticed also that Antonius did not answer. Then Arbaces came to them, shook his head slowly, and led Antonius away.

Curious, he thought while he moved toward the object which haunted him nightly in his dreams.

Ione saw Glaucus approaching and drew in her breath as she studied the handsome planes of his face.

"Good day, Ione," he said when he reached her side.

Ione hesitated, trying to understand what emotions warred within her whenever she saw Glaucus. "Good day," she whispered. "You worship Isis also?"

Glaucus slowly shook his head. "I worship instead she who worships Isis."

Blushing, Ione turned from his intense gaze, while she fought to control her emotions. "I should have thought your sort would favor Bacchus."

"My sort?" he asked innocently. "And what sort is that?"

Ione gazed openly into his large, liquid eyes. "The sort who spends his life in vain pursuits and idle pleasures."

Stiffening under her words, Glaucus kept the smile firmly affixed on his lips. "But you are my pleasure—and my idol."

"And you are as vain as your pursuit," she snapped, falling quickly into their strange banter.

"Well said!" Glaucus declared with a full smile. "Ione, I . . ." But he stopped when he saw her features tense and her

eyes dart past his shoulder. A second later he heard Arbaces'
distinctive voice in his ear.

"Noble Glaucus," Arbaces called politely.

Glaucus turned, his smile still fixed, and bowed politely to
the priest.

"You are welcome to the temple. And if you care to know
something of our religion, perhaps I can help you," he
offered, his gaze shifting from Glaucus to Ione, and back to
Glaucus again. "As I am certain that you have no interest in
disturbing the worship of *any* of our members," he added
pointedly.

Smiling tightly, Glaucus nodded. "Forgive me, Arbaces. I
didn't realize I *was* disturbing." On his last word, he flicked
his eyes to Ione. "Good day," he said to both of them as he
turned and walked from the temple. On the street, he stopped
and looked back just as Ione glanced over her shoulder. He
thought he saw a sad expression on her face, but she quickly
drew her eyes away from his and followed Arbaces away.

Perhaps there is a chance after all, he told himself. He
wanted to go home now, to exercise until his passion for Ione
was abated. And after that, he was to meet his friends and
attend a play.

Sighing at the foolishness of life, Glaucus started home.

Within the sacrarium, the priests and priestesses of Isis
gathered in a dark chamber. The walls were draped in a
black, shiny material which reflected the light of the single
candle placed in the center of the altar.

The chamber was silent except for the sound of breathing
as Antonius knelt at the base of the altar before a young priest
dressed in white.

Antonius looked up at him, and the priest nodded. Then he
placed a small amount of white powder on Antonius' tongue.
Staring deeply into the youth's eyes, he handed him a golden
goblet.

The voices of those gathered in the room rang out in a
droning, repetitive chant that was both eerie and hypnotizing.
Antonius drained the goblet and returned it to the white-robed

priest, who slowly stepped back while Arbaces took his place before the kneeling initiate.

"Antonius," Arbaces said, "for forty days you have kept your vow of silence and have purified your soul with fasting, partaking only of the holy food and drink of Isis. Now the time has come for you to take your vows. First, the vow of poverty, to which all must ascribe."

Arbaces lifted a stylus and vellum, which he offered to Antonius. "My son, with this you offer all your worldly goods to Isis."

Antonius took the vellum and reached for the stylus, but Arbaces drew it back as he stared into the dull, drugged eyes of his wealthiest disciple. "But Isis, in her wisdom, accepts only what is freely given. Antonius, think well! Search your heart and enter this with a clear mind."

Antonius' eyes were half lidded and vacant. His face remained slack and uncaring as the drug he had just taken turned his mind into fog, stealing away the last of his free will. Antonius slowly nodded in his effort to please Arbaces.

"Do you freely give, my son?" he reiterated.

"I freely give," Antonius replied in a hollow voice.

Arbaces handed him the stylus, and after Antonius had scribbled his name Arbaces helped him to his feet. "Isis loves you," he said as he embraced the newest of the cult's priests.

With this cue, everyone in the chamber rose and came toward the two men. Each priest and priestess, in turn, embraced Antonius, welcoming him into their ranks. When it was done, Arbaces lifted his arms and the room became silent again.

"Now let him be taken to the Hall of Mysteries, as is his right." When Arbaces stepped back, the others took Antonius into their midst and carried him from the chamber, leading him to the Hall of Mysteries. But Arbaces did not follow them; instead, he motioned Calenus to him.

"That girl this morning was good," he said to his assistant when they were alone. "She played her role well."

"And she was paid well, too," Calenus rejoined. "Xenia is greedy, but of good use."

"They are all greedy, Calenus, which suits our purposes. Come," he ordered imperiously.

With a nod, Calenus followed the high priest from the chamber and down a long hallway, with Arbaces carefully holding the signed document giving him sole rights to all of Antonius' wealth and property. Two large eunuchs followed behind them, struggling with the large coffer laden with the day's offerings.

The group stopped at an ornately carved door. Arbaces unlocked it and motioned the eunuchs to enter. Once they had placed the coffer on the floor, he waved the eunuchs from the room and closed the door behind them.

When the two men were alone, Calenus spoke. "Young Antonius had estates a bird couldn't fly over. No doubt Ione will give the same when she is initiated."

Arbaces shook his head. "You miss the point, Calenus. Their wealth is useful, true, but better still is the fact that they're from old stock. Their father's name is still beloved, respected . . ."

Calenus understood then, and his eyes sparkled greedily. "Which makes them very useful in attracting other nobles to the temple."

Arbaces took a torch from the wall and held it high. From every direction, gold and jewels glittered under the flickering light. Ropes of gold spilled from coffers, and carelessly strewn plates of silver shone like full moons.

Arbaces withdrew a dagger from within the hidden folds of his robe and held it in the air. The golden handle was ornately carved with twining serpents. "Lovely, isn't it?" Arbaces asked as he gazed at the unusual dagger.

Without waiting for a reply, he turned and used the dagger to open the day's coffer. When he had replaced the blade in its sheath, he motioned the other priest forward. While Calenus worked, Arbaces replaced the torch in its notch and paced within the room full of treasure.

"Antonius looks upon you as a god," Calenus said while he sorted the coins.

"He's the perfect choice to take my place in Pompeii, when I am done here."

"Arbaces . . ." Calenus cried, stung by the words.

Arbaces, a calculating smile on his thin lips, shook his head slowly. He lifted a large jewel from a table and went to Calenus, where he stuffed the sparkling gem into his robe. "Pompeii is but one step toward a much larger goal. I need a man like you along the way. A man who understands expedience . . . and certain necessities."

Calenus looked at him knowingly as he nodded. "Sometimes you sound more like a politician than a priest."

"Today one can hardly tell the difference. I *do* have a great concern for the empire. Look at the rulers we've had since Nero, who was himself unspeakable."

"No real leader among them," Calenus agreed.

"A leader is he who is supported by the people. The man who will control the empire is the leader who can bind the people together with a deep belief in which they all can share."

"Like the belief in Isis?" Calenus whispered. When he saw the shrewd look covering Arbaces' face, Calenus had his answer. "Arbaces," he said carefully, "you mean to be that leader."

"How smart you have become," Arbaces said with a smile.

As the applause faded, people began to leave the theater, spilling into the street. Glaucus, disturbed by some of the unexpected undertones of the comedy, reached the street in the company of his three friends.

"Good old Plautus; his comedies still hold up," Clodius commented.

"Although it's not easy work, making sport of marriage," Sallust agreed.

"But is contentment truly worth more than a dozen pots of gold, as he says there?" Lepidus queried.

"Never!" swore Clodius. "But a dozen pots of wine—now that's something else. Shall we?" he asked the others.

"Who's buying?" asked Sallust.

"Glaucus, of course," Clodius stated jovially. "And later, perhaps a look at the ladies?"

Glaucus shook his head at this. His mood was too heavy, and he wanted to be alone. "I won't be joining you," he told them.

Clodius looked at him, his face set in worried lines. "What's come over you? You're dour as a Christian. Or have you lost your pot of gold, the gods forbid?"

"Life is more than money and games," Glaucus snapped with a marked lack of humor.

"Now I know you're ill," Clodius joked, hiding his surprise at Glaucus' words.

"Or at last offended by our grossness?" Sallust asked cheerfully.

"Nonsense!" Lepidus declared. "It's plain the man is in love. He shows all the signs: sighing, incivility, philosophizing, moralizing . . ."

"Forgive me, but I must go." Without a backward glance, Glaucus walked away, wondering why he had been so rude, but suddenly not caring. He knew that it was his money that attracted the three, but he had long ago accepted that fact. He believed also that beneath their carefree surfaces they were basically good men.

Before he could get more than half a block from the theater, Glaucus encountered Diomed and Julia, the merchant greeting the passing people with the smiles and speeches indicative of his sudden political aspirations.

"Ah, Glaucus," Diomed called, elbowing Julia into attentiveness.

"Diomed, Julia," Glaucus said in turn, bowing to them.

"Wonderful, that Aristophanes! I like his stand on marriage. A fool with money, though . . ."

"Daddy, Plautus wrote the play, not Aristophanes."

Diomed waved her statement away airily. "A Greek at any rate. No doubt you've met him," he said to Glaucus.

"He was a Roman, actually," Glaucus said, controlling his face carefully.

"And I doubt that Glaucus knows him," Julia cut in again. "He's been dead three hundred years."

Glaucus cast Julia an amused look and began to edge away. Diomed, however, was not yet finished.

"Why, what a clever pair you make," he said as he wagged his finger before Glaucus' face. "I know young men set great store by passion, but as the years go on, a clever wife is an enormous comfort."

"Who would know better than you, Daddy," Julia said, her words laced with irony. "We must go," she added to Glaucus.

"As I must," he replied.

"No, you must join us," Diomed offered. "I'm speaking to the baker's guild this evening, a most important political group for me."

"Thank you, but I promised Clodius . . ." He spoke the lie easily but paused when he saw Julia's expression change at the sound of the name.

"But . . ." Diomed began.

"Goodbye, Glaucus," Julia said.

Glaucus bowed formally and went on his way. As he walked he wondered just why Julia always reacted so strongly to Clodius, whom she seemed to detest. Or did she?

Nighttime in Pompeii could be peaceful and pleasant, or loud and raucous, depending where you were and which night it was. This early summer night on the waterfront was a quiet one, the fishing boats having been tied up hours ago and the dockworkers and slaves long gone to their homes.

The shops were shuttered for the night, most locked against the possibility of thievery. But one shop, although shuttered, was not dark and empty inside, for the secret room within Olinthus' shop was filled with people who waited for the sailmaker to lead them.

Medon, sitting near Olinthus, gazed at Chloe and at the young baby in her arms. The young prostitute spoke proudly to the sailmaker. "Olinthus," she said, "I'm so grateful that you'll bless my child—in spite of what *I* am."

"No, Chloe," the large, bearded man said, "Christ has taught us that we are all equal in the sight of God. I cannot judge you. Yet I cannot but hope that one day you will change your life, so that you may take Christian vows."

Blinking, Chloe tried to find the right words with which to answer him. "I tell myself that when I know my baby is provided for, then I will start a new and better life. But inside, I know the world will always see me as Chloe the whore. What chance have I to change that?" she asked in a sad whisper.

A sharp rap on the door startled everyone, and as Olinthus rose he signaled everyone to silence. "Petrus?" Chloe asked Medon in a low voice.

Medon closed his eyes and shook his head. "I'm sorry, Chloe. I tried, but . . ."

Chloe nodded in understanding, and did not show the pain she felt. When she looked up again, she saw Olinthus leading the boy Catus inside.

"You're sure you weren't seen?" he asked.

"It's all right, Olinthus," the boy reassured him.

Olinthus sighed and approached Chloe, taking the baby from her and pulling him close to his chest. Turning, he gazed into each of the faces before him.

"Dear friends, how brave you are for coming here tonight, despite the danger, so that we may keep faith with one another, and with God. The loss of our loved ones has been hard to bear," he said as he held the baby out in front of him in an evident offering to the people. "But see how God blesses us with *new* life! See how he sends this precious likeness of his own son to remind us of his promise."

Medon rose suddenly, his hands outstretched, stopping Olinthus. "Someone," he whispered. All eyes turned toward the door. Olinthus handed the baby back to Chloe and went forward. Fear charged the room with tension, and one person began to edge toward the secret exit.

Olinthus went to the front of the shop, and as the gentle

rapping sounded again, he peered through the small spy hole. Exhaling in sharp relief, Olinthus opened the door to Petrus.

"It's all right," he called when he walked back to the others, his arm around Petrus' shoulder.

Chloe gasped when she saw her lover. Petrus stared at her for a moment, and then a change came over his face. He walked to her and, taking the baby in one arm, drew her close with the other.

Olinthus, seeing that Petrus had finally come to terms with his plight, smiled and took a deep breath. "Let us pray, as Paul has taught us," he said as he fell to his knees and bowed his head solemnly.

After Chloe and Petrus had knelt, the baby still in his father's arms, Olinthus' voice rang out clearly. "The Lord is my light and my salvation; whom shall I fear? The Lord is the strength of my life; of whom shall I be afraid?"

Several weeks after the day of the games and the stormy events of that night, Glaucus again strolled with Clodius in Pompeii's open market. Walking aimlessly about, they watched the vendors who sold what they could, the thieves who stole what they could, and the merchants who profited from all the others.

They passed the slave traders' stall and eyed the naked female slave being offered. They walked on, stopping when they saw Diomed astride a large stool in the center of the cloth sellers' market.

"Again?" asked Clodius.

"Always," replied Glaucus, staring at the now familiar form of the fat merchant as he orated to the gathered throngs, casting about for the votes that he hoped would make him magistrate of Pompeii. To Glaucus, this familiar sight would have been depressing, if not for Diomed's comedic appearance and gestures.

"How can you vote for him?" Diomed asked. "He is an ordinary bureaucrat. What can he understand? But *I*, I am a businessman, as are you. I know your problems; they're mine as well. I've felt the threat of increased importation. These are my ships, remember, that should be sending *your* cloth abroad.''

Clodius nudged Glaucus and tilted his head toward the edge of the crowd. Glaucus looked in that direction and saw Arbaces, with a group of priests in tow. He saw Diomed nod to the high priest, even as he spoke, and watched the priest favor the merchant with a slow inclination of his gold-banded head.

"We can work together," Diomed continued, "to make Pompeii prosperous. . . .''

"Let's go," Clodius urged, and started to move away.

Glaucus followed. Behind him, Diomed's words continued to ring out, pleading with the citizens for their votes. A few blocks later they stopped in a weaponmaker's stand, and Glaucus looked through a fine display of daggers.

Spotting one that stood out from the rest, he lifted it and gazed at the intricately carved handle, coated with smooth gold. The twining serpents, spaced just right for a man's hand, called to Glaucus strangely. He held it toward Clodius, to see what his friend thought of it.

"Very fine," Clodius said. "Unusual also."

"Yes, it is. I'll have it," he told the weaponmaker.

While Glaucus paid for the dagger, Clodius looked out onto the street where a richly dressed, elegant woman of sixty was exiting a shop across from him. She stopped, and Clodius saw her eyes roam about anxiously.

"The Lady Fortunata," he whispered.

"Who?" Glaucus asked when he'd finished the transaction.

"It's not often that she leaves the villa."

"Who is she?" Glaucus repeated, his curiosity piqued.

"The wife of Gaius, an old senator. Hmm, I wonder if he is ill? I should pay him a visit soon," Clodius said, with a greedy glint in his eye.

Clodius, aware of Glaucus' stare, turned back to the weaponmaker and began to look at other things. Glaucus stayed where he was, watching the elegant noblewoman walk toward the weapons shop, noting also the nervousness that was like an aura surrounding her.

She stopped suddenly, and Glaucus saw her turn pale. Then he saw Arbaces come up to her with a smile on his face that did not reflect in his eyes.

"My . . . Lady Fortunata. What a rare pleasure," Arbaces said loudly enough for Glaucus to hear. "And your noble husband, Gaius. Is he not with you? Surely he has not left his villa for any reason . . . ?"

Glaucus heard the underlying threat in the priest's voice, and saw also the way Fortunata stood stiffly, as though in fear.

"You know he never speaks to anyone, Arbaces, nor will he."

"That is good, but do give him my greetings. And please, assure him that I have not forgotten him. Indeed, I will never forget him."

Fortunata nodded her head and turned suddenly, just as her litter came to her side. When she stepped toward it, Arbaces reached out his hand to her, but one of her massive Nubian slaves stepped quickly between them and stared at him openly and without fear.

Fascinated by what was happening, Glaucus continued to watch. Arbaces stepped to the side and gave Fortunata a low bow and a wry smile. *Strange*, Glaucus thought, *very strange*.

"Come," Clodius called. "I think it is time for some food and wine, no?"

"Are you always hungry or just thirsty?" Glaucus asked.

"When you're buying, I'm both," Clodius said with a laugh.

Glaucus shook his head and put his arm about Clodius' shoulder. "All right, my noble-born friend, food and wine it shall be, but a story to go with it."

"Story?" asked Clodius.

"I would hear of Fortunata and Gaius," Glaucus said, his interest still strong after what he had witnessed.

A frown creased Clodius' forehead. "Perhaps," he said, carefully keeping his face straight, and wondering if he dared tell Glaucus about them.

Chapter Six

"Oh, Petrus!" Chloe cried as she arched her back, thrusting herself up to him, her long legs locked around his strong thighs, her hands digging into the flesh of his back.

His lips covered hers as he pushed himself deeper into her, savoring the moist heat that captured him, caring not for the past, or the future, but only for the present.

Her full breasts were crushed to his chest, and his arms held her captive, but her body would not be still as it twisted beneath his, her muscles gripping him tightly, holding the length of him within her. Then, in a way that never happened with another man, her muscles contracted, squeezing him, forcing her breath to explode outward.

Yet Petrus still rode her, his hips moving rhythmically, his mouth searching across her neck, dipping down as he lifted himself on his arms while he caught one taut nipple between his teeth. Then Chloe's hands did their magic, floating along his buttocks. He thrust deeply one last time, and poured his seed within her.

He lowered himself atop her, their breathing harsh and loud in the silent room above Burbo's tavern. A few moments later, Petrus lifted his weight from her and rolled on his side, while Chloe kissed him deeply. Several quiet minutes passed, and when their breathing returned to normal, Chloe slid from the bed, covering him with a light sheet as she looked at him lovingly.

She crossed the room, lifted the robe from the table, and slipped it over her head, pausing for a moment to gaze at her lover's contented face. She tensed as she heard footsteps in the hall, then relaxed as they continued past her room.

She realized, however, that too much time had gone by. Smiling, she walked toward the bed. "Out, out! Out!" she laughed, playfully pulling the cover from his body, yet unable to resist one last longing look at the smooth, muscled body of the man she loved.

"Cruel woman!" he cried as he tried to reclaim the cover. Then he stopped fighting and grabbed her wrist, pulling her down to him and kissing her passionately.

"You'll be missed," she said when she drew her mouth from his. "Even old Diomed can't spend the *whole* day giving speeches in the market." She pulled away when Petrus tried to kiss her again. "Petrus! Even Medon can only cover so much for you."

Petrus shook his head and sighed. "True," he whispered. Then his eyes locked with Chloe's in a deep, searching gaze. "But perhaps Diomed will win the election, and . . ."

"No. Let's hope not. With Arbaces supporting him, all will go even harder with those who believe in Christianity," she stated.

"Possibly. But I've been thinking. Sometimes when a master has good fortune, he frees some of his slaves as a show of generosity, and . . ."

"Petrus, when did Diomed ever free a slave?"

"Why not?" Petrus demanded. "I've served him faithfully. And Chloe, think of all the freedmen who've done well for themselves. If I were free, we could . . ." His voice trailed off as Chloe laid her fingers across his lips.

"A dream, Petrus, just a dream."

"You don't know that! Those things do happen," he protested, but without real conviction.

Chloe leaned forward and embraced him tenderly, drawing his head to her breasts in a timeless gesture of understanding and comfort. "Yes they happen sometimes. Petrus, I love you for your dreams. But I can't bear to see you hurt again. You are a slave. I am a slave and a prostitute. Such is our lot, and that is the very reason why I'll stop at nothing to see my child grow up a free man!''

"I know . . ." Petrus began, but a loud cry of pain echoed into the room, cutting off whatever he was going to say.

"Nydia," Chloe said as she rose and ran to the door. Petrus left the bed, pulling on his toga as he followed Chloe into the hall. There he and Chloe stopped when they saw Stratonice and the blind slave girl.

"No!" Nydia cried, holding out her hands protectively.

"I warned you!" screamed the hulking figure of Stratonice. "I told you what I would do! Get down those stairs, you lazy slut!"

Nydia tried to move, but she was too slow, and Stratonice swung her massive hand again, knocking Nydia backwards, sending her crashing down the stairs.

"Oh, my God, Nydia," Chloe whispered, burying her face in Petrus' chest. Stratonice raced down the stairs after the blind girl as Petrus moved to go after them, but Chloe held him back. "We can't," she said bitterly. "You're a slave. I . . ."

They moved to the edge of the landing and watched what was happening below. Stratonice hauled Nydia to her feet, pulling her close to her face. "Too refined to please the men for me, are you? We'll see how you like it on the block."

"Please," Nydia begged, tears spilling from her unseeing eyes.

Suddenly Philos, the artist, ran from the serving bar to face Stratonice himself. "You don't want to sell Nydia," he said in a placating voice. "She won't bring any kind of price. And, Stratonice, she does give this place an air."

"I'll give you an air, you little whelp!" Stratonice shouted, sending Philos spinning with a backhanded slap.

"No!" Nydia screamed, renewing her struggles to free herself from the woman's grasp.

Unable to stand more, Chloe rushed down the stairs. "Stratonice. No. You can't do this!"

Again Stratonice's hand snaked out, her plump fingers

winding into Chloe's hair, dragging her face close to hers. "Stay out of this unless you prefer whoring on the street."

With that, Chloe was flung back, barely managing to grasp the railing and break her fall. Looking up, she saw Petrus staring at her, about to charge down to her aid. She shook her head fiercely at him, stopping him in his tracks.

Chloe stared helplessly while Stratonice dragged Nydia from the room. When the door slammed behind them, she turned to Philos, who was just getting to his feet.

"Philos," she cried, running to the dwarf. "You must help me, help Nydia."

"How?" he asked groggily, his head still spinning from the blow he had received.

"Go to Lydon. Tell him what is happening," she pleaded.

"Yes," Philos said quickly. "Poor Nydia."

Then he too was gone, and Chloe looked back up at Petrus' sad face.

Since early morning the gladiators of Pompeii had been hard at their practice. Swords flashed in the air. Groans and cries were rife as the fighters swung at the straw dummies that were today's foe. The men had been paired off by Marcus to work in teams, and while Sporus and Melior trained at one spot, Lydon helped Gar at another.

"Thrust!" he shouted to the German, watching the clumsy fighter attack the dummy. "Now at me!" he shouted.

Gar turned, raised his sword high, and charged. Swinging hard, he aimed his blow at Lydon's head, but the champion deflected the stroke easily, at the same time flicking his wrist to rid his blade of Gar's. Then Lydon lunged, his sword tip resting a hair away from Gar's throat.

Stepping back, Lydon nodded. "That's how it's done. Now again!" he ordered.

Sporus signaled Melior to wait, and they both watched as Gar attacked Lydon over and over, never getting past the champion's guard. Then Marcus was there, yelling even more instructions at the ponderous fledgling gladiator.

"I can't think why Lydon wastes his time with that over-grown barbarian," Sporus said.

"Not jealous are you, Sporus?" Melior asked with a grin.

Sporus sniffed airily at the question, but his eyes returned to Lydon. "It's not like him. He never involves himself with anyone. And Gar . . . He's hopeless."

Shouts and laughter broke out behind them. In the midst of another group of gladiators, Philos was being tossed into the air like a ball.

"Let me alone!" he screamed in terror. "I must see Lydon! Lydon! Help me!" he cried over and over.

"Enough!" Lydon ordered. "Let him go."

The last gladiator to catch the dwarf held him firmly aloft and walked over to Lydon, where he carefully placed Philos on his feet.

"What is it, Philos?"

"Lydon," Philos said urgently, "you must come. It's Nydia!"

"What has happened to her?" Lydon asked, as a warning chill raced along his spine.

"Stratonice is selling her in the market today," Philos said, almost cringing when the words were out.

Lydon stared at him for a moment, then he shook his head. "It can't be."

"It's true! Lydon, Chloe sent me after you. You must help Nydia!"

"I will," Lydon promised. He whirled on those who were watching him, his face dark and angry, his heavily muscled chest rising and falling with his strain. "I need money," he shouted to Marcus.

"I'm sorry, Lydon," Marcus replied, turning his grizzled face from Lydon. All the men did the same, except for Sporus.

Lydon approached the gladiator solemnly. "Sporus, please. You know I'll repay you."

"You always have to be the hero, don't you? You stand all the drinks at Burbo's and blow all the lucre you win on trifles. And now you need me to help you buy a woman . . . of all things!'' Sporus said contemptuously.

Angered, but controlling his pride, Lydon spoke to Sporus again. ''I can't let them take her. I'll . . . I'll pledge you my full purse from the next games. Sporus, you know how much I'll earn in Campania.''

''Unless you're killed,'' Sporus said icily. Then he smiled and placed his arm intimately around Lydon's shoulder. ''Forget this slave girl.''

The moment the words were out, Lydon spun, pushing Sporus from him. Taking a deep breath, he ran from the practice field toward the crowds heading to the market.

''She doesn't give a damn for you, you fool!'' Sporus shouted as he stood. *But I do,* he said silently to himself.

After a pleasant few hours spent over lunch, Glaucus and Clodius were again walking to the market place. Clodius, happy with the way he had managed to avoid any discussion about Gaius and Fortunata, veered them toward a silk merchant. While Glaucus looked over the man's wares, Clodius glanced across the stall to see Julia examining a length of blue silk. A moment later, Julia turned, her eyes widening when she saw him. Her face reddened, and though his smile was not a cruel one this time, she turned her back on him anyway.

''A handsome girl, that Julia,'' Glaucus said as he watched his friend.

''I've noticed that you appear to think so,'' Clodius replied, his voice sharper than he'd intended.

Glaucus arched his eyebrows in surprise. ''Are you jealous?''

Clodius forced a laugh from his dry throat, and shook his head sadly. ''Really Glaucus, of a merchant's daughter? No background—and all her coin new-minted. I was simply questioning *your* taste.''

''Does it never give you pause to think you aristocratic poor could be outstripped in time by these industrious freedmen?'' As he spoke, he waved away a pretty vendor who was offering beautiful cloaks, one of which had caught Clodius' eye.

"You are cruel, Glaucus," Clodius said suddenly.

Glaucus heard the change in his friend's voice and paused. "Here, I'll make it up to you. The cloak is yours."

Clodius' smile was dazzling as he reached for the cloak, while Glaucus dipped his fingers into his purse. But his hand stopped when he saw a terrible sight in the distance.

"Nydia," he shouted, forgetting Clodius and the vendor as he watched Stratonice dragging the blind slave along. A second later he was running in the street.

Before Glaucus caught up to Nydia, Stratonice had reached the slave trader and had whispered something into his ear. The man smiled and hauled Nydia up onto the block.

Glaucus stopped at the edge of the crowd, staring at the hapless girl the trader now offered for sale.

"She's blind, you robber," shouted one customer.

"Yes, but what she's best at needs no eyes. Come on, my dear," he said, pulling down one side of her robe.

"No!" Nydia screamed, trying to draw away from him.

"And she has spirit too," he cried out with a laugh. "Tell me, where can you find any better!" Finishing the last word, he whirled on Nydia, his hand snapping out to catch the edge of her robe and rip it from her body.

Nydia stood there, her arms crossed in front of her just budding breasts, her body trembling with a fear she had never before known. Then, with a keen sense possessed only by the blind, she heard her name being called from a distance and instantly recognized the voice as Lydon's.

Glaucus flinched when the trader tore Nydia's robe from her. His usual aloof detachment disappeared, and his heart—and anger—burst through. Pushing all those near him out of the way, he ran to the block, jumped upon it, and covered Nydia with his own cloak.

"Your sale is made," he snapped angrily, tossing a money bag at the slave trader.

The crowd laughed and applauded good-naturedly at the nobleman's gesture, but Glaucus paid it no heed as he drew the frightened girl to him and lifted her down from the block.

Glaucus took Nydia with him, brushing past the crowd. He

was still so angry that he did not notice Olinthus staring at them, his face twisted with fury at what he had just witnessed.

From the moment Glaucus had called out her name, Nydia's heart had found new life. Now, with his arm tight around her, she spoke. "It is you, Glaucus, isn't it?" she asked in a sobbing voice.

"We must get away from here," Glaucus stated.

"Are you mad?" Clodius said in a hissing whisper when he finally reached Glaucus' side after witnessing the unbelievable act of his friend.

Ignoring Clodius, Glaucus continued through the crowd. "You'll be all right now. I'll take you to my house," he assured Nydia.

"Oh, Glaucus," Nydia whispered, her voice still choked with emotion.

As they turned the corner, Glaucus did not see the gladiator who stared at them so fiercely—the veins on his forehead and neck throbbing wildly. Lydon, with his heart pounding, and his mind a confusion of sadness and jealousy, knew he had lost Nydia forever. And worse, he had lost her to the only nobleman who had ever shown him a kindness.

Whirling, Lydon fixed his heated glare on the slave trader, now whipping a manacled Nubian who was defiantly refusing to mount the block.

"Get up there, you black bastard!" he shouted. Then he cracked the whip across the man's back.

Lydon started to turn away but stopped when he saw his father's friend Olinthus charge forward and grab the slave trader's wrist.

"This is a man! A human being," Olinthus cried, "not a beast. He is not a piece of goods to buy and sell."

"Get out of here, you madman," yelled the trader as he pulled his wrist free.

Olinthus, a full head taller than the trader, knocked the man off his feet and, just as swiftly, bent and took the bulging money bag that Glaucus had given him.

"Guards! Guards!" cried the trader, "arrest him!" The

man's words were echoed by the crowd which was now shouting at Olinthus.

"Yes!" Olinthus called out, louder than any in the crowd. "Yes, people, howl! But howl and weep aloud for the miseries that shall overtake you! You think your gold is god," he cried, opening the purse and flinging its contents into the air. The golden coins arched upward, sparkling in the sun, until they fell into the eager faces of the crowd.

"But as it so flashes in the sun, so too will it burn into your very flesh as this man's chains burn into his! For with your gold, you store up the fire for your last, pitiful days!"

Lydon watched the bronze-armored guards approach Olinthus. He was paralyzed by what he saw, knowing that if he went to the man's aid it would cost him everything he had worked for. Then the most fearful of all cries filled the air, even as the guards seized the sailmaker's arms.

"Christian! Christian! Christian!" the crowd cried, their voices combining into a lethal chant. Then the guards dragged Olinthus through the crowd, allowing the people to pummel him with their fists or whatever else they had at hand.

But the sailmaker refused to flinch; rather, he carried on in his oration. "Hear my warning! Those last days are coming! Those last days are coming soon!"

Far beneath the streets of Pompeii, a lake of molten lava began to climb its way upward, reaching toward the high ceiling that was the very ground of the city above. It rose steadily, angrily, as if in answer to the sailmaker's distraught warning. But soon it fell back upon itself, boiling, hissing, steaming, not yet ready to make its final thrust. That would wait for another day.

Glaucus waved his household slave away, preferring to pour the next glass of wine for himself. After returning from the market, he had spent the day in the gymnasium, exercising his muscles until they ached and throbbed with pain.

His mind was troubled, caused in part by his irrational behavior at the market. He knew he'd had no business interfering at the slave sale, but something in him had snapped, cracking his shield of indifference, and his heart had gone out to the blind girl.

He sipped the wine, and thought about the day, over two months ago, when he had returned to Pompeii, and the strange sense of change that had gripped him then. *Was today a part of it?* he wondered. So much had happened since he'd returned, but Glaucus realized very little had changed. Pompeii was still the same—falling a little into decline, perhaps, but still the same. *I am seeing everything in a different light,* he thought suddenly. *Everything, and everyone, including myself!*

His attention was drawn to the door, which opened to reveal Nydia, dressed in a fine Grecian robe of blue and white.

"That's much better. You look very pretty, Nydia."

"Thank you," Nydia replied with her usual shyness, while she reached out to find the wall.

Glaucus rose and went to her, taking her hand and leading her within.

"I'm sorry to trouble you. But I will learn my way about very soon."

"I'm sure you will. Sit here," he said when they reached a bench. He sat across from her, gazing at her young face. For a moment, neither spoke.

"Glaucus, I . . . I don't know how to thank you."

"You already have. To see you safe is thanks enough," he said, surprising himself with the truth of his answer. "But the real question is, what shall we do with you?"

"I'll do anything!" Nydia replied anxiously.

He gazed at her young face for a moment more, and then made his decision. "You shall be in charge of the garden— officially, as you are already quite the expert," he declared.

"My mother taught me as a child," she said, her voice catching with the memory.

Glaucus gazed intently at her for a moment before he spoke. "Then you haven't always been a slave?"

Nydia shook her head in a slow movement. "No, I am

Judean. When''—she paused to fight off the sadness of those memories—''when Vespasian's soldiers came, they killed my father and took my mother and me away; I was just a child.''

You still are, Glaucus thought. ''What became of her?''

''There were crowds of people being pushed onto the ship. She lost her grip on my hand, and . . .'' Her words ended when a teardrop rolled down her cheek.

''Nydia, you will always be welcome in my home. You will be safe here at last,'' he said, touched by her story, and by her tears.

Nydia was unable to stop the timid smile that formed; the words he had spoken had rekindled a flame that was ready to burst forth in love for her new master.

Olinthus, after spending a long night in the jail, where he had maintained a vigil of prayer that had calmed his tortured soul, was led by two guards into the Hall of Justice and brought before the magistrate, Quintus, and the second magistrate, Tibius.

Drawing his shoulders back, he met Quintus' stare without showing either fear or regret for being there.

''So, Olinthus,'' said Quintus in a low drawl, ''once again you are before us. You are charged again with disturbance of the peace. How say you?''

''If the truth disturbs the peace, then you must name me guilty of the truth, Magistrate.''

''You're cool for a man whose fate rests in our hands,'' stated Tibius.

Olinthus gazed at the man for a moment, then nodded his head. ''I meant only that you must do your duty, as I do mine.''

''Our duty,'' Quintus stated, ''is to carry out the *people's* will, to help the empire prosper, and to keep the peace. While you, Olinthus, have made it yours, I gather, to disrupt it. You speak of freeing slaves. You offend the people with wild talk of their doom and destruction. You know, do you not, that some are even calling you a Christian?''

"I have heard them say it, yes."

"And you know how the people hate Christians," snapped Tibius.

"I know the people fear the Christians. They believe them responsible for all disasters—if there is a shipwreck, an earthquake, a drought, or if Rome is burned."

"And you believe this?" Quintus cut in.

Olinthus stared openly at the magistrate for a moment before he spoke. When he did, his voice was low. "As a man of justice, do you?"

They stared at each other for a moment before Quintus broke the gaze. In an angered voice that could not hide a hint of apprehension, the magistrate spoke again. "Do not force me to ask the question which will send you to your death," he snapped. Sighing wearily, he turned away from Olinthus.

"By 'the question,' do you mean is the Christian god my god?" Olinthus asked bravely. "But, as you know, the Christians say their god is the god of every man, whether he will it or no. Therefore, Quintus, he is the god of you as well as me."

Quintus' breath hissed in rage. "You mock me!"

"Nay, I know your role is a hard one, when justice must fight with the need to please the people," Olinthus said in a gentle voice.

Stiffening, Quintus stared into the unfearing eyes of the man before him. Olinthus' words were confusing him, and his anger grew out of proportion. "Guards! Take this man for punishment!" Then he was again trapped by Olinthus' deep eyes. His mouth became dry as he formed the final words, but he paused and rethought the punishment. "For disturbing the peace," he finished.

Olinthus did not resist the guards when they took his arms and marched him from the room, but when he was gone, Quintus looked at Tibius, in whose eyes he saw disapproval. "He warranted nothing more."

"He is a Christian," Tibius stated.

"We do not know it for certain," Quintus replied. Standing,

he went to the window and looked on while Olinthus was tied
to the posts in preparation for his whipping.

Quintus watched the whip strike its first blow across the
tall man's back. Olinthus' body arched, but his face remained
calm and did not show the pain that the whip produced. "Too
brave for his own good," Quintus muttered just as the high
priest Arbaces stepped into the public square.

"Tibius, go out and ask Arbaces to see me. Then stay
outside." Quintus looked back to the scene in the square and
continued to watch while he waited for the priest.

"You wished to see me, Quintus?"

Quintus turned at the sound of Arbaces' voice. "Yes,
Arbaces, with no one around us to overhear. Have you not
prospered here in Pompeii under my administration?" he
asked suddenly.

"If you are referring to the growth in the temple's
membership," Arbaces began amiably, "then certainly it is
so."

"And yet, I understand you support Diomed in the coming
election?"

"I am a man of religion, not politics."

"Do you deny you have swayed your own people in favor
of Diomed?" Quintus challenged.

Shrugging, and with a calculated smile on his face, Arbaces
replied in a low voice. "If my people are . . . interested in a
new government, perhaps it is because they feel you have not
favored Isis these past years."

"We have been impartial to *all* cults in Pompeii! And we
will continue to be, so long as they do not allow their beliefs
to conflict with their duty in observing state religion—and
pay homage to the Roman gods and the emperor."

"Indeed, such is the duty of us all. We of Isis have not
failed in that obligation, but . . ."

"And that is why you are allowed to continue—and grow."

Arbaces held up his hand and then nodded his head. "But
the point is that the people's hearts are with *my* temple. They
see that belief in Isis is belief in good. They want as their
civic leader a man who shares that belief." Arbaces paused to

stare deeply into the magistrate's face. "Magistrate, do you realize how members of Rome's *noble* class worship Isis? And also, what their approval means to you?"

"Of course I realize it," Quintus snapped. "But I must uphold the official gods, and only those!"

Arbaces studied Quintus, and then his mind took yet another tack in his quest. "But are you doing that?" he asked quickly.

Quintus looked at him, and shrugged hopelessly.

"Look at your treatment of this man Olinthus. All Pompeii knows him to be a leader of Christians. Yet, once again, you've let him off with a flogging."

"We have no proof that he is a Christian."

"Really?" Arbaces said as he raised his eyebrows accusingly. "You have but to insist he burn incense to the image of the emperor and curse the name of Christ. His refusal is your proof."

"You need not teach me Roman law," Quintus said stiffly. "Have you forgotten the Christians I condemned to the last games?"

"No, I did not forget those token few. And your reluctance even with those was well noted. Especially by the nobles who do not want uncontrolled rabble spreading their dangerous ideas throughout the empire," Arbaces replied in a level, yet threatening voice. "Think upon that, gracious Quintus."

Quintus stared at the priest as the man bowed to him, turned, and left the room. Only when he was gone did Quintus speak. And then, it was only one word.

"Damn!"

Chapter Seven

Since the day Antonius had been initiated as a priest of Isis, Ione had found her existence to be the loneliest she had ever known. Each day, after the morning prayers at the temple, and before the afternoon devotions, she would walk alone to the Street of Tombs, bringing with her a small urn of oil to pour in libation at the tomb of her parents.

There she would stand for endless moments, trying to bring peace to her mind and to prepare herself to follow her brother's footsteps. Until recently it had been an easy thing for her to do, but when the winter had ended and the spring had come, it brought with it doubt and confusion in the form of the handsome Greek noble Glaucus.

From the moment she had seen him, she had been captured by his handsome face and his beautiful, questing eyes. His voice had been deep and pleasant, and she had sensed that behind the courtliness there lurked an abundance of seductive charm, as well as a sensitive and caring man who was searching for deeper meanings in his life. He had about him, she thought, an air of mystery, an aura of the unknown.

Chasing away the haunting thoughts of Glaucus, Ione leaned forward to pour the final libation upon the tomb. While the oil rained onto the marble, footsteps sounded behind her and she turned to see who it was. She froze, stunned momentarily at the sight of the very man she had been thinking of.

"Forgive me, I did not mean to intrude," Glaucus said.

"I have finished," she whispered as her eyes locked with his. For a moment neither spoke, then they both tried at the same time, turning their words into nonsense.

They both laughed, and Ione held back, deferring to Glaucus.

"Ione, I . . . I must confess, I followed you here." He hesitated when he saw her flush, but quickly picked up the pace of his words. "I have been reflecting a great deal of late on your opinion of my—my character. I gather you see my life as only a search for toys and pleasures, and that I aspire to little else."

"No!" Ione said, too quickly. "I mean . . . I was much too harsh the other day. You must think me . . ." But she could not find the right words, and shrugged helplessly.

"What I think, Ione, is that you were right. I offer no excuse for my life. Only that perhaps I have yet to find that thing which commands my attention." He smiled then, his eyes filling with understanding. "I admit that I can take no great pride in my life. My poor parents, they gave me everything, and then died too soon to keep me on an even path." As he finished, his voice was low and emotional.

"I, too, know what it is like to lose a mother and a father," she whispered, her eyes sweeping across the tombs.

Glaucus, following her gaze, read the names engraved on the marble, and even as he did, his eyes widened in recognition. "Your father—his statue stands in Rome, with other senators'. . ."

Ione cut him off, her voice both bitter and sad. "Nero dared not throw it down, though he dared to kill him." She took a deep, calming breath before looking at Glaucus again. "But I know that I will see him again, and my mother too. Isis tells us that."

"It must be comforting to believe that."

"And you do not?" she asked as she began to walk from the tombs, with Glaucus keeping pace at her side.

"By all the gods of Greece and Rome," he said fervently, "I cannot tell you what I believe! I wish I had your certainty, but I don't. I'm like this fellow here," he said, stopping to point out a stone, and reading its engraved message. " 'My life is over. Whither now?' "

Ione shook her head, reading the words engraved on the stone next to it. " 'There nothing is beyond this grave.' How sad," she whispered. "Oh, Glaucus, I do wish I could make you understand how happy it would make you to believe in something higher than yourself," she said wistfully, again gazing into his eyes.

"I do, Ione," he said, fighting the sudden constriction in his throat. "I believe in you."

Tensing, Ione turned from him, unable to bear the look in his eyes. "No! I don't want your courtly speeches."

Glaucus reached out and placed his hands on her shoulders, feeling the heat of her satin skin on his palms while he gently forced her to face him. "Then let me speak plainly. I've told you that until now my life had no purpose. But you could change that."

Ione closed her eyes against his words, willing them away. When she opened them again, he was still staring raptly at her. "No," she whispered.

Glaucus' hands tightened on her shoulders for a brief moment before he took a deep breath, willing himself not to move too fast. He sensed that to do so would push her from him. Carefully, he released her shoulders.

"You talk of happiness in your beliefs, and yet you're always so sad."

"I'm not!" she said quickly. "It's only that I miss my brother since he has become a priest."

"Ione," he whispered, but she turned and walked away.

"Ione!" he shouted to her retreating back, afraid to go after her, yet afraid to let her go.

He stood on the Street of Tombs for a long while after she was gone, wondering why he had not followed her and forced her to face him. His mind was churning, and his body filled with a restless energy that forced his thoughts to focus only on Ione and the way she had looked at him before she'd fled his words.

Needing some outlet for his tense thoughts, Glaucus began to walk. He saw nothing of the streets he passed nor of the people in them. His mind saw only the beautiful and patrician face of the woman he now knew he loved, as he had never before done.

When he stopped his directionless steps, he found himself standing on the flat ground of the palaestra, which was deserted except for a few gladiators at the far end. The exercise field looked inviting, and the equipment lying on the ground called out to him.

Glaucus stripped off his robes and, wearing only a loincloth, picked up a long, shiny javelin. He hefted it and drew his arm back. Taking five exact steps, he launched the sleek missile. His eyes followed its arcing path carefully, until it landed in the earth, its shaft quivering from the impact.

Soon Glaucus was lost in the exercise, and after throwing the last javelin, he worked with the discus until his body shone with a film of sweat. Yet, no matter how hard he pushed himself, his mind was still roiled and confused. He picked up another discus, but paused when he saw one of the gladiators walking in his direction. Then he whirled his body around, extending his arm, and let the discus fly.

He watched it soar into the air, floating as if held up by the breath of Zeus, until it reached its highest point, and then, like a spinning platter of silver, floated to the ground at the far side of the palaestra.

"Well thrown," came a deep voice. Glaucus turned to find Lydon smiling at him.

"Thank you."

"Glaucus, I've never thanked you for the kindness you showed to me at Diomed's."

Glaucus grimaced and then laughed. "That banquet! Not very sporting of Diomed."

Lydon smiled with the noble, and then, forcing his voice to sound casual, he spoke. "How is your new slave? The blind girl."

"Nydia? You know her? Lydon, I hardly think of her as a slave," he said truthfully. "She's happy now, I think. Come and see her whenever you wish," he offered. He glanced at the remaining discs and then looked at Lydon. "Join me?"

"Thank you, but I know little of Greek contests."

"They're very different from yours, and—forgive me, but I much prefer them."

Lydon appraised the noble again, pondering what he had just heard. "You don't hold with killing men for sport?"

"I can see the skill it takes; but when a man, with flesh and blood like my own, is cut down as a pastime for the mob . . ."

"The mob merely imitates the empire," Lydon said civilly, "which teaches them that life is cheap."

"Lydon, your words make me yearn for Athens as it was long ago, where man himself was the measure of all things. The people here," Glaucus said pensively, "are restless, always searching outside themselves for meaning."

Lydon smiled openly, realizing for the first time that Glaucus was much more than a joy-seeking nobleman—that they shared similar feelings. "Teach me some of your sport," he offered.

"Wonderful! Let's wrestle," Glaucus declared as he dropped into a crouch and began to circle the bigger man.

Lydon met the challenge eagerly by feigning a slap to the nobleman's cheek.

Glaucus dodged the blow easily, and the others that followed. Then he laughed and held up his hand. "Here, let me show you," he said in a friendly tone as he put his hand on Lydon's shoulder. The gladiator stared at him, waiting for Glaucus' next move, when suddenly the Greek slipped his foot behind Lydon's leg and in a swift, smooth motion, pressed back on the bigger man's shoulder and pulled his foot forward, sending the gladiator tumbling to the ground.

As soon as he felt Glaucus move, Lydon knew he had been tricked but could do nothing about it. When he hit the ground, he spun quickly and leaped to his feet. His laugh was loud, and his eyes sparkled with merriment. "Well done!" he shouted, advancing on Glaucus. Lydon was, if nothing else, a fast learner. He'd had to be.

The two men met again, and this time their movements were in earnest. They wrestled madly about the palaestra, shouting, grunting, and laughing as one tried to better the other. Within a few moments the other gladiators had formed a half circle around them, their voices cheering the men on.

Glaucus maneuvered around Lydon, enjoying the sport,

unaware of the piercing eyes that watched him from across the palaestra. Ione stood at the foot of the statue of Isis, having just risen from her prayers. If he had been close enough, Glaucus would have seen a strange light in her eyes while she watched his finely muscled body move so gracefully. He would also have seen Arbaces, behind Ione, glaring at him as if he were a dreaded enemy. Glaucus would have seen, too, the desire that eventually filled Ione's eyes, and the way she started when Arbaces' hand fell on her shoulder, turning her away and leading her back inside the temple.

But Glaucus saw none of this while he wrestled with Lydon, enjoying the harsh physical contact which allowed him to finally clear his mind of Ione.

They fought smoothly, bantering back and forth as each sought arm holds and body holds for a quick victory. Both men were quick, and both had tasted the dirt beneath their feet several times, but each time the fallen one had sprung to his feet, laughing and joining again.

Spotting his chance, Glaucus reached for Lydon, but when his hands gripped the other's shoulder, they slipped, putting him off balance. Quickly, Lydon spun, lifting Glaucus and then throwing him to the ground, landing on top of him a second later.

"Surrender!" he called as he pinned Glaucus to the ground.

Glaucus thought of refusing, but realized he had been defeated. "I surrender! Thank heaven you know nothing of Greek games!" he said laughingly.

Lydon stood and helped Glaucus up. "No, no. You were a worthy match for me," he stated.

"Just the same," Glaucus said in mock severity, "I never want to meet you in your *own* arena!"

Lydon laughed loudly and slapped Glaucus on the shoulder.

"I'm off to the baths, join me?" Glaucus asked.

"Thank you, but no, too many nobles," he said truthfully.

"True," Glaucus replied as he picked up his clothing and waved goodbye. But when he reached the street, he stopped as his eyes fell on the statue of Isis and the dark-skinned priest who stood before it, leading his followers in prayer.

Their eyes met briefly, and a chill raced along Glaucus'
back when he saw the hatred burning within Arbaces' eyes.
The sensation was so strong that it wiped away all thoughts
of the match he had just finished, and of the friendship that
he had felt building between himself and Lydon.

A few minutes later, with the memory of the priest's glare
heavy in his thoughts, Glaucus stepped into the entrance of
the Stabian baths. The sprawling and cavernous interior always startled him, with its ornate and luxurious fixtures
already fading, already badly in need of repair. But he remembered also the times his parents had taken him here when he
was only a child. The baths had been the finest in the empire
then, a great lure that drew noblemen from far and wide to
enjoy its luxuries. In the past seasons, however, the crowds
had thinned, and the baths lost some of their charm.

Inside the huge building Glaucus walked past a steaming
pool along the side of which fat old men were throwing dice.
At another pool, five men played a ball game while others
cheered them on. Then, as he made his way toward the pool
he favored, he heard himself hailed, and turned to see Diomed
smiling up at him.

"Glaucus, my boy, how are you?"

"Fine. How goes your campaign?"

Diomed drew himself to a sitting position and nodded his
head weightedly. "Very well indeed. I'm expecting an easy
victory. But enough of politics. We have missed you of late,
and my poor Julia—why she's shut out all her other suitors in
hopes that . . ."

"Do give my respects to her," Glaucus said, forestalling
what he knew was to come, "and to your lovely wife as well."

"Glaucus, I . . ." But again Diomed was cut off, this time
by Clodius, who had spotted his friend and was calling to
him.

Glaucus bowed to Diomed politely and started toward
Clodius, breathing a sigh of relief at the ease of his escape.

"Thank you," Glaucus said with a smile. "And Clodius, I
want to talk to you about . . ."

But Sallust, who was sitting next to Clodius, interrupted

with a laugh. "The game's up. He's going to ask you for the money you owe him!" he warned Clodius.

Feigning a hurt expression, Clodius threw himself into his act without really seeing the serious set to Glaucus' face. "Oh, Glaucus, you know how difficult my life has been. If only you could give me a few more days . . ."

"I don't give a damn about the money," Glaucus snarled, his eyes hard as they swept across first Clodius' face and then Sallust's. "If you would have the courtesy to let me speak, I would appreciate it," he said abruptly.

Sallust stood suddenly, his tone sarcastic yet wary. "Certainly, my liege. A thousand pardons. Come, Lepidus," he said to his friend who had not yet spoken, "we shall take our business elsewhere."

Glaucus glared at them as they walked away, then silently stepped into the pool five feet from where they had been lying. He looked back at Clodius; his friend's features had changed from incredulity to concern.

"What is it? You're not yourself today."

"Clodius, what do you know of Arbaces?" he asked suddenly.

"Arbaces? Not you too? Are you becoming religious?"

Glaucus ignored this remark as he pressed on. "No one seems to know much about him."

"Nor do I," Clodius stated, "except that he's most certainly a rascal. But if you're really serious, I could ask Gaius."

"Gaius? Fortunata's husband? The man you would not talk to me about?"

"The same," Clodius replied. "He was a friend of my father's in Rome. I visit him sometimes. I may be the only person on earth who does. And I seem to remember him speaking of Arbaces."

Glaucus remembered the day he had seen Fortunata, and the fear he had seen in her eyes when Arbaces had spoken to her. "She was afraid of him," Glaucus whispered.

"Ah . . . perhaps," Clodius said, then he hesitated. "It . . . it may require a bit of money to make the arrangements."

"I expected no less from you," Glaucus said evenly as he turned and went to the pool, diving into it and washing the sweat from his body.

It was just before noon when Chloe, dressed in a plain robe of pale yellow, neared the Stabian baths. She knew that Diomed had gone to the baths, as had been his daily habit since becoming a politician. She hoped that Petrus would be in the vicinity of his master, for she wanted to speak with him today.

At the entrance to the baths she saw a young boy about to go in. She recognized him although he was bent almost double under a load of wood he was carrying. "Catus," she called, "have you seen Petrus?"

"No," he replied without looking up.

"I had hoped he'd be here," she said sadly. "Diomed is, isn't he?"

"Yes." But even as he spoke, four men came out of the baths, looking at each other and not where they were walking. Before Catus could get out of the way, one of the noblemen walked into him, knocking him down and spilling the load from his back.

"Damn!" Clodius exploded, glaring angrily down at the boy.

Catus scrambled to his feet, his eyes downcast. "Forgive me, sir," he begged Clodius.

With a disdainful glance Clodius waved him away and looked at Glaucus. "I'll meet you in an hour," he said, drawing his shoulders back and shaking his head at the boy and at the woman who was now helping him pick up his scattered load.

Chloe glanced up, gasping when she recognized Glaucus, who approached and began to help them.

"Glaucus! By the gods," cried Clodius, shocked by what he saw. "What are you doing?"

Glaucus turned a sardonic eye on Clodius. "What you would not."

Then Chloe saw one of the other men staring at her.

"Hello," Sallust said to her with a leer. "I almost didn't recognize you in an upright position." Sallust laughed loudly at his humor, and was joined by the others as they cast one last glance at the three bent-over figures before walking away.

"Please, sir, I can do it," Catus pleaded, afraid of what might happen if his master saw a nobleman helping him.

"Glaucus!" Clodius shouted from a few feet away, but when Glaucus did not turn he sighed and led the other two toward the market.

After Catus had gathered his wood and gone into the bath, Glaucus brushed himself off and silently smiled at the girl. But just when he was about to leave, Chloe hesitantly spoke.

"Sir," she began. She saw Glaucus raise his eyebrows, and she went on. "I want to thank you for your kindness just now."

Glaucus shrugged uneasily under her gaze. "The load was too heavy for a lad of his size. Poor boy, he'll sweat out his life in that hole beneath the baths so that my kind can have pleasures."

"But no, you're not like the others."

Glaucus' bark of laughter was bitter. "Am I not?"

"*They*," she said, pointing in the direction his friends had gone, "would not help Catus as you did. Nor would they have given Nydia a home." Chloe paused when Glaucus cast her a surprised look, but she made herself continue while she still had the courage to speak. "To them, people like Catus, like Nydia, or me—we're . . . we're just cattle. No, you're not like them at all."

As she finished, a burst of noise issued from the baths, and Chloe saw a group of men coming out. Rather than compromise the kind nobleman by allowing him to be seen with a common whore, she fled down the street, aware of Glaucus' eyes following her every step.

Only when she was gone did Glaucus recognize her as the dancer at Diomed's banquet on the day he had returned to Pompeii.

* * *

Clodius, mindful of following through with his offer to
Glaucus, and conscious also that his need to continue his
friendship with the rich Greek nobleman was as important as
anything else, made his way to the bookseller's stall deep in
the heart of the market place. His friends Sallust and Lepidus
followed behind him, absorbed in their own conversation for
the moment, leaving him free to think.

He was troubled by many things, especially his inability to
gain a foothold with a woman wealthy enough to support
him. He was bothered too by his feelings for Julia, and of his
disgust that she was common born and not his equal, for he
knew, no matter how much he tried to disbelieve it, that he
loved her.

Reaching the bookseller's stall, Clodius watched the man
working meticulously, transcribing an epic poem onto fresh
vellum. Then he turned to look at the sheets of poetry dis-
played within the stall.

Lepidus spoke: "I don't understand why you must buy a
poem. You're a poet, Clodius. If you need a gift for a lady,
write something yourself."

"This lady is an old friend of the family. Old enough to be
my mother."

"What about this?" Sallust asked, proffering a scroll which
Clodius glanced at quickly and shook his head.

"She's already the wife of a Stoic. Why make her suffer
through Seneca as well?"

"Something lighter perhaps. Petronius? Martial?" suggested Lepidus, but Sallust's wry laughter made them both
look at him.

"Why should Clodius buy their work? He's already *stolen*
most of it and put his name on it."

Sincerely insulted, Clodius glared at Sallust. He was about
to speak when someone else came into the stall. Wisely, he
held back his acidic retort when he heard Lepidus speak.

"Julia, good day."

Clodius whirled to find himself looking unguardedly into
Julia's eyes. It was a moment before his usual mask slipped
into place. Then he favored her with a sad, mocking smile.

Sallust spoke first, turning to Julia with a knowing look. "Perhaps you can help. It's a question as to what to give a lady."

"Well," she began, trying to ignore the emotions that the sight of Clodius brought out, "it depends upon the sort of lady."

"Elegant, refined. A true patrician," he said.

"Fortunate man," she said to Sallust, "to know such a lady."

"Oh, no, not I. It's Clodius' lady."

Julia swung her eyes to Clodius, staring at him and fighting away the jealousy that rose quickly, sharply. "Is it? Well then, Clodius," she said without quite hiding the hurt she felt, "I recommend a Greek."

"A Greek?" Clodius asked, hardly able to either disguise his anger with Sallust or his discomfort with Julia's presence.

"Of course! If it's for a lady, you'll want poetry of love. And who's more expert at love than a *Greek*?" she asked, knowing full well how Clodius would take this. "Good day," she said with a sweet smile to the three men, ignoring the angered look that Clodius flashed at her.

But when she was gone from the booth, Clodius did not see the sad, desolate look that quickly transformed her features. He saw nothing except that Glaucus was both Greek and rich, and that Julia must have meant him.

Picking up a scroll at random, he tossed the bookseller several of the coins he had gotten from Glaucus and stalked angrily away, leaving Lepidus and Sallust behind, to stare at him in wonder.

The sun had passed its zenith, crossing the top of Vesuvius in a graceful arc, while beneath it, on the green slopes, the people worked and played, enjoying the warmth of the late afternoon.

Lydon was in an especially good mood. After exercising with Glaucus he had taken the nobleman at his word and had gone to his house to see Nydia. From the moment Glaucus had extended the invitation, Lydon's hopes had soared. Nydia was no longer denied him.

When he had arrived, she had just been leaving with an empty basket hanging on her arm. He had greeted her and then accompanied her on the walk to the base of Vesuvius and into the fields of flowers which she had visited each day when she was owned by Stratonice and Burbo.

They talked freely there, while Nydia picked flowers. Lydon gazed at her with eyes that were filled with love, eyes that she would never see for herself.

"I was frightened for you when I learned that Stratonice was selling you," he said, picking up the conversation from a few moments before. "But it was worse when I saw you on the block. Nydia, I learned then that I must change my life. I did not have the money to save you—I was desperate."

Nydia straightened a delicate flower and put it into the basket. She shrugged her shoulders. "It worked out for the best; I'm quite happy. And even if you had bought me, I would still be a slave."

"Not my slave! Never that!" Lydon swore passionately. "Oh, Nydia, I love you," he said, for the first time expressing his true feelings.

Stunned, Nydia caught her breath in surprise. "Lydon," she whispered after collecting her thoughts, "you've always been good to me—since I was a little girl. But you can't, you mustn't, confuse your desire to protect me with love."

"I have always loved you!" he stated hotly. "And as you have grown and changed, so has the nature of my love. Nydia, I want you for my wife."

"You can't mean that," she said, her voice filled with tension and her mind praying for the sight she never had, to help her to see his face, to help her understand. "With so many women desiring you. I . . . I can't even see you."

"Can you not?" he challenged, unwilling to accept her words. "You have always seen me better than the others. Nydia, I will leave the arena," he promised.

"You've already tried that."

"I had no money then, no reason either." Lydon paused to

gaze at her, then he turned and looked at the mighty mountain towering above them, ablaze under the powerful light of the afternoon sun. When he spoke again, his voice was subdued, his words deep and serious.

"When I was slave to Diomed, I worked with my father in the vineyards. We used to dream of having our own home. That was before Diomed sold me to the ring. But I could have that home now, Nydia; we could have it, and soon. I'm leaving on a tour of contests—when I return I'll have more than enough to . . ."

Nydia's startled, incredulous laugh stopped his words. "You, a farmer?"

"Yes!" he declared. "Imagine it, my father and I in the fields, and you there with us. I could teach you," he said, bending to scoop some earth into his hand, and then putting it in Nydia's.

"No. For you, it would be but another form of slavery. You'd miss the crowds, and the cheers."

"They do not cheer for me, only for my death! How long can I stay champion, even if I wanted to? It has to end soon. It only takes one misstep, one younger, faster opponent."

"I've never known you to fear death," she whispered.

"I never have, until I fell in love with you."

His words whirled madly in her mind, and her heart reached out to him. "I'm honored by your feelings for me; but I *am* a slave, in my heart as much as in fact."

"Nydia, I know you're not promised to another," he stated, unwilling to understand what she was trying to say.

"No, not promised, and I never will be," she said, no longer able to hide her sadness, or the true meaning of the words.

Lydon shook his head in sad denial, understanding then that there was another man for whom she had feelings. He grabbed her hands, drawing them to his lips. He kissed first one, and then the other, before he spoke again. "I won't let you say no to me. If this love of yours is as hopeless as you think, then I'll conquer it, in time!"

Nydia drew her hands away, shaking her head. "You think, because you're champion . . ."

"No! Because I'm offering you what you have never had. Love—and freedom!"

Nydia shook her head again, trying to think of how to explain the foolishness of what he proposed. Before she could, however, his laughter rang out, and his hands were on her waist, lifting her high into the air, spinning her around and around.

"Love and freedom, Nydia. Think of it!"

Chapter Eight

The sun was halfway between the zenith and the horizon when Glaucus and Clodius turned off the neatly kept pathway and onto a stone-lined walk. Behind them, and far below, lay Pompeii in all its splendor. From where they stood on the side of Vesuvius, they could see the entire city and its labyrinthine maze of streets.

Clodius gestured toward the sprawling villa ahead, pointing to it with the hand that held the elegantly wrapped scroll he had purchased earlier. But when he turned back to Glaucus, his eyes clouded for an instant. "You're a strange one," he said.

Glaucus merely smiled secretively.

"And I suppose that means you're still not going to tell me why you want to know more of Arbaces."

"Let's just say that he interests me."

"I can't promise that Gaius will tell you anything, or even if he'll see you."

"I understand, and the money is still yours."

"That's generous, seeing that I've spent most of it on this," he said, waving the scroll in the air. "Ah," he added, "were almost there."

Unseen yet by the two nobles, an old, frail man, his short white hair swept forward in a futile effort to hide the ravages of time, walked slowly along the edge of the wall surrounding his villa. He was gazing along Vesuvius' slopes when he heard voices in the distance and turned his tired, watery eyes in that direction. He froze for a moment, and then spun when he heard footsteps behind him.

Shaking his head at his wife, he pointed a trembling finger at the approaching men. "Fortunata," he said, his voice underlined with a tremor of fear. "Look."

For a moment, Fortunata's face became taut, but she relaxed when she recognized Clodius. "It is only Clodius, with another man."

Gaius gazed at her pleadingly, but she chose to ignore the plea. "I'm sure it will be all right. Clodius wouldn't bring anyone who isn't safe."

Together they went toward the young men. When they were only a few feet apart, Fortunata spoke in a melodic voice. "Welcome, Clodius."

Glaucus noted well the full smile with which Clodius favored her as he bowed politely to her. "Thank you, Fortunata," Clodius replied. "Gaius, Fortunata, my friend Glaucus, late of Athens, Rome, and Naples."

"So many places," Fortunata said wistfully.

"But only Athens is my home," Glaucus stated.

"Be careful that the emperor doesn't take your property for that," came Gaius' tremulous voice.

Glaucus tried to smile at Gaius, but he wasn't sure just how serious the old senator was.

"What brings you this high on Vesuvius?" Fortunata asked.

"My friend here," Clodius said with a nod, "wanted to speak with Gaius."

"Oh?" Gaius asked, his eyes studying Glaucus intensely.

"If I may?" Glaucus asked.

"Perhaps. Come," Gaius said, as he started to walk away.

"For you, lovely Fortunata," Clodius said, handing her the scroll when Gaius and Glaucus started off.

After opening the wrapping, Fortunata smiled brilliantly. "The odes of Pindar. How lovely."

"And much better than my own, I'm afraid."

As he walked, Gaius shook his head at the words he had just heard. He spoke just loudly enough for Glaucus to hear. "Oh, yes, I can see what Clodius is about. But he's amusement of sorts for Fortunata." Stopping suddenly, he stared up at Glaucus. "But you? Surely you have nobler ambitions than such vain pursuits?"

Caught unprepared, Glaucus laughed to cover his embarrassment. "Is it so apparent? You are the second one to chide me of late on my lack of direction."

Gauis' voice gentled at this admission, and his weary eyes sparkled for the barest of seconds. "Wasting life is a pity. But then, the empire's left few pursuits of worth to those it has conquered . . . nor, indeed, to anyone. It seems only earthly pleasures are a youth's ambitions."

Before more could be said, Clodius and Fortunata had caught up with them, and Clodius, overhearing the old man's last remarks, spoke out as if it were meant for him. "But Gaius, when you live in such splendor, and set feasts upon your table, how can you say ambition and pleasure are unimportant?"

"I say so, when compared with the moral ideal of living a rational life of the mind."

Clodius held the old man's eyes and laughed. "Yet you say so from the comfort of this palace!"

Gaius continued to stare at Clodius in a thoughtful way. Glaucus, feeling a sense of responsibility for Clodius' argumentative words, spoke out. "Clodius, no one says a stoic has to suffer."

Glaucus stopped speaking suddenly, seeing Gaius' face freeze with anxiety at the sudden appearance of a slave from around a corner. He sensed too that nothing should be said until the slave passed by.

When the slave was gone, Gaius acted as though nothing unusual had happened, picking up the conversation from the point at which it had been interrupted. "But Clodius is correct, Glaucus. I live my life in quiet contradiction, which all my study of philosophy has failed to resolve. When I think back to my days at Nero's court, days filled with every kind of evil and corruption . . ."

"But you're well out of that, my dear," Fortunata said quickly, before her husband became more agitated.

"Of course I am!" he snapped irritably. "But I cannot

deny how much I miss the power I had then! Oh, I see the vanity of the world and know that death would be a welcome respite. Yet I fear that void, that . . . nothingness.''

Glaucus stared at Gaius with excitement. He had found a way to bring up his questions, but he knew he must be careful. ''Then you do not believe in immortality?'' he ventured.

''If there is such a thing, it is in our deeds, whose consequences live on after us,'' Gaius declared gravely.

''And is there, then, no higher power?''

''Who can deny some godlike spark within us?'' Gaius responded with a shrug. ''Some idea of good, despite the evil that we do? But—is this God? That I do not know.''

''Such deep questions, Glaucus,'' Clodius cut in. ''Now I understand your interest in priests.''

Gaius grimaced contemptuously before he spoke, and when he did, his voice was harsher, tinged with anger. ''Priests spring up these days like poison weeds on deserted fields of battle—feeding on the corrupted spoils of peace. What more do you need to know of priests!''

''My interest lies only in one special priest,'' Glaucus confided in a low voice. ''I understand that you know something of this man Arbaces?''

Fortunata gasped, and a strange, fearful look passed between them. ''Who told you this?'' Gaius demanded.

Taken aback at the urgency of his question, Glaucus glanced at Clodius, who was looking from Gaius to Glaucus. ''Well, I thought that . . . that you know so much of the world. I . . . I was certain I'd heard you speak of Arbaces,'' Clodius said lamely.

''You are mistaken, Clodius,'' Gaius stated in a cold voice as he turned from them and walked angrily away.

''You must forgive him,'' Fortunata said a moment later. ''He needs his rest.''

Gauis, who had reached the entrance to his house, turned back to stare at them. ''Yes, do I not . . . if it were but to be found. Fortunata, we must not keep these gentlemen any longer. It is growing late.''

Fortunata looked apologetically at Glaucus and Clodius for a moment but did not say anything.

"Thank you for your generosity," Glaucus said politely. "It *is* late. We need to get back to town."

"I . . . Thank you. And Clodius, thank you for the scroll." With that, Fortunata went after her husband, while Glaucus and Clodius exchanged looks, and started toward the gate of the villa. The sun was just falling behind the horizon.

By the time Glaucus reached his house, he had replayed the old senator's words over and over in his head. He remembered the open fear in Gaius' face, and the startled reaction to the mere mention of Arbaces' name. Glaucus had no doubt that Gaius knew perhaps too much about the high priest, and feared him to no small extent.

Beneath Gaius' large, ornate villa, and even as Glaucus and Clodius reached their homes in Pompeii, yet another passage opened within the heart of the earth. Thousands of tons of boiling lava quickly filled it, snaking upward along the myriad crevices, rushing higher and higher as it fought to rise toward the surface.

Steam and gases mixed in the giant caverns the lava created along its way, hissing angrily, impatiently searching for a way to escape. As if in echo to their pleas, the giant plates, the foundations of the world above, inched further apart.

Two days later, at midday, Lydon stood on the practice field, ignoring everyone and everything around him while he swung his sword in a variety of patterns. His body gleamed with a heavy coat of sweat, yet he was unconscious of either the heat or his exertions as his thoughts continued to haunt him.

Two nights ago, after leaving Nydia at the nobleman's house, he had gone to Olinthus' shop. He found his father there and had poured his heart out, telling Medon of his love for Nydia, his intentions for the future, and how he planned to buy both Medon's and Nydia's freedom and someday settle them all on a farm.

But his father had turned away from him, saying that what he wanted could never be. "Why?" Lydon had demanded.

"Because killing is against God's laws," Medon had responded sadly.

"It is my trade! It's all I know. What other choices are there?" he'd asked.

His father replied only that he could quit the ring immediately and find something else. But Lydon knew that was impossible, because if he did, he would lose everything, including Nydia.

Unable to reason with his father, he had left, dispirited by his failure. Etched in his mind were Medon's parting words: "You need not buy my freedom, especially with the blood of others, for when I found God, I became a free man."

Marcus, the lanista of the gladiators, shouted loudly in the foreground, his voice cutting into Lydon's thoughts. Glancing over his shoulder, he saw the man yelling at a slave who was putting armor into a wagon. The final loading was being done; they would leave for a tour of Campania tomorrow.

Turning, Lydon began to walk across the field to the barracks. Halfway there, he paused at the sound of Sporus' rough voice taunting Gar, who was training with the revolving jump pole, learning how to jump more quickly so that he might possibly live to fight yet another day.

Lydon flinched when the pole caught the big German's shin, but nodded his head when Gar refused to be beaten and went back to jumping again.

"Behold the dancing bear," laughed Sporus.

Melior, standing next to Sporus, ignored him and waved to Lydon. "Lydon, by the gods, you've been working like a slave. Come and stand us a drink. You'll vanquish all Campania anyway!"

Lydon shook his head and again started for the barracks, but was stopped by Sporus' taunting voice. "The man's become a fanatic!" the gladiator said disdainfully.

Melior, unaware of the sudden tension coursing through Lydon's body, played along with Sporus. "He's very changed of late," Melior laughed. "It must be love!"

"Quite so!" declared Sporus. "Our *champion's* become the slave of a slave. And, I'm told she does her new master's bidding wonderfully well!"

Lydon, his anger mounting to a dangerous level, turned to face Sporus. He pointed his sword at the man, and stared for several silent seconds. "Be careful of your tongue, Sporus," he warned. When he turned away from Sporus, he saw Gar staring at him. "Come, Gar, I'll practice with you."

Before he could take three steps, Sporus' voice rang out again. "Lydon, you're so perverse. In love with a girl who cares nothing for you, and with a boy who's determined to get himself killed shortly."

"Shut up, Sporus," Melior whispered suddenly when he saw Lydon's muscles tense. But Sporus, as usual, refused to listen.

"But it's so cruel of Lydon, telling poor Gar that he'll be a champion someday . . ."

Lydon saw Gar's puzzled reaction, and whirled to face Sporus. "I never said that!" Turning to Gar, he said the same thing to the German.

"But," Gar began, trying to understand what was happening, "you're always helping me, training me."

"I've been trying to teach you how to stay alive, boy!" Lydon snapped, his anger at Sporus' stupidity lending an edge of cruelty to his own words. As soon as he had spoken, he regretted it. But it was too late, as Gar, a stricken look on his face, backed away.

"Gar, I tried to tell you . . ." Lydon began.

"No!" Gar spat. "No! You don't *want* me to be champion. You're afraid I'll be better than you! And I will, damn you! I will!" Spinning on his heels, he strode angrily away.

"Don't fret, Lydon," Sporus called in a suddenly feminine voice. "I'll talk to Marcus. Perhaps he'll sell Gar to me. *I* know how to keep him alive."

Too many things had happened in the past days, too many things had confused and confounded him, and suddenly anger tore reason from Lydon's mind. Spinning, he brought his sword high and advanced on Sporus. "Oblige me, Sporus. I need a sparring partner,'' he said when the tip of his sword touched Sporus' neck.

"Fight the champion? I couldn't,'' Sporus said with a smile.

Lydon pressed the sword forward as Sporus' eyes widened and his face turned ashen. "I think you shall.'' Lydon's whisper was icy with rage. Lowering the sword's tip to the center of Sporus' chest, Lydon pressed sharply, a hard smile forming on his lips.

Sporus stared at Lydon, and then down at the blood seeping from around the sword's tip. His arm trembled, but he fought his fear as he realized the man he loved, the man he wanted above all others, was about to kill him.

Calming himself, Sporus tightened his grip on his own sword and, moving quickly, brought the blade up, knocking Lydon's away. "Have your way then,'' he whispered, whirling to strike his own blow. Their blades locked and the sound of metal rang loudly in the field.

Suddenly the other gladiators stopped what they were doing, realizing that what was happening was not a game. Silence fell as the men surrounded the two who fought.

They moved with the grace and speed of the trained men they were, swinging, thrusting, and meeting blade with blade as each tried to get past the other's guard. The sound of steel upon steel was loud, but the quiet control of the two fighters seemed even louder.

They danced around each other, circling guardedly, their bodies coiled, ready to strike at the first opportunity. Lydon feinted to his left. Then he spun and lunged at Sporus. But Sporus saw the move and countered it. Their blades met and locked. For a second they stood frozen, staring at each other across the span of inches. But to them, it was a distance that could no longer be measured in seconds or in inches.

All of Lydon's frustration and rage surfaced, feeding directly into the powerful arms that wielded his sword.

"Enough, Lydon,'' Sporus begged. His eyes echoed his plea, but behind them lurked something else. "I have a better way for you to stab me.''

"Damn you!" Lydon screamed, his fury lending even more power to his body as he pushed his blade against Sporus' sword, forcing him back. Acting with the reflexes of his years of training, Lydon lunged, and his sword bit into Sporus' waist.

Both men froze, and Sporus' eyes widened at the feel of the blade's penetration. Then Lydon withdrew the sword, and Sporus stared into the eyes of his death.

Spinning from Lydon, Sporus raised his sword and charged, but Lydon was prepared for this and easily countered the attack. A second later, Lydon renewed his own attack, lunging recklessly from a low position.

Unprepared for the thrust, Sporus stumbled and tripped. The force of landing knocked the wind from his lungs and tore the blade from his numbed fingers. Suddenly Lydon was standing above him, his face a mask of hatred, his sword poised two inches from Sporus' chest.

"Thrust, Lydon," he whispered, staring up at him.

Lydon saw Sporus through eyes filmed with rage. He wanted to kill this man, to end it now, but something stayed his hand.

"Please, Lydon, thrust," Sporus begged, his voice now a bare whimper. "End it for me, please!"

Lydon lowered the sword, knowing that he could not kill the man who had once been his friend. Sickened by the twisted desire he saw in Sporus' eyes, he turned and walked away. Behind him, the defeated gladiator's sobs echoed in the air.

The Temple of Isis, for all its preaching of good and all its surface piety, was as filled with inner disturbance and chaos as was the roiling, moving mass upon which Pompeii itself rested. On this hot summer morning it was no different, as a small child lay on a simple woven bier at the feet of the statue of Isis.

The child's mother knelt at the bier, clothed in a tattered robe that had once shone with beauty and gave voice to a grief that she was unable to contain. Her moans for her dying child rose upward to haunt everyone who listened.

Surrounding her were the priests and priestesses of Isis, with Antonius standing off to one side, his heart going out to the pitiful mother and child. He watched the head priest take a small box from the woman, and heard its few coins rattle hollowly within. When her gift was given, she looked up at Calenus, her eyes hopeful.

"Mighty Isis," he intoned, "look favorably upon this woman's offering, and take her child's soul to thy eternal breast." Saying this, Calenus waved his hands over the altar fire. An instant later, a flaming green tentacle shot skyward. He looked at the woman, and slowly, meaningfully, shook his head.

Seeing the refusal of her gift, the woman brought her hands together in anguish. "I have no more to give," she sobbed, collapsing at the feet of the priest.

Antonius, deeply affected by her anguish, moved to comfort her, but a priestess stopped him with a firm grip on his arm. "She'll come up with more. They always do."

Antonius stared incredulously at her, but sounds from the street stopped what he was about to say. Everyone rose to stare at the parade of gladiators leaving for the games throughout Campania. All watched the procession—except for Antonius, who was still trying to understand what he had just witnessed.

Out on the street the gladiators waved to the people who ran out to them, smiling with confidence and accepting the praise and good wishes offered them.

The parade turned the corner, heading toward the waterfront, and as it made its way onward, the name of Lydon raced ahead, carried on the air by the shouts of the people. A few blocks away, sitting in Glaucus' garden and weaving a garland, Nydia heard the first faint noises. A few minutes later she clearly heard Lydon's name being hailed and knew that the gladiators were leaving for their contests.

Standing, the garland forgotten in her hand, Nydia walked to the iron grill of the gate that separated the garden from the street and waited for the procession to draw near. The noise was so loud now that she did not hear Glaucus emerge from the house and walk to where she stood. But when he whispered in her ear, she turned to him. Just then, the wagon holding Lydon passed the gate.

If she were not blind, she might have seen the pain and hurt flash across the gladiator's face. She might have seen the jealousy which creased his mouth in an angry grimace when he spied the blissful expression on Nydia's face, revealing irrefutably whom Nydia loved.

But Nydia could not see Lydon. And even if she could, the mere magic of Glaucus' voice would have been enough to make her smile. She had not been so happy since those days long ago when she had been a small girl, and free.

After the gladiators were past and the street had regained its quiet, Glaucus and Nydia walked back to the stone bench. Nydia sat quietly, her hands hidden behind her back.

"The gladiators are off on their tour of Campania. Dreadful business," Glaucus commented. "But let's wish Lydon well; he's such a good sort." When he paused, he glanced at Nydia, expecting a comment but receiving none. Shrugging, he continued on. "You look so pretty, sitting there with the sun on your hair." Then he noticed that her hands were hidden from him. "Are you hiding something?"

Flushing, Nydia brought out the garland. "I wanted to surprise you," she said shyly.

Glaucus accepted the gift and, looking at the perfection of the flowers, wished that Nydia could see them also. "It's lovely. Thank you. I'll wear them to Diomed's tonight. I must go," he added with a weary sigh. "I've run out of excuses for declining."

Glaucus studied Nydia for a moment, wondering if the plans he had made would work. He knew that he must try, for if he did not he would be unable to live with himself any longer.

Taking a deep breath, he spoke. "Nydia, I too have a surprise. Two, in fact. First," he said, extending a thin golden necklace and placing it around her neck.

"What is it?" Nydia asked, her face animated with pleasure while her fingers explored the golden strand. Her fingers
touched his, and she quickly pulled them away. "Oh,
Glaucus," she cried when she realized what he had given
her. "Thank you, I'll treasure it."

"I wish you could see yourself. It suits you perfectly."

"You're too good to me," Nydia told him, her voice filled
with emotion.

"No, it pleases me to see you happy. And I have news
which will make you happier still."

"My second surprise?" she asked, not really believing that
what she dared hoped for might come true.

"Yes. I want to send you to live with Ione."

Nydia gasped. "You're sending me away? You're selling
me?" The world began to close in on her, and she could not
stop the sudden onset of tears. She had been so close to what
she wanted, only to learn it was not to be.

"No, Nydia, I am not selling you to her. But," Glaucus
said, startled by the emotional change in the girl, "Ione is
gentle and kind, and you will keep each other company.
You'll come to love her, I'm sure."

"As much as you do?" she asked bitterly.

Glaucus did not hear the bitterness in her tone as his
thoughts went to Ione for a moment. "Am I that transparent?"

"You said I'd always have a home with you!"

"I know, but there's been talk. It's a question of your
reputation," he lied in an effort to ease what he now saw
becoming a difficult situation.

"Slaves don't have reputations!"

"Enough! You know I've never looked upon you as a
slave."

"What's this, then, but a symbol of that very thing,"
Nydia snapped, uncaring now of what he thought of her,
knowing only that she was about to lose the one person she
loved above all others. Grasping the necklace, she ripped it
from her neck and flung it away as another sob tore from her
throat.

Glaucus tensed, stunned by her actions. His anger was

under control, but his senses had been badly offended, and he could not understand why. "Very well, Nydia," he said at last. "I will set you free if that is your wish." Saying that, he started away.

His words echoed painfully in Nydia's ears. Crying out, she spun and ran after him, stumbling crazily over the things in her path. "Glaucus, no! I'd rather die than be freed from you." She fell, landing on her knees. When she realized she could not go on, she pressed her head to the ground and begged for forgiveness.

Glaucus, turning when she cried out to him, watched helplessly as she tried to reach him. When she fell to the ground, he moved toward her, alarmed that she might hurt herself, yet humored by her melodramatic pleas. He knew that even though she thought herself in love with him, she could not really be; she was barely grown, still a child.

Reaching down, he lifted her gently to her feet. "Enough of this foolishness," he said patiently.

Nydia held her head down, willing her tears away. "I am sorry. I have been behaving like a child."

"But soon you'll be a child no longer. Nydia, you must learn to control these gales of ill-placed passion." Looking around, Glaucus spotted the necklace she had thrown away. After he retrieved it, he fastened it around her neck again.

"How do you find it so easy to control your passion? Your love for Ione?"

"Love is quite another matter than passion," he intoned. "You'll soon discover that when you're grown to womanhood."

Then Glaucus reached into his robe and took out yet another necklace, one far different than Nydia's. Suspended from the chain was a golden key encrusted with glowing emeralds, deep-blooded rubies, and shining sapphires.

Carefully, he took Nydia's hand, and then placed the necklace in it. "You will be happy with Ione. Nydia, go to her. Give her this necklace and tell her I send it with my love."

Rather than speak, Nydia nodded her head, sensing intuitively that nothing she could say would matter and that the love she had for him would be forever unrequited.

*   *   *

An hour later Nydia stood before Ione. Although she could not see the woman who would be her new mistress, she could almost hear the woman's strained breathing as Ione studied the necklace that Nydia had given her.

"I don't understand," Ione said. "It's exquisite, but much too lovely to accept. Please tell Glaucus . . ."

Nydia shook her head, interrupting Ione. "I'm to say it's sent in friendship and appreciation, should you care to welcome me to your home."

Ione looked at the slave girl for a moment longer, wondering why Glaucus had sent her here. Then she placed the necklace around her neck, feeling the subtle play of the gold on her skin. When it was secured, she sighed, suddenly understanding Glaucus' gesture. He had sent the young girl to her because of her loneliness.

"Then I won't offend by refusing it, because I do welcome you, Nydia. I . . . I want you to be happy here. You're not to think of yourself as my servant, but as my companion."

"It is my duty to serve those my master loves," she stated.

"Loves?" Ione asked sharply, taken aback by the girl's words. "That's just his way of speaking, don't you think?"

"Perhaps . . ." Nydia said in a cool, even voice.

Ione gazed at her for a moment, the hope in her eyes fading at Nydia's strangely lethargic response. But then a smile softened her beautiful features as she went over to Nydia and placed her arm around the younger girl's shoulders. "Glaucus is right, Nydia. I have been very lonely, and I think you have, too."

Nydia refused to be drawn in by Ione's apparent kindness, but she could not help sensing the truth that she heard underlying Ione's words. "But," Nydia began hesitantly, "you won't be lonely when you've been made a priestess."

Ione stared at Nydia, even as her hand moved without her volition and touched the necklace she had just put on.

"I don't know, Nydia," she whispered, as a peculiar and unknown sadness spread through her mind. "I don't know."

Chapter Nine

Far beneath the city of Pompeii, within the twisted pathways of the lower strata, flowed rivers of molten lava, continually seeking a passage out of their deep, dark prison. Throughout the early part of the summer the boiling monster beneath the surface sent out warnings in the form of small tremors. Occasionally, a small pocket of steaming gas would find a crevice that led upward to the peak of Vesuvius, where it would leap high into the air, shooting skyward, like a herald announcing an impending arrival.

The summer was progressing well for Glaucus. He had finally come to the realization that he loved Ione as he had never before thought it possible to love a woman. He had thought, and it was proving to be correct, that in sending Nydia to Ione to help ease her loneliness, Nydia would also be a constant reminder of him.

And as the days grew hotter and longer, Glaucus began to spend more time with Ione. He was careful of what he said, and careful also not to offend or to be overly demonstrative. Glaucus knew he was in a battle for something more than just sport. He was fighting for Ione, and for his life as well. If he lost this battle to Arbaces and the cult of Isis, he would lose Ione, forever.

So whenever Ione was free of her obligations to the cult, Glaucus would make sure that he was near her. They would spend some afternoons walking in the vineyards on the slopes of Pompeii, while others would be spent sitting in Ione's garden, talking of whatever was of interest to them.

And while the days passed, Glaucus came to the understanding that he had found what he had been searching for. He had finally learned the reasons for his apathy toward life, and he had come to understand the deep passions and desires which ruled him now.

Then a day blossomed like none before it. It was a magnificent and exquisitely beautiful morning of golden sunshine and turquoise sky that signaled, unbeknownst to him at the time, the start of a an even deeper change within him. It was to be a transformation brought on by circumstances and by his desires to prove himself to Ione. It was a change which worked as well upon the very fabric of Pompeii; by the time another day would dawn, its repercussions would affect a great many people.

On this beautiful day Glaucus surprised Ione by taking her to the waterfront where his ship was docked. He had planned a day of sailing to celebrate the beauty and warmth of the summer itself. While Glaucus' ship pulled away from the docks, Nydia stood with Olinthus.

After the ship was gone, Olinthus put his arm through Nydia's and guided her toward his shop. "A handsome couple, those two," he said as they walked.

"So I'm told," Nydia replied cynically, unable to hide her bitterness at Glaucus' betrayal of her love. "But hardly a *couple*. Ione's to become a priestess soon."

Olinthus gazed at the young girl for a moment, surprised by the tension in her voice. "Perhaps," he said thoughtfully. "But let us hope that Glaucus can prevent that particular tragedy."

When Nydia made no reply, Olinthus stared at her again, moved by her sad and innocent face but not understanding the source of her melancholy. "No doubt you're missing Lydon. Come and sit with me," he suggested when they neared his shop, leading her to the stone bench outside it.

They sat quietly for a few moments before he spoke again. "Now I'm eager to hear about your plans."

"My plans?" Nydia asked, confused by his question.

"Yes. Medon tells me that you and Lydon hope to marry when he returns from his tour."

Nydia forced herself to stay calm. "I have promised no such thing! Indeed, I am not free to make any such promise. I'm a slave, Olinthus; I belong to Glaucus."

Olinthus, startled by the passion of her statement, tried to understand what lay beneath the words she had spoken. He wondered if it was fear or something else. He stared at her young face, her beauty reminding him of times past.

"Nydia," he began in a low voice as he took her hand within his. "I am an old man now, and I have been blessed in many ways. But my one regret is that I have neither wife nor child. There was a woman once, but I said no to her."

When he paused, he saw that he had gained her interest, and he continued on, hopeful that his experiences in life could help her. "I wanted to be free. And so I watched her marry another, and have his children. Sometimes, Nydia, when it is late at night, and I'm lying in my bed, I can see the way her hair shone in the sun when she tossed her head back. I can hear the soft melody of her voice. I chose to be free," he repeated, pressing her hand tightly. "But the truth is, I have never been free of her, ever."

Thoughtfully, Nydia took a deep breath and nodded her head. "Perhaps you did not truly want to be free," she whispered.

"Perhaps. And you?" he asked suddenly.

"I . . ." But Nydia didn't know how to answer; instead, she stood. "Thank you for sharing your thoughts with me." And abruptly she was off, her staff sounding the way for her.

Olinthus watched her go, saddened yet hopeful at the same time. Because he was so immersed in the memories his words had invoked, he did not see a man of at least seventy walk past him and go into his shop. But a few minutes later Olinthus rose, setting aside the memories of years ago, and returned to the work which awaited him.

Entering his shop, Olinthus saw the visitor and paused. Something about the white-haired man was vaguely familiar.

"May I help you?" he asked, staring into the man's open and friendly eyes.

"Don't you know me, Olinthus?"

Olinthus frowned, his memory prodded by a familiar lilt in the man's voice. Then his heart beat faster and a bright smile creased his face. Going to the man, Olinthus embraced him tightly. "Joseph!" he cried.

When he released the older man, Olinthus stepped back. "It has been so long, so long. I must send word to the others. They will want to see you."

"Yes," Joseph said. "I haven't much time. Can it be done this very night?"

"It shall be," Olinthus promised rashly, uncaring of the dangers that filled Pompeii.

The water in the bay was as gentle as the day was beautiful. The boat's motion was soothing to the occupants who sat on soft cushions and gazed quietly around. To their left was Vesuvius, rising high into the sky, and beneath it sprawled Pompeii in all its splendor.

Near the prow, a single slave tended the sail, and as he worked he sang a tender, sweet love song, his voice low and haunting. Ione listened to the words while her fingers absently traced the surface of the gem-encrusted necklace and her eyes gazed into Glaucus' handsome face. When he smiled, she smiled in response.

She stood up and went to the side of the boat. "Oh, look, Glaucus," she said, pointing to the shoreline. "Pompeii seems so far away. I can't even see the temple from here. . . . It makes me want to float on forever."

Glaucus came to her side, pausing to study her face before speaking. When he did, his voice was as gentle as the water on which they sailed. "We could, Ione, we could. Think of all the wonderful places we might go—Byzantium, Carthage, Alexandria!" He saw her dart a quick, half-believing look at him, and he smiled again.

"I *should* like to go to Egypt, to see the birthplace of Isis."

Hiding a quick surge of annoyance, Glaucus laughed slyly. "We could float down the Nile, like Cleopatra and Marcus Antonius."

She was conscious of his closeness, and of the intense way he looked at her. The warmth of his breath brushed gently across her cheeks, and she tried to find a way to stop what was happening within her mind and body.

"Do you suppose he truly loved Cleopatra? Or did he merely want a crown?" she asked, again looking out at Vesuvius.

"But of course he loved her! How could he help it? She was Greek." Ione turned back to him, unable to mistake the meaning of his words even though they seemed to have been said half in jest.

"She was only half Greek," Ione replied, trying to ease the tension enveloping them. "Although it does make for a better story. But Glaucus"—her voice grew serious once more—"the best love story I know is that of Isis. She was married to the great god Osiris. But her jealous brother murdered him and threw his body into the Nile. Isis, weeping, went in search of him—throughout the land, across the sea and back again—never stopping until at last she found Osiris, and restored him with her healing powers."

When she finished, Glaucus took her hands in his. "It is a beautiful story. And I see better why you worship her." His eyes locked with hers, and he drew her close. "But there is one thing you must tell me," he demanded suddenly. "How can you believe that a goddess with such passion wants *you* to be cold? To sacrifice *your* chance for a love that might be as great as hers?"

Ione shook her head, but she could not deny what was happening within her own mind and heart. She drew her hands from his and turned her back on him. "Please, Glaucus," she whispered.

Unable to stop himself, Glaucus put arms around her narrow waist, drawing her to him, feeling her softness pressed against him.

Her hands covered his, pressing them tightly to her. She

could feel the strength of them, their heat burning through her robes as if she wore nothing.

Then his lips were on her neck, gentle and seeking. She cried out against the hunger that was fast consuming her and pulled away from him, her breasts rising and falling rapidly. "No, Glaucus," she whispered.

"I love you, Ione; you cannot deny us for too long."

Staring at him, Ione saw the truth of his words written on his face, and also knew once again the impossibility of her situation. Yet, as she realized this, she understood too that she could not cut Glaucus from her life—at least not yet.

Throughout the day, word of Joseph's arrival and the time and place of the special meeting was passed from Christian to Christian, be they slave or freeman.

Petrus, on his way to see Chloe, was stopped by Catus at the side door to Burbo's tavern and told of Joseph's arrival. Petrus, both excited and doubting, questioned the boy about the old man and about what Olinthus had said. Then, still wondering if it was wise to meet with so many others, he voiced his concern.

"But Joseph is here to help us," Catus responded with the rash voice of youth. "Olinthus says that tonight, at the foot of Vesuvius, Joseph will tell us of his experiences with Jesus! Olinthus says he is here to let us reaffirm our faith in the Lord Jesus. He is here to seek new followers and to spread the Christian beliefs."

"It is still risky," Petrus said adamantly.

"We won't gather until very late," Catus argued, undaunted by Petrus' doubts.

"All right," Petrus replied at last. "I swear, Catus, every day you sound more and more like Olinthus. Go ahead, spread the word among the others," he said, patting the boy's shoulder.

When Catus had gone, Petrus entered the tavern. His own excitement at meeting someone who had actually known Jesus began to build, lending force to his legs, and letting him fly up the stairs. He knocked loudly at Chloe's door.

When she opened it, he stepped inside, lifted her up, and whirled her around. Then he closed the door with a bang, and began to tell her what he had learned of Joseph's visit, without thinking about the woman he had just passed in the hallway.

It was Xenia who had been standing there, half in and half out of her room. She saw Petrus, excitement written on his face, rush past without saying hello. But when she saw the way he greeted Chloe, she sensed something out of the ordinary was happening.

She quietly closed her door and went to Chloe's. There she put her ear to the wood and listened intently. When she straightened up, a smile was etched firmly on her lips, and her thoughts centered around the rewards she would soon be able to claim. Walking just a shade faster than usual, Xenia, one of the many prostitutes of Pompeii, was about to reshape her life—and her social status.

As the sun dropped below the horizon, and even as Glaucus and Ione left his ship for his villa, and dinner, Xenia returned to Burbo's tavern with a mysterious look of satisfaction on her face.

Meanwhile, Arbaces and Calenus sat across from each other in the high priest's quarters within the sacrarium. They had been there for fifteen minutes, and so far Calenus had done all the talking. But now Arbaces interrupted him: "I still have trouble accepting this good fortune. Tell me again about the man."

"He is an old man named Joseph," Calenus explained. "He is from Palestine, and travels about the empire, spreading the word of the Christians' so-called god."

Arbaces pondered his assistant's words while he absent-mindedly played with his dagger, studying the twining golden snakes. "The Christians must think highly of him, to risk gathering in such large numbers," he said at last.

"If I'm not mistaken, *all* of Pompeii's Christians will be gathered there tonight, because this Joseph is supposed to have known their Christ before his execution."

"How certain are you that this information is correct?" Arbaces asked after gazing at Calenus for a moment.

"Very certain. Xenia told me herself. She overheard two Christians talking. And you know how eager she is to become a priestess."

"In time she may become one," Arbaces said noncommitally. "Well, Calenus, shall we see just how much our magistrate wishes to be *reelected*?"

As the high priest and Calenus stood, they exchanged confident smiles. They both knew that Quintus, the magistrate, would accept their information and act on it quickly, for Quintus was, above all else, a politician and would not hesitate to use whatever would help to assure a continuance of his authority. Nor would he refuse to acknowledge, in the future, those who helped him to maintain his position.

Arbaces smiled with satisfaction. He had no doubt that the Christians would be destroyed tonight.

It was almost midnight when all but the last of the Christians arrived in the wooded glade that Olinthus had chosen for tonight's meeting. When Olinthus himself joined the assembly, after speaking with the lookout, the people grew silent.

A few moments after Olinthus passed the sentry, another couple did the same, walking through the woods, aided by the low glow of their oil lantern. Reaching the edge of the clearing, they paused, and Chloe turned to Petrus, skepticism evident in her voice.

"Petrus," she began, but he stopped her with a gesture.

"I am glad you decided to come here with me," Petrus said gently, trying to ease Chloe's tension.

"But I'm not certain that it's right. Petrus, I don't want to offend Joseph by . . ."

"By your presence? By what you are? If he is truly a man of God, then surely he will see that in your heart you want to be a Christian."

"But I can't call myself a Christian until I take the vows. And I can't do that—not if I'm a whore," she stated sadly, sighing and turning away. "Oh, why talk about it any more?"

But Petrus would not be denied this night, and he made her face him. "You always call me a dreamer, and say I hope for miracles. Maybe this Joseph is the miracle I've waited for. He knew Christ! Oh, Chloe, maybe he can help us change our lives."

Saying that, he gripped her hand and led her toward the others. A moment later they were standing in line, waiting their turn to meet Joseph and to listen to the words he had come so far to say.

They sensed the powerful mood of the people, united, gathered together as never before. Oil lanterns dotted the open glade, and small groups stood around talking, their voices excited and happy. Petrus watched Joseph welcome each of the group individually, embracing every man, woman, and child.

When all had been greeted, Olinthus stood before the people, calling them together and smiling warmly. "It is time now, brothers and sisters, to listen to the words that Joseph has traveled so far to tell us." He turned to the older man. "Joseph," he said.

With an air of confidence and grace, Joseph walked to Olinthus' side and embraced him once again. Then he turned to the people, and with his arms raised, and a smile on his lips, he began to speak.

Standing on the basilica's steps, Quintus took a deep breath of the nighttime air. "The forum is unusually quiet tonight. It is as if the people sense what is happening," he said to Tibius, the second magistrate.

"More likely they're sleeping or fornicating," Tibius said in an offhanded way that annoyed Quintus.

Instead of replying, Quintus shook his head and turned away just as the captain of the guard arrived in his gleaming armor. Quintus noted the sword that hung at the man's waist, and the scarred breastplate the man wore only for battle. He saw, too, in the man's stance and the tilt of his head that the captain was more than ready for tonight's duties.

"There is to be no killing tonight," Quintus ordered, the

moment the man saluted him. "You are to arrest all those at this meeting. Nothing more. I won't have it said that I've condoned lawlessness. Arrest them! Bring them to me! They will be accused as Christians, and tried—legally."

"Understood, sir!" Then the captain saluted Quintus again and turned, unable to suppress the cynical smile that had formed as the magistrate spoke. He took it for granted that Quintus was only mouthing the words. He knew where his duty lay.

When the captain reached his men, Drusus, second in command of the guards, saluted. "Sir, we are ready."

"Mount," the captain ordered as he climbed onto his horse's back. When the troop was ready, he signaled them forward, but was stopped once again by Quintus, who had stepped in front of the horses.

"No massacres!" Quintus reiterated. "Is that understood?"

"Yes, sir," the captain replied.

Kicking his horse harshly, the captain led his men from the forum. When they reached the road leading to Vesuvius, he looked at Drusus. "The magistrates!" he swore sarcastically. "They're like all petty politicians. They want order and safety, but we are told not to abuse the poor, suffering criminals!"

"And need we ask who'll take the credit for ridding Pompeii of the Christians?" Drusus asked with a short, barking laugh.

An ugly sneer twisted the captain's face, followed by a quick snort. "Oh, we'll be rid of them—but in *our* way! Now, let's get them before they split up," he said, laughing loudly as he spurred his horse forward.

When the troops were a quarter of a mile from the meeting place, the captain signaled them to halt and dismount before he gave Drusus his instructions. Once Drusus disappeared into the darkness, the captain ordered his men to silence and slowly led them toward the Christians.

Drusus knew what was expected of him and was more than willing to comply. He walked quietly until he reached the most likely spot on the road. Then, drawing his dagger, he went into the first line of trees, moving stealthily, his senses fully alert.

A moment later he stopped dead. Another step and he would have been face to face with the Christian sentry. But the man was straining to listen to the faint sounds filtering from the glade, and his attention was fixed therein.

Moving soundlessly, Drusus sneaked up behind the sentry. Covering the man's mouth with his hand, he pulled him back. He felt the fear in the man's body, and smiled as brought his knife to the man's neck.

"Pray to your god," Drusus whispered in a voice that reached only the sentry's ears. Then the razor-sharp blade flashed in a deadly semicircle. As the blood gushed over his hand, Drusus held the lookout until he felt the man's lifeless body sag against him. Then he lowered it to the ground. This act of murder had taken Drusus only half a minute, and in that time not one sound had gone out to warn the Christians.

As quietly as he had entered the woods, Drusus left. Three minutes later the captain and his men appeared, and Drusus nodded his head, signaling them into the woods.

Within the glade, the Christians sat facing Joseph. To one side was Olinthus, with Medon, Petrus, Chloe, and Catus. Although his attention was on Joseph, Olinthus' senses were alert to the surroundings.

He thought he heard a rustling behind him and turned cautiously, but he saw nothing except the dark, impenetrable woods.

"The first time I saw Our Lord was by the sea of Galilee," said Joseph, his voice strong and firm. "I was a young man and had heard much of this Jesus of Nazareth. It was said he could work miracles of healing, that he had raised the dead. And that he told strange stories with deep meanings, to teach people how best to live in the sight of God."

Petrus glanced at Chloe's rapt face and, seeing her thus, took her hand in his.

"I believed very little in all of this. Yet, I was most curious to see this man who I thought was probably some sort of magician. Or perhaps yet another of the many prophets who went about promising that a messiah would come." Joseph paused to take a breath and to gaze benevolently at the faces before him. "When I arrived at the shore that long ago day to see and hear Our Lord," he continued, "I could scarcely believe my eyes. A throng of people had gathered such as I had never seen! I was far back in the crowd, and I could not see Jesus. I had almost despaired, when suddenly from the crowd emerged a man. While the crowd held back, he walked alone toward the water. . . ."

Olinthus sat straighter. His mind raced with excitement at what he hoped was to come, but still he remained alert. Then he heard more rustling from the woods, and he turned toward it, again trying to see who or what was there.

He looked at Petrus, who was also staring at the woods. Exchanging quick glances, Olinthus signaled Petrus to continue to watch the woods while he turned back to Joseph.

Joseph, too, seemed to have heard the noise. He met Olinthus' eyes and nodded his head imperceptibly. As he did, he raised his voice, letting his words grow louder. "I looked at Jesus as he walked toward the water. He seemed no more than an ordinary man. And yet, as they watched him, there came a great hush over the crowd, and within me, unaccountably, a wonderful feeling of peace. . . ."

Olinthus tensed again when the rustling in the woods grew more pronounced. Joseph's voice grew louder, and Olinthus knew what the old man was doing. Moving quickly, the sailmaker signaled Petrus to his feet, even as many of the other Christians stirred in alarm.

When Petrus stood, Chloe grabbed his arm, her eyes wide and her face fearful. Petrus half-motioned, half-pushed her toward the far trees, but Chloe refused to release her hold on him, and followed him as he moved through the people, silently urging them toward the far woods. All the while, Joseph continued to speak as if nothing out of the ordinary was happening.

Before they were halfway across the clearing, the guards burst out of the woods, mounted the horses they had been leading, and raised their swords high as they charged. The screams of the Christians pierced the night as they ran in panic from the oncoming troops.

Joseph, however, had refused to move until all the people were fleeing. Only then did he start away.

Olinthus saw this and, after pushing two women into the woods, turned, yelling to Joseph and running toward him in an effort to save him from the certain death that charged madly down at him.

At the edge of the woods Petrus stopped to look for Olinthus. Next to him were Medon and Chloe, holding each other in fear. "Olinthus!" Petrus called. Then he saw the big sailmaker running near him.

"Joseph!" Olinthus cried, pointing to the old man.

Petrus saw what was about to happen and, shrugging off Chloe's restraining arm, raced on ahead of Olinthus.

Then the guards were upon them. Olinthus stumbled over a man's body, falling to the ground just as a guard rode past. Then he saw that Petrus was almost at Joseph's side, and he knew he could do no more.

Running to the others, he grabbed Medon and Chloe and forced them into the woods, all the while struggling with Chloe, who wanted to go back to Petrus.

Petrus ran madly, fear goading him onward, but when he was a scarce ten feet from Joseph, he saw Drusus' sword arc downward, and watched helplessly as Joseph fell to the ground.

Then his mind grew dark with fury. He screamed wildly as Drusus' charge carried him within Petrus' reach. Launching himself from the ground, Petrus leaped onto the horse's back. His arm snaked around the burly guard's neck and locked into his other arm, even as both men crashed to the ground.

They tumbled wildly, and just as Petrus regained his feet he saw another mounted guard approaching. Realizing that to stay and fight would mean certain death, Petrus lunged across the narrow opening between Drusus and the charging man and raced into the safety of the woods.

Behind him came the the mounted guards as he rushed deeper into the trees, searching for Chloe. The charging sounds of horses and guards mingled with the terrified cries of those who had not been able to escape.

With his heart racing and his breath almost gone, Petrus stumbled ahead blindly. Suddenly a hand grabbed him and he whirled, his fist outstretched and ready.

"It is I," Olinthus whispered.

Petrus' arm dropped and he gasped for breath. "Chloe?" he asked.

"Here," she said, going into his arms.

"Thank God," he said.

"Joseph?" Olinthus asked in a fearful voice.

"He is with Jesus," Petrus stated, drawing Chloe tighter.

Olinthus was silent for only a moment. "We must make our way back, carefully." Saying that, he led them from the still hunting guards, and out of the woods on the far side from which they had originally entered. An hour later, in the heart of Pompeii, Petrus and Chloe bid Olinthus goodnight.

They were a block from Burbo's tavern when they heard the sound of horses. "Quick," Chloe whispered urgently, pulling Petrus into a doorway. There she wound her arms around him and began to kiss him, moaning loudly as she pressed her hips wantonly to him. Just then the guards came abreast of them, Drusus and the captain arguing loudly. Petrus' muscles knotted with tension, but Chloe held him close. His blood burned with anger, and his throat tightened with disgust when he heard them speak of all the dead. But suddenly everything became silent.

"Now there's a hard-working girl," shouted the captain as he pointed to the doorway.

Drusus laughed, then moved closer. He felt something prick his mind when he saw them. "You two! Come out here!" he ordered.

Chloe, holding Petrus' head to her neck, looked out at Drusus with a bold smile. "Good evening," she called.

"Step aside, woman. You," he shouted to Petrus' back. "Come out here." When the man didn't move, Drusus dismounted and started toward them, his hand on the hilt of his sword.

"But sir," Chloe said, "we've done nothing. This is my friend, we don't have much . . ."

"Get away!" Drusus snapped. He grabbed Petrus, yanking him roughly away from Chloe. "You!" he shouted, his sword slithering from its scabbard as recognition flooded his mind. "Here's one for the magistrate," he shouted to the captain. "He's the Christian who fought me in the grove, by the gods!"

Petrus shoved Chloe into the street, his eyes pleading for her to run.

"What about her?" Drusus asked the captain as he eyed Chloe.

The captain moved his horse and grabbed Chloe, lifting her up to him. When she was across his lap and his arm was around her, his hand coarsely caressed her breast while he looked at Drusus with a smile. "No need to be fanatical. You have your Christian prisoner. I'll take charge of her!"

"She's done nothing wrong!" Petrus shouted, trying to break away from Drusus. "She's just a whore," he pleaded.

"I know," whispered the captain, just as Drusus pushed Petrus ahead of him with his sword's tip. "Aren't you, my dear?" the captain asked as his hand slipped inside her robe and rubbed across her nipple.

Chapter Ten

The day after the massacre of the Christians dawned as brightly as the day before. The sun rode majestically in the sky. News of the events of the previous night was not yet widely spread, so for most, life in Pompeii continued as if nothing had happened.

For Glaucus, the day was another step toward his winning of Ione, and to that end he had invited her to visit him before she went to the temple. She arrived, accompanied by Nydia, and they went into the garden. Nydia went to the far end and sat by the flowers, while Ione stood next to Glaucus as he ordered a slave to get wine.

"No," Ione said, "I mustn't. I'm already late for services."

"But you can stay for a few more minutes."

Ione's heart was torn. With each day she found herself falling deeper and deeper within Glaucus' hypnotic spell, wanting nothing more than to be with him. But she knew also the dangers. "I've been neglectful in my duties at the temple," she said.

Glaucus began to protest, when a commotion in the front of the house reached their ears. Turning quickly, both Glaucus and Ione saw the house slave chasing after Chloe, dressed in the same garments she had worn last night and carrying her baby in her arms.

"I must see Nydia," she screamed at the slave. Then she stepped into the garden and froze at the sight of the two nobles. "Oh, sir," she pleaded to Glaucus. "I must speak with Nydia."

Glaucus, taken aback by the woman's sudden and untimely

intrusion, glared angrily at her. "What is the meaning of this?" he demanded, recognizing the prostitute immediately.

"Forgive me, but I didn't know where else to turn except to Nydia," Chloe cried, her eyes widening as she saw Nydia walking toward her. She started forward to her friend, but was stopped by the anger in Glaucus' voice.

"How dare you come into my house! And in the presence of this lady!" he shouted, embarrassed that Ione should be in the same place with a whore.

"Chloe?" called Nydia in a low voice.

Suddenly Chloe didn't care what the nobleman might do to her. She ran to Nydia. "They've arrested Petrus," she sobbed. "They'll kill him. I know they will! You must speak to Lydon. . . . Perhaps he can speak to Diomed. Maybe the magistrate. Nydia, he is their champion, please, they respect him."

Glaucus was about to throw the prostitute out, but Ione stepped between them. Holding out her hand, she motioned Chloe to her. "Come, tell me your trouble," she said.

Chloe stared at the noblewoman, recognizing her for the first time. "I . . . Forgive me, my lady," she began, but her tears stopped her.

"Who is Petrus, and why was he arrested?" Ione asked in a gentle voice as she took the child from Chloe's arms and held him to her chest.

"Petrus is the man she loves," Nydia began for Chloe.

"They'll . . . They'll accuse him of being a Christian. They'll kill him," Chloe finished.

"A Christian?" Glaucus cut in, glancing from Chloe to Ione. "Why do you come to us? Do you know how much trouble this can be to Nydia, and even Lydon, were he here and not in Campania?"

"I came because I don't know what else to do. I had to try to find some way to help. Please," she begged.

"I will try to help you, Chloe, but Lydon . . ." Nydia began, knowing the futility of Chloe's request.

While Nydia spoke to Chloe, Ione walked to Glaucus, the

baby still cradled in her arms. When she stopped, she stared at him, her eyes searching his face.

"Glaucus," she said in a low voice, "you have told me that you seek a purpose in your life."

Knowing what she meant, Glaucus looked away from her. "But Christians? Ione, do you realize the danger? I can't get involved in this. Nor can I allow you to either!" he stated adamantly. Then he shrugged his shoulders. "I'll give the poor girl money, of course, but . . ." He stopped because Ione's eyes clearly reflected her disappointment.

"Oh, Glaucus, I thought that you were different," she whispered as she turned, handing the baby back to his mother. Without a backward glance at Glaucus, she walked out of the garden and into the street.

"Damn it!" Glaucus snapped when she was gone. "Damn the whole world!" he shouted loudly at no one in particular. Then he turned to stare at the source of his problem. "All right, out with it all. And I mean all!" he ordered Chloe.

Half an hour later, his thoughts jumbled, his mind confused, Glaucus arrived at Diomed's villa. When Chloe had finished her story, Glaucus had sat in stunned silence, shocked by what he had learned. It had taken him only a few minutes to realize that he did care, and hardly no time after that to devise a plan of action. The ornate door opened, and Glaucus quickly told Medon he must speak with his master. A moment later he was following the servant into Diomed's garden, knowing that he might make a fool of himself, but strangely uncaring at the same time. He was so determined to succeed that his body seemed to hum with a new and strange excitement.

Medon stopped within the entrance, and Glaucus saw the overweight merchant staring at a dying plant, his wife Lucretia looking just as downcast as he. "Sir, Glaucus to see you," he informed his master.

Diomed smiled broadly at Glaucus. "Noble Glaucus, what an honor. Lucretia, fetch Julia!" he ordered his wife. Then he motioned Glaucus toward him. "Do forgive us, but we're quite at odds today. I'm afraid we've a runaway slave,'' he said.

"Petrus. Yes, I know," Glaucus said without showing any emotion.

"You know?" Diomed echoed, still unsure of what was happening.

"That's why I've come. Your Petrus has been arrested . . . as a Christian."

"A Christian? Petrus?" Diomed said, genuinely astonished.

Glaucus nodded slowly as he spoke. "I gather he's to be tried immediately."

"As well he might be!" Diomed declared righteously. "And condemned as well! A Christian, indeed! Fancy my harboring a Christian in my very own house," he thundered mightily, falling into his politician's pose of righteous indignation.

Glaucus had counted on just that reaction, and the instant Diomed finished he made his move, but did not let his mask of stoicism slip as he spoke: "And one can only imagine what the magistrate will make of *that*, with the election coming."

Diomed's head snapped up at these words. He paused, his mind racing. "Oh. . . . Ye gods, I hadn't thought of that. What . . . ?"

"Yes, I thought you might not have . . . an honorable man like yourself. And that is why I've come. I believe I might have a solution for you." Glaucus was now even more certain that Diomed, in his quest for the magistrate's seat, would not think too deeply about the events surrounding this strange conversation.

Diomed looked at Glaucus with a mixture of desperation and sad hope. "Anything, noble Glaucus!"

A sudden whirlwind of feet and costly robes announced Julia's arrival. She stopped three feet from Glaucus, smiling shyly at him before speaking to her father.

"Not now, Julia, not now," Diomed said, waving her away as he looked at Glaucus. "Tell me, please, how can I rectify this situation?"

Glaucus stepped next to the merchant, and in a low conspiratorial voice advised him of what should be done. A few moments later, Diomed, smiling with pleasure, called for Medon to bring him his writing materials.

Quintus stared at the captain of the guard, his mood angry and tense. He and Tibius had spent almost an hour questioning the captain and had gained no satisfaction from the answers.

Quintus thought he had made his position clear last night. "I told you to arrest the Christians. There was to be no killing. And what did you return with? A stack of bodies and one miserable slave! A slave you didn't even arrest at the scene!"

The captain hid his annoyance, speaking calmly. "This slave *was* at the meeting. Drusus," he said, pointing to the other guard, "can testify to that."

"We've been over this a dozen times," Quintus said stonily. "Very well, Captain, have the prisoner bought in." When the captain nodded to Drusus, Quintus glanced around at the chamber as if he was bored with the whole procedure.

"The slave's name is Petrus," said the captain after Drusus had left to fetch the man. "He's the slave of Diomed."

Suddenly Quintus was no longer bored, and his eyes were riveted on the captain's face. "Of Diomed? Is he indeed!" His thoughts were interrupted as one of his scribes came into the chamber, with the noble Glaucus, and another man, a slave, trailing a few paces behind him. *Now what?* he asked himself wearily.

The scribe went to Quintus and whispered in his ear, while Glaucus and the captain exchanged brief nods. Then Quintus straightened in his chair and looked at Glaucus with puzzled interest. "Lord Glaucus, you have business with the court?"

"I understand you have arrested one of my slaves, Lord Magistrate. A man named Petrus?"

"Your slave?" questioned Tibius. "I thought the man belonged to Diomed."

Glaucus looked from Tibius to Quintus before he spoke,

and when he did, his voice, although low, sounded very loud in the chamber. "And so he did, until three days ago."

Glaucus motioned to the slave who had accompanied him, his eyes locking with the slave's pointedly. "Or was it two days ago?" he asked. "I don't really remember exactly when I bought him. Give the magistrate the bill of sale," he instructed his slave in an offhanded manner.

The slave withdrew a roll of vellum and went to the magistrates, where he extended it. Tibius, fully cognizant that a nobleman of Glaucus' position was not a man to be trifled with, or to have his word questioned, waved the slave away.

"I must say," Glaucus continued smoothly, enjoying the game, "that Diomed warned me about this fellow. I gather he enjoys himself with the women of a certain sort. But I shall cure him of that!"

"Did good Diomed also warn you that your man was a Christian?" asked Tibius smugly.

"A Christian?" Glaucus asked with a puzzled shake of his head.

This time it was Quintus who spoke for the court. "He is under arrest for attending a meeting of Christians last night. Therefore, even though he is your slave, I'm afraid he must be tried."

Glaucus stared at Quintus blankly. "Last night?" he asked, looking steadily at the magistrate, and knowing that his acting must be the best ever. "Forgive me, Quintus, but I don't see how that's possible. He was in attendance the entire evening. I was entertaining, you see."

"Yet he was arrested in the street, just before dawn," cut in Tibius.

"Yes, I sent him out myself," Glaucus stated. Then he walked closer to the magistrates and lowered his voice to a barely audible level, making them lean forward in order to hear him. "My visitor was a lady, you see. I had Petrus accompany her to her house. I shouldn't like to involve her, but if it's necessary, I shall give you her name, of course. I guess it was then that Petrus took the opportunity to meet with a prostitute. But after this, I believe he will think twice before he schedules unauthorized trips.''

The chamber door opened again, and Drusus entered with Petrus, who looked dazed, confused, and frightened.

"Lord Glaucus, is this the man in question?" Quintus asked.

Taking a deep breath, Glaucus turned to look at Petrus, the warning in his eyes unseen by the others. "So, Petrus, is this how you embarrass your new master? Perhaps a good whipping will remind you of your station in life!" he said angrily, ignoring the confused look reflected by Drusus as well as Petrus.

"So," Quintus said sarcastically to the captain, "your man was certain that Petrus was at the meeting, was he?"

The captain stared first at Quintus, and then at Glaucus. When his eyes returned to the magistrate, he shrugged his shoulders and spoke in a tired, cynical voice. "It was very dark," he said.

Drusus stepped forward, a protest on his lips, but an angry gesture from the captain silenced him quickly.

Glaucus nodded to the captain, smiling bitterly as he spoke. "I'm sure your man meant no harm. After all, who really looks at a slave?" Glaucus said sagaciously.

A short time later, Glaucus brought Petrus into the garden where Chloe had been anxiously waiting. The moment she saw her lover, Chloe cried out and ran to him, embarrassing him as the tears fell from her eyes. "Oh, Petrus," she whispered.

Then she drew herself straighter, looking at Glaucus through a veil of tears. "My lord, I have no words with which to thank you. You have given me back my very life. But on that life, I swear to you that someday, somehow, I will repay you."

When Chloe finished and turned to Petrus again, Glaucus saw that Ione had returned to the garden and was sitting on a bench, watching him. It was then that he saw the proud, loving look on her face, and realized just how important it was to him, and how close he had come to losing her.

It was only the sight of her face that wiped away the memory of the way the guard, Drusus, had looked at him in the magistrate's chamber—of the way he had stared, his face a grotesque mask of venomous hatred.

It was a look that Glaucus would have cause to always remember.

PART
II

Chapter Eleven

The noon sun poured down, stifling the almost deserted streets of Pompeii with unremitting heat. On this August afternoon, most houses in the city were shuttered against the sun's strength. The buildings surrounding the forum were quiet, and the forum itself was almost deserted. A low, faraway sound of thunder rumbled through the streets, but to those few hapless souls who were out in the midday heat there were no clouds visible to offer even the hope of relief. Yet the sound returned again, waking one beggar from his sleep on the steps of the temple of Isis. As he opened his eyes, a pitcher on the ledge above him began to rattle, and a moment later it crashed to the streets.

Shrugging, the beggar closed his eyes and lay back again for a few more minutes of sleep. But his rest was disturbed again by the sound of pounding feet. He glanced up to see the priest Calenus race past, sweating, a look of apprehension on his face. The beggar watched until the man disappeared into the sacrarium. Then once again he closed his eyes, hoping for sleep.

Calenus did not tarry upon reaching the cooler interior of the sacrarium; rather, he ran even faster, until he was at Arbaces' door. Knocking once, Calenus opened the door and stepped inside, pausing only long enough to let his eyes adjust to the darkness of the room.

Arbaces' private apartment was windowless, lit by burning tapers on black-curtained walls. Incense burned within a golden tripod, above which hung a globe covered with myriad Egyptian astrological symbols. Several richly embroidered couches lined the wall. Tables of wood, brass, and silver held many of Arbaces' possessions.

When his eyes were acclimated to the darkness of the room, Calenus could see Arbaces lying on a couch, staring at him.

"Well? Where is Ione?" asked the high priest somewhat impatiently.

"The blind girl says Ione is out with Glaucus."

"Again? She has been with him all too frequently in these past weeks," Arbaces muttered angrily.

Calenus shrugged but could not hide his look of triumph. "I warned you."

"You did," Arbaces agreed. "We must initiate her soon. Until we do, Calenus, keep close watch on her."

Calenus nodded his head, his eyes studying the high priest. "And Glaucus? My brother Burbo could take care of him."

"No! That would be too dangerous," Arbaces said. "Besides," he added in a milder voice, "I have *better* plans for Glaucus."

The two priests stared at each other, smiling. "As you wish," Calenus said.

Arbaces stood then, nodding his head. "And to implement my plans, I must visit Diomed. Isis see me through that!"

As if in answer to his sarcastic words, the floor of the sacrarium trembled slightly.

In the depths of the earth the huge masses shifted again, blocking old fissures and closing the ancient steam vents that had maintained the tenuous balance between the further depths below and the thin crust above.

Molten lava pooled angrily. Steam and gas hissed urgently against the barriers. Slowly, the pressures began to increase.

High above this turbulence, on a gentle slope of great Vesuvius itself, Glaucus and Ione sat on a woven blanket, talking to each other. The food on their gold-edged plates was forgotten, the wine in the silver goblets untouched. A mound of cheese sat in a platter on the edge of the blanket, and an intricately designed bowl held moist fruit. But for all this abundance, Glaucus and Ione saw only each other.

"My father brought me here once, as a child," Ione said. Lifting her eyes, she looked around at the mountain. "I loved it when he could come down from Rome to see Antonius and myself."

Then her eyes focused on Glaucus' handsome face again, and her breath became strained. Forcing herself to think of something else, she smiled. "My father said there was a legend of Vesuvius . . . but it's silly."

Glaucus, unwilling to allow her lilting voice to stop, shook his head. "Tell me."

Ione's crystal blue eyes became unfocused, and a moment later she spoke. "It was said that there was a battle between the giants of the earth and the gods of heaven. And the gods forced the defeated giants down into Vesuvius, burying them alive. They lie there, year by year gathering their strength."

Glaucus smiled and took one of her hands into his. "And now and then they shake themselves, in a wild frenzy to get free. And that is what we feel as earthquakes," he declared.

"No one knows," Ione said with a sly smile, her eyes playfully wide, "it could be giants after all."

Glaucus looked about in alarm. Then he grabbed her other hand tightly. "Quiet! They may hear us!" he whispered, and then burst out laughing. But with the heat of her hands burning into his, his thoughts turned serious and the smile left his face.

"What is it?" Ione asked, sensing his sudden change of mood.

"You," Glaucus said. "You seem so different these days. So free and happy."

Flushing under his powerful gaze, Ione pulled her hands from his and twisted away. But Glaucus moved swiftly, catching her shoulders, turning her so that she was forced to look into his eyes.

"This time you will hear me out," he said in a passionate voice. "The first day I saw you, in the spring, I fell in love with you. Ione, I want to be good enough, worthwhile enough, to make *you* love me.''

Ione's heart beat faster, but she shook her head nonetheless. "You are good! You've shown me that."

Glaucus leaned forward, drawing her to him at the same time. When their lips met, fire raced through their bodies. Ione stiffened, trying to push him away, but the feel of his mouth on hers threatened to rob her of her will.

"No, Glaucus!" she cried, forcefully breaking the kiss.

"Ione, life without you would be barren. As barren as your life as a priestess would be."

Closing her eyes, Ione tried to make him comprehend her needs. "You don't understand, because you don't believe."

Glaucus shook her slightly, forcing her to open her eyes and look at him. His blood raced, and his desire grew even more powerful as he stared at her. "I can't believe in a goddess who would entomb you in some deadly temple! I believe in nothing that would keep you from me!" he declared.

He drew her to him again. Their eyes locked and his arms tightened about her. This time when their lips met he felt Ione's resistance stay firm, but he no longer cared. Shifting, he forced Ione down onto the blanket, and a moment later lay above her.

She struggled but could not fight his greater strength. Nor could she fight the heat that blazed so suddenly within her. In that very instant, her lips softened, and Glaucus' tongue darted within her mouth. A low moan issued from the back of Ione's throat. Her mouth opened wider to his probing, and her arms wound around him as she returned his passionate kiss with her own.

Her hands became explorers, racing madly along his back, rising upward, caressing his neck, weaving through the thick abundance of his curly hair. Her passions exploded wildly, and for the first time, Ione realized what she had been holding back—from him, and from herself.

Then his mouth left hers, to journey along her cheek, to kiss and caress her satin skin, brushing over her closed eyelids before traveling to her neck. His hands moved everywhere, making slow, maddening circles.

Glaucus inhaled the scent of the woman beneath him. He heard her low moan of desire when his hand caressed her full breast and the nipple hardened beneath his palm. When his fingers slipped beneath the fold of her robes he almost gasped at the silken feel of her skin. He kissed her again, deeply, passionately, his hand encasing her breast. Then he drew slightly away, gazing into her now open eyes.

"I love you, Ione. I want you."

"Glaucus," she whispered, aware of his hand on her breast and of the deep agitated aching need within her. Suddenly she realized how much she loved him—how much she wanted him too. But in a far corner of her mind a small voice of reason called to her, reminding her of her obligations. "No. . . . Glaucus, I ca—"

But Glaucus would not listen; instead he bent to kiss her again. His mouth was so passionate and demanding, and his need so evident, that all thought of protest was driven from Ione's mind. Her final resistance crumbled; she knew their passion could no longer be denied

Her blood raced wildly and her breathing became forced. His mouth was everywhere, kissing her, searching every secret place on her face and neck. Then he slipped her robe from her shoulders. A moment later she cried out, arching her back when her nipple was captured by his searing lips.

Heat exploded across the surface of her breast, and a strange, pleasant warmth spread low in her belly. Moisture formed in the juncture of her thighs, even as Glaucus' mouth left her breast to travel across her skin.

Glaucus, lost within the touch and taste of Ione, did not feel the first tremor shake the ground. The loud cracking noise which followed, however, did startle them from their passion. Lifting his lips from her skin, Glaucus stared blankly around. Two feet from where they lay a large crack was opening in the earth.

Glaucus willed his fear away. Forcing himself into action, he grabbed Ione's hand and pulled her to her feet. "Run!" he shouted, dragging her with him, racing against the fast-moving cracks that sped at all angles toward them.

Everything seemed to be happening as in a dream. The entire side of the mountain shook crazily, rocks and pieces of earth pelted them with every step they took, and more than once they lost their footing, tumbling madly in their effort to escape.

Stealing a glance behind him, Glaucus saw a giant boulder trembling and realized that if it were shaken loose they would most certainly be killed. Urging Ione to run faster, Glaucus pushed her ahead of him, keeping himself between her and the large rock. Then, as suddenly as it had started, the trembling ended, and an eerie quiet descended.

They stopped, their breathing loud and jagged as they looked around at the mountain slope. But once again the ground began to shake. Glaucus saw the fear on Ione's face and pulled her to him for a brief moment. "Courage," he said. Then he released her, taking her hand again, leading her down the slope.

"Come, I know where to find shelter," he said, pointing off to one side of the mountain, to the far distant speck that was the roof of Gaius' villa.

Although the full force of the earthquake ravaged one slope of Vesuvius, only a minor trembling was felt in Pompeii, where Arbaces had just stepped into the atrium of Diomed's villa. He was looking at a statue when the ground beneath his feet quivered angrily. Holding onto the base of the sculpture, he waited the quake out. When the ground was still again, he straightened himself.

A moment later, undaunted by the passing tremor, Diomed came into the atrium, his face wreathed with a smile. "This is an unexpected pleasure. The campaign is going very well, you know," he said, assuming the election to be the reason for Arbaces' visit.

"Is it?" the priest asked coldly.

"Why, yes," Diomed replied, puzzled by Arbaces' tone.

"What a pity then, if it should all prove worthless."

"Arbaces, I don't understand what you mean."

"Glaucus." Arbaces said the word as if it were an anathema.

Diomed sighed noisily. "I cannot understand that man! Arbaces, we have spoken about this before. He has been most helpful to me, but when it comes to interesting him in Julia . . ."

Arbaces shook his head, his eyes still hard. "If you're to prove your standing with the people—and especially old families—*and* if you're to get to Rome . . ." Wisely, Arbaces left the rest unsaid.

"Don't you think I know that I need a noble, monied son-in-law? And Glaucus always seemed the best choice."

"If you expect the temple to continue supporting you, Glaucus is the *only* man!" he stated tersely.

"Arbaces, Julia is plagued by other noble suitors. Why must it be Glaucus?"

"Because Glaucus is in love with Ione!" Arbaces snapped out of exasperation. Then, seeing the puzzled expression on Diomed's face, Arbaces explained: "Just as you need Glaucus to become magistrate, I need Ione for the temple. To strengthen its position with the nobles."

It took Diomed a moment, but the logic of Arbaces' words finally sank in. "And the stronger the temple . . ."

"The stronger are your chances," Arbaces said with his first smile of this meeting.

"But how am I to accomplish this marriage?" Diomed asked wearily.

"Find a way!" Arbaces ordered. Pivoting on his heels, the priest walked out of the atrium. Diomed remained where he stood, pondering the many possibilities of accomplishing the impossible.

It took them almost a quarter of an hour to reach Gaius' villa, but when Glaucus and Ione stepped onto the front porch they breathed a sigh of relief.

Fortunata rose from her seat and came toward them, her face changing from surprise to concern when she saw their disheveled clothing and dirt-lined faces. "Glaucus?" she asked hesitantly.

"We were caught in the earthquake," he said by way of explanation.

"We felt the shaking, but I've grown accustomed to it, though it did seem stronger this time," Fortunata said as she motioned for them to follow her.

Glaucus paused for a moment when he saw Gaius staring at him. "This is kind of you," he said to Fortunata.

"We feared it might start up again," Ione added.

Fortunata smiled at her and then led the two toward Gaius, whom Glaucus eyed uneasily. "Gaius dear, come and see who is here. It's Ione!"

Glaucus and Ione exchanged startled glances as the old senator came eagerly forward, a wide smile on his weathered face. "Good day, sir," Ione said politely.

Gaius stared openly at her and his old eyes seemed to grow younger. "Little Ione, grown into a beautiful woman."

"Forgive me, but I . . ." Ione began, confused by his words.

"You were too young to remember me. Your father was at Nero's court with me, poor man. There was a boy?" Gaius asked.

"Antonius, my brother," Ione answered. "He's become a priest of Isis."

Glaucus tensed at Ione's words, and watched the old senator's expression change. "Ione wants to follow him into the temple," Glaucus said pointedly before Gaius could speak.

Gaius held Glaucus' gaze for a moment before he nodded his understanding of what was not spoken. "I see," he whispered, looking quickly at Fortunata, who had gone to Ione's side and gently taken her arm.

"Come, you need to clean up, and then you must have some refreshment."

When Fortunata had led Ione into the house, Gaius glanced at Glaucus, alarm clearly written on his features.

"What is it?" Glaucus asked quickly.

"It's . . . nothing. Only that I see you love her very much," he said with a forced smile. "And now I understand your interest in Arbaces . . . as he calls himself."

Glaucus sensed that Gaius was still afraid to speak to him, but his concern forced him to insist. "You must tell me! If there's any . . ."

"I don't hold with religion," Gaius said, cutting Glaucus off. "The gods were born of fear. And high priests profit from it."

"Gaius!"

Gaius stared at Glaucus. The eyes of both men were filled with the same look of pleading. "Don't ask me more. Glaucus, if you love Ione, do not let her join Arbaces!"

Glaucus wanted more, but the look of finality on Gaius' face stopped him. He nodded his head slowly.

"I think you should clean up too," Gaius said, pointing at Glaucus' dirt-stained tunic.

"There is more than dirt that must be cleaned. Is that not so?" he asked the senator in a whisper that the old man ignored as he led him into the house.

Later Glaucus sat as though detached, sipping wine, while he watched Ione converse with Fortunata. What had happened before the quake seemed to have been an illusion, possessing no point in reality. Whenever their eyes met, Glaucus felt a curtain had fallen between them.

After finishing their wine, Glaucus and Ione thanked the older couple and returned to Pompeii. They walked back to Ione's villa in silence, both aware of the tension swirling around them.

Ione was lost in her thoughts, afraid to even think about what might have happened had it not been for the intervention of the earthquake. She had allowed her emotions—and her body—to betray her, almost to the point of madness. But now she was no longer sure of anything.

"Ione," Glaucus said in a low voice when they reached the entrance of her home.

Instinctively, Ione knew what Glaucus was about to say. Raising her hand, she tried to ward off his words. "Please. Let's not discuss it again."

"Ione, I have so many doubts about Arbaces . . ."

"Because you don't understand him!" she snapped. Then,

in a softer voice, she tried to make him see the truth of her feeling. "From the time our father died, Arbaces has been like a father to Antonius and myself. He has given me so much, Glaucus. He taught me the love of Isis."

Pausing, Ione stared into the depths of Glaucus' eyes. She lifted her hand slowly and stroked his cheek. "And you . . . you hold out such different hopes."

Glaucus covered her hand and then brought it to his lips. He kissed her palm gently and then released it. "I have never asked you to give up your love of Isis."

"Not that, but to give up my intended life as a priestess."

"Because I love you, Ione. I want you for my wife!"

Under the intensity of his gaze, Ione felt her resolution waver. Steeling herself, she shook her head sadly. "You . . . you must give me time to think. Glaucus, it's better that we don't meet for a while."

"Are you so afraid of yourself?" he asked in a low voice. "Look at me, Ione!" he ordered, cupping her chin and lifting her face to his. "On the mount, we were almost one. Our hearts had joined, as had our lips. Stop fighting your heart."

Turning away, Ione took several deep breaths. His words had struck her with both their truth and their hopelessness. With her back still to him she undid the necklace he had given her; when it was cradled in her palm, she turned back to him, her hand outstretched.

"I must return this," she said, opening her hand to reveal the coiled golden rope.

He did not take it. Instead his hand covered hers once again, closing her fingers over the beautiful piece of jewelry. "No. I'll respect your wishes if I must. I'll give you whatever time you need. But keep this as reminder of my love. And Ione, send for me when you have made your decision."

Their eyes locked, and many unspoken messages passed between them. But when Glaucus drew her to him, Ione pulled away and shook her head. Quickly she stepped back from him, spun, and hurried into her house.

*   *   *

Many blocks away from Ione's villa another argument was in progress. This confrontation was taking place in Diomed's atrium, and the combatants were Diomed himself and his daughter Julia. The argument had continued for a half hour already, and as the minutes went by their voices grew louder and more heated.

"No!" Julia screamed, whirling to face her father again. "I'll tell you for the last time! I won't try to lure Glaucus for you!"

"Enough!" Diomed shouted, his face scarlet with a rage Julia had never seen before. "And I say you shall, or I'll know the reason why!"

"Why?" Julia asked. Then, unable to stop a bitter laugh from escaping, she shook her head at him. "Because I'm as much a fool as my father. Because I'm in love with Clodius."

Diomed stared incredulously at her, unwilling to believe what he had just heard. "Clodius," he repeated inanely. "How could you do this to me?"

Another hollow laugh reverberated from her lips. "You needn't look so worried. Clodius would never have a merchant's daughter," she stated factually.

As prideful as ever, Diomed exploded foolishly. "Why that . . . that pompous scoundrel!" Then Diomed drew himself straighter, suddenly smiling at Julia. "But you won't be a merchant's daughter when I am elected magistrate. *We* will be the *new* nobility!"

Diomed's words registered in Julia's mind, and her anger dissolved as quickly as her father's had. "I know. I'm counting on that."

Diomed gazed at his daughter, realizing exactly what she meant. "You are the clever one, aren't you. You think that if I'm elected, Clodius will come round."

"I can only hope."

"You are my daughter, clever girl!" Diomed declared expansively. "Well, now you and I are in each other's hands. Julia, without Glaucus I cannot get elected."

Julia stared at her father, trying to puzzle out his last words. "I don't understand."

"You will. Listen to me carefully, Julia, for at least this once. I see a way for both of us to have what we want. All *I* need is for the world to *think* that you're promised to Glaucus," he said pointedly.

"Father, I've told you," she began, but Diomed stopped her with a dismissing wave of his hand.

"Do this for me, Julia, and when I win the election, you may marry whomever you choose. . . . Even Clodius, if he'll have you," he added contemptuously.

Julia's breath caught, but her mind was saddened by the knowledge of what he really wanted. "You would even let me prostitute myself for your ambitions, wouldn't you?"

Diomed's face turned scarlet with rage, and his eyes narrowed dangerously. "How dare you! Look at yourself! You're spoiled! Privileged! Your every whim is granted! And why? Because I've spent my life working, pulling myself up from nothing. Yes, I'm ambitious! And because I am, you can forget my family came from slaves! Because I am, you may one day be a Roman lady, where the smell of fish sauce can't cling to those silk robes you love so much! So don't you presume to judge me, my girl!"

Julia was startled, stung by his words. Slowly, however, she realized the extent and the truth of what he *thought* he wanted. She knew that her father could not help being what he was, just as she could not help being his daughter. She laughed again—that same haunting, bitter laugh of moments before. "Quite right, Daddy! One whore should never judge another." Knowing she no longer had any choice, Julia fled the atrium for the safety of her own bedchamber. Had she turned back she would have seen the shame that was so evident on her father's face.

Chapter Twelve

On the hot summer morning following the minor earthquake, the Stabian baths were filled with the rich women of Pompeii. The only men in evidence were the eunuch masseurs who lavished the women's bodies with soothing oiled massages.

Every inch of available space was taken by the women, their hairdressers, and their slaves. At one small bathing pool, five women surrounded a fortune teller, waiting their turn to learn about the faithlessness of their lovers. At another pool, only a few yards away, two women soaked in the heated salt bath, talking about the orgy they had attended last night.

Near the entrance to the bath, a solitary figure paced back and forth, impatiently waiting for someone's arrival. Then she turned and stopped, her orange-hennaed hair bouncing in emphasis to the sudden movement.

Julia sighed as she watched Nydia argue with the doorkeeper. Calling out, she signaled him to admit the blind slave girl. A moment later, Julia took Nydia's arm and led her into a private alcove.

"I'm sorry, Nydia," she began, apologizing for the doorkeeper's brusque attitude. "How shocking for you to be treated like a *common* slave."

"I am a slave," Nydia said evenly.

Julia smiled. "You needn't be! Nydia," Julia began, choosing her words carefully. "I asked you to come here because I want to offer you a trade—your freedom for your help with Glaucus."

"Glaucus has already offered me that," Nydia said, her face expressionless.

Surprised, Julia tried another approach. "I can see to it that you will be well paid."

With these words Nydia understood what was happening, but she did not really care. "What I want, you can't give me," she said simply. "Does this mean you love Glaucus too?"

Julia snorted disdainfully. "No, Nydia, it doesn't. But I must find a way to make Ione break with him."

Nydia, tempted as she had never been before, thought for a moment before speaking. "Julia, Ione is good to me. She trusts me."

It was the tone of her voice, not the words, which gave Julia the insight she had been seeking. "Is that worth your freedom? Freedom to do anything you want—to have any man you want! And you wouldn't have to be Ione's handmaiden anymore!"

Tortured, Nydia struggled with her own conscience. "No, please don't say any more. I . . . I cannot help you. I can't!" she cried, upset by the thoughts and desires Julia had brought out in her mind.

Before Julia could stop her, Nydia stumbled toward the entrance where the doorkeeper took her arm and guided her out. Shrugging her shoulders, Julia turned back to the baths, ignoring the disapproving stares of several women who had witnessed the scene between her and the slave girl. Undaunted, Julia returned to her place by the side of the pool.

While the Stabian baths continued to fill with women, the various chambers within the sacrarium of the temple of Isis filled with people as well. In one chamber stood a group of priests and priestesses, relaxing in their usual manner after the morning prayers, taking full advantage of their leisure.

One priest in the center of the group, still dressed in the robes he had worn at the morning service, arched his head back suddenly and threw his arms wide. "Oh mighty Isis," he prayed, "send more wine!" With that he fell backwards, into the waiting arms of the other priests and priestesses, who, laughing drunkenly, began to pair off. Wine passed from hand to hand, and as the drinking progressed, the level of noise increased. Soon, clothing fell to the floor and a full-scale orgy replaced the pious prayers of minutes before.

Antonius stood off to one side of the chamber, refusing to join the writhing mass of bodies sprawled around the room. Since he had become initiated, he had learned of the baseness of his peers. It had been only Arbaces' cautioning words that had kept him here this long. Arbaces had explained how so few men and women could live the life required by Isis. How so few could hold to their morality and rise above the petty needs of the flesh.

Arbaces had even explained the reasons he allowed the priests to continue on in this manner, assuring Antonius that his future would go along a far different path. But at this very moment Antonius wasn't sure of anything beyond the disgust he felt at what he was witnessing.

"Come, Antonius," called a young priestess, her large breasts bobbing as she neared him. Her arms went around him and she pressed her body eagerly to him in an open invitation.

Sickened, he tried to pull away. Nonetheless, his body began to react to the heat of the woman's closeness. Stunned by his reaction and fearing he would give in against his will, Antonius pushed her roughly away and looked about for a way to escape. The priestess went back to him, but stopped when another voice rang out.

"Let him go," ordered one of the older priests. "We wouldn't want to hurt our little virgin!"

Blushing at the sounds of laughter directed at him, Antonius sped from the room, seeking the safety and solitude of his small bedchamber. So much shame filled his mind that he did not see Ione, dressed in a pale blue robe, walking a dozen feet ahead of him—nor did he see that Arbaces was leading her to his private quarters.

When Arbaces had closed the door behind him, he motioned Ione to a seat. Then he stepped next to her, his face a mask of pious concern. "Your absence from the temple has concerned me. For Isis has spoken to me of you, Ione," he said. He paused for a moment, assured now of her full attention. "The time of your initiation has arrived."

Ione gasped loudly at his words, but could not find her tongue to reply.

"It is modest of you to think yourself unworthy," Arbaces told her, his voice still soft and kind.

"Arbaces," Ione began hesitantly, searching carefully for each word. "I do believe in Isis, and you know that I've been happy in her worship. But . . . but I don't think I can be a priestess," she whispered.

Arbaces' eyebrows arched, lending credence to the look of feigned surprise that filled his face. "Ione?"

"I've prayed to Isis. I've searched myself for answers, but . . ."

Arbaces, a veteran of empire politics, knew how and when to act. "A question of faith is always necessary on the path to true commitment," he said smoothly.

"It is not that. Arbaces, I love him!" she admitted aloud for the first time.

"Him?" Arbaces asked innocently.

"Glaucus. I love Glaucus!"

"Glaucus," Arbaces repeated. "But of course he has turned your head. He's a handsome, dashing man. He has turned the head of many a girl." Pausing for just a moment, Arbaces held Ione's gaze with his own warm look. "Ione, you are at an age when one might expect such an infatuation."

"It's not infatuation," Ione insisted. "I want to marry him. He wants the same."

Arbaces remained silent for a moment as he looked at her with pity. "Think, Ione, think! Surely you must see what Glaucus is—a rich noble, spoiled and quickly bored. He is a man who buys new pleasures when and where he wants."

"He has changed, Arbaces," Ione pleaded.

Arbaces sighed loudly and placed his hand on Ione's shoulder. "You know you are like a daughter to me. And like a foolish father, I had hoped to spare you pain. But I see now that I cannot.''

"What?'' Ione asked, alarmed by Arbaces' words.

''I had hoped not to have to tell you, but . . . Well, it is about Glaucus and . . . Julia—Diomed's daughter. Ione, he may have been attracted by you for the moment, but it is still Glaucus and Julia, as it was before he met you,'' Arbaces said, the lie rolling smoothly from his tongue.

Ione's mind whirled, unable for the moment to grasp what he was saying. "Glaucus and Julia? What do you mean?''

''Oh, my innocent dear, it's common knowledge that they . . .''

But Ione refused to accept his words. "No,'' she whispered hoarsely, as a tear escaped her eye. "He loves me!'' Unable to sit still under Arbaces' pitying stare, Ione stood and walked around the chamber.

Arbaces, keeping his face emotionless for a moment, went to her and gently made her face him. "Don't waste your tears on such a man. I saw in you, long ago, that you had a strong purpose in life. Ione, you're destined to be not just a priestess but the high priestess! Your destiny is to help me carry out my mission through the empire, and to spread the word of Isis to all.''

Ione, still confused, drew back from the high priest. "I can't believe what you have said about Glaucus. I . . . I'm so confused,'' she cried.

''Then come with me now,'' Arbaces counseled, seizing the opportunity he had created. "Come into the temple. You'll be safe from such ill use there. You will find solace.''

''No, not yet,'' Ione said. "I can't accept what you've said. Arbaces, please, give me just a little while longer.''

''Would you like to see your brother?'' Arbaces asked, undaunted by his failure.

''No!'' Ione cried in alarm. "Don't tell Antonius. He'd be so disappointed; you know how his heart is set on my confirmation. Please, just give me a little more time.''

''If you insist,'' Arbaces agreed reluctantly, knowing that he must not push her too far. "But promise me that you'll stay away from Glaucus. He has hurt and confused you terribly. To give him the opportunity to fill your head with more lies can only hurt you again."

Arbaces saw fresh tears spring into her eyes, but smiled when she nodded in obedience. Then, without another word, Ione turned and left. Arbaces stood in the archway of his chamber and watched her disappear from sight.

"You let her go?" Calenus asked as he stepped from the shadows.

"Would you have me bind and gag her? She must return of her own free will. If I must force her, or rush her, she may always have doubts. No, I want her to be completely *mine*."

Hearing the emphasis in Arbaces' voice, Calenus nodded, then spoke with a deceptive innocence. "When you say *yours*, you mean, of course, you want her devoted to Isis." Arbaces' hard stare did not bother the other priest as he smiled and continued. "But will she return?"

"I have several means left to me. And most importantly, I have Antonius. When I tell him that Glaucus has broken his sister's heart, Antonius himself will convince her to enter the temple."

After Calenus had gone, Arbaces stared vacantly down the hall. *I have come too far to be stopped now,* he told himself. *Too far!*

For several hours following her conversation with Arbaces, Ione sat alone in her garden, thinking of what had been said. But she thought also of what Glaucus had told her. She believed in his love for her, and in her love for him. She wondered, over and over, why Arbaces had told her such lies.

Not once since she had met Glaucus had he even mentioned Julia. *No, it was not possible.* But Arbaces had planted the seeds of doubt in her mind, and when she thought back to her first meetings with Glaucus, and her impressions of him, her doubts increased.

Suddenly, she knew she must find the truth, one way or another. If Arbaces had lied to her, she would find out. If he was right, then she knew that she did not belong anywhere but with Isis. Rising, Ione called out for Nydia. A moment later the blind girl came into the garden.

"Nydia," Ione whispered, "I need your help." With that she told Nydia about her meeting with Arbaces, and what he had said about Glaucus. When she was finished she waited for Nydia's response, but the blind girl remained silent.

"Nydia, please, you know Glaucus. Could he do such a thing to me?"

"Arbaces has upset you," Nydia said, unwilling to be drawn in by Ione's desperation.

"Nydia, please, answer me!"

Jealousy and anger flared in Nydia's mind, and she was soon fighting a harsh battle of her own. "It . . . it doesn't seem like Glaucus," she replied, reluctantly speaking the truth.

Ione stared at Nydia for a long moment, accepting the girl's words, but still filled with doubt. She remembered last night, when Glaucus had told her that when she was ready she was to send for him. With sudden determination, Ione unclasped the necklace Glaucus had given her and placed it in Nydia's hand.

"Take this to Glaucus," she instructed, "tell him that I will redeem it only from his hands. That if he loves me, he is to come to me." Unable to bare any more of her thoughts to Nydia, Ione walked slowly from the garden.

"And he will," Nydia whispered to the empty garden. For a brief instant, her heart had gone out to Ione, but then her own needs had surfaced. *He would come to you, if he were to know of your need,* Nydia thought as her own unrequited love for Glaucus rose to taunt her.

She remembered her conversation that morning with Diomed's daughter. Suddenly, Nydia realized what she must do. Her fingers curled around the necklace, and she knew that she held within her hand the means for Julia to gain her wish, and also the possibility that she, too, might win at the end. With those thoughts controlling her, Nydia left the garden.

Instead of going to Glaucus, she turned west on the street and walked steadily toward Diomed's villa.

It was well after midnight when Julia finally went to bed. For hours she had been making plans, rethinking them, and then setting them straight in her head. With the aid of a faintly flickering oil lamp she stared at the jeweled key suspended from the golden necklace. She had not believed her good fortune when Nydia had come to the villa earlier. But now, with the heady feeling of victory within her grasp, Julia laughed to herself. Not two hours before she had sat with her father and Arbaces, and had learned of Arbaces' conversation with Ione and of the way Arbaces had described Glaucus' character to the young priestess.

When the priest had left, Julia had walked alone in her garden knowing that she must plan every detail perfectly if she were to be successful. Julia wanted Clodius so badly that she knew she would make her plan work.

"Soon, Clodius," she whispered as she dangled the necklace before her.

Throughout that day, and all during the long hours of the next morning, Ione waited for Glaucus to come to her. By midday her doubts were growing stronger, and Arbaces' words were becoming easier to believe. *Why has he not come?* she asked herself for the hundredth time.

When Nydia returned from delivering the necklace, Ione had waited to hear what the girl had to report. But Nydia said nothing, only that the necklace had been delivered.

"Ione," Nydia called in a low voice.

Turning from the window, Ione stared at the young girl. "Glaucus has come?" she asked.

"No, but you have another visitor. Julia, daughter of Diomed."

"Julia?" Ione asked, barely managing to keep her voice on an even level. "Why?"

"I . . . I don't know," Nydia replied hesitantly.

"Very well," Ione said, forcing herself to stay calm and to

fight the jealousy that surged within her breasts. "Send her in."

Ione stared vacantly out the window until she heard footsteps come to a halt behind her. Girding herself to face her rival, Ione turned and stared at Julia.

The merchant's daughter was dressed in a robe of white silk which amplified her full figure and barely concealed the ripeness of her jutting breasts. To accent the simplicity of the white robes, a long piece of blue silk was tied loosely around her neck. Her mouth was shaped in a worldly smile, and her heavily made-up face seemed out of place within the sanctity of Ione's home.

"Thank you for seeing me, Ione. We have much to discuss."

Ione took a deep breath and prepared herself for confrontation. "I don't understand," she said icily. "What is it that you want?"

"I come but in simple kindness—to spare you further pain." Julia's smile widened, and she took another step toward Ione. "Believe me, I know well how Glaucus can break a woman's heart. He has done it often."

Ione stiffened, staring coldly at Julia. "And you presume to think he has broken mine?"

"He doesn't mean to," Julia said in a kind voice. "He's just thoughtless and spoiled. Usually I overlook his, ah, indiscretions—they're generally just . . . little common things. But this time I am upset. I mean, you are a priestess!" Julia sounded indignant.

"I am not a priestess."

"Well, almost. But it's all the same thing to him, isn't it? The challenge and all? Glaucus really is harmless . . . and his charms defy my anger."

Ione refused to accept Julia's words, and suddenly her love for Glaucus rose above it all. "I don't know what cruel game you're playing, but I'll believe nothing until I talk with Glaucus!"

"I suppose you won't. But I expected that. You're so predictable, just like all the others," Julia said with a tired sigh. "But this time everything has gone too far. A priestess of Isis! For shame! My mother is deeply dedicated to your goddess. That is the reason I came here today.''

As she spoke, Julia assessed Ione's tense stance, and knew that she was close to winning. Slowly, and as casually as she could, Julia undid the material about her throat, pulling it away. She was rewarded by Ione's involuntary gasp.

''Where did you get that!'' Ione demanded, appalled by the sight of her necklace on Julia's neck.

Arching her eyebrows in surprise, Julia's hand went to the necklace. ''This? Why Glaucus gave it to me.'' Julia paused when she saw the look of pain which flashed across Ione's face. She almost faltered at that point, but composed herself as she thought about Clodius and what her act here meant to them. ''Don't tell me Glaucus offered it to you first and you refused it!''

Ione looked away, unable to bear the sight of the necklace, anxious to have the woman go away. ''I don't want it,'' she whispered.

Julia stared at Ione's back, loathing herself for what she was doing, but refusing to turn back now. ''I've upset you enough. Ione, I won't wear it again,'' she promised, taking the necklace off and putting it on a table. ''Try not to feel too wretched. You can see now that he isn't worth it. I can't even tell you why I put up with him, except that my pride seems to diminish where he's concerned.''

She could see Ione's back tremble and could hear her low sobs. Silently, Julia left the room, stopping only when Nydia opened the front door for her. Looking at the blind girl's downcast face, she tried to speak, but a sickening rush of self-revulsion prevented even that small gesture. Instead, Julia left the house and stepped into whatever future she had created for herself.

When Nydia closed the door and wiped the tears that fell from her eyes, she heard Ione call her. Walking slowly, she entered the room where her mistress still stood.

''Nydia, if Glaucus should call, do not allow him entrance.''

"Ione," Nydia whispered in a choked voice.

"No, say no more about him. He is not welcome in my house."

Glaucus left the baths feeling as restless as he had when he arrived two hours before. He regretted his foolishness in telling Ione she must send for him, wishing now that he could take back his words. He had composed a note and planned to send it to Ione, accompanied by a gift. Realizing that he was walking away from the forum and the merchants' stalls, Glaucus changed his direction. He was forced to stop, however, when he reached a cross street bordering the forum and found himself in the midst of a procession of screaming, jovial men and women who surrounded a large transport cart.

Watching, Glaucus recognized the returning gladiators, back from their tour of Campania. He saw Lydon standing in the center, his powerfully muscled body aglow in the sunlight, the wide belt of the champion of the games still clasped around his waist.

Good, Glaucus thought, happy that the man had returned unharmed. As he began to walk again he realized he was approaching the temple of Isis. He paused when he saw Ione's brother, Antonius, standing by the statue of the goddess. The young priest was deep in conversation with Arbaces and did not see Glaucus. Arbaces did, however, and quickly guided Antonius toward the sacrarium.

Angered, Glaucus turned and began to walk toward Ione's home. The gift he intended to buy her was forgotten in the wake of his anger. He would see her now and convince her to marry him and to give up her plans to become a priestess.

Five minutes later he banged on Ione's door. When Nydia opened the door, he demanded to see Ione.

Nydia stepped outside and closed the door behind her. "I'm sorry, Glaucus, but she does not want to see you."

"I must see her. Surely, Nydia, even if she means to refuse my love, she would tell me herself. Unless Arbaces has gained complete control of her, as he has with Antonius!"

"I'm sorry, Glaucus. Ione has said that you are no longer welcome in her home."

Glaucus stared as he tried to adjust his thoughts. Then, taking a deep breath, he reached into his toga and withdrew the note he had written at the baths.

"Give this to her, Nydia; perhaps she will relent." Then he drew Nydia to him and tenderly kissed her on the forehead before he walked away.

When his footsteps were gone, Nydia crumpled the note in her hand, even as the tears poured from her eyes. "I'm sorry, Glaucus," she whispered. "So sorry." Then she leaned her face against the hot stone of the wall, waiting for her sobbing to end.

The instant the cart stopped, Lydon jumped down and started away without a backward glance. He had already learned that Nydia was now living with Ione, not Glaucus, and that had cheered him to a small degree.

Tucked within his toga was a purse almost bursting with the gold of his winnings, coins which he had refused to spend foolishly as had always been his habit. He wanted to prove to Nydia that he could buy not only her freedom but a farm as well.

His pace quickened when he neared the street where Ione lived, and he pushed aside the only sadness that had marred his return home. His old friend Melior had met his death during the tour. It had affected Lydon severely, but it taught him also just how precarious his life was. And just how much he wanted Nydia, and his farm.

Turning the corner, Lydon froze. Not a hundred feet ahead of him were Glaucus and Nydia. He watched Glaucus hand her a note, and then tensed when Glaucus pulled Nydia against him and kissed her forehead. He stayed where he was until the nobleman had gone, and only then did he walk toward Nydia, who leaned against the house, crying softly.

"Nydia," he called when he was near.

Nydia stood straighter when she heard her name. "Lydon?"

she asked, trying to hide the unhappiness in her voice. "You've returned safely!"

"What is it, Nydia? What's wrong?"

Ignoring his question, Nydia wiped the tears from her face. "We've all heard such wonderful tales of your triumphs."

Before she could finish, Lydon grasped her shoulders tightly. "Yes, damn it all, I won! And all so that I could have you, Nydia!"

Nydia cringed in his large, strong hands, unable to stop from crying. "Please, Lydon," she whispered, "can't you understand that I don't love you?"

Lydon released her, rage filling his every thought as his eyes cast along the street where Glaucus had disappeared. "Then it is he."

Nydia, hearing the anger and jealousy in Lydon's voice, lifted her head proudly. "Go ahead and laugh! I love him! Lydon, I cannot choose not to love him."

Lydon stared at her once again, overwhelmed by the child-like beauty of her face. "Then you're a fool," he snapped, using his words to strike back at her. "Nydia, you are more blind in your heart than in your eyes!"

Reacting to the bitterness of Lydon's words, Nydia threw her own defiance at him. "Then let me stay a fool!" she spat as she pulled away from him and walked toward the safety of Ione's house.

Lydon watched her walk away, regretting the heated words he had uttered. Then Nydia stumbled, and Lydon rushed to her aid. Reaching out to steady her, Lydon spoke. "Here, let me . . ."

"No!" Nydia yelled, jerking away from his touch. "Let me go! Lydon, let me be alone."

Lydon stood still, his mind once again numbed by her words. "Be alone then," he whispered. "Be alone!" he yelled. Lydon knew then that all his dreams and all his hopes were useless, that there was nothing left for him except the arena, and eventually, inevitably, his death.

Chapter Thirteen

Glaucus tossed and turned, unable to sleep, groaning at a shooting pain that lanced through his head. He opened his eyes in the dim light of the just dawning day and gasped at what he saw. Lying not a foot from him was a woman. Closing his eyes, he tried to remember what had happened, and why *she* of all people was in his bed.

Yesterday afternoon, after leaving Nydia, he had returned home and—to the surprise of his house slaves—had ordered wine brought to him. His anger had turned to depression, and all he'd wanted to do was to drink enough wine to blot out the memory of Ione.

By nightfall he had become pleasantly drunk and had refused the meal his cook had prepared. His thoughts ranged widely, and whenever they had returned to Ione he had taken another drink of wine, forcing himself to think of Athens and his childhood home. At some point in the evening, Petrus, Diomed's former slave, had come to him, a strange expression on his face.

"What?" Glaucus had asked.

"Mistress Julia wishes to see you."

"Me? Why?" Glaucus had asked, puzzled by this new development.

"I . . . I don't know," Petrus had responded.

"Very well, show her in." Glaucus had tried to stand, but his legs had not obeyed him.

"Please, don't rise," Julia had said when she entered.

Glaucus had gestured for her to join him on the couch, very much aware of the soft blue silk that barely covered her body.

"Wine?"

"Please," Julia had replied with a smile.

But when Glaucus had looked for another goblet, all he had found was his own. "I'll get you a goblet," he had said, his words slightly slurred.

"No," Julia had said in a husky whisper, "I'll drink from yours." Then, as she lifted the goblet and sipped, she whispered, "Glaucus . . ."

Glaucus had become mindful of the subtle scent radiating from her, and conscious too that he could see the darker tip of one breast when she bent to pick up the wine. He had realized then that it had been a long time since he had been with a woman—a very long time.

"Yes?" he had prompted when she'd seemed to hesitate.

"I don't want to seem forward, but . . ." She had paused again to take another sip of wine. When finished, she leaned toward him. "I've waited for you to come to me. To . . . to be with me. . . . Do you find me so unattractive?"

Glaucus had been taken aback by her words, yet at the same time he felt his desire stir heatedly. "You're beautiful," he had whispered drunkenly, seeing not Julia but Ione.

"Show me," she'd commanded.

And then they had come together, their lips meeting hungrily, their arms winding about each other, their hands exploring, seeking, searching.

It had all turned into a blur of limbs and heated cries, and only for a brief instant before Glaucus entered her did he realize that he was making love to Julia, not Ione. But that reality had been wiped from his mind when her hands had coaxed him onward.

The rest of the night had formed into a hazy kaleidoscope of flashing memories and sounds, as they drank more wine, made love again, and finally ended up in his bedchamber. The last thing he had been aware of was the sound of her voice, whispering her love for him, over and over.

Glaucus opened his eyes again. When he saw Julia's face, he realized the mistake that he had made last night. But he did not know what to do about it now. Then he saw her eyes

open. A funny look flashed across her face, and then she
smiled at him.

"Glaucus, I'm so happy," she whispered. "I must run
home and tell Father."

"Father?" he echoed in surprise.

"Oh, silly, he thinks I'm spending the night with a friend
. . . a lady friend. Oh, I can't wait to tell him about us, and
our plans."

"Plans?" Glaucus asked, altogether confused at this point.

"Our marriage! Oh, Glaucus, when you asked me last
night, I was so thrilled."

Glaucus stared at her incredulously. "I asked you to marry
me?"

"Of course you did," Julia said, her eyes suddenly not
meeting his.

"Julia," he began, his voice cracking from a night of
wine. "We . . . I made a mistake. . . ."

"Mistake? Glaucus, what happened was no mistake." With
those words, she began to sob loudly.

"I'm sorry, Julia," he said helplessly.

Julia rolled away from him, stood, and glared down at
him, her breasts jutting out proudly. "You've shamed me! I
love you, and you took advantage of me. You've ruined
me!" she screamed. "I didn't believe what I'd heard about
you, but it must be true! You . . . You . . ."

Glaucus' anger got the upper hand of his reason. Standing
quickly, he glowered across at her. "I may have been drunk
last night, but I never asked you to marry me!"

"Liar!" Julia shouted as she raced from the room. She
went into the room she had found Glaucus in last night;
gathering her clothing, she dressed quickly.

Glaucus followed her and stood silently while she dressed.
Only when she had finished, did he speak. "Julia, I am
sorry."

"Please allow me to keep some of my dignity. Glaucus,
please pretend that you love me, for just a little while. I . . ."

Glaucus, touched by her distress, went to Julia and embraced her. "What can I do?" he asked in concern.

"I. . . . Let me keep my dream for a few days. Please, Glaucus, don't tell anyone about this. I want people to look up to me. I want to say I will be your wife, even if it's just to tell my father."

Glaucus wiped away the tears that streamed down her cheeks. He saw the desperation on her face and remembered that, since Ione would no longer see him, nothing mattered anyway. "All right, Julia, tell your father. Have your dream for a little while."

Glaucus did not realize that the fullness of Julia's sudden smile was not for his gracious gesture but for her victory.

"Thank you, Glaucus," she said sincerely. "Thank you." In an instant, Julia was gone, leaving Glaucus to wonder if the whole thing had really happened. But as he turned, another lancing pain in his head reminded him all too sharply that it had indeed been real. Walking slowly toward the couch, Glaucus stopped when he saw several splotches of dried blood on the covering. "She was a virgin," he groaned.

Picking up the goblet of wine, Glaucus drained it. When he went to pour more from the pitcher, he found it empty. He was about to call for Petrus when he realized that it was still too early for anyone to be up. And thankfully so, he realized, for then no one would see Julia as she made her way home.

Shrugging his shoulders, Glaucus decided to go back to bed—and hopefully to sleep—to forget how much of a fool he had become in the past few days.

Shortly after Glaucus had returned to bed, and the sun had begun its ascent into the sky, a ship bearing the purple sail of the emperor docked in Pompeii. A few minutes later three men dressed in the cloaks and armor of the imperial services stepped onto the dock. As they were met, the message they carried was spread to all who were near.

These men were the bearers of ill tidings, come to Pompeii to announce the death of the emperor Vespasian and the accession to the throne of his son Titus.

By midday the market was more crowded than usual as word of Vespasian's death spread through the streets of Pompeii.

Everyone crowded around the stalls, buying incense and medallions to use in the mourning ceremonies that would continue throughout the day. Every citizen of the Roman Empire would be required to kneel at the statue of Vespasian and pray to him, as he was now a god.

In the center of the forum, at the statue of Vespasian, the masses gathered to hear the various priests call out to their deities and to worship for the first time the new god, Vespasian.

Clodius, Lepidus, and Sallust stood as usual on the fringe of the crowd, making fun of everything and everyone, trying to look as bored and disinterested as possible.

"So Vespasian is dead," Sallust commented. "And now he has become a god. And I suppose we must go and do this business of worshiping at his feet like the rest."

Lepidus, never one to be left out, puffed up his chest and spoke with foppish eloquence. "But of course! It's the duty of every man, woman, and child! Sallust, you don't want to be accused of sacrilege, do you?"

"A pretty pass we've come to, when a commoner can become an emperor, and then a god—with never once being a noble, eh, Clodius?"

Clodius turned to Sallust, his expression blank. "Sorry, I missed that."

"Really, Clodius, you grow worse daily. If you are in love, at least confess it. Who is the lady?" Lepidus asked good-naturedly.

"Leave off, can't you!" Clodius snapped, annoyed with their petty game. "I've told you there is no lady!" Turning, Clodius gazed out at the crowd just as Petrus walked by. "You! Petrus," he shouted to the slave. "Is your master at home?"

Petrus stopped in front of the nobleman and nodded. "Yes, sir, I'm fetching wine for him now," he replied. When he saw that Clodius wanted nothing more, he went on his way.

"Did he say wine?" Sallust asked. "In that case, we should pay Glaucus a visit."

"That's Glaucus' slave? I thought . . ." Lepidus began.

"He got him from Diomed," Clodius stated.

"And I understand that's not all Glaucus got from Diomed —or his daughter, anyway. I can't believe the rumors of late. Clodius, do you think Glaucus is really going to marry Julia?"

Clodius glared at Sallust, but before Sallust could make anything of it, Lepidus cut in. "Nothing surprises me these days. And I overheard Diomed telling someone just a little while ago that Glaucus was indeed going to marry Julia. Clodius . . . ." Lepidus stopped when he saw Clodius walking away from them. Glancing at Sallust, he saw his friend was as puzzled as he.

A commotion a short distance from them took their attention from Clodius as they saw the burly guard Drusus begin to push Petrus around. They drew closer to learn what it was all about.

"Stand still!" Drusus ordered.

Petrus, his eyes lowered, tried once more to walk past the man, but the guard's hand was on his chest, stopping him.

"So, you thought you could make a fool of me before my captain and the magistrate too, did you? You and your conniving master!"

"Please, sir, I have no quarrel with you."

"Oh, haven't you, *Christian*! Nor with our new god Vespasian either, I trust." Drusus' voice had grown louder, and a large crowd began to form around the two. Near the front of the crowd was Calenus, flanked by several priests of Isis.

"I haven't seen you praying at his altar yet," stated Drusus, his face an ugly mask of hatred.

"I'm a slave. I have no money to buy incense," Petrus pleaded.

The hollow laughter of the crowd rang out at his feeble plea. Calenus, laughing louder than anyone else, drew out a coin and flung it in Petrus' face. "There's your money, Christian! Pick it up," Drusus growled.

Petrus stood still, refusing either to look at the coin on the ground or to obey the command.

"Why waste your time?" Calenus yelled. "You've got a sword, use it!"

Drusus smiled at Calenus but shook his head. "Oh, no, not I. They want it legal, and by the gods, that's what they'll get. Priest, will you testify in court that this man refused to worship an official god?"

"Most willingly," Calenus replied with a sly smile. "As will we all," he added, gesturing to the other priests.

Smiling broadly, Drusus grabbed Petrus by the arm and jerked him forward, knocking the wine vessel from his hand and laughing again when it shattered on the stones.

The amused jeers of the crowd followed the two men until Drusus and Petrus disappeared into the high-windowed jail on the other side of the forum.

"Sir," called a slave, forcing Glaucus to abandon his thoughts of Ione.

He glanced absently at the slave, while he toyed with the golden dagger he had bought at the weaponmaker's stand in the forum. "What is it?"

"Clodius is here to see you."

"Send him in," Glaucus said, pleasantly surprised by this visit. Clodius entered a moment later, and Glaucus immediately sensed a strong tension emanating from his friend.

"Is that how you greet a friend?" Clodius asked when his eyes fell on the serpent-handled blade.

Glaucus set the dagger down. "It's good to see you. I've been neglectful of my friends of late," he said as he poured a goblet of wine for his friend.

Taking the silver goblet, Clodius held it up before him. "Well, when a man is in love I suppose his friends must expect neglect."

"Are there no secrets in Pompeii?" Glaucus asked with arched brows.

"Then what they're saying is true?" Clodius asked, his voice tight, betraying his anger. Then he quickly laughed, trying to disguise his jealousy. "Well, why should it be a secret! Unless, of course, you're having second thoughts."

Glaucus, puzzled by Clodius' words, gazed at his friend

for a long moment. "You're in a strange mood today, Clodius."

"I? Strange?" Clodius shook his head at the unwanted image of Julia which formed in his mind. "But then, she is lovely—albeit beneath you," he added sharply.

Angered at this attack against Ione, Glaucus' hand tightened around the goblet. "Clodius, at times your wit strays from its mark."

Clodius held Glaucus' accusatory stare, wanting to physically strike out at the Greek. However, before he could form his next words, muffled, argumentative voices disturbed the air around them.

"What now?" Glaucus asked irritably, slamming the goblet down just as his slave came in.

"Sir, the priest Antonius insists on seeing you."

"Antonius!" The name almost exploded from Glaucus' mouth. "Has he a message?" he asked the slave while he turned back to Clodius. "Clodius, forgive me; I must speak to this man." Without waiting for a reply, Glaucus left the room.

Behind him, Clodius stood, holding his goblet high, directing it at the spot Glaucus had just left. "Don't let me detain you, *noble* Glaucus," he said sarcastically, his anger and jealousy growing steadily with each passing minute. "Well, Julia," he whispered, "here's to you." Clodius drained the goblet and set it on the table next to the ornately sculpted dagger. He studied the expensive weapon for a moment before he shrugged and started out.

At the entrance Clodius paused, his curiosity piqued when he heard Glaucus and Antonius arguing. Their voices were loud and their words sharp. Sensing something sorely amiss, Clodius edged closer to the room where the two men argued. However, Glaucus' slave reappeared and, clearing his throat, nodded to Clodius. Embarrassed at being caught, Clodius walked stiffly from the house, wondering what Glaucus and Antonius had in common.

*   *   *

"I'm telling you I won't stand for this!" Antonius shouted, just as Clodius was leaving.

"Will you stop yelling at me? Antonius, you don't understand."

"I *do* understand. Arbaces told me everything this morning!" Antonius stated, his young face drawn tight by anger and tension.

"Antonius, please listen to me."

"How could you do this to Ione?" Antonius asked furiously.

Glaucus held back his stinging retort, forcing himself to take several calming breaths. He realized that Arbaces had planned well. "Can't you see that Arbaces has lied to you, and to Ione?"

"How dare you!" Antonius, his face chalky white with anger, swung his fist at the Greek.

Moving quickly, Glaucus blocked the intended blow and, at the same time, grasped Antonius' wrist tightly. "Antonius, listen to me! You and Ione are being misled. You must make her see me!" Saying this, he released the young priest.

"Do you think I'd let you see her, just so you could lie to her again? She believed you when you said you loved her."

Glaucus shook his head helplessly at Antonius, wondering how everyone in Pompeii but himself knew what was going on between him and Ione. "Antonius, whatever is happening with Ione, and with you, is the doing of Arbaces. You must believe me!"

"Never!"

Glaucus froze under a sudden sharp flash of memory. *Gaius!* "Antonius," he said quickly. "I know you don't believe what I am trying to tell you, but there is another whom we must see. He knows the truth about Arbaces. We must get him to talk!"

"I'll go nowhere with you!" Antonius stated.

A film of red rage curtained Glaucus' eyes. Whirling on Antonius, he grabbed the priest's shoulders and pulled him close. "And I say you will!" Glaucus spat between clenched teeth. "Damn it, if you're so sure of the greatness of Arbaces, then you have nothing to fear from the truth." Then he said in a calmer voice, "If I'm wrong, I swear to you I'll never set eyes on Ione again. Now, must I call my slaves, or will you come willingly?"

While Glaucus was leading Antonius to Gaius' villa on the slope of Vesuvius, hopefully to learn the truth about Arbaces, Petrus was also being led to a confrontation. But for Petrus there was no hope.

Drusus pushed him harshly into the Hall of Justice, there to face the icy gaze of Quintus himself. Behind him he heard several people mocking his helplessness, and he turned to see Calenus and his cronies standing there.

"Petrus," Quintus called.

Petrus stared at the silver-haired magistrate. Suddenly, resolve and courage filled him, and he drew himself straighter as Quintus went on. "You are charged with impiety, and accused of being a Christian. These witnesses have sworn that you refused to practice the state religion. How say you?"

Petrus held his eyes steady on the magistrate's, but no word passed his lips.

"Are you a Christian?" Quintus demanded, glaring at him. Petrus maintained his silence. Quintus shook his head, conscious of the eyes of the priests of Isis upon him, and spoke in a voice filled with resignation. "Very well! If you think that by your silence you can avoid punishment, you are mistaken. You are a slave, Petrus, and it is legal to torture a slave to obtain testimony."

Petrus' stomach churned at the horror of Quintus' statement. But he also remembered the way Joseph had raised his voice and remained calm in order that the others might escape. Taking a deep breath, Petrus decided he could do no less.

"Take this man away," Quintus ordered when he saw the resolve grow firm in the slave's eyes. "I do not want to see him until he is prepared to speak—unless, of course, he should die first!"

Drusus, his eyes sparkling with menace, grasped Petrus' arm and dragged him away, satisfied that at last he would have his way with the arrogant slave.

"Well done!" called Calenus. Without replying, Quintus stood and swept out of the chamber.

He didn't know how he had managed it, but the moment he and Antonius had arrived at Gaius' villa, and he had seen the fear rise once again in the old man's face, Glaucus had faced him, arguing and pleading until Gaius finally gave in.

Once Gaius had begun to talk, it seemed as if the weight of a century were being slowly lifted from his shoulders. Fortunata stood a short distance away, watching her husband with a mixture of pride and love. Glaucus stood to one side, fascinated by the old senator's words. But it was Antonius who was transfixed before the white-haired man, staring wide-eyed into his lined, weathered face.

"It began slowly, but then it was all too evident. He was a madman. Nero was vicious, frenzied, and above all suspicious. He trusted only one man, his astrologer. This astrologer was born a slave, a foreigner who was laughed at and looked down upon by the nobles.

"But he had his revenge. A word to Nero that the stars foretold disaster from some noble, and that man would exist no more. He would either be executed, exiled, or forced into suicide, his lands and goods seized by Nero." Gaius broke off his monologue for a moment, his watery eyes suddenly bright. "Nero shod his mules with silver. Did you know that?"

"The astrologer," Glaucus asked, sensing the direction Gaius was going. "He had his share, no doubt."

Gaius stared at Glaucus, and then looked at Antonius before nodding his head. "Indeed he did. This astrologer was this man you call . . . Arbaces."

"No!" Antonius yelled. Then his hate-filled eyes blazed at Glaucus. "You put him up to this!"

"Damn it, boy!" Gaius shouted, grabbing Antonius roughly by the shoulders. "Do you know how your father died? *Do you?*"

"Nero murdered him!" Antonius answered defiantly.

"Not Nero, boy! Arbaces! He hated your father because

your father did not fear him. Because your father was the one *just* man in Nero's court. Arbaces vowed to ruin your father's name, and have his fortune as well. The only thing preventing him from attaining it is Ione, and he plans to *have* her as well!''

Antonius tried to break free, but Gaius' frail hands held the young priest tightly. ''You're lying! My father left his fortune to Ione and me.''

''Yes! Because I stopped Arbaces. The one and only good thing I have ever done! Antonius,'' Gaius said, his voice quieting even as he lifted his hands from the youth's shoulders, his eyes imploring. ''I couldn't save your father, I couldn't even save my own children! But I did save you and your sister. If you could only guess what the cost of that action was. . . . But now, despite all my efforts, Arbaces will have his way, for he has already gained half the fortune.''

''I won't listen to any more of these lies!'' Antonius cried, spinning on his heels and running away from them.

''Antonius!'' Glaucus shouted at the priest's back.

''Go after him. Make him listen,'' Gaius commanded.

''Gaius,'' Glaucus said, trying somehow to express his gratitude for the trust Gaius had bestowed upon him this day.

''Go,'' Gaius said gently.

Glaucus ran then, forcing his feet to fly over the ground, knowing that he must catch Antonius and make him understand. A few minutes later Glaucus reached the dirt pathway leading down the slope toward Pompeii; he saw Antonius glance back and then begin to run faster.

However, the youth was no match for Glaucus' trained body, and soon Glaucus was upon him. Reaching out, Glaucus caught Antonius' robe. Both men stumbled but did not fall.

''Antonius, we must talk.''

''No!'' Antonius cried, jerking away from the Greek's hold, but strangely not running off.

Glaucus saw the defeated slump of his shoulders, and his heart went out to him. ''You must let me help you. Antonius?''

Antonius turned, and Glaucus saw the pain and confusion

on his young face. When he spoke, Glaucus heard his uncertainty in the husky crackling of his voice.

"I . . . I don't know what to do," Antonius admitted, lifting his eyes in a silent plea. "I can't believe what that old man told me. I don't want to believe. . . . But I have seen things in the temple that I question . . . that frighten me. And Gaius, he has no reason to lie, does he?"

"None," Glaucus replied in a low voice. "We'll go to Ione and tell her what we've learned."

Antonius drew himself up. His eyes, the same blue as his sister's, were clear. "No. I must take care of this my way. Please."

"How can I wait helplessly by?"

"Just give me time. A day or two cannot matter now. Please," Antonius implored.

Glaucus studied the young priest for several seconds before he nodded his agreement. "I love her, Antonius. Don't make me wait too long."

Chapter Fourteen

Calenus stood at the altar of Isis, not officiating, but watching everything carefully. An hour before, his spy had returned from the mount and had told him all. Then Calenus—knowing that with each passing day he was getting nearer and nearer to what he wanted—went to Arbaces and gave the high priest his own version of the final report.

"Everything is in readiness?" Arbaces had asked.

"Everything," Calenus had stated with a smile.

"Good. When Antonius returns, he will come directly to me. When you see him, prepare the chamber. You see, Calenus, did I not tell you exactly how everything would happen?"

Calenus had left him then, returning to the temple where he had waited patiently. A low chant began, and as Calenus mouthed the words he saw Antonius skirt the temple itself and go directly to the sacrarium. When the young priest entered the corridor, Calenus slipped away from the others and followed him inside.

Calenus paused to listen at Arbaces' door. When he heard Arbaces and Antonius talking, he went to the next door; opening it, he poked his head inside: "Soon," he whispered. Then Calenus went to yet another door, opened it, and stepped inside.

One low taper burned, illuminating various forms of strange machinery. There was a small stool in the center of the room and Calenus went to it. He sat and waited for the proper signal.

* * *

"I don't understand, my son," Arbaces said, smiling benevolently after listening to Antonius' disjointed words. "Suddenly you're ridden with doubts, but you won't say who or what is their source."

"Not sudden, Arbaces!" Antonius declared vehemently, summoning courage with every means he possessed. "I've seen things, things I've tried to believe aren't true. When . . . when you excited my desire to join the temple, you spoke of virtue, knowledge, companionship with gods. But the temple is filled with cheats and tricksters!"

"It is for just this moment I have waited," Arbaces said, throwing Antonius completely off stride. Then he stepped close to Antonius, his arms going around him, embracing him fondly.

"I knew my faith in you was not misplaced! I saw your purity—that search for the ideal that burns within you. And it was I who fanned that sacred flame."

Antonius stepped back from the high priest. "And told me nothing of the deceits!"

"Had I done so, Isis would have lost her priest. Antonius, I left you to discover and be sickened by the things that dazzle ordinary men, so that you would know you are meant for higher things."

Unwilling to accept this version of events, Antonius held his hand before him, waving it in emphasis to his words. "But you still blind the people."

"Because they must be blinded!" Arbaces asserted in a pious voice. "For their own good, Antonius, for their own good. They don't want the truth. They want oracles, ceremonies, and rites. They need pageantry to lift them from their dull lives. The people need a belief, a faith, a *fear* of something greater than themselves. And we are the ones entrusted to instill and control that fear." Arbaces' face was now glowing with holy fervor. "Antonius, we are the ones who bring peace and order and harmony to what is called civilization, and we do it in the name of Isis!"

For the first time since entering the chamber, doubt crept

into Antonius' mind, clouding his thoughts and making him vacillate. "But . . . I can't live with those deceits."

Arbaces smiled kindly now, his mind filling with the taste of victory as he sensed the doubt within Antonius' voice. Arbaces slowly raised his hands, as if he were about to offer a prayer. Behind him, a rope drew tight. "You are not intended to, my son. For those like you, whose higher natures demand truth, the doors are opened on secrets that give power to the wise, on the enigma that is life itself." With that, Arbaces dropped his arms, and the chamber was plunged into darkness.

Arbaces slipped silently from the room, going through a black curtain in the rear to join Calenus for the completion of his plan.

"Arbaces!" Antonius cried, startled by the sudden darkness. "Arbaces, please!"

He froze, however, when the darkness was filled by Arbaces' voice, which seemed to issue from the very air above his head. It was a hollow, faraway sound that sent a chill of fear racing along his spine.

"Antonius, you are like a child now, fearful of the dark, terrified of what it may contain; frightened that everything you've believed will be swept away. Let it go! For your faith, your vows of abstinence and chastity were made in ignorance. Leave them and go toward the light of understanding, where they can be remade in wisdom."

In the small room filled with machinery, Calenus and Arbaces began to move wheels and tug on ropes and pulleys.

Antonius stood perfectly still when Arbaces' voice had faded, but suddenly he saw a spot of light appear. He watched it, fascinated, as it began to fly around. Soon there were dozens of small, flitting spots of light, chasing each other all around the room. Then the faraway sound of music filled the air. The dots of light coalesced, forming a wavy vision. Antonius saw planets and suns and stars floating in a vast universe, and knew he had been given a rare privilege by Isis.

"Look at this world, Antonius. Observe its order, its

regularity. Someone must have created it. But what, or whom? Isis, you will say."

A sudden gust of wind blew across his body. With it came a low moaning cry.

"No!" Antonius screamed in unbridled fear. "No."

"Isis is the power of the mind," whispered Arbaces' hollow voice. "Isis is the power of the body, power that will destroy you unless you master it." Loud claps of thunder accentuated the high priest's words. Then a flashing bolt of lightning shot across the room.

Antonius, unable to stand any more, sank to the floor. "Stand up, Antonius! Be fearful, and you are lost, like the most ignorant of men! Rise, Antonius, for this power is all a part of you. It is within you, not without. It is yours to command! Stand, Antonius, stand!"

The wind died as suddenly as it had risen, and the sounds faded with it as well. Stunned, Antonius struggled to his feet, drawing in deep, ragged gasps of air. From the far distance came a faint shimmering of light, which grew steadily brighter until it was an all-encompassing entity of pure white power.

"Now, Antonius, you have taken your first step toward wisdom. Wisdom that you will use to turn the ignorant to good." Arbaces paused to nod his head at Calenus. A moment later music played in the chamber. A curtain opened near Antonius, revealing a bubbling fountain surrounded by cushions set neatly in place on the floor.

"But there is a wisdom of another kind," Arbaces continued. "The wisdom of the senses. Without it, all your vows are meaningless. For how, Antonius, can you renounce what you do not know?"

Then, like an apparition, Antonius saw a beautiful woman come toward him, swaying in rhythm to the music. Beneath her thin veils he saw the lushness of her hips and the fullness of her breasts. Her dark hair bounced enticingly, and her sensual lips smiled seductively at him. Then another vision appeared, dressed in only a loincloth about her hips, her breasts exposed and oiled. In her hand was a goblet of gold, and in her eyes was an invitation. As she reached him, she offered him the golden cup.

But Antonius shook his head and stepped back, his eyes unable to leave her face.

"Take it! Taste it! Feel its flames," coaxed Arbaces' faraway voice. The woman placed the goblet to his lips, forcing him to taste of its contents.

As the first of the fiery liquid raced across his tongue, Antonius stiffened, but an instant later he opened his mouth, greedily accepting the gift of the wine.

The moment the woman drew the goblet away the luminous spot of light began to fade. But Antonius' ravaged mind was already reacting to the drugged wine. It no longer mattered to him where he was or what he was.

Then he felt hands behind him, running upward along his back, caressing and gentle as they traced his skin through his robe. The woman in front moved closer, pressing her naked breasts to his chest even as the woman behind pressed against his back.

The room began to spin, but not unpleasantly, and Antonius felt a powerful surging within his loins, even as he heard Arbaces' voice, sounding further away with each word.

"You must plunge yourself into the fires that lesser men mistake for pleasure, to know how to lead them into purity."

Antonius' hands were being lifted by the woman before him. Slowly, with a sensual smile on her mouth, she brought his palms to her cheeks, letting them rest there for a moment before forcing them slowly down her body. For an eternity Antonius stared at the wavering image he was touching. Then his breathing deepened as she lowered his hands to her chest, moving them slowly, inexorably over the rich fullness of her heated skin.

"Feel the passions which enslave lesser men, in order to see how to free them. Surrender, Antonius, to learn how to conquer. Surrender," whispered Arbaces for the last time.

One set of gently roaming hands flowed down his back, sliding over his buttocks, caressing and teasing, while the woman in front of him came closer still. Lifting on her toes, she covered his mouth with hers.

His drugged mind spinning with passion, Antonius let himself be lowered to the floor, where he was covered by the women, who brought his passion to unimagined peaks. Eventually darkness enveloped him and he could not feel, or see, or think anymore.

Much later, the two women carried Antonius to his small cell-like chamber and placed him on the simple pallet. When Xenia left, Chloe lit the room's single candle and then drew a coverlet over Antonius' naked chest. She studied his innocent face for a moment. She was disgusted by her own actions and saddened by the way he had been drugged and mistreated. Chloe had sensed the evilness all around her, and had overheard the words that Calenus and Arbaces had spoken. She knew that something here at the temple was very, very wrong.

"Poor boy," she whispered just as Xenia returned, shaking two well-filled purses.

Revulsion filled her at the blatant greed reflected in Xenia's face. Standing quickly, Chloe spoke in an angry whisper. "You should have told me! I don't like this type of business."

"Money is money, Chloe. Come on, let's get out of here," she said, offering Chloe her share of the money.

Chloe stared at the purse as if it were a snake, but slowly, reluctantly, she reached out and took it. *For my son,* she told herself. "But I'm staying. I want to be certain he's all right," she said, again looking at the shallow rise and fall of Antonius' chest.

Xenia shrugged stoically. "You're a fool, Chloe." She stopped again at the door. "Lock it when you go. I promised Calenus I would."

When the door closed, Chloe brushed her hand across Antonius' brow and was rewarded by a small moving of his head. Then his eyes, still glazed from the drug, blinked open. Chloe stared helplessly as she watched Antonius' face twist with hatred, his eyes filled with tears. Unable to bear it any longer, she drew him to her.

"It's all right," she whispered soothingly.

Antonius stiffened, then struggled free of Chloe's arms. "Get away from me."

Reacting swiftly, Chloe covered his mouth with her fingers, whispering urgently for him to be quiet. "You're not safe here. You must come with me."

Antonius tried to focus his eyes, but he could not. Only the sense of urgency in her voice lent him any hint of life.

Chloe lifted his robe from the floor and helped him into it. She saw in his eyes that the drug seemed to have taken hold again, but she refused to let this unfortunate young man languish hopelessly within the cult's clutches.

Twenty minutes later Chloe was hurrying along the empty streets, half carrying, half dragging Antonius with her. By the time they reached Olinthus' door the stars were fading and the first gray band of dawn was rising in the east. Turning to look at Antonius, Chloe saw that the effects of the drug were lessening.

Just as the door opened, Chloe heard a horrifying moan of pain, and as she brought Antonius inside, her eyes fell on the bleeding, ravaged back of a man lying on the floor. "Olinthus, I have someone who needs your help," she began, but stopped when she recognized the injured man. "Petrus!" she screamed. Releasing Antonius, Chloe ran to Petrus, dropping to the floor next to him.

"What have they done to you?" she cried, tears pouring from her eyes, but all Petrus could do was stare at her through swollen eyes. "Oh, Petrus, my darling," Chloe sobbed, cradling Petrus' head while she looked at Olinthus for an explanation.

But Olinthus wasn't looking at Chloe. Instead he stared wide-eyed at the man he knew to be a priest of Isis. "You are Antonius, Arbaces' priest."

"He left the temple of Isis; he has broken from Arbaces," Chloe said quickly. "I helped him escape." When she had spoken, she felt Petrus draw away from her. Turning back, she leaned close to him.

"No," he whispered weakly. "Leave me."

"Petrus, what happened?" she asked, not allowing him to turn his face from hers again. "Petrus?"

"Drusus. . . . He arrested me, and I couldn't hold out, Chloe. . . . They kept on beating me. They said they'd kill me if . . . if . . . if I wouldn't curse the name of Christ. And I did. Chloe, I denied Him."

"Oh, my God," Chloe whispered. Then she gently kissed his lips and gazed into his eyes with all the love, understanding, and forgiveness she had within her. But even then, Petrus broke down, sobbing with such heartwrenching sounds that Chloe drew him to her breasts and rocked him back and forth, uncaring of the strange tableau that was unfolding three feet from her.

"Is what Chloe says true?" Olinthus asked Antonius bluntly.

"I . . . yes," the young priest said groggily.

Olinthus nodded and stepped closer to Antonius. "Then you're welcome here, my son."

Antonius' head jerked up sharply. " 'My son'! Arbaces always called me that. But I'm the fool—for listening to his lies."

"He has seduced all Pompeii," Olinthus said quickly when he heard the distress in Antonius' voice. "But the living God will judge him."

"Don't speak to me of gods! There is one truth Arbaces taught me. They are all false!" he cried, his voice breaking on the last defiant word.

Olinthus gazed at Antonius in sympathy. Suddenly he felt a rush of compassion fill him, and suddenly he knew what he had to do. Turning, he looked at Chloe and Petrus.

"I'm taking Antonius with me; can you tend to Petrus?" he asked in a gentle voice.

Chloe looked up at the large, bearded man and nodded slowly.

Olinthus took Antonius' arm, but the young priest resisted. "I want to go to my sister. I must tell her what has happened, and together we will expose Arbaces."

"Yes," Olinthus agreed. "But later, when you're calmer

and can think more clearly. Arbaces is a dangerous man. You must prepare yourself for what must be done."

"My sister and I are of noble birth. Surely we can bring this Egyptian to justice."

"Perhaps," Olinthus cautioned. "But for now I want you to come with me."

"Where?"

Instead of replying, Olinthus smiled at him. "To a safe place."

As the sun brought light to the people of Pompeii, the shifting masses far below the surface groaned again. Lava coursed over the plates of the earth, seeking their escape from the caverns.

A trembling filled the interior of the planet, and yet more fissures were closed off. The steaming gases, once again diverted from their only routes to the surface, began to search desperately for other avenues. As they did, the pressures increased within the shell of the earth.

The morning sun warmed the air pleasantly, especially out in the bay, where Olinthus and Antonius now sat, rocking gently in the sailmaker's small skiff. They had been out for over an hour, and for the first part of that time Olinthus had sat silently, waiting for Antonius to grow more comfortable with his presence.

Before taking the small boat out, Olinthus had found a change of robes for Antonius. Now, dressed in a plain toga, the youth looked more relaxed than he had for many, many weeks.

"When I was as young as you," Olinthus began, looking not at Antonius but at the sea, "I traveled all over the world. I worked at anything, whether it was honest or evil. I could cheat a man, rob his purse, steal his name, or even his life—for what could it matter? Like you, I knew there was no God."

From the corner of his eye Olinthus saw Antonius look at

him with a startled expression, but he did not acknowledge the young man's stare.

"And then one day a prisoner was put on my ship, bound for Rome. He was a maker of tents, and I was a maker of sails, so naturally we spoke of our crafts. Curious isn't it, how work binds men together?" This time he did look at Antonius, and accepted the tentative smile the youth gave him.

"But as we traveled a gale struck us. So powerful a storm was it that every man aboard the ship gave up all hope. Every man, except this man. While I saw every moment as my last, he talked to me of his God, and of salvation. He told me of Christ, the Son whom God had sent to save mankind. He said there was no evil I had done or could do that God would not forgive, if I were only to believe."

"And . . . did you believe him?" Antonius asked in a husky voice, drawn fully into the story.

"I, who believed in nothing?" Olinthus smiled and slowly shook his head. "But you know, that storm without was nothing to the storm that raged within me as God fought for my soul. And then, on the blackest of nights, our ship was hurled onto the rocks of Malta. I cried out in rage to him, 'Can your God save me now?' Then I was swept overboard." Olinthus paused when Antonius leaned eagerly forward.

"When I awoke, I was on the shore. The sun shone in my eyes, and the tentmaker was nearby, kneeling and praising God. And I rose up and went to him." Olinthus ignored the tears that fell unashamedly from his eyes as he relived that fateful day.

"Olinthus," Antonius asked in a low voice, "who was he?"

"His name was Paul. He was one of Christ's disciples. Nero killed him, and when he died, I made a vow to carry on the word of God." Sighing, Olinthus reached up and tugged one of the sail's ropes, changing the direction of the boat.

"It must be wonderful to believe. . . . Yet you believe in your God no more than I believed in Isis."

Olinthus stared at the young man for a long moment before

he shook his head slowly in denial of Antonius' mistaken conclusion. "You think that you are lost because all that you've believed has played you false. But can't you see that God has found you? He has led you to me, as surely as he cast me up onto that shore. Antonius, you have never needed to search, but only to lift up your head and look around. God has found you, even as he did me on that long-ago day."

Antonius gazed at Olinthus for several minutes, pondering all the man had said. Slowly, without realizing it, he began to understand. "You . . . you've been very kind to me, Olinthus."

"I have only treated you with honesty and the love of God. But enough rhetoric, let's go in now, before the streets are swarming with Arbaces' spies. When the night comes, we will take the next steps."

After they had returned to Olinthus' shop, Antonius went to sleep in the secret room, lying on the floor across from the pallet that held Petrus, who was also asleep. Chloe, meanwhile, went to Burbo's tavern, where she wrapped her son in blankets. She sneaked out before anyone saw her, and returned to Olinthus' shop with her proudest possession.

Later, she sat across from the sailmaker and smiled sadly at him when he began to speak. "We'll have to get him to Glaucus' house."

"No," Chloe said with a strong shake of her head. "He's not going back. Neither am I. When he's able to travel, I'm taking him away."

"Where?" Olinthus demanded. "Where can the two of you go?"

"I don't know! All I know is that if they arrest him again, they'll kill him. He won't denounce Christ again. Olinthus, he's so ashamed."

"Chloe," Olinthus said in a calmer voice, "they'll kill him if you're caught. Petrus will be a runaway slave."

Chloe smiled again, but this time her smile held a tinge of irony. "It's curious. I've always been the one to say that we can't change our lives. But now I know that I would rather die with Petrus than go back to what I've been. Olinthus, whatever happens will be God's will."

"I . . ." Olinthus began, but Chloe's hand covered his, and he suddenly felt the confidence of her words.

The rest of the day was spent quietly. Olinthus worked in the shop while the others slept in the secret room. Antonius had come out once, and he and Olinthus had talked about what steps might be taken. But a customer had come into the shop, and Antonius retreated to the hidden room, where he stayed for the rest of the day.

Once night had fallen, Antonius came out of the room again, dressed as he had been on the boat. His face was washed clean of sleep, his stride purposeful once again.

"Thank you, Olinthus," he said, putting his hand on the larger man's shoulder.

"I should stay with you until you reach your home," Olinthus began, but Antonius quickly cut him off.

"I cannot spend the rest of my life in fear of Arbaces."

"Neither can you fight him by yourself."

"It's better that I go to Ione alone. It will be hard for her to accept the truth about Arbaces. But we are still of a noble house, and together we will be able to make Arbaces leave us alone."

Olinthus studied the determined set of Antonius' face. "All right," he said reluctantly. "But remember that I am here to help you whenever you need me."

"Olinthus," Antonius began, but he could not go on, as emotion choked off his words. "Thank you for today," he said finally.

"God go with you," Olinthus whispered as he pulled Antonius to him. A moment later he released the young man and went with him to the door. Opening it, he looked out. Seeing the street was empty, he motioned Antonius out. When the young nobleman was barely a shadow in the distance, Olinthus spoke in a whisper. "And do nothing foolish."

Chapter Fifteen

Glaucus paced aimlessly through his house, trying to make himself relax but failing with every step he took. Too much had happened in the past few days—too many things that he had little control over.

Chief among them had been Ione's refusal to see him, followed by Julia's untimely arrival while he had been trying to drown his emotions in wine. He had been foolish to allow that to happen. Now he could only hope in the long run it would prove to be of little consequence. All these events had been upsetting, but it had been Antonius' accusation of betraying Ione with false words of love that had finally broken through the emotional barriers he had erected.

A full night and day had passed since he had last seen Antonius, and Glaucus was angry at his inability to act on what they had learned from Gaius. Only one other thing had added to his concern: the disappearance of Petrus.

When Glaucus had returned from Gaius' villa the night before he had discovered that Petrus was missing. He had sent another of his slaves to inquire as to Petrus' whereabouts and had learned that Petrus had been taken before the magistrate and charged with Christianity—again.

He learned also that Petrus had been tortured until he had finally denounced the name of Christ, and had been released. That was all the slave had been able to learn. Where Petrus had gone to no one knew. Glaucus suspected he knew his whereabouts but had decided to wait before acting.

A sudden, horrible thought made Glaucus stop in midstride. *What if Arbaces has prevented Antonius from seeing Ione?*

Glaucus stared at nothing while pondering this thought. Then, with a determined nod of his head, he walked out onto the nighttime street. He could wait no longer for others to take care of matters for him. He needed to see Ione, to speak with her and make her understand his love—and her danger.

As he walked to her house, Glaucus was forced to stop and brace himself against the side of a building for support as another of the ever-increasing tremors struck the city. He waited until the shaking streets calmed before he continued on.

He paused for a moment when he reached Ione's house, as renewed indecision mixed with his needs. Then he rapped sharply on the door, no longer caring about protocol or the stupid promise he had made to Ione.

A few seconds later Nydia opened the front door. "I must speak with Ione," Glaucus told her before she could ask who it was or move to prevent his entrance.

"Glaucus," she whispered, shaking her head and stepping back within the entrance hall, half blocking him from entering further. "Glaucus, Ione won't see you. Please go."

"She must! Has not Antonius been here? Didn't he tell her?" Glaucus asked urgently.

"Tell me what, Glaucus? Surely there's nothing more to be said," Ione stated as she walked into the entranceway, staring openly at Glaucus.

Glaucus' eyes roamed across her face, momentarily stunned, as always, by the serene beauty that radiated from her. He noted the dark circles under her eyes, and the downturned corners of her mouth, but even these signs of sadness only served to add yet another vision of her beauty to his mind. Before he could speak, Ione held out her hand, from which dangled the necklace he had given her. An instant later it was in his hand, and Ione was walking away.

"Ione! Wait!" Glaucus called. "Please, I must talk with you."

She stopped, turning to stare at him with haunted eyes. "Julia has already said it all. She returned the necklace to me, in person, with her sympathy."

"I don't understand," Glaucus whispered truthfully. "Ione, didn't Antonius speak to you?"

"What do you know of my brother?" she demanded, concern tinting her words.

"He was to come here . . ."

"Only Calenus has been here. He, too, was searching for my brother. He told me that . . . he said Antonius has not been seen since yesterday."

"Yesterday?" Glaucus repeated, thinking back on how he had left Antonius just two short streets away from the temple of Isis, and had watched him disappear in that direction. Suddenly a strange racing chill of alarm coursed through his mind, but he fought against letting his fear show on his face.

"What is it, Glaucus?" Ione asked, taking a step toward him. "Is Antonius in trouble?"

"Don't . . . don't be concerned. I'm sure it's a misunderstanding. Ione, I'll try to find him," he said as he turned and started for the door.

As he reached the archway, he paused. Looking over his shoulder, he gazed deeply at Ione. "And, Ione. No matter what you've heard, no matter what may happen, I love you. Remember that!" he stated. Then he stepped into the night again, his worry about Antonius lending speed to his feet, while it wiped caution from his mind.

"Glaucus! Wait!" Ione shouted.

He turned quickly. She stood in the doorway as though she planned to follow him. "Stay here, Ione. I'll bring Antonius to you. He'll explain everything."

"Glaucus!" Ione cried again. But Nydia, sensing Ione's pain, led her into the house. Meanwhile Nydia fought her own dark battle. For the first time, she realized just how badly she had betrayed Glaucus and Ione.

When the door to Ione's house closed, Glaucus did not hear the sound. Nor did he hear the footsteps that followed a short distance behind him, as Calenus slipped from his hiding place and began to follow Glaucus, just as he had been instructed to do by Arbaces, in hopes that the Greek would lead them to Antonius.

*   *   *

From the moment Antonius left Olinthus' shop, he moved unerringly toward the home that he and Ione had shared since their birth. Because his mind had been filled with the thoughts of his newfound knowledge—of the wonderful story Olinthus had told him, and the sudden finding of a faith that he could believe in—he paid scant attention to his surroundings.

Only a subconscious warning stopped him before he crossed the forum; he quickly realized that he had taken the wrong pathway home. Freezing to the spot, Antonius stared across at the temple of Isis. He could see that it was filled with a multitude of praying people.

Revulsion and anger welled up within him so intensely that he knew he could no longer hold it back. He felt that now would be the time to speak out against Arbaces, to expose him to the world for what he was. Here, in the temple itself, before the beguiled masses Arbaces had deceived—it was here that Antonius must begin.

With increasing determination, Antonius started forward. But as he did a strong hand fell upon his shoulder, startling him and making him turn about.

"Antonius, we have been looking for you," Arbaces said in a low voice.

Antonius shook off the Egyptian's hand and glared defiantly at the high priest. "I'm sure you have. Arbaces, I intend to expose you for who and what you really are! I will denounce you to all of Pompeii unless you leave us alone and give back to me my estates!"

Arbaces' eyes narrowed, and when he spoke, his voice was dangerously taut. "My son, think well on what you are saying!"

"I have thought well. More clearly than I've thought in my entire life. Take heed, Arbaces; the people of Pompeii will listen to Antonius and Ione!"

"Who will believe you, you fool," Arbaces said with a sneer.

"Oh, they'll believe me, and the Greek noble, Glaucus."

Arbaces' hand shot out, grabbing Antonius' rough tweed

toga. He drew the youth close to him, and when their faces were barely an inch apart he spoke. "What does Glaucus know of this?"

"Everything! Everything that Gaius had to say—who you really are, what you've done!" Antonius stated triumphantly.

Arbaces' face twisted with anger before he finally released Antonius. Forcing himself to gain his self-control, Arbaces spoke in a tone of reason. "You can't believe that senile old fool. My son."

Antonius cut him off with a sharp laugh of victory. "No more! Oh, Arbaces, there is a God! I know it now, I learned that fact today. A true God," he proclaimed. Then he started to walk away.

Antonius had taken only two steps when Arbaces moved. His hand dipped into the folds of his priestly robes, then his arm swung up. Moonlight glinted off the steel blade he had withdrawn from its sheath. Taking one more step, Arbaces' arm arced downward.

"Then go to your God!" Arbaces declared as the steel sank into Antonius' back.

Antonius stiffened with a strange, twisting sensation. His eyes widened in disbelief, and his legs buckled. For an endless moment he thought he was in a dream. But then the ground came toward him and he faded into darkness.

Quickly Arbaces looked around. He saw no one. But had his eyes been able to penetrate the dark he would have found that there was a witness to his crime. Standing in the shadows nearby was Calenus. The priest had raced ahead to warn Arbaces of Glaucus' approach. He had arrived just in time to see Arbaces plunge his dagger into a man's back. Now, drawing himself further into the shadows, he watched as Arbaces stood over the body of Antonius.

Just then, Glaucus turned the corner. In the dark he could make out a white-robed figure that was about the same size as Antonius. Glaucus raced forward. "Antonius?" he called.

The white-robed figure turned toward Glaucus and then began to back away. Glaucus, afraid that Antonius would elude him, ran faster. Just as the man disappeared completely into the shadows, Glaucus stumbled and fell to his knees.

Spinning, Glaucus looked at what had tripped him. He realized with sickening dread that it was a man's body. Reaching out, he turned the body onto its back; when he did, his breath hissed out.

"Antonius," he whispered as he bent over the youth. "No," he whispered, cradling Antonius' head in his arms. Bending close, Glaucus tried to see if any life remained in Antonius' body. His attention was so intense that for a moment he did not hear the footsteps behind him. Then he looked up quickly.

The only thing he saw was a blurring golden orb. Suddenly the world exploded in a brilliant flash of colors that was soon replaced by utter darkness as he sank across Antonius' unbreathing chest.

Arbaces waited until he was sure Glaucus was unconscious. Then, with a dark smile on his lips, he bent and placed the gold-serpentined dagger in Glaucus' hand. Straightening quickly, he looked around. Satisfied that no one had witnessed his murder of Antonius, Arbaces ran to the temple to wait, with all apparent innocence, for news of the murder to be brought to him.

Calenus still stood in the shadows. Ideas churned within his mind. He felt no revulsion at the murder, only a twisted admiration for Arbaces. At the same time, he also realized that what he had been waiting for—for so long—was now at hand. With the events of this night, Calenus knew that his position within the temple of Isis was about to rise higher.

As he was about to leave his hiding place, he heard footsteps approaching. From one direction he heard people walking silently; from another direction he heard several men carrying on a drunken conversation.

It was the silent ones that reached the scene first. Calenus saw a man and woman stop when they reached the prone figures. The man bent, and then stood quickly, just as Glaucus began to stir, a low groan issuing from his throat.

Yet it was the woman who reacted first. She gasped, and then her voice rang out tremulously. "He's dead!" she screamed at the unmoving body beneath Glaucus. Then she saw the bloodied dagger in his hand. "He killed him!" she cried loudly, just as three men turned the near corner.

Calenus saw them stagger to a halt for a moment before the slim man in the center of the trio started forward. He recognized him instantly as Clodius, the moneyless noble.

When Clodius reached the screaming woman, he stared in shock at Glaucus, who was still kneeling over the body, the dagger still clutched in his hand.

"Glaucus?" he called, unable to believe the sight before him. "By the gods," he whispered, still staring wide-eyed as Sallust and Lepidus reached his side.

"Seize him!" ordered the husband of the screaming woman. "Guard! Guard!" he shouted in a thunderous voice.

Calenus watched everything, and as he did, a broad smile formed on his lips. Glaucus, still groggy from the blow to his head, was staring up at Clodius. The other man grabbed the dagger from him and hauled the Greek to his feet just as several guardsmen raced to the scene.

"It was murder," cried the woman, who pointed a quivering finger at Glaucus. "He killed the man!"

"What?" asked the first guard, drawing his shortsword and staring at everyone. "Murder?"

The other guards reached them then, and one bent to the fallen figure. "This one's dead," he stated. "Stabbed in the back!"

"Killed him, did you?" the first guard asked Glaucus. Glaucus did not answer. Instead, he stared into the shocked eyes of his friend.

Calenus, still smiling, waited until everyone had left the scene before he emerged from his hiding place and raced toward the temple.

There he pushed through the milling people, waving his hands high and running toward Arbaces, who stood at the

altar. "Arbaces!" he shouted to the high priest. Just before
he reached the Egyptian's side, he saw a startled, alarmed
expression cross the man's features.

Arbaces recovered quickly and glowered at the rushing
priest. "Calenus! How dare you interrupt our ceremony. You
are a priest of Isis, and . . ."

Calenus nodded, even as he twisted his face into a mask of
mock sorrow. "Oh, Arbaces, Antonius has been murdered!"
he cried in a voice loud enough for everyone to hear. Then he
ducked his head, unable to hide his smile. A multitude of
voices cried out in disbelief. Quickly Calenus wiped away his
look of triumph, knowing that it was not yet time for Arbaces
to learn that he now held within his grasp the power to
control the high priest.

Within the depths of the earth, molten lava washed thunder-
ously against the barriers that blocked its progress. Churning
upon itself, the superheated molten river continued its search
for a path of escape. Then it reached a thin barricade that
could not withstand its furious onslaught, and after a short
time a sheet of rock collapsed.

The lava boiled through the opening, accompanied by steaming gases. It began to snake its way through a wide cavern,
slowly rising upwards toward a small pinpoint of light. Before the lava could reach it, however, the plates in the earth
groaned, and the rushing river was recalled to the depths.

For now it receded. But this time the passageway toward
freedom remained open. A thin stream of white gas sped
toward the light and escaped through the small crevice at the
peak of Vesuvius. Leaping mightily in the air, the advance
scout had finally reached its freedom.

Fortunata, her long hair falling across her shoulders, stood
by the old stone fence and gazed down at the sleeping city of
Pompeii. Only a few torches still burned within its streets.
Far off on the horizon a few tentative streaks of gray and pink
rose into the black night sky, heralding the coming of the new
day.

Her thoughts were on only one thing, and it was that which had awakened her. Ever since Glaucus and Antonius had come, and Gaius had finally spoken the truth about Arbaces, Fortunata knew that Arbaces would be seeking revenge. What was bothering her even more, however, was that she was starting to welcome those thoughts.

They had been in hiding for too many years, afraid of everything and anything. Now that their lives were drawing to an end, she did not want it to be an inglorious one. She wanted Gaius and herself to be free, to be proud of themselves one last time.

But could they? Would they be strong enough? *We must!* she told herself. Suddenly Fortunata froze at the sound of footsteps. Whirling, she found herself face to face with a priest of Isis, and could not stop the startled gasp which escaped from her mouth.

"Forgive me, Lady Fortunata; I did not intend to startle you," Calenus said with an oily smile. "I am sent by Arbaces, with a message for Gaius."

Holding back her fears, Fortunata drew herself straighter while she gazed at the priest with a practiced and patrician air. "Whatever message you bear, you may give to me."

"My pardon, but Arbaces was most insistent that Gaius should hear."

Fortunata arched her eyebrows imperiously and stared silently at the swarthy priest for a long moment. "Shall I call my slaves?" she threatened in an icy, regal voice.

Calenus shook his head quickly and drew a deep breath. "In that case, I am afraid I must tell you that *our* young priest, Antonius, is dead."

"Dead. . . . No!" But after those first disbelieving words, Fortunata fought off the wave of dizziness that gripped her. "How did he die?" she asked after gaining control of her emotions.

"Sadly, he was murdered . . . by a man named Glaucus, a Greek nobleman."

Fortunata stared at him, knowing that what he had just said

could not be true. Before she could question him further, Calenus spoke again.

"Arbaces also extends his regrets that he could not personally come to inform Gaius. But he wishes to assure Gaius that, indeed, he will come to visit him—very soon."

Fortunata took a deep breath and then nodded to the priest. A moment later the man bowed to her and left. She waited until he had disappeared into the darkness before allowing herself to sink to her knees on the soft earth. She leaned her head against the stones of the fence, and only then did she let her grief loose.

Later, when her sobs had quieted, Fortunata stood and went into the villa. She knew what she had to do now. It was as if all her fears had come to realization, and with them had come also the knowledge that she must act. She could not let events continue without somehow finding a way to help those who needed her help the most.

Inside her bedchamber she knelt by Gaius' side and watched the even rise and fall of his chest. Bending, she brushed his forehead with her lips. At the entranceway of the villa, Fortunata put on a hooded cloak and stepped outside. As she began her walk toward Pompeii, she knew she was taking the first of many steps that should have been taken years before.

Within a dark cell, deep in the heart of the jail, Glaucus sat on a straw pallet. The wound on his head was bandaged and no longer bleeding. He stared at the single burning torch without seeing it. His blue eyes were vacant and distant—his lips formed over and over again a single word. "Ione."

Ione paced nervously before turning back to the woman whom Nydia had admitted a few moments ago. Ione's robe was covered by a long mourning veil that proclaimed her loss to all. Off to one side, sitting on a small stool, Nydia wept, her low sobs accented by the all-pervasive silence within the house.

Since the captain of the guard had brought Ione the news of Antonius' death, and had informed her also that Glaucus was her brother's murderer, she had been in a state of numbed shock. And now, with the appearance of the older woman and the words she had spoken, her shock and her sense of loss had deepened.

"I must thank you for coming to share my grief," Ione began in a faltering voice as she gazed into Fortunata's lined face.

"Please, Ione, you must listen to me, to the truth. You cannot believe that Glaucus murdered your brother!" Fortunata said for the second time.

"I must! He was seen by witnesses! If . . . if only I could understand why," she whispered in confused helplessness, tears springing suddenly from her eyes. Then she pulled her shoulders back and smiled tentatively at the older woman. "Will you come to my brother's funeral with me?"

"Ione, please!" Fortunata said urgently. "I cannot go, and you must not go either." Fortunata paused when Ione's eyes clouded with confusion, but she let her determination push her on. "You must get away from Arbaces! He is dangerous. He will destroy you, as *I am sure* he destroyed Antonius!"

"Arbaces? Fortunata, what are you saying?" Ione asked, her voice coarsened by desperation.

Fortunata drew the hood over her head and looked sadly at Ione. She turned and went to the door, but paused to look back once more.

"I can't tell you anymore. But Ione, I am going to take Gaius away from Pompeii. You must get away too. Now! Go to Rome, where your father's name can still protect you from this madman. Leave immediately. Ione, leave now!"

"Fortunata," Ione called, her confusion increasing with each word the woman spoke. This time Fortunata did not answer; instead, she opened the door, stepped through the archway, and closed it quickly behind her.

"Nydia," Ione cried, "come, we must catch her. She must tell us what she knows." With that, Ione went to the front door. Nydia stumbled behind her, moving as quickly as possible, her face still awash with tears. Just as they reached the street, another woman, her dress disheveled, came up to them.

"Lady Ione! Nydia!" she declared in an urgent voice.

"Chloe?" whispered Nydia, recognizing her friend's voice.

"Thank God I'm not too late. Please, you must both come with me," she pleaded.

Ione, her mind still dazed and confused from the events of the night and from Fortunata's distressed warnings, stared at the prostitute, finally remembering who she was.

"The funeral . . ." she began, but Chloe cut her off.

"You must not go. Not yet. Please, Lady Ione, there is someone you must speak to first. Someone who knows the truth of your brother's death."

Hearing those words, Ione flinched. Then she slowly nodded her head and allowed Chloe to lead her and Nydia to wherever she must go.

By the time the sun had risen, the funeral preparations for Antonius had been completed. Under Arbaces' firm, guiding hands the priests and priestesses of Isis had laid out Antonius' body on a bier at the foot of the statue of Isis. The bier itself was set upon a two-foot thickness of the wood that would soon become Antonius' funeral pyre.

His body was dressed in a fresh white robe. Flowers were sprinkled in his hair, and two golden coins covered his closed eyelids. In a semicircle around the dead youth stood the priests and priestesses, draped from head to toe in their traditional black veils, chanting a dirge to the beat of drums and the rattle of sistras.

Off to one side, Arbaces watched the ceremony impatiently. "Where is Ione? The rite is about to begin," he said to Calenus.

"You are certain she will come?" Calenus asked, half in disbelief.

"To her own brother's funeral?" Arbaces replied, his face growing dark. "Get her! She must be here!"

"Of course, Arbaces," Calenus said with a slow and irreverent bow that the preoccupied high priest missed.

Calenus returned to the temple ten minutes later. "Ione is gone," he whispered in Arbaces' ear.

Arbaces stared at the other priest for a moment and then shook his head slowly. "Then she knows."

" 'Knows,' Arbaces?" Calenus asked, feigning more innocence than was called for.

But Arbaces did not detect Calenus' false tones as he realized he had spoken aloud, and had not just thought the words. Arbaces stared at the priest for a moment, thinking about what must be done. Then Arbaces took a deep breath, his eyes darkened, and his voice echoed with all the blistering fury that raged within his mind. "Find her, Calenus! Find her and bring her to me!"

Then, moving with the jerky strides of anger, he snatched a torch from one of the priests and marched toward Antonius' funeral bier. He paused for only an instant before he threw the torch onto it. A moment later a single flame leaped upward, signaling the start of the funeral pyre.

Chapter Sixteen

For a half hour, Ione had sat silently and listened to the burly, kind-eyed sailmaker as he explained the circumstances surrounding Antonius' death. He told her how Chloe had brought Antonius to him, and what had happened to her brother to warrant the prostitute's actions and concerns.

He told her too of their morning sail, and of the strength and convictions Antonius had discovered. It was then that Olinthus had handed Ione the priestly robe Antonius had left behind.

When Olinthus finished, Ione held the robe in her hands and looked around the secret room. Off to one side sat Chloe, cradling her son. Petrus sat next to her; his back was still bandaged, but he was able to sit up this morning. Ione gazed at them for a long moment, slowly comprehending that everything Olinthus had told her, and everything Glaucus and Fortunata had warned her of, was true.

Turning back to Olinthus, she blinked away her tears. "Arbaces has taken everything," she said in a broken voice. "He took away my family, Glaucus, even my faith." A deep, wrenching sob tore through her, but a moment later she lifted her head proudly. "We must do something! I will go to the magistrate, tell him of our suspicions. I will tell him what Fortunata said. Surely," she said as her eyes locked with Olinthus', "I have nothing to fear from *him*."

Olinthus wanted to reach out and comfort the beautiful young woman, but instead he spoke in a soft, sympathetic voice. "Ione, we only have suspicions. And you cannot count on the magistrate. Quintus is interested in the election, not in justice. I'm sorry, but he'll do whatever Arbaces wants."

"He can't," Ione argued, shaking her head defiantly.

"No, Ione, we have no choice but to pray to God for guidance. That, and to plan a way to get you out of Pompeii before Arbaces' assassins find you." Then, while he stared at the noblewoman, he made up his mind. "I must get to Medon. We have done such things before," he added.

Before Ione could protest, Olinthus left the room, closing the door behind him. She stared at the space where he had been, but quickly another curtain of tears veiled her eyes as she thought of her dead brother, and of Glaucus, who lay helpless in the jail. She knew also that his execution would be immediate, because the elections were drawing near and Quintus would need this public spectacle to recoup his position in the peoples' minds and make them forget Diomed for the time being.

In Diomed's villa there was also strong reaction to Glaucus' arrest. Diomed, his round face suffused with scarlet blotches, stood glaring at his daughter, while Lucretia went to the front door where Arbaces waited. As Diomed's wife led the high priest toward the garden, both could hear Julia and Diomed as they argued.

"And you can forget this silly business about Clodius— forever! I'll never let you marry him, even if he'd have you!"

"But I kept my bargain about Glaucus!" she retorted angrily.

"If you had done it properly, I wouldn't be a ruined man today!" Diomed snapped irrationally.

Julia, her face ashen, stared with loathing at her father. "Is that all you can think of? Just yourself?"

Before more could be said, Lucretia stepped into the garden, with Arbaces a half step behind her. "Diomed," she called.

Diomed turned but did not see Arbaces. "I'm lost, Lucretia," he wailed to her.

Lucretia smiled at him. "Now, now, dear, it can't be that bad."

"When the whole town's laughing at me over Glaucus? And now they'll all go over to the magistrate if he condemns him."

When Julia glanced past her mother she saw the high priest staring at them. Stiffening, she turned and walked out of the garden. Just then Diomed saw Arbaces. "And he *will* condemn Glaucus, if you say so, Arbaces," Diomed declared.

Arbaces favored Diomed with a sarcastic smile. "You can hardly hold me responsible for a hotheaded Greek."

"It's all very well for you. You'll have your Ione now! But what of me?" Diomed whined. "You've used me!"

"Diomed!" Lucretia exclaimed, shocked at her husband's accusation against her priest.

"Diomed," Arbaces said in a conciliatory tone, "listen to me. No one is laughing at you. In fact, you're seen as deeply injured by Glaucus."

"Or a fool!" Diomed snapped, ignoring Arbaces as he fed his self-pity. "Now that Vespasian is dead, how will I ever get to Rome?"

Arbaces, unwilling to close off any possible aid he might need to carry out his plans, knew that he must placate the fat merchant. Keeping his voice soothing, he stepped closer to Diomed and put a friendly hand on his shoulder. "Diomed, the new emperor, Titus, plans to carry on his father's schemes of bringing new men to Rome."

"There, you see, it's not as bad as you thought," Lucretia said, coaxing her husband with a shallow smile.

"Yes, Titus is a man who likes his pleasures. He has made it his first project to complete the Colosseum, just because he has such a passion for the games!"

Diomed, still unmollified shook Arbaces' hand from his shoulders. "A pity I'm not a gladiator. Really Arbaces, I fail to see . . ."

"You know, don't you, that it is said that any man who also loves the games is bound to be smiled upon by Titus."

"Well, Diomed, it's simple isn't it?" Lucretia chimed in. "Titus will look with favor upon Pompeii, won't he, as mad as our people are for the games? And if you host them, well . . .''

Diomed stared at his wife, and then at Arbaces. Slowly a smile returned to his face as both Lucretia's words and Arbaces' meaningful gaze filled his mind with the various possibilities for the future.

Unable to listen to her father and Arbaces plot some new horror that would eventually ensnare her, and disheartened that Diomed now refused to honor their agreement, Julia walked disconsolately in the back garden of her villa with her small dog jumping around at her heels, unaware that someone was watching her.

But then the little dog barked and ran toward the rear gate. Watching him go, Julia's gaze lifted, and then she froze. Standing at the gate staring at her with dark, brooding eyes, was Clodius.

Slowly, almost afraid of what his appearance signified, Julia went to him. He bowed slightly to her.

''I came to offer my condolences,'' he said in a gentle voice.

Julia, so used to Clodius' sarcastic words, reacted as if she had been slapped. ''You always mock me, even now.''

''I only wanted to offer what comfort I could about Glaucus.''

''Oh, Clodius! You don't believe that lie too? How could you when you know . . .'' But she stopped herself before saying anything else.

Looking away, Julia tried to force back the flush she knew was coloring her face. Not wanting to be hurt any further by the man she loved, Julia took a deep breath and spoke coldly to him. ''Well, I suppose it amused you to believe that story.''

Clodius stared openly at her, his eyes searching across her face. ''Be honest with me, Julia. Are you in love with Glaucus?''

Suddenly Julia didn't care what her father might say. ''No,

nor was he in love with me. Ione had captured Glaucus' heart, totally!''

"But he is a noble, and wealthy.''

"You've always done me that injustice. Thinking that money is my measure of a man.''

"Just as you've always thought that lack of birth is my measure of a woman,'' Clodius said in a low voice, his eyes locked with Julia's. "Especially a woman who could forgive lack of money,'' he said as he stepped through the gate and came next to her.

Julia gazed into the tortured depths of his eyes, and for the first time understood him. "I . . . I can forgive,'' she whispered.

Clodius took her hands in his and squeezed them gently. "Julia,'' he said hoarsely.

But Julia withdrew her hands and spoke sadly. "What good does this do us now?'' she asked as she tried not to look into his puzzled eyes. "You may be the only noble in the empire whom my father will never allow me to marry. Oh, Clodius,'' she cried. Then she was against him, and their mouths met for too short an instant before Julia pulled away. Turning, she ran back into the house.

Clodius stared at the door that closed behind her. Then, holding himself back from charging after her, he turned and left the villa.

He walked for a long time, replaying their conversation over and over in his head until he could stand it no longer. Returning to his small apartment, he went to his desk and dipped his quill into the inkwell.

Then, as he stared at the blank sheet of vellum, he began to write.

To Julia—Who, when I look into your eyes

But he could not go on. He stopped and glanced around at his quarters. The single room was barren except for a desk, stool, and pallet. One small wooden wardrobe stood in the far corner; a small table with a basin and a pitcher completed the meager furnishings.

Clodius looked down again, studying what he had written.

Snorting with disgust, he scratched out the words just as a knock sounded on his door.

"Go away! I haven't got the rent," he stated angrily. But as he stared at the door, it opened, and Arbaces came inside.

"I must speak to you of Glaucus," the high priest stated.

"Glaucus? There's a sad case," the nobleman replied too quickly, conscious that he was trying to cover his own feelings.

Arbaces, his face creased with grief, nodded slowly. "Antonius was like a son to me. And it must be terrible for you also, to have seen Glaucus murder him."

Clodius gazed at the priest before he shook his head. "I did not see the deed itself."

"But the guards say you recognized the unusual dagger that he . . ."

Clodius shrugged. "I was with him when he bought it. Oh, there's little doubt he did it. Only . . . it's just so unlike him."

"But you were his closest friend. Surely you knew he was in love with Ione?"

"So I've just been told," Clodius stated, sighing with the irony of his admission.

"Antonius was bitterly opposed to this."

"I know. They had a fearful row about it. Of course, at the time I didn't understand what it was about."

"You heard this argument?" Arbaces asked eagerly, barely managing to mask his excitement.

"At Glaucus' house," Clodius volunteered.

"You must testify to what you heard!" Arbaces stated.

Clodius stepped back from the priest, eyeing him with sudden suspicion. "You seem very keen on this."

"Antonius was a holy priest of Isis! Can I let his death go unpunished?" Arbaces' voice was one of pious certitude.

"I understand how you feel, Arbaces. And I have no reason to protect Glaucus. Far from it," he said with a bitter laugh. "But to testify against him—that is rather low."

"Low? To merely tell the truth? To see justice done?" Arbaces prompted.

"Oh, justice is it?"

Arbaces was silent for a moment before his expression
changed yet again, and when he spoke his words were sympathetic and direct. "I suppose you've seen little enough of
justice. Living like this, when upstart foreigners like Glaucus
live like princes."

Arbaces' words were like an echo of Clodius' own distant
thoughts. He gazed at the priest, then slowly nodded his head.
"It's true. I could live for a year on what he spends in a
day."

"Well"—Arbaces smiled once again—"I suppose when
one lacks money, one must marry it."

Clodius' quick snort of derision was followed by a sudden
and unexpected admission. "I have always looked to marry
for money. And yet I would marry Julia if she were a
pauper."

"Julia? Clodius, surely you know I have Diomed's ear."

Clodius stared hopefully at Arbaces. Gradually the reality
of his words and the piercing gaze of the priest's eyes told
him what would be expected. "Of course. And if I will testify,
Julia is the prize."

"Your reluctance in this becomes you. After all, Glaucus
was your friend. But consider that I ask only that you tell the
truth. Nothing more."

"But to send Glaucus to his death . . ." Clodius protested.

Arbaces shook his head meaningfully. "Clodius, even as
outraged as I am, I wouldn't wish for a man's death. Glaucus
is rich and high born. They would never execute him. At
worst, he'll be banished back to Athens."

Clodius thought about that for a moment. Then he nodded
his head. "Yes, that is justice these days." Turning away
from Arbaces, he went back to his desk. His eyes swept
across the vellum, and fastened on just two words.

To Julia

Suddenly Clodius knew what he had to do. "Well, if I
must speak only the truth. . . . That's no dishonor, is it?"

"None," Arbaces said. "You shall not regret this decision,
Clodius, nor will I forget what I have said this day."

Clodius stood still for several minutes after the priest had left his small room. Julia's image floated in his mind, but suddenly that image was torn apart as the memory of Glaucus' face, covered with blood, stared helplessly at him.

By late afternoon, a large crowd had formed at the steps of the basilica, noisily awaiting the verdict from the swift trial of Glaucus. The forum was filled with all manner of people, from slaves to priests to noblemen. Near the foot of the steps several white-robed priests of Isis milled together, their voices low as they asked each other if it was time to send up the cry for Glaucus' death.

But the senior priest shook his head. "We must wait a few more minutes. I will give the signal; be patient," he said as he looked across the forum toward the building where Quintus was holding court.

Inside the magistrate's chamber, Glaucus stood between Drusus and the captain of the guard. Across the room stood Clodius, speaking quietly and answering each of the questions put to him. The other witnesses—Sallust, Lepidus, and the man and woman who had first discovered the murder— had already testified that Glaucus had killed Antonius.

Then Glaucus' eyes fell on the knife that Quintus held. Its distinctive twining serpent handle glowed from the light filtering in through the window. From the moment he had recognized the dagger he had been confused as to how it had gotten into his hands, for Glacus knew he had left it at home before going to see Ione.

"Is this the weapon that killed young Antonius?" Quintus asked Clodius.

"It is the dagger I saw in Glaucus' hand last night."

"Have you ever seen it before?"

Clodius looked at the dagger again, and then at Glaucus for a brief moment. "I was with Glaucus when he bought it."

"I see," Quintus said. "Do you know whether Glaucus and Antonius knew each other?"

"Yes, Lord Magistrate, they did."

"Have you ever had any occasion to overhear them fighting before last night?"

"Yes. I overheard a rather nasty fight the other night, when I was visiting Glaucus," Clodius said, his voice dropping lower.

"Thank you, noble Clodius, for speaking so candidly. You are free to go."

Clodius turned, and when he did, his eyes locked with Galucus' lighter ones. Then Clodius took a deep breath and started out of the room.

"Glaucus," Quintus called, "do you have anything to say in your behalf?"

Glaucus stared without passion at the white-haired magistrate. During the questioning of the witnesses, he had come to the realization that Quintus could do nothing other than what he was doing. He knew that Arbaces, who was sitting in the rear of the chamber, was the real source of evil, controlling everyone with subtle pulls of his ever-lengthening strings.

"Would that it could help me, Lord Magistrate, but there is nothing I could say that would change the course you have already set. You have questioned all the witnesses. Arbaces himself has told you that Antonius and I were bitter enemies, made so by my love of Ione." Glaucus paused to turn his gaze on Arbaces before continuing. "Yet, though he spoke only lies, I cannot prove it. I know only that it is Arbaces himself who is guilty!"

"Murderer! Shut him up!" Arbaces shouted as he stood.

"He is entitled to speak," Quintus said benevolently, but Glaucus knew better than to harbor false hope.

"All of the witnesses, my friend Clodius included, were telling the truth, for none of them saw the act of murder itself. They did come upon me, holding that dagger, but I did not kill Antonius. Another killed him! When I found him, and bent over to aid him, I was struck on the head by someone—the knife placed into my hand without my knowledge."

"Strange that it was your knife, is it not?" asked Tibius, the second magistrate.

"It is not mine. Send someone to my home. You will find my dagger there!" Glaucus shouted.

"Do not insult this court with your lies," Tibius sneered.

"Glaucus, it is unfortunate that a nobleman such as yourself has fallen to such base acts as murder. You will be taken to your cell. I will send word to you when we weigh all the evidence, and your guilt—or innocence—is decided upon. Captain," Quintus said with a dismissing wave of his hand, "take Glaucus back to his cell."

Glaucus glared at Quintus, and then his eyes locked with Arbaces'. Within their darkness he saw the high priest's triumph. "It is not over yet," Glaucus said to Arbaces just as Drusus and the captan pulled him from the room.

Quintus and Tibius stood, and Arbaces went to them. "Listen!" he commanded. As they did, the voices of the mob filtered in, calling for Glaucus' death.

Quintus glanced at Arbaces and shook his head slowly. "What Clodius says is most persuasive. I have no doubt of Glaucus' guilt," he said, motioning Tibius and Arbaces toward the door.

"*He* made fools of us in the matter of that Christian slave," stated Tibius.

When Quintus reached for the door, Arbaces' hand stopped him. "Quintus, you have bungled every opportunity I've given you to win this election. Are you now going to tell me that you won't condemn Glaucus?"

"But to give him death?" Quintus asked in a hushed tone, knowing how heavy the responsibility would be to order the death of a noble.

"You would do the same to a common murderer. Glaucus is much worse! He killed a holy priest of Isis, and the people will not stand for that! The people, Quintus! The same people who will reelect you—or not," Arbaces declared. Their eyes met for a moment, and then Arbaces opened the door and stepped back so the magistrate could pass through first.

Quintus, although he had heard the angry shouts of the mob, was unprepared for its size. The forum was jammed with a multitude of people, all of whom had turned when the chamber door opened.

Knowing how little choice he now had, Quintus went to

the basilica steps, and with Tibius and Arbaces leading the way, he went to the top and prepared himself to face the crowd.

He held up his hands for silence, but the people would not quiet down. Then Arbaces stepped to Quintus' side and held his arms up.

"In the name of justice, let Quintus speak," he ordered to the noisemakers. When everyone was quiet, Arbaces nodded his head and stepped back to give Quintus the stand. When he did, he saw Diomed edge toward the bottom step. They exchanged knowing glances, and then Arbaces began to walk down the steps and into the crowd where his priests waited.

"My friends, you call for justice," Quintus said in a loud voice. "And justice will be done. I have always sought peace and justice for Pompeii, and shall do so in the future, with your support."

"You want support?" shouted a man in the crowd. "Then punish Glaucus!" In accent to his words, the crowd began to chant anew, crying for Glaucus' death.

Quintus gazed at the people, his eyes falling on Clodius on the far side of the crowd. He saw the man's face register fear at the cries from the crowd. Again, Quintus signaled for silence.

"Glaucus has committed a sacrilege, flying in the face of the deep moral and religious feeling of all Pompeii! He has taken a holy life. And for this, I decree, he must pay with his own!"

The crowd erupted spontaneously at this announcement, cheering and screaming their approval to the magistrate.

On the far side of the basilica, Olinthus stood with Medon, staring at the ferocious crowd, feeling a deep sorrow for what was about to happen to Glaucus. He stepped toward the crowd, but Medon pulled him back.

"You can't," Medon whispered.

"I can take no more of this," Olinthus declared. "Medon, you must not be seen with me. Carry out our plan to take Ione out of Pompeii. Do it now! This city has gone mad."

"You have gone mad! There's nothing you can do. In God's name, Olinthus . . ."

"In God's name I must try. Medon, for how long have I done nothing when they killed our brothers? Have I not stood silent when they said I was a Christian?"

"Would you throw your life away?" Medon asked fearfully.

"Not *throw* it away. I would *give* it, if I must."

"Olinthus," Medon cried when the large man pulled free of his grasp and entered into the thick mass of people.

Olinthus' mind was made up. He knew he had to do something, and do it now. But even as he fought his way through the crowd he saw that Diomed was walking up the steps toward Quintus.

"Lord Magistrate, I salute you," Diomed declared in a loud voice. "And I salute the people of Pompeii," he added, turning to smile at the mob.

"Diomed, what . . ." Quintus began, but Diomed cut him off quickly as he faced the crowd again.

"You all know this worthy man and I oppose each other. But there comes a time when politics must yield to justice—when right-thinking men must stand together."

Seeing what Diomed was about, Quintus laughed derogatorily as he gestured to his opponent. "People! Here's the man who would have Glaucus for a son-in-law!"

Amid the hoots and laughter from the crowd, Diomed sucked in his girth and raised his hands high. "Yes! Glaucus deceived me, just as he deceived everyone else with his foreign, princely ways. He is an outrage to us all; and I say a *public* show of feeling is in order. I say he must die in the arena!"

Another wild cheer resounded, and while the words bounced against Olinthus' ears he continued to fight his way closer to the basilica steps.

"People! People!" shouted Quintus, trying to maintain a semblance of order. "You'll remember we had a show only a few months past!"

"And they deserve another show!" Diomed cried, sensing a victory

"Pompeii cannot afford more games yet!" Quintus pleaded, more to Diomed than the crowd. But the crowd heard him and began shouting out their dismay at this announcement.

"Really, Magistrate!" Diomed said, his voice suddenly loud and powerful. "Surely not *all* the taxes that we pay have been drained into your pockets?"

The crowd was now clearly on Diomed's side, cheering him on as he faced the magistrate.

"How dare you," Quintus hissed, as he failed in his efforts to silence the crowd.

Smiling, Diomed raised his hands slowly, and the crowd fell still. "My friends, you call for games, but our lord magistrate will have none of it. Very well," Diomed said. He took a deep breath and nodded his head dramatically. "Then *I* shall give you games!"

Another powerful roar greeted his words, and soon his name was being hailed by the crowd.

But while Diomed preened himself, accepting the ovation, Olinthus burst through the crowd and bounded up the steps of the basilica, coming to a stop an inch from Diomed, who backstepped quickly to get out of the big sailmaker's way.

"People," Olinthus yelled to the crowd. "People, hear me! This man is playing you like puppets."

Olinthus' words were met with strident boos. Then, slowly, the most dreaded cry of all was heard. "Christian!" The single word was soon picked up and amplified by a thousand throats. "Christian!" they shouted. "Get him down!"

Once again, Diomed saw an opportunity and took it boldly, before Quintus could step forward.

"No!" he called to the crowd. "I'll answer him! Olinthus, would you oppose the people's right of justice?"

"Justice? Or is it power you see?" Olinthus first asked Diomed and then the crowd. "Power that he tries to buy from you with games, like children! And once he has it, do you think he'll show *you* any justice?"

"It's true!" Quintus said, suddenly backing Olinthus' words. "It's all a cheat to sway you."

"Listen to the magistrate, siding with the Christian!" Diomed cried, drawing further protests from the crowd.

Olinthus drew himself taller and swung his arm to encompass both men. "Look at these men. Both of them are pathetic fools. Both are tools of Arbaces, as you are tools of them!"

As Olinthus spoke, the ground began to tremble, announcing that yet another of Pompeii's earthquakes was about to strike. Olinthus' eyes met and locked with Arbaces', who stood within the crowd, whispering frantically to his priests.

The priests set out a new cry, which the crowd quickly picked up, calling for Olinthus' arrest as a Christian. But the sailmaker shook his head slowly and pointed his finger directly at the high priest.

"God knows you're evil, Arbaces. He will punish you! And"—he looked out over the crowd—"all who follow him in wickedness!"

His words were punctuated by an ominous rumbling. Then the ground of the forum shuddered madly. "I have warned you," Olinthus cried out loudly, "that your last days are at hand. Then you will feel the wrath of God upon you!"

The earth's shaking grew more pronounced, and cries of panic filled the air. Soon the mob became a pushing, swarming mass of frightened humanity. It seemed that the only person unaffected by the quake was Olinthus, as he stood at the top of the basilica, his feet firmly planted, staring at the chaos below him.

From the corner of his eye he saw Diomed bolt, racing unsteadily down the steps, while Quintus stood almost as calmly as Olinthus, holding his arms up, trying to restore order.

Another violent shuddering tore across the forum, rattling the buildings, and knocking people from their feet. "Yes! Cry for mercy!" Olinthus shouted.

"No!" Quintus yelled, seeing the perfect opportunity to regain some of his losses at Diomed's hands. "Calm yourselves. You must stand firm against this Christian evil!"

As suddenly as it had come, the tremor ended. For a

moment, silence blanketed the forum as the people picked themselves up and looked at Quintus. "It is Olinthus who has brought this upon you. You've heard the tales of Christians' evil powers. Now you've felt it!"

Suddenly people began to scream, their fingers pointing to Olinthus. "Kill him! Kill him! Kill him!" came ther cries.

Quintus smiled and looked down at Diomed, who had reached the lowest steps. "And where's Diomed now, my friends? Look at the coward! Can he save you from Olinthus?"

"Not from me—from God's wrath!" Olinthus challenged. The moment he had turned to face Quintus, several people in the mob broke free and raced up the steps, grabbing at Olinthus and holding him fast while the rest howled for the sailmaker's death.

"No! Stop! I command you!" Quintus ordered, afraid of what the crowd might do.

"Friends! Please!" Diomed pleaded, sensing also what would happen if the crowd were let free.

Always alert to the mob's feelings, Arbaces knew it was time for him to act. Moving quickly, he went to the steps and then turned to the crowd, his arms flung wide. "Wait, good people, wait!"

The moment he spoke, another, lighter tremor struck. It lasted for barely a heartbeat before fading away. But it had brought silence again, and attention to Arbaces.

"People of Pompeii, listen to me. Is this the face you would show Isis and the world? Would you be no better than the mobs in Rome?"

"He's a Christian!" yelled one unseen face.

"Yes. We must rid ourselves of Christians. But we have laws for that. Let your magistrate condemn Olinthus legally. Then let him die in the games that Diomed will give you!"

While Arbaces spoke, five guards climbed the basilica steps in answer to Quintus' signal. They took Olinthus from the men who had captured him and led him off.

Before he was taken from the basilica steps, Olinthus planted his feet solidly and looked out at the masses. "God help you all!" he shouted, not in anger, but in sadness.

Chapter Seventeen

It had been a remarkably volatile day for Pompeii, and for many of its citizens as well. Olinthus had been summarily tried and found guilty of practicing Christianity. Quintus had sentenced him to death in the arena—tomorrow. Glaucus, already sentenced, had been transferred to the arena's dungeon and had found himself sharing a cell with the sailmaker.

Diomed, sensing a possible victory, had gone to Marcus and ordered the lanista to stage the best games of his career, sparing no one in his attempt. He had also given the gladiator's manager specific orders about Glaucus' death, leaving Marcus no choice in the matter.

Arbaces, having come yet another step closer on the road toward fulfilling his ambitions, had only one thing left to do so far as his business in Pompeii was concerned. Issuing instructions to Calenus, Arbaces ordered his adjunct to find Ione and to return her to the temple. He also told the greedy priest to utilize the still-frenzied mob to capture as many Christians as possible. Arbaces wanted tomorrow's games to be remembered for a long, long time, and also for the people of Pompeii to remember that it was he and the cult of Isis who provided their entertainment.

To implement this, Calenus had gone to his brother, Burbo, and offered him a huge sum of money to lead the priests and the mobs to the secret hiding places of the Christians. Burbo, ever greedy, was anxious to comply.

So, as the day faded and night came to Pompeii, the streets of the city were filled with people. The explosiveness which had marked the day was but a mere shadow of what the later hours of the night would bring.

As word spread throughout the city of the games and the sacrifices tomorrow, the gladiators, who would be the main show, were being feted by Marcus—with the compliments of Diomed.

They were in the barracks dining room, and most were enjoying themselves fully, as was their wont. The frenzy which gripped the city seemed to be contagious, and the banquet this night was an especially raucous affair, with the big-boned, heavily muscled gladiators tearing huge pieces of meat from the roasted haunches set on the tables.

Wine flowed freely, and all but one of the men threw themselves into the spirit of the banquet. That one was Sporus, who watched the mayhem with the cynical eyes of a man who had seen too much, especially of the big German who had recently become a foolish braggart. Eyeing Gar, Sporus slowly shook his head.

Gar, seeing Sporus' gesture, turned away self-consciously and grabbed a piece of meat, while another gladiator called out to Sporus.

"Enjoy yourself, Sporus. This may well be your last meal!"

Sporus shook his head in a sad, dramatic gesture. "I never eat with men the night before I have to kill them," he said as his eyes fell on Gar's broad back.

Gar, ignoring Sporus' words, stood up and slammed down the piece of meat. Then he left his seat to strut boldly around the room, a sneering smile on his face.

"Lydon won't be champion much longer!" he declared bravely. "I'll get him in the arena—if he's sober enough to stand—and I'll stalk him!" he shouted, crouching low and pretending to stalk an adversary. "He'll back away from me, the coward, but I'll keep coming."

Gar lunged forward at an empty table. Gripping its edge, he yelled and lifted it in the air. A moment later he flung it from him. The sound of shattering wood echoed noisily in the hall while the other gladiators cheered him on.

"And then I'll grab him. I won't even need a sword! I'll

grab him and . . ." Gar whirled, picking up a bench and lifting it over his head. His eyes grew wide, and his muscles began to bulge.

"And I'll break his back . . . like this!" he stated as he brought up his knee and slammed the bench across it. A loud crack resounded in the room and the bench broke in half. Once again all the gladiators, except for Sporus, cheered the German on.

Gar, finished with his theatrics for the moment, returned to his seat and the goblet of wine which waited for him. The moment he lifted it to lips, voices floated into the room from the hallway, and everyone quieted down just as Marcus and Lydon entered the room, arguing heatedly.

"I won't fight Glaucus!" Lydon stated.

"Why let pride prevent you from an easy kill and a heavy purse? Are you that much of a fool?" the lanista asked.

Lydon stopped when they entered the dining hall. "Pride has no part in this," he told Marcus.

Marcus stared at Lydon for a moment, and then looked at the others. "Perhaps cowardice then?" he said in a sneering voice. "Has our champion soaked in wine so long he's afraid of the untrained man?"

Laughter was the gladiators' response, and Gar's laughter rang the loudest. "Marcus," Lydon said in a low voice, "I won't fight him."

Gar rose swiftly at these words and strutted toward Lydon. "Then I will, if the champion's too . . . unsteady." Gar's eyes locked with Lydon's. The room turned silent, and tension grew thick in the air.

"Sit down, boy," Lydon said in a husky whisper.

Their eyes remained locked for several seconds, but while Lydon did not blink, Gar did, and gradually the cocky self-assurance began to slip from the German's face. Unable to hold Lydon's open stare, Gar slowly stepped back and returned to his seat.

Lydon whirled and raced to a wall where several swords hung. Freeing one from its hooks, he spun to face the others.

His chest rose and fell angrily. His blood pounded in his temples.

"Now all of you *heros,* hear and understand me! Whoever feels like killing Glaucus, let him! But first that man kills me!" Pausing, Lydon glared at each man in turn, until all of them, one by one, dropped his challenging gaze. "What?" he asked sarcastically. "Not one of you wants to be Pompeii's champion? Not you, Gar?" He pointed the sword at the German, who still refused to meet Lydon's eyes.

"Fools," he spat, turning quickly and walking out of the room.

Marcus shook his head and followed, calling to him urgently. When he had caught up with him, he said, "Lydon, if you love your father, you will not be so hasty."

Lydon favored Marcus with a chilling stare. "What are you talking about?"

"Diomed has told me that if you fight Glaucus, your reward will be your father's freedom. If you refuse, Medon will be sold so that you will never find him again."

Lydon stared at Marcus, refusing to believe the man's words, his eyes narrowing dangerously. "Liar," he whispered.

"No. Diomed means to win his office. And he *will* have his show. He'll give the people Glaucus *and* Olinthus."

"Olinthus? Olinthus is to die?" Lydon asked, cutting Marcus off.

Marcus nodded his head slowly. "And all the other Christians, when they find them." Marcus paused for a moment as a sarcastic laugh escaped his mouth "That Arbaces! He talks law, then sends his priests out to stir up the mob, again and again."

"You're sure?" Lydon asked, his eyes searching Marcus' face desperately.

"Oh, I'm sure all right. The priests are out with the mob. They're rounding up anyone who had any Christian ties. After tomorrow's games the lions won't be hungry for a long, long time." Before Marcus had finished, Lydon had turned and raced away, the sword still clenched in his hand.

Marcus watched him until he disappeared. When he was gone, Marcus shook his head sadly because he knew that when the games went on tomorrow, Lydon would indeed face Glaucus. Of that, there was no doubt.

Within the secret room behind Olinthus' shop many Christians huddled together. Most were refugees, fleeing the ever-closing net of the mob. They huddled in small groups, some praying, some shaking with fear, and some just holding each other for whatever comfort they could derive.

To one side of the group sat Chloe, Petrus, and their son. They did not look at the others but instead gazed deeply at each other, their conversation low and intense, with Chloe trying to reason with Petrus.

"We must get out of here quickly," she reiterated. "They won't be satisfied with Olinthus. Not with the games tomorrow. Listen to the sounds in the streets! They're trying to get all of us."

"We must wait for Medon. He has the only plan for escape. Chloe, we must wait," Petrus insisted.

She sighed and then nodded her head. The baby stirred, giving vent to a plaintive wail. Smiling at her son, Chloe lifted him, adjusting the top of her robe so that the child could reach her breast and feed himself. While the baby suckled, Petrus put his arm around Chloe and drew her against his side. He kissed her cheek lightly, watching the child he now fully considered to be his son.

Across from Petrus and Chloe, sitting off by themselves, Ione and Nydia were engrossed within their own conversation. It had taken Ione almost the entire day to marshal her thoughts and to understand all that had happened. But when word came of Olinthus' plight, and of the sentence of death upon Glaucus, she had withdrawn into herself.

It had been Nydia, sitting next to her for hours, who had finally broken through Ione's wall of silence and gotten the noblewoman to speak again.

"But Nydia," Ione asked sorrowfully, "how can I live if

Glaucus dies? I love him, but he believes I blame him for Antonius' death.''

Nydia, hearing the abject misery in Ione's voice, could no longer hold back her own guilt. For hours she had coaxed Ione with gentle words, but this last admission tore through her heart. ''Ione,'' she cried, ''forgive me.''

''Forgive you?'' Ione asked, startled by Nydia's words and the sobs that followed them.

''It was I who betrayed you . . . not Glaucus! I gave Julia your necklace. It was I who let you believe that Glaucus did not love you,'' she admitted, her tears flowing freely, her sobs deep and wrenching.

Ione stared at the blind girl, her mind racing, her body tensing. ''Why, Nydia? Why?''

Nydia sat straighter, wiping her tears. ''Because I loved him too. I couldn't bear it when he was with another! Oh, Ione, there were moments when I hated you, only because he loved you.''

Ione, suddenly understanding what Nydia was trying to say, reached out and gently touched the girl's shoulder. But Nydia pulled away from the touch, shaking her head harshly. Refusing to be put off, Ione reached out to embrace the young slave girl, pulling her close and holding her sobbing body.

''Forgive me, Ione, forgive me,'' Nydia cried, her head buried against Ione's breasts.

''No, Nydia, I'm the one who needs forgiveness,'' she whispered in an emotion-choked voice as her hands rubbed Nydia's back gently. ''I poured out my joys and sorrows to you, and never once wondered if you had any of your own.''

''But I am just a slave,'' Nydia whispered, forcing herself to gain some control over her emotions.

''You are a *person*, Nydia,'' Ione stated.

There was a sharp rapping. All conversations died as every eye turned toward the door. Catus, Olinthus' ten-year-old disciple, went slowly to the door and looked through the small spyhole.

Everyone watched him breathlessly as he opened the door and stepped back. Some people cried out in choked voices, others stared in shock when the powerful form of Lydon, a sword in his hand, stepped into the room.

Before Catus could close the door, the room was filled with sounds of the mobs in the streets. All suddenly realized that their world was about to end.

Chloe was the first to speak. Handing the baby to Petrus, she stood. "Lydon! What are you doing here?"

Lydon turned toward the familiar voice. "Chloe, quickly, you must go! Where is Father?" he asked as he looked around the room. "Nydia!" he cried, his breath catching in his throat when he saw this unexpected sight.

"Who is it? Who's coming?" Ione stood too, pulling Nydia to her feet as she did.

There were loud sounds of people breaking into the shop. Lydon glanced at the door, and then back at the others, signaling them to silence. Moving quickly, he put out the oil lamp and rushed to the rear door. Using all his strength, he lifted the heavy iron bar that secured it.

When the door was free, Lydon pushed it open and stepped out of the way. "Run!" he commanded them as he returned to brace the door that the mob was now battering.

"Lydon! Ione!" Nydia cried when several people rushed past her, knocking her about. Then Ione grasped her hand and led her from the shop.

Chloe, her baby in her arms, pulled urgently at Petrus, but Petrus shrugged her off. "No! Hurry, Chloe, watch out for our son," he said as his eyes searched her face.

"Petrus!" Chloe pleaded, tears pooling in her eyes.

"Take her!" Petrus ordered the last of the fleeing Christians. He pushed Chloe into their arms and watched her taken from the shop. Only when she was gone did he go to Lydon's side.

Lydon, holding his sword at the ready, stared at the door as it began to splinter under the assault from without. From the corner of his eye, he saw Petrus come to his side. "Petrus, go while you can!" he ordered.

"Not this time," Petrus said calmly, his voice filled with determination.

Lydon glanced at the firm set of his jaw and slowly withdrew the dagger from the sheath at his waist. He extended it to Petrus, who grasped it firmly.

A moment later, the tortured wood gave way in a thunderous crash. Lydon raised his sword and Petrus readied the dagger as the first of the mob charged through.

Lydon, his body trained to move instinctively, wielded the sword with all the efficiency of his strength, never wasting a move, making each swing of the sword a killing stroke. Man after man charged, only to meet the flashing death that Lydon wielded. But as formidable a fighter as he was, he could not hold the doorway forever and was slowly forced back.

One man charged through the widened opening, skirted past Lydon, and turned, his dagger ready to plunge into the gladiator's back. Petrus lunged at the man, ignoring the sharp pain from his not-yet-healed wounds. Before the man reached Lydon, Petrus' dagger had found its mark and the assailant stiffened and fell to the floor.

There was no time to think. Petrus moved closer to Lydon, knowing that all in the shop must be killed or Lydon too would end up dead in the arena, labeled a Christian.

The world seemed to stop for Lydon as the dead piled higher on the floor. Then two men with shortswords charged through the doorway. Everything moved slowly, almost dreamily, as the distorted features of the attackers grew close. Lydon's muscles knotted with tension a second before his arms uncoiled. The flashing blade bit into flesh and bone, and the first man's dying scream rang out. Lydon pulled the sword free and swung at the second, striking him in the neck, half severing his head from his body.

Then he heard Petrus' scream of rage and turned quickly to see him face to face with the hulking mass of Burbo. Anger and disgust filled Lydon's mind, even as Petrus lunged at the tavern keeper, sinking his dagger into the evil man's heart.

"Behind you!" Lydon yelled in warning, but it was too

late. One of Burbo's men stabbed Petrus in the back. Lydon leaped across the body-littered floor, and with one mighty stroke plunged his sword through the murderer's neck.

When he withdrew the blade, the man slowly toppled to the floor, falling next to Petrus, whose eyes stared vacantly, glazed with death.

With a scream of fury and denial, Lydon turned back to the doorway, but he froze, his sword slowly dropping to his side, for there were none left to attack. He and Petrus had beaten them for now, but he knew that more would follow.

Kneeling at Petrus' side, Lydon reached to close the dead man's eyes. "You're free now, Petrus, go with your God, and be at peace," he whispered. Then he stood again and started toward the rear door. Behind him he heard shouting voices as more men entered the sailmaker's shop. Taking a deep breath, Lydon stood and raised his sword again. Then he shook his head slowly. Whoever had escaped was free; he knew it would be pointless to stay. He had two things yet to do: to find his father and to make sure that Nydia was safe. With tears forming in his eyes, Lydon raced from the shop and into the night.

In the midst of their frenzied rush, Nydia's hand was torn from Ione's, and she stumbled unsteadily until another hand reached out to steady her.

"It's me," Chloe whispered while she guided Nydia out of the frenetic rush. When the fleeing Christians turned a corner, Chloe led Nydia straight ahead to a sheltering doorway.

"Ione," Nydia cried. "Where is Ione?"

"I don't know," Chloe said, shifting the baby in her arm and pressing him tighter to her as she put her other arm around Nydia. "She will be all right," she added reassuringly.

They were quiet for a few minutes, listening to the sounds of the street, waiting until they felt it was safe to continue on. Just as Chloe started to move, loud, racing footsteps echoed in the night, and she shrank back into the darkness of the doorway.

As the running man drew closer, Chloe leaned out to see who it was. "Lydon!" she cried in relief.

Lydon stopped, turning to Chloe, his face softening when he saw that Nydia was there also. But with Chloe's next desperate words, his muscles filled with tension.

"Petrus? Where is Petrus?" she asked, turning and looking down the street frantically.

"Chloe . . . I'm sorry," he whispered.

Chloe stared at him and slowly sank to the ground, her baby clutched tightly in her arms. Her body shook horribly, and soon the agony of her sobs filled the street with their mournful, chilling wail.

Lydon gazed at her, his fist clenching and unclenching helplessly. "He was a good man, Chloe. A brave man who died so that you and your son might live."

When Ione found herself separated from Nydia, she fought to return to her friend's side, but the rushing, frightened people would not give way, and she was swept a good distance along before she was able to break free.

When she stopped, taking deep lungfuls of air, she glanced around and saw that the street was empty. Walking back a little, she tried to see if she could spot Nydia, but realized that it was hopeless.

Then she realized she was only a short distance from the ampitheater where Glaucus was imprisoned.

I must go to him. I must tell him the truth—tell him I love him, she said to herself. With her mind made up, Ione started toward the arena, moving stealthily along the street, pausing to duck into darkened archways whenever someone came near.

When she finally reached the amphitheater, she stopped at the entrance only long enough to let the guard pass by on his rounds. Then she raced through the entrance, cutting directly across the arena's field toward the line of barred dungeon windows. A flock of peacocks screamed when she ran through their middle, but Ione paid them no mind. Nor did she notice the three men, dressed in the robes of Isis, who were hidden in the shadows, marking her progress with satisfied smiles.

Deep in the bowels of the earth a low groan echoed through the endless caverns. The hot lava continued to churn, seeking out the new passages that the earlier quakes had opened. Slowly, inexorably, the lava rose higher, gaining entrance at last to the maze of passages that led to the very center of the towering mountain named Vesuvius.

Heated gases, long trapped within the earth's core, broke free when the shifting plates contracted, racing ahead of the lava to press at the very tip of the sealed mountain, trying, again and again, to find whatever small crevices were available to allow its escape.

All the while, the pressure continued to build. More and more explosive gases, created by the lakes of flowing lava, raced toward the highest point in the mountain above.

The dungeons of the amphitheater were baleful, dirty places, fit only for animals. It seemed appropriate, however, since the people in the dungeons—the prisoners condemned to death in the arena—were treated no better than the lowest form of animal.

In one such dungeon, with only dirty piles of hay to use for beds and one fetid pail of brackish water to drink, Glaucus and Olinthus paced aimlessly, silently about, their eyes by now well adjusted to the low sputtering of the single burning taper. Rats ran freely within the cell, caring for nothing except whatever food the humans might drop.

Glaucus forced himself to ponder the night's events, for all of his hopes and desires had been crushed when the magistrate had played into Arbaces' hand. Glaucus had not wanted to admit it, not even when his friend Clodius had turned on him, condemning him with his words, but Glaucus knew certainly that his life was over.

His biggest regret was that Ione would never know the

truth about her brother's death, and that Glaucus' own death would leave nobody to stop Arbaces from taking her and her wealth.

Glaucus turned away from the slime-coated wall and went to the center of the dungeon and sat, ignoring Olinthus, who looked out the high window.

Olinthus, kicking away a brave rat who was trying to nibble at his sandal, turned away from the window and looked at Glaucus. His heart went out to the handsome man who had so bravely defended himself earlier but who now had a forlorn look on his face.

Sighing, Olinthus spoke in a low voice to the Greek noble. "When Paul came to die, he said, 'No one helped me, all deserted me. But God stood by me and gave me strength. My life has been poured out, and the time has come for my departure. But I have had a part in the great contest. I have run my race. . . . I have preserved my faith.'"

Glaucus glanced at the burly sailmaker, looking into his kind, bearded face. "It must be wonderful to have such faith. To be able not to feel despair."

Olinthus shook his head slowly in understanding. "You despair because you think your fate is death, instead of a new and better life."

Glaucus smiled sadly as he studied the sailmaker's face. "Without Ione, there is no life."

"But Ione will be there with you, in time to come," Olinthus stated with deep feeling.

"My lot would be easier if I could truly believe that," Glaucus admitted.

"You have only to open your heart."

"No, Olinthus, for me it takes more to play the coward's part and pray for heaven now that death's upon me." Unexpectedly, he saw a soft grin spread across Olinthus' face, allowing the big man's teeth to shine against the darkness of his beard.

"Oh, Glaucus, there's no better time for it." Stepping closer, Olinthus knelt by his side. His eyes glistened as he stared at Glaucus, and then he began to pray.

Glaucus listened to the moving words, but flinched when a peacock screamed loudly outside his cell. He started to relax again, but tensed as he heard his name being whispered from the window.

Glaucus looked up and saw Ione's face pressed to the bars. Standing, his breath escaped in a loud hiss. "Ione . . . What . . ."

But Olinthus had risen also and reached the window at the same time as Glaucus. "Ione! What happened? Medon was to take you away."

But Ione did not hear Olinthus' question, for her eyes were fastened on Glaucus while her arms stretched through the bars. When Glaucus reached up and took her hand, she spoke in a low voice. "I couldn't leave you. Glaucus, I love you."

Although he had waited so very long to hear those words, Glaucus could not respond as he wanted, for he was aware of the danger she was now in. Squeezing her hand tightly, he rose onto the balls of his feet. "You must leave now. Ione, your life is in great danger."

"I won't leave you again!" she whispered adamantly. "Glaucus, Fortunata came to me and warned me about Arbaces. She feels he is responsible for Antonius' death. If only she would expose him to the magistrate. With what she knows, you would be set free."

For the first time since he regained consciousness on the street last night, Glaucus felt a faint stirring of hope. He stared deeply into Ione's crystal eyes, and smiled openly at her.

"Not the magistrate—he is Arbaces' puppet! But Ione! Gaius knows everything about Arbaces, everything! He can turn the nobles against the magistrate and make him spare us. You are one of them. Even Arbaces cannot challenge the combined strength of the nobles. Gaius is our only hope."

"Then I must go to him," Ione stated, smiling lovingly at Glaucus as she started to draw away.

"Wait. . . . Ione, I love you," Glaucus stated simply.

"I know that now," Ione said softly. A moment later her

footsteps faded, while Glaucus tried vainly to see her through the darkness of the night.

From the direction she had taken came another frightened cry of a peacock, rising chillingly in the air. Glaucus glanced at Olinthus, but neither man spoke. Neither could they know that in Ione's eagerness to help Glaucus, she had run straight into the arms of Calenus and the priests of Isis, who had been waiting in the shadows for just that opportunity.

In yet another section of Pompeii—a squalid, rundown street of ramshackle wood and stone houses that had once, many years before, been the vacation homes of wealthy nobles—Lydon, Nydia, Chloe, and her son were ushered into the home of Philos.

The dwarf had stared unintelligently at the trio who had knocked on his door, but had quickly regained his wits, and big them enter. When they were seated and he had heard their story, he had taken out a pot of wine and poured each of them a glass, while Chloe had laid her sleeping child on a small thatch of carpet.

Nydia spoke after taking only the barest of sips. "It is kind of you to take us in, Philos. We didn't know where to go."

"There is always room for friends. Arbaces is a monster!" Philos delcared angrily as he gazed at Chloe, empathy for her loss strong within him.

"If only I knew that Ione were safe," Nydia whispered sadly.

Suddenly Chloe rose, looking from Nydia to Philos, and then at Lydon. "I'll find her."

"No!" Nydia almost shouted the word as her head snapped up, and her unseeing eyes eerily centered on Chloe. "It's not safe for you. And after what you've already suffered . . ." But she couldn't finish her words, because the too fresh memory of Petrus' death was reaching out to haunt her.

"Yes! My Petrus died because of Arbaces. He may be gone now, but I made a vow to Glaucus to repay him for what he did for Petrus and me. I intend to keep my word," Chloe stated. "And to repay Arbaces!"

Saying that, Chloe gazed down at her sleeping child for a moment, looking at the infant as though to memorize its every line. Then, sighing softly, she turned and started out.

"Wait," Philos called suddenly. "I'll go with you."

When they were gone, and Lydon and Nydia were alone in the silent house, Lydon moved toward the blind girl.

Nydia, hearing Lydon move, turned in his direction. "Poor Chloe. She loved Petrus so much," she whispered in a faraway voice. "Lydon, you once loved me."

"And I still do. You know that," Lydon replied when he reached her side.

"If you still do," Nydia said in an emotion-filled plea, "then I beg you not to fight with Glaucus."

Lydon laughed bitterly, thinking of the irony of his situation. "So many offers for the head of Glaucus! Diomed bids my father, little Nydia offers herself."

Nydia stiffened at his words; drawing her shoulders back proudly, she shook her head. "You don't understand. I must save him, for Ione's sake."

"*Her* sake? Not your own?" Lydon asked doubtfully.

"Yes. Lydon, you must believe me."

Lydon's eyes softened when he looked at her. His confused jealousy of Glaucus changed when he heard her words, and suddenly he accepted both his love for Nydia and his loss of her.

"Nydia, if you think I could kill Glaucus willingly, you don't know what I feel for you. I would spare him. I would even let him finish me, only because you love him."

"Oh, oh, Lydon! No!" Nydia cried.

"But there is no saving him. If I refuse to fight him, he'll go to the lions with Olinthus. And my father will be lost to me forever. Nydia, the best thing I can do for him is to kill him quickly, mercifully. And then I shall never kill again."

When he stopped talking, he stared at her and at the silent tears that rained from her eyes. His heart ached with his loss and her pain, but there was nothing he could do. Reaching out, Lydon started to touch her cheek, but he stopped himself and withdrew his hand. "I must go now, to see that my father's safe. Goodbye, Nydia," he whispered.

Nydia, her throat constricted with sorrow, reached out her hand to him, wanting him to take it, praying that he would, but she heard him turn and walk to the door. Only when she heard the door close, and she knew she was alone, did Nydia give in to her grief, releasing the deep sobs that had been blocking her words.

"Oh, Lydon," she cried. "It is you I love."

Chapter Eighteen

The madness that had captured Pompeii seemed to have eased as the night wore on. The wandering bands of armed men, led for the most part by the white-robed priests of Isis, had broken up and gone either to their homes or to the taverns. The evidence of their night's work could be heard in the cries and wails coming from the jail, which now housed scores of Christians, awaiting certain death.

But on the dark street, across from the temple of Isis, all was quiet as Chloe and Philos waited in the shadows. They had been there for an hour, standing silently, waiting for something to happen.

"How can you be certain that they will capture Ione?" Philos asked.

"It's a feeling, that's all," she said. She looked up at the moonless sky and saw that the night was almost gone.

"But what if they have her already?" the dwarf asked.

"Then I must find a way inside. Hush," she whispered.

Several figures were approaching the temple from across the way. Chloe and Philos marked their passage, and noted that they were but four priests. Chloe recognized Calenus as he led two other priests who supported another between them. But when they took the first step up toward the temple, the priest in the middle sagged, his head going back and his hood falling off.

Chloe gasped when she saw a woman's long hair fall free, and instantly she recognized Ione's drugged face. When the priests dragged Ione up the temple steps, Chloe started out of her hiding place, but Philos' small, strong hand stopped her.

"It will be day soon," he whispered. "We must have a plan or we will not be able to free her."

Chloe relaxed, but her eyes never left the priests. Even after they disappeared into the sacrarium, she stared vacantly after them.

"There is a way," she said. "There is one way."

Arbaces stood in the treasury room of the temple, listening to Calenus report on the capture of Ione, who was now sleeping in one of the small locked cells that lined the corridor of the sacrarium.

Several torches burned on the walls, illuminating the room and the gold and silver that filled the coffers to overflowing. Within the treasure room was enough wealth to buy half the empire, and Arbaces had plans to do just that and more.

"Your night's work was well done, Calenus," Arbaces said as he extended a bag stuffed with coins.

Calenus took the purse and hefted it in his hand. "You are generous, good Arbaces. And my brother Burbo? Has he pleased you also?"

Arbaces shrugged. "He hasn't yet returned. But that is nothing. Most important is that you have brought Ione safely back. I will speak to her tomorrow."

"Yes," Calenus agreed with a strangely twisted smile. "To see how safe she *really* is . . . or how wise." Calenus was not frightened by Arbaces' piercing stare; rather, Calenus gave him a knowing nod of his head. "I saw you kill Antonius. I saw it all."

Arbaces was stunned, scarcely able to believe what he heard. He forced himself to break Calenus' suddenly hypnotic gaze. Then he smiled when he saw the greed in the other man's eyes. "You do understand I had to do it. I killed him for the good of the temple."

"Of course," Calenus said as he rubbed his hands together. "And for the temple's treasury. Why else have I remained silent? A man like you must have discretion to do what is necessary—and discretion, too, in a partner."

Although strained past endurance, the smile clung to Arbaces' lips. His eyes, however, turned into cold, deadly orbs. Then he laughed, shaking his head at Calenus.

"You have learned well from me. All right—partners!"

"In everything," Calenus demanded boldly.

Arbaces nodded his head and withdrew the key to the treasury, tossing it carelessly to Calenus. "In everything," he agreed.

Calenus' eyes widened as his hand gripped the key and he looked avariciously around the treasure room. Seeing this, Arbaces bent to one coffer and chose a beautifully designed bracelet. He held it up, jingling it purposely until Calenus' eyes were drawn to it.

"Exquisite, isn't it?" he asked with a knowing laugh. "It would look well on Xenia. Look, see how beautifully the emeralds are matched." He handed the bracelet to Calenus.

Calenus took it quickly, holding it toward one of the torches while he studied the intricate workmanship. "It is magnificent," he whispered, unable to take his eyes from the glowing gems.

Unnoticed by Calenus, Arbaces had slipped behind him, and as he listened to Calenus murmur about the bracelet, his hand closed around a heavy golden statue of the goddess Isis.

"Look closely at the engraving—there is none other like it," Arbaces told him.

Calenus brought the bracelet closer to his eyes. As he did, Arbaces swung the statue which sparkled like a deadly scythe as it arced in the air and struck Calenus' head with a sickening thud.

Calenus stiffened, his back arching, his eyes widening at the bolt of pain that exploded in his head. He tried to turn, but even as he did his eyes glazed and were unable to focus on Arbaces' laughing face. For a long, endless moment, Calenus stood, his eyes staring blankly. Then his legs buckled and he crashed to the floor, one hand grasping a coffer and pulling it down with him. Its heavy contents spilled over his fallen body in a grotesque mockery of scintillating greed.

"Fool!" Arbaces whispered when he bent to pry the treasury key from Calenus' curled hand.

* * *

By noon, the bloodred sun which had risen over Pompeii
that morning had changed to its familiar yellow glow, bathing
the city and the surrounding countryside with a pleasant heat.
And as the sun grew to its midday strength, the streets of
Pompeii were crowded with throngs of people walking steadily toward the amphitheater and the special games that Diomed
was giving.

But on the slopes of Vesuvius, none of the merriment or
sounds reached as far as Gaius' villa. Within the gently
winding vineyards, everything seemed peaceful. Birds called
to one another and sparrows flew daintily from branch to
branch as Gaius walked in his garden.

In his hand was a silver goblet, and while his old, watery
eyes surveyed the land around him, he took a deep sip. Then,
when he looked up at the peak of Vesuvius, a change came
over his face. The lines of fear seemed to ease, and his eyes
grew stronger. Soon, a long-absent smile appeared on his
lips.

Fortunata emerged from their villa and, seeing Gaius nearby,
walked slowly to him. When she was near, he turned to look
at her, the smile holding firm.

"I have been watching the tip of Vesuvius these last few
days. Have you noticed how a plume of smoke has appeared?
It is as if whatever gods dwell within are beginning to stir.
For everything, dear Fortunata, there is a first day, and a final
day. Much as I have tried to study man and nature, that is all
I know. Except for one thing more. That, while we may not
choose but to be born, we may choose a thousand ways to
die." Pausing, Gaius gazed lovingly at his wife's patrician
features. "And I have chosen mine."

Hearing the words she had always dreaded, Fortunata reacted swiftly, her face etched with both pain and love. "Gaius,
no! You must not speak this way. There is still a chance for
us, if only you'll come away with me."

"And go where?" he asked in a strong voice. "Look at
me, Fortunata. See me as I am. You are witness to how my
past acts of cowardice have told upon my mind . . . waiting

for death, fearing I shall see Arbaces in every shadow. Then hoping he'll come swiftly and end it for me. No, you must not ask me to go on.'' Gaius paused, but did not take his eyes from Fortunata. ''Let me cheat Arbaces in this, at least, and steal what dignity I can from it.''

Fortunata stared at him, trying to deny his words and to ignore the pain they caused. But suddenly the pain changed, and her mind hardened with anger and resolve.

''You may call yourself a coward, but never have I thought so. Never, Gaius, until now! Please, there is still some good you might do in this world. If you won't save yourself from Arbaces, then you must save Glaucus!''

''How?'' Gaius asked sadly. ''I have no certain knowledge of the murder.''

''Do you not?'' Fortunata challenged in a harsh voice. ''You know in your very soul that Arbaces did it! You alone know enough to ruin him, to throw doubt upon this execution. Your name still commands deep respect among the aristocrats, even in Rome. If you seek dignity in death, then die fighting!''

But Gaius refused to answer her. Instead, his eyes filled with the total desolation that he felt. Slowly, he shook his head.

''Very well,'' Fortunata said in a tight voice, ''*I* shall go! The magistrate might listen to me.''

''Fortunata,'' Gaius called when she turned from him. ''My dear Fortunata, if I had ever had your courage . . .'' He stopped as he held the silver goblet before him. ''But it is too late for me now.''

Fortunata stared at him. Her eyes widened with understanding when she glanced at the goblet. With her head shaking in denial, she began to back away. ''Then die!'' she cried out, her words charged with agony. ''But I won't stay to watch.''

''No, you cannot desert me now,'' Gaius pleaded.

''You have deserted me!'' she whispered, tears beginning to pool within her eyes. ''I've given you my life, my sons, and my loyalty, And all to see you, in the end, embracing death instead of me.'' She could say no more. The finality of his act washed heavily through her mind, forcing her to succumb to the tears that would not be denied.

Gaius rushed to her then, throwing away the goblet and pulling her into his arms. But Fortunata fought him, pummeling his chest with her balled fists until Gaius' arms tightened around her and she could no longer fight. Her arms went around him then, and she buried her face on his shoulder, her sobs ringing in the air.

"Forgive me, my old love, forgive me," Gaius pleaded as his own tears joined hers.

In the distance, the only sounds that could be heard were the birds who called to each other. Then one bird, its red and ochre feathers glistening in the sun, left the branch above Gaius and Fortunata and flew to a tree that stood on the edge of a small, shallow pool.

When it landed it began to sing, but it suddenly became still, as did every living creature on the slopes of Vesuvius. An instant later a deep, low moaning echoed hauntingly, barely audible to Gaius and Fortunata but loud to the animals on the slopes of Vesuvius.

The mirror-calm surface of the pool began to ripple. On the far side of the pool, several marble statues began to vibrate. Another wave of ripples stirred the water, and one statue trembled violently. A sharp cracking filled the air as the statue's base crumpled and the statue itself fell into the pool.

Everything froze in time for several seconds afterward, but then the red and ochre bird began its song again, and soon the entire vineyard called out with life.

Pompeii was undisturbed by this latest tremor, but in Diomed's villa the walls shook with the sounds of a heated argument.

"You will do as I say!" Diomed shouted angrily to his daughter.

Julia shook her head vehemently and stalked out of the house and into the garden, where she turned back and shouted at her father. "Do you think I would go to watch Glaucus die?"

Diomed stepped into the garden, resplendent in the finest of gold-trimmed robes, his face dark with anger. "Yes!" he screamed. Then he paused to take a calming breath. "Julia, how will it look without my daughter beside me?"

Julia's face reflected the amazement she was suddenly feeling. "It will look just as it is—as if you no longer had a daughter," she said in a low, determined voice.

Diomed cut off his angry retort as he was struck with the meaning of what she had just said. He stared at her, shocked, trying to find some way to reason with her, but Lucretia's high-pitched voice called out, interrupting him.

"Julia," he whispered, understanding perhaps for the first time what he had done to his daughter.

"Diomed, do come!" Lucretia ordered as she stepped into the garden, dressed even more richly than Diomed. "They're all waiting for us."

Diomed continued to stare at Julia for another moment, but then he saw the determination in his daughter's eyes and knew that he had lost her. Turning, he looked at his wife and nodded to her. "All right, let's go, Lucretia."

Julia watched them go, releasing her breath only when she heard the front door close behind them. Unable to hold back her tears, she looked at the soft bed of roses near her feet. She didn't know how long she had stared at them, but it was only the sound of her name being called that brought her back to reality.

Turning, she looked toward the back gate. "Clodius," she gasped. "What . . . ?" She stopped when she saw his tightly drawn face and red-rimmed eyes. His sad features called out to her, and she ran to him.

When their hands met, Clodius gazed deeply into her eyes. "Julia, I . . . I have come to say goodbye."

"Goodbye?" she asked, startled. "Where are you going?"

Clodius' eyes filled with tears, and he blinked several times before he spoke. "I swear to you I didn't know they'd kill Glaucus! Arbaces promised they wouldn't. I . . . I only did it because I wanted you."

Julia withdrew her hands from his and raised them to his

face to stroke his cheeks tenderly. Clodius grabbed her hands again, pressing them to him for a moment before he pulled away.

"I betrayed Glaucus—for you," he admitted finally.

"And I for you. Whatever comfort there may be in that," Julia replied bitterly, unable to take her eyes from his. "And worse, there's no way to help him now."

"Julia, I must leave Pompeii," Clodius stated.

"Then take me with you!"

"Me? How can I? I have nothing."

"I don't care. I never cared! Clodius, I won't stay here without you." Her words left no doubt in his mind that she meant just that. Carefully, as if it were the first time he ever held a woman, Clodius brought her to him, his arms winding around her. When they embraced, he kissed her deeply, with passion, but most of all with love.

While the throngs of people continued to wind through the streets and pour into the amphitheater, the priests and priestesses of Isis formed into a large procession led by Arbaces. In their midst was a litter, and seated upon it was a woman dressed in the costume of Isis. Her long hair was covered by a flowered veil, a golden, serpentined mirror was affixed to her forehead, one shapely shoulder was bare, and the other was covered by a black cloak adorned with the silver symbols of the cult.

At first glance one might think the woman to be Ione, but a closer inspection revealed her to be Xenia, the prostitute. With their stringed sistras humming loudly, the priests and priestesses followed Arbaces into the streets. Moments later they were swallowed within the hordes of people heading toward the arena.

Five minutes later the street around the temple was deserted, except for one lone priest who stood on guard at the sacrarium door—and two people hidden within a nearby doorway.

Chloe glanced out once again. Seeing the street deserted, she sighed in relief. "All right, Philos," she began, but the dwarf cut her off.

"Why can't I come to help you find Ione? It's too dangerous to go in there by yourself."

"No!" she stated with finality. "I need you here. Philos,
if I fail to return within the hour, go back to your house and
get my baby from Nydia. Take him to Fulvio, the wine
grower who sells to Burbo."

Saying this, she reached under her shawl and withdrew two
bags of coins. Speaking quickly, she handed him the first.
"Give him this. He will understand." Then she handed him
the second bag. "And use this one for yourself. Philos, I
want you to run from this danger we are in, run as far as you
can . . . and may God be with you."

Philos gazed up at her, silent at last. Hesitantly, he nodded
his head in agreement. Chloe left the doorway and began to
walk casually toward the temple, and its single white-robed
guard.

Just before she reached the sacrarium, her walk changed
and her hips began to undulate sensually. She opened the
shawl to reveal the full swell of her breasts, which she had
powdered lightly before leaving Philos' house. The guard at
the sacrarium entrance turned and saw her. His eyes flickered
across her face before traveling over the inviting mounds of
flesh.

"What are you doing here, Chloe? Everyone's gone to the
games."

Chloe smiled seductively, stepping closely enough to the
priest for him to smell the heavy scent she had applied—and
for him to feel her breasts against his chest.

"Calenus said I'd find you here," she whispered throatily.

"Calenus?" he asked in surprise. "What . . . what did he
want?"

'He wanted me to keep you company. Poor boy," she said
as she ran the tip of her tongue in a slow circle around her
hips. "All alone here while the others have a holiday. Calenus
sent me so that you could have one too." Then she took his
hand and led him inside.

The priest took her to his small cell. Smiling at his good
fortune, he offered her wine. Chloe stepped between the

priest and the wine and kissed his neck softly. Then she
pushed him away.

"Let me," she said with a twinkling laugh. Turning, she
lifted the pitcher of wine, and then, when he couldn't see her,
she reached into a small secret pocket within her shawl and
brought out a pinch of white powder, dropping it into his cup
as she poured the wine.

Turning back to him, she handed him his cup while she
lifted her own to her lips. "To Isis," she toasted.

"To Calenus, and to you," he replied, quickly draining the
cup.

When Chloe went to pour him another, the priest shook his
head and motioned her to him. Smiling, Chloe shook her
head. "Let me dance for you."

The priest's eyes widened, for he had heard of Chloe's
ability with dance, and he nodded his head eagerly. Chloe
began to move without the benefit of music. Her body swayed
sensually, her eyes never leaving his. As she danced, her
hands began to run along her body, cupping her breasts,
offering them to him and then pulling away.

Before she had even removed the shawl, the priest's eyes
began to close. Chloe stopped and stared at him, smiling
broadly now as his head dropped lower. "Be glad you are
only sleeping," she hissed, as the memory of Petrus grew
strong in her mind. She had returned to see him one last time.
And so she had found him, lying dead on the floor of
Olinthus' shop, the dagger that had slain him lying at his
side, still covered with his blood.

Chloe had picked up the dagger and hidden it within her
robes. Now, staring at the drugged priest, she found it hard to
resist plunging the blade into his heart. But she didn't. Instead,
she began to search the empty sacrarium, calling loudly for
Ione, stopping at every door, locked or not.

Then she reached an archway that led to an underground
passage. Walking slowly, Chloe descended into the depths of
the sacrarium, still calling Ione's name.

Halfway along the underground passage she heard a low,

muffled call, and raced toward its source. Before her was a massive wooden door, locked securely.

"Ione!" she cried.

Within the room, Calenus moaned as he pulled himself closer to the door. His head spun with the effort, but when he had awakened in the darkened treasury and realized what had happened, he had sworn vengeance upon Arbaces, and would not give up until he saw it accomplished.

"Let me out of here," he cried to the muffled voice on the other side of the door.

"Who's there?" Chloe asked, unable to recognize the voice through the thick wood.

"Calenus! I command you to open the door!"

Chloe hesitated a moment and then smiled. "Calenus, where is Ione?"

"Chloe? Is that you, Chloe?" Calenus asked. "Hurry, Chloe, I'll pay you well."

"Not until you tell me what you've done with Ione!"

Calenus hesitated until he remembered his resolve to see Arbaces pay for his duplicity. At the same time, however, his wounds had not robbed him of his ability to manipulate situations. "I'll tell you, Chloe. Let me out and I'll tell you everything," he shouted.

"Where is Chloe?" she asked again.

"Let me out!"

"I can't, I have to get help," she said truthfully. "Prove to me that you are not lying."

"If I tell you where she is, you'll leave me to rot."

"Calenus!" Chloe threatened.

"You can't get her out without a key. I have that key. But if you get me out, I'll free her, and I'll testify that I saw Arbaces kill Antonius," he said in a clear voice.

Chloe held her breath for a moment. Calenus' tone told her she had no choice. "I'll get help," she told him.

Ten minutes after Chloe had promised Calenus help, Philos burst into his house, calling excitedly to Nydia, who was holding Chloe's son in her arms. Her told her what had transpired at the temple, and of Chloe's predicament.

"And Calenus told her everything! He saw Arbaces kill Antonius. He'll even swear to it!"

Nydia sat still for a second as she digested the news. Then she carefully placed the baby on its blanket. "We have to get them to stop the games before it's too late. Philos, somehow we've got to get Calenus to the arena, to swear before the magistrate that Arbaces is the murderer."

"How? Calenus is locked in the temple. We can't get him out," Philos cried.

Nydia bent and retrieved her staff. "I know who can help us. Philos, stay here with the baby," she ordered as she stepped through the door, her staff sounding the way.

"But, Nydia!" Philos called helplessly as he stared at the baby, who was just beginning to stir.

Many blocks away from where Philos was rocking Nydia's baby in his arms, Diomed, at the arena, gazed out from the seat of honor at the center of the ringside dais—the seat that usually held Quintus, the magistrate and the elected giver of the games. His eyes searched everywhere, looking at the almost full amphitheater with satisfaction.

The crowd was already loud, and the vendors were selling their goods so quickly that it seemed as if they would not have enough food and drink to last until the lions devoured the last Christian. Diomed rose several times, standing pridefully to wave at an important nobleman or merchant, nodding with the secret knowledge that with these games his ascension to the office of magistrate was almost assured.

Then he gazed down at the arena and toward the tunnel from which the gladiators would appear. "That Marcus had better put on a good show," he said to Lucretia. "Do you have any notion of how much this is costing?"

"Think of what it's buying you, dear," Lucretia replied in a wise whisper. "Rome."

Diomed smiled. Then he turned slowly to watch Quintus and the second magistrate go to their seats. With a supercilious smile on his lips, he waved to the man whose position he had usurped today, and would hopefully replace completely as the lord magistrate after the next elections.

Glancing around once more, Diomed saw that all the important people had arrived. Arbaces was seated off to the right, and the nobles' boxes were filled. Not caring whether the rabble had gotten to their seats, Diomed waved his hand. In response to his gesture, a blast of trumpets sounded and the gladiators started onto the field. The crowd went wild, calling and cheering madly in anticipation of what was to follow.

In a small cell, deep within the lower levels of the sacrarium, Ione lay silently in the darkness. Her breathing was shallow, her eyes closed. The drug Calenus had given her still controlled her system, keeping her sedated and quiet. Although she could hear sounds in the hallway, she could not open her mouth or make a sound herself, not even when she heard her named being called in the faraway distance. Try as she might, Ione could not move at all.

Struggling against the powerful drug, Ione concentrated on forming a word, but her throat and mouth refused to obey. Then she felt a single tear fall from the corner of her eye and slowly trace its way down her cheek.

Chapter Nineteen

Julia packed a small bag, taking only enough clothing for a few days. Although she was leaving her home, she was truly happy. Turning, she smiled at Clodius, who stood to one side watching quietly.

"Come," she said. "I must speak to Medon. Then we will be free."

Nodding, Clodius followed her from the chamber. He would not argue with her now—not after he had at last spoken his heart. They met Medon in the hallway near the front entrance, and Clodius stood silently while Julia said her goodbyes.

"Medon," Julia informed the slave, "when my father returns, tell him I have gone away with Clodius." But then she paused, shaking her head. "No, his anger will come back at you. Please tell him only after he sees I am gone that I took *nothing* of his. Nothing!"

Medon gazed at her with wise eyes, and then looked at Clodius before nodding his agreement.

"Julia," Clodius called, uncaring that Medon was there, "I ask you again to think well. You know I love you. But how will we live? It will be hard for you. Are you sure?"

"We'll live," Julia stated, her eyes filling with strength and determination.

Clodius gazed at her for a long moment, feeling the truth of her words. "Yes, we will."

Before anything else could be said, someone was calling out Julia's name. Medon opened the door and stepped back quickly as Nydia rushed in.

"Julia," Nydia called. "Julia! You must go to your father and stop the games!"

"Nydia? I don't . . ." she began, but Nydia's words cut her off when Clodius' tense hand settled on her shoulder.

"Glaucus is innocent—and we have proof! Calenus, the priest, saw Arbaces do the murder. He will swear to it."

Clodius' hand tightened suddenly on Julia's shoulder. His eyes widened and his breathing turned shallow. "Nydia, where . . ."

"Who is that?" Nydia asked, straining forward to better hear him.

"Clodius," he said quickly. "Nydia, where is Calenus? We must take him to the arena."

"He is imprisoned in the temple."

"Medon," Clodius said as he gazed at the older slave, "are there more slaves about the house?" Medon nodded, and Clodius went on. "Send them to me! Julia, go to your father. Try to stop the fight."

"If it's not too late," she whispered, her hand covering his for a moment. Then she turned and started out the door, knowing that she must run if there was any hope for Glaucus.

Medon ushered three slaves to Clodius, who hurriedly led them toward the temple—and the faint chance that he might be able to save Glaucus.

The call of the trumpets echoed hauntingly within the gladiators' tunnel, where Lydon, dressed only in a simple leather breastplate, watched the other gladiators walk to the exit and step onto the arena's field. The chilling cries of the mob sent a shiver coursing along his spine, and Lydon closed his eyes against this new feeling of revulsion.

When he opened them again, he saw Sporus staring at him. The grizzled gladiator's eyes were filled with concern, but Lydon did not react to Sporus' unvoiced question. A moment later, Sporus went to the exit and stepped into the sun.

Then Gar stood next to him, but the young German looked straight ahead. Shaking his head, Lydon reached out and touched Gar's shoulder. "Good luck, Gar," he said in a low voice.

Gar stared at him, his eyes hot and proud as he jerked his shoulder away and continued to the exit. Then the crowd's cries grew louder and louder, and Lydon heard his name being hailed.

"Lydon," Marcus called as he brought up the end of the procession with Lydon's engraved golden helmet cradled in his arm, his face dark and angry. "Get out there and show yourself! They're calling for you."

"Who is Gar fighting?" Lydon asked, ignoring Marcus' angry words.

"Sporus."

Whirling to face Marcus, Lydon's anger flared. "He's a dead man. You've killed him."

"He's not a dead man, and I'm not a fool," Marcus said, dismissing Lydon's anger with a wave of his free hand. "Diomed did not pay me enough to let my men die. I'm giving him one or two of the new convicts, nothing more— except for Glaucus. Now get out there!" he ordered, thrusting the helmet into Lydon's midsection.

Lydon, his anger still unabated, grabbed the golden helmet from Marcus and flung it away. Turning as it clattered along the tunnel's floor, Lydon moved toward the archway that led into the arena.

A loud roar of approval greeted his appearance on the field, but he did not bother to raise his arms. Instead, he stood with his arms crossed, watching the line of gladiators standing at attention before Diomed.

A sudden hush fell over the amphitheater. As if they were one, ten pairs of gladiators raised their right arms high, their weapons gripped tightly in their fists as they saluted the giver of the games.

"Hail, Pompeii!" they called loudly. "We who are about to die, salute you!"

The crowd erupted with throaty cries at the same time that the roar of a single lion rang out, its ferocity blend-

ing with the bloodlust released by the twenty thousand
screaming citizens of Pompeii.

Glaucus watched the procession of gladiators walk toward
Diomed. Until this very moment he had held out the hope
that Ione would find a way to help him. But when the
morning had passed, and the afternoon arrived without word
from her, his concern about his life had lessened, overwhelmed by his fears for her safety.

But what would it matter? he asked himself. In an hour he
would be dead. Sighing, Glaucus glanced at Olinthus. His eyes
widened momentarily when Olinthus took a step toward the
window and stopped directly in a beam of sunlight. For an
instant the big sailmaker had seemed to be bathed by a strange
glow, but when Olinthus spoke, the magic of the moment
disappeared and reality again set into Glaucus' mind.

"Glaucus," Olinthus said in a strong, comforting voice,
"our last day has come. And as evil as this world can be
made by man, it is hard for me to leave its wonders. To no
longer see the shining of the sun on the waves at sea; the
winds that blew me to a thousand unknown shores; the joy
that came of fashioning a simple piece of work. And all the
things I've missed or left undone."

Glaucus stepped closer to the sailmaker, his eyes searching
the bearded face. "And I—I could look upon this last day
with peace . . . were it not for Ione. But to die, Olinthus,"
he said as he placed his arms on the other's broad shoulders,
"never knowing what her fate is. To think that if she's dead
or suffering it's because she tried to save me, when she could
have saved herself."

Olinthus' arms went around Glaucus, drawing him close,
embracing him as a father would a son, and trying, without
words, to give him whatever comfort he could.

Lydon stood at the mouth of the tunnel watching the
gladiators fight. It was all too obvious to him that the men
were not giving their all, and he saw that the crowd had
drawn the same conclusion.

But when his eyes went to the center of the arena he saw that Gar was swinging madly at Sporus, his face set in strong and determined lines as he charged the more experienced man.

Lydon silently applauded Sporus' attempts to act out the drama of a hard fight while at the same time holding back from striking Gar with any of a dozen strokes that could have penetrated the clumsy attack of the large German.

Victor after victor stood above their fallen foes, and the crowd cheered and booed as their whims dictated. Finally there were only two men left on the field.

Because of the attention that Sporus and Gar drew, the fallen gladiators—most showing splotches of blood from light wounds—were able to escape the field before the crowd called for their deaths.

But then Lydon stiffened when the crowd began to chant his name, for he knew that soon he would have no choice but to face Glaucus. Forcing himself not to think about it, he concentrated on Sporus and Gar, wincing as Gar took another awkward swing at Sporus' head.

On the field, Gar swung ineffectively at Sporus. He stiffened when the crowd booed him and called out Lydon's name instead of his. Angered at this insult, Gar screamed at Sporus and then flailed his sword wildly. He had put so much strength into the blow that he was pulled off balance, and when Sporus ducked the sword, Gar spun and fell to the ground.

Sporus' trained reflexes took over without conscious command. The instant Gar struck the ground, Sporus was astride him, his sword at the German's throat. Then Sporus turned and stared at Marcus, who stood next to Lydon.

Marcus nodded, then looked at Diomed, giving the fat merchant a quick, surreptitious thumb's up.

While Marcus and the gladiators stared at Diomed, the corpulent vote-seeker leaned forward, his arm extended, his fist closed. Before he could give the final verdict, the crowd began to shout wildly, crying out and calling for Gar's death.

Thousands of arms were outstretched, their fists clenched,

their thumbs pointing down. "Death! Death! Death!" they chanted. Diomed surveyed the crowd, and then swallowed to force his suddenly dry throat to open.

Slowly Diomed's thumb descended. The crowd roared its approval.

Sporus stared at Lydon for a long second, the regret written plainly on his face as he held the sword tensely, not yet obeying Diomed's command.

Seeing that protest would be wasted on the mob this day, Lydon nodded his head grimly, accepting the fact that Sporus was waiting for *his* approval and assent, and not Diomed's.

Sporus' face changed then. Looking down at Gar, he spoke in a soft, regretful voice. "Damn you, Gar, for being such a fool." He thrust quickly then, ending the German's life without pain or torture.

As the blade passed through his opponent, Sporus felt the ground shake fiercely. Turning quickly, he saw the amphitheater itself tremble madly, and heard the crowd's first panicked screams.

Glancing at Lydon, he saw the champion of Pompeii holding onto the frame of the archway, staring not at the stands but at the high-peaked mountain in the distance, and at the flume of smoke that spurted angrily into the air.

Diomed sat as though frozen in his seat while the entire amphitheater shook around him. He saw the ground vibrate violently and heard the terrified screams of the people. Then he turned and saw Quintus rising, his features set in grim lines as he held up his hands. Suddenly Diomed found the courage to do what must be done. Rising swiftly, he turned to face the citizens of Pompeii, his arms outstretched, his hands open.

"Good people," he called loudly, "good people, it will pass! Calm yourselves," he shouted. "Calm yourselves," he called again, just as the tremor subsided. He saw in the faces of the people that he had won them for the instant, but only for that long if he did not act quickly. Seizing the opportunity, he shouted across the field to Marcus.

"Lydon! Bring on Lydon!" he commanded. Instantly the

multitude picked up the words, chanting them as if they were a litany. Their cries grew louder and louder, and not one man, woman, or child bothered to look behind them at the angry plume of smoke which still spewed from Vesuvius' peak. Their concentration was on one thing only—the coming death of Glaucus.

"Again!" Clodius ordered. Charging forward, he and the three slaves slammed their shoulders into the treasury door. The hinges splintered, but the door still did not give in.

"Once more and it's done," Clodius said. Together, the four men hit the door, and a loud groan of tortured and breaking wood and leather resounded in the half-lit hallway.

Then the door fell inward, collapsing on the floor. Clodius was the first inside. Oblivious to the wealth that surrounded him, he leaned down to grasp Calenus' robes.

Hauling the priest to his feet, Clodius stared at him for a long moment. "Will you tell the magistrate the truth of Antonius' death?"

"Yes," Calenus stated, his eyes meeting Clodius'.

At his signal the other slaves grasped Calenus' arms and led the injured man away. When they passed one of the sputtering torches, they all saw the heavy mat of dried blood caked on the priest's head and face.

At the entrance of the sacrarium, Chloe ran up to them. "What about Ione?" she demanded. "I know where Ione is, but I can't get her out!"

Clodius looked at her, and then at the priest. "There's no time now if we're to save Glaucus. Stay here until we come back," he ordered as he motioned the others onward toward the amphitheater.

Chloe stared at him for a moment, and then nodded her head in agreement. Turning, she raced back to the cell Ione was locked in, to call her name again and pray for an answer.

The first tremor struck the arena just after two slaves had entered Glaucus' dungeon cell, carrying armor and weapons. When the shaking started, they braced themselves against one wall to wait out the quake and to avoid being hit by shards of stone breaking loose from the ceiling. As they watched, a narrow crack split the wall from floor to ceiling. Then the shaking subsided again, and the two slaves approached Glaucus.

Olinthus, watching them carefully, slowly sank to his knees, his fingers entwined together, his hands held before him as he began to pray. His words rang out, carried by his deep voice.

"It is time," the first slave stated as he held out a piece of armor.

Glaucus stepped away from him, shaking his head adamantly. "I want none of it."

"Of course you do, sir," said the slave. "Who knows, the gods may favor you." Saying this, he winked at the other slave knowingly, and both men burst out with sly laughs. They advanced on Glaucus again, forcing the leather shielding upon him.

Olinthus watched it all as he prayed, and when the slaves laughed, his voice grew louder. After the second slave had closed the last buckle, he whirled on Olinthus, his finger pointing at the sailmaker's bearded face.

"Yes, you devil, mumble for more earthquakes! But we'll soon be rid of you."

Undaunted, Olinthus continued to pray, his eyes meeting Glaucus' at the end of his prayer. "And I shall dwell in the house of the Lord forever."

Glaucus held Olinthus' gaze for a long moment, grateful that he had spent his last hours with this man, and regretting only that he must now go out to die without knowing Ione's fate. He stiffened at the sudden call of another coarse voice.

"It's time," said Marcus, who opened the cell door and grasped Glaucus' arm.

Julia, her knee bleeding from a fall in the street when the earthquake struck, rushed into the amphitheater and began pushing her way through the crowd, moving in a direct line toward the center of the stands where her father sat. Twenty feet behind her, Medon led Nydia forward, trying to help the blind girl keep up with Julia.

* * *

The crowd's clamor turned thunderous while they waited
for the match to begin. Lydon, standing in the mouth of the
tunnel, surveyed the masses and knew that their bloodlust
must be satiated, but he knew also that he had to try and
figure out a way to help Glaucus, and perhaps turn the mob's
favor.

The people began to jump up and down madly when
Glaucus appeared on the field, stepping from the mouth of a
tunnel fifteen yards distant from Lydon.

Glaucus took several more steps but stopped, his stomach
churning sickeningly under the assault of the enormous wall
of sound the crowd was creating. Straightening his shoulders,
and tightening his grip on the sword's handle, he turned to
look at Lydon as the gladiator walked across the field, his
hair pulled back tightly, glistening with oil.

The crowd's calls changed then, and twenty thousand voices
began to chant for Glaucus' death as Marcus came onto the
field, carrying Lydon's trident and net.

Lydon stared at Marcus and shook his head. He slowly
lifted his arm into the air, hefting his sword high as a signal
to Marcus that he would fight with the sword alone.

Then a trumpet's plaintive wail sounded. The mob grew
silent while Lydon and Glaucus slowly finished their walk
toward the center of the arena. The tension grew steadily, and
even the procurator who was walking to them slowed his pace
when he saw the tight, haunted look upon Lydon's face.

A moment before the procurator reached them, Lydon and
Glaucus were face to face. The procurator stopped at their
sides and looked back toward Diomed.

The crowd's roaring began again, building slowly toward a
thunderous crescendo as Diomed stood to accept their applause.

The procurator touched both men on the shoulder as was
the custom, but Lydon ignored him, keeping his eyes locked
on Glaucus'. "Glaucus, listen to me . . ."

"Quiet!" ordered the procurator. "Begin the . . ."

Lydon whirled on him, his sword flashing in the air
threateningly. "Leave us," he hissed at the procurator who

had already stepped back in fear. As the man edged away from them, Lydon faced Glaucus again.

"I know what you must do. Lydon, I won't oppose you," Glaucus whispered.

Keeping his voice as low as the nobleman's, Lydon spoke quickly and urgently. "No. Fight bravely! Get them to your favor. They may let me spare you with just a wound."

"Listen to them, Lydon," Glaucus said as the cries for his death grew even louder. "They'll have blood, and if not mine, then it will be yours!"

"Then let them have it!" Lydon declared heatedly.

"No! How can I?" he whispered, knowing that he could not take any life, much less this man he respected so deeply.

"Damn you, Glaucus! Help me save you! Fight me!" Lydon pleaded as he raised his sword and swung at the Greek.

Glaucus reacted instinctively to the attack, bringing his own sword up and parrying the blow. The sound of metal rang in the air, accented by the quick roar of approval from the mob.

"Good! Fight me!" Lydon commanded, swinging at Glaucus again. But the Greek barely managed to deflect the blow, and Lydon whirled to face him again. "Now, Glaucus," he hissed, "thrust!"

Glaucus did as he was told, lunging half-heartedly at the gladiator, who easily sidestepped the attack but in so doing made it look like a very close call.

Julia, her breath ragged from the long run, burst through the crowd not five feet from her father. She froze for a moment when she saw Lydon's sword flash toward Glaucus, but willed her feet to carry her forward, just as Medon and Nydia reached the entrance to the box of honor.

Medon held Nydia back then, making her wait as Julia called out to her father. He saw Diomed turn a startled face toward her and half rise from his seat.

"Stop the fight, Father!" she demanded.

"J-Julia!" he stuttered. "Why?"

Behind Diomed, Quintus sat straighter, taking in everything, intuitively sensing that something was badly amiss.

Before Julia could reply, the crowd exploded with a derisive uproar of boos and hisses as Lydon deflected another ineffectual blow from Glaucus, and then turned from the Greek to strut in his old, cocky manner toward the stands, his arms held high for applause. The crowd, dissatisfied with what they were witnessing, booed Lydon even louder. "Kill him! Kill the Greek!" they shouted over and over.

Arbaces, sensing what Lydon was trying to do, rose to his feet, signaling his followers to join him as he began to run toward the very edge of the arena, his voice rising in a chant that his followers picked up. "Kill the murderer! Kill Glaucus!" Soon the people in the stands spilled out to join the priest, and the guards were suddenly hard-pressed to hold them back.

Julia, undetected by the crowd, cried out to her father. "Glaucus is innocent! He did not kill Antonius!"

Diomed tore his eyes from his daughter to look at the crazed mob. He shook his head slowly at Julia. "They'll kill us all if I try to stop it," he pleaded.

"Lord Magistrate," cried Clodius, who now barged through the crowd. Behind him came the slaves carrying Calenus.

Arbaces, near the rear of his priests, turned just in time to see Clodius bring Calenus toward the magistrates. He stared at the men and knew instantly that his reign was over. Reacting quickly, he lowered his head and began to weave his way through the crowd, calling to several of his followers to join him as the mob swelled against the guards protecting the field of the arena itself.

"Arbaces killed Antonius!" Clodius shouted, pushing Calenus forward. "Arbaces, not Glaucus. Ask him!" he yelled, thrusting Calenus to his knees before the magistrate.

On the field, Lydon saw the danger in the mob and turned to Glaucus. He advanced on the man, knowing that there was nothing else he could do.

Glaucus, fearing not only his death but Lydon's as well at the hands of the bloodthirsty mob, knew that he could not let

Lydon sacrifice himself uselessly. Slowly, as Lydon neared him, Glaucus sank to his knees and stared up at the gladiator.

"Get up!" Lydon ordered, his anger bursting forth as he raised his sword.

"I will not allow both of us to die needlessly."

"Get up, damn you!" Lydon cried, emotion tearing through him when he saw that Glaucus was prepared to face his death so that he could survive.

"Lydon, if you can, save Ione," he whispered. "Now! End it!"

Lydon stared at Glaucus, his muscles knotting painfully. Then the crowd was suddenly still, sensing that death was near. Drawing in a deep, shuddering breath, Lydon tensed his muscles for the final stroke.

Deep within the core of the earth, the giant plates shifted once again, but this time their movement released a mile-deep well of gas which shot upward in a rush to escape its ancient prison.

The gas pushed through the boiling lava, pulling it along as it struck barrier upon barrier. But nothing could stand in its way now. At every barrier, the gases fought against the stones, until the stones shattered and opened even more pathways toward the surface.

Then all the gases, followed by the rushing, boiling lava, merged together and battered at the very base of the mountain called Vesuvius. With a loud cracking explosion, the final obstacle was battered away and the newly formed ocean of lava rose within the waiting shaft, led by the gases as they sped toward the pinpoint of light at the very peak of the mountain.

Then, like a virgin within the throes of her first orgasm, Vesuvius exploded with a cataclysmic roar that blew the peak of the mountain high into the air.

Lydon's arm froze when the ground buckled and the loud, blasting explosion shook the earth. The ground trembled wildly, growing more violent with each passing second. Then Lydon, his body frozen to the spot, saw a thousand-foot

flame shoot into the air; as he watched, Mount Vesuvius'
peak shattered and was blown apart.

Standing in the center of the arena, Lydon watched wide
eyed as the roof of the stands began to collapse. Columns
split apart, falling on the mob below. People were thrown
into the air as their screams for death changed into terrified
cries for mercy.

Lydon threw his sword from him and spun, dragging Glaucus
to his feet. "We may live yet!" he shouted, pulling Glaucus
with him. But when he looked at the entrance to the tunnels,
he saw that a large mob had already formed near them.
Staring at the center of the stands, Lydon thought he saw his
father.

The instant Vesuvius erupted, the tiers of stands began to
break apart. Julia stood paralyzed as Quintus, just standing to
go to Calenus, was knocked from his feet and buried beneath
a large stone that had broken loose from above him.

Behind them, Medon tried to protect Nydia from the panic
around them. He saw Arbaces as he broke free from the mob
and started toward the exit. Medon tried to stop him, but the
priest pushed the slave and the blind woman roughly aside in
his frantic bid for freedom.

Clodius, hearing Nydia's scream, whirled in time to see
Arbaces racing away. Without thinking, he charged after
him, but was thrown from his feet by yet another bucking of
the stands. Willing himself to rise, Clodius staggered after
Arbaces, finally reaching him and grabbing his robe.

Arbaces whirled, brandishing a dagger. He lunged at Clodius
and sunk the blade into the nobleman's stomach.

Clodius screamed, staring unbelievingly at Arbaces. Jerking the dagger free, Arbaces raced from the amphitheater
while Clodius sank slowly to his knees.

"Clodius!" Julia screamed in horror as she started toward
the man she loved. But Diomed grabbed her.

"Julia! Come with us!" he ordered.

"No!" she screamed defiantly. Pulling her arm violently
from her father's grasp, she ran to Clodius' side and knelt

beside him. "Clodius," she cried, cradling his head in her hands and drawing him to her breasts. Just then Glaucus and Lydon reached the stands and raced toward them.

"Father!" Lydon shouted as he guided Glaucus through the horror of what was happening. Explosion after explosion ripped through the air. The ground bucked violently as though trying to dislodge everything upon it.

Lydon finally reached Medon's side, grasping him in a tight embrace even as he looked at Nydia's fear-stricken face. When he released his father, he started toward Nydia but saw that Glaucus had reached her first and was holding her by the shoulders.

"Nydia," Glaucus said, "what happened to Ione? Where is she?" he asked.

"Come! Quickly!" Lydon ordered, grabbing Nydia's hand and freeing her from Glaucus' hold.

"No!" Nydia said, refusing to be pulled along by Lydon. "I must help Glaucus get Ione," she cried.

"She's alive?" he asked.

Lydon stared at Glaucus, and then at Nydia, sensing that even now, with death raining upon them from every direction, she would rather be with Glaucus. "Then we will get her together," he said at last. Turning, Lydon gazed imploringly at his father.

"We can't leave Olinthus," Medon stated with finality.

"Oh, dear God!" Glaucus cried as he stared from Medon to Lydon. "He's trapped. Lydon, please, listen to me. I'll go with Nydia. You must help free Olinthus. Then come to my ship. I will have Ione and Nydia there, waiting."

They stared at each other for a moment. When another eruption split the air, Lydon nodded his head. With one last regretful gaze at Nydia, he turned and led his father back into the frenzied mob.

"Where is she?" Glaucus asked again.

"Locked in the temple of Isis," Nydia replied as he grasped her arm and began to lead her through the panic-stricken mob.

Glaucus stopped suddenly when he saw Julia leaning over Clodius.

"Go, Julia, please," Clodius whispered. Then he coughed, and bloody spittle oozed from the corner of his mouth.

Shaking her head, Julia drew him closer to her. "No, I won't leave you now," she cried.

Releasing Nydia's hand for a moment, Glaucus bent down. "Clodius," he called in a choked voice.

Clodius moved his eyes and saw Glaucus, realizing that the friend he had betrayed was alive. "Glaucus," he called in a barely audible voice. "Forgive me."

"Clo—" Glaucus began, shaking his head in dismissal of the words, but Clodius cut him off.

"Ta—take Julia with you," he pleaded.

"No!" Julia declared, drawing Clodius tighter to her breast and shaking her head defiantly at Glaucus.

Glaucus, understanding what Julia was doing, nodded his head. "Rest well, my friend," he said to Clodius. Tightening his hold on Nydia, he joined the frightened, screaming crowd exiting from the arena. For the moment the earth had stopped its violent trembling.

Chapter Twenty

Vesuvius' eruption shook the very foundations of the earth, shooting tons of earth, boulders, and pieces of molten lava high into the sky. As it burst forth, Gaius and Fortunata were thrown to the ground. For a moment they lay on the ground, stunned, while giant cracks opened in the crust of the earth.

The land cried out as it was torn apart, and trees, centuries old, groaned in protest as they were torn from their roots and swallowed into any one of a hundred fissures.

Then a huge boulder—one of the many Vesuvius had spat into the sky—plunged back to the earth, shattering the villa that Gaius had constructed thirty years before. The roof collapsed under the weight of the giant rock, and Fortunata cried as she watched the walls of her home crumble to the earth.

Gaius, although growing weaker from the poison he had consumed earlier, gathered his strength and drew his wife into his arms. It was then he saw that she cried not in fear but in sorrow for all that was being taken from her.

Dozens of smaller rocks began to fall around them as Vesuvius erupted again, shooting gas and flames thousands of feet into the sky. They watched as an ocean of molten red lava gushed from what had once been the mountain's peak. It quickly formed a river that began to cascade down the slopes, eating everything in its path. As he saw it come toward them, Gaius spoke in a gentle, level voice.

"I had thought, at last, to take a stand, to end my vacillation between cowardice and courage. But you see how even nature mocks me—with her *own* suicide. All my idle speculation was as useless as my life has been."

Fortunata stared at him, her tears ending now as she listened to his words. "No, Gaius, my love, not useless. We had each other," she said before brushing his taut lips with hers.

Gaius tried to lift his hand to her face, but the poison was working more quickly now, and his arm fell back uselessly. He sighed with the exertion but did not lose the tender smile he had for his wife.

"But all is well, Fortunata. Cleansed of this world's corruption, the universe may someday bring forth a better." Gaius laughed, but a racking cough seized him. When it stopped, he blinked away the darkness. "Yet how can it be better, unless devoid of man himself?"

Then his eyes closed, and he became still. Fortunata buried her head upon his chest. Her sobs grew loud, and her grief made her deaf to the rushing river of lava that poured down the slope, not twenty yards from where she lay.

The hordes continued to rush from the amphitheater, running in panic, not caring who they trampled as they searched for escape. Above them a dark cloud of ash was forming, lit by bits of still red and burning rocks that fell randomly upon the city and its people.

Diomed, holding his wife close, edged his way from the arena, keeping his bulk between her and the shoving masses. He paused at a wall just as another tremor hit. The wall vibrated madly, and Diomed pulled Lucretia away an instant before it split, shattering into hundreds of pieces and tumbling down upon the terrified people.

"We must get to the water. To your ship!" Lucretia cried when they were out of reach of the wall and of the panicked people.

Diomed stared at her, his mind vacillating between what she had said and what he knew would happen later. "There will be looting. Our fortune is in the villa. Your jewelry . . ."

"I . . . Do we have the time?" she asked, realizing she could never go back to what they once were.

"We must," Diomed said, his greed and stupidity overwhelming the last of his good sense. Together, hand in hand, they ran toward their villa. Behind them, another fault opened in the street, swallowing several people.

The fumes grew thicker. Ashes and burning rock fell relentlessly from the sky as Lydon pulled Medon with him across the arena's field. They reached the first tunnel and found it partially blocked. Pushing aside some rocks that partially blocked the entrance, Lydon stepped inside with Medon close on his heels.

A rumbling started then, and Lydon held on to his father until it passed. Part of the tunnel's ceiling gave way with a thudding crash. With the dust whirling around them, Lydon heard a groan of pain and ran toward the sound. There he found Sporus, trapped beneath a pile of rubble.

"Sporus," he called, bending over the blood-soaked face of his former friend. Lydon could see the edge of death in Sporus' eyes. Moving quickly, he began to remove the stones that pinned his colleague, but the gladiator opened his eyes and cried out in a cracked voice.

"No. Lydon, get free. Oh, Lydon, I did love you," he whispered.

Lydon reached down to Sporus' exposed hand and grasped it as the gladiator closed his eyes for the final time. A moment later, feeling his father's hand on his shoulder, Lydon stood, unashamed of the tears on his cheeks.

"He was a good man, despite himself," he said to his father. With a final glance at Sporus, Lydon and Medon continued through the tunnel.

Just as they stepped into the hallways that led to the dungeons, another tremor—the most severe yet—jerked Lydon and Medon from their feet. Even as he fell, Lydon reached out to his father, but Medon had been hurled away from him.

Forcing himself to his feet, Lydon called out, but a loud cracking resounded in the hallway. He looked quickly at the ceiling, where he saw a large support beam break away.

Reacting instinctively, Lydon ducked his head and rolled out of the path of the crashing beam. He regained his footing at the end of the somersault and, coughing from the dust that filled his lungs, began to search desperately for Medon.

"Father!" he shouted over and over, until at last he heard Medon's low cry. Moving carefully through the debris-strewn floor, Lydon reached him, but almost turned away, sickened by the sight that greeted his eyes.

Only Medon's head, arm, and shoulder were visible from under the huge wooden beam that pinned him to the floor. Without hesitating, Lydon bent and put his shoulder to the beam. The veins of his neck bulged and the highly trained muscles of his body knotted powerfully as he pushed against the beam with every ounce of his strength. But his valiant effort failed, and the beam held steady.

"Lydon," Medon gasped when he opened his eyes and saw his son trying to free him. "Lydon, you must save yourself."

Ignoring his father's plea, Lydon again set himself against the beam, summoning up the last of his strength in a maddened attempt to rescue his father. A moment later he realized that he was defeated, and sank back.

Then he looked at his father, and saw Medon's eyes caressing his face lovingly. Lydon's throat constricted and pain filled his chest. "If I can't save you, Father, then we'll end our lives together."

"Please, Lydon . . . Son," he began, but stopped as a cough racked his body. When the spasm passed, his eyes were clear. "I can't let you die here," Medon whispered.

Drawing in a deep, tortured breath, Lydon shook with anger. "Where's your all-powerful God now, Father?" he demanded. Once more Lydon struggled to his feet and threw himself against the beam.

Medon, watching his son's anguished efforts, closed his eyes and began to pray. Even as the words left his lips, he heard Lydon shout loudly and felt the beam shift minutely.

Olinthus, having seen the destruction of the amphitheater from the barred window of the dungeon, knew that at last God had come to the aid of his people. Turning carefully, while the tremors savaged the ground he strode, Olinthus knelt on the soft dirt of the cell and began to pray. He remained there for a long time, praying even after the third wave of quakes had struck.

As the screams of the people faded and his prayers flowed upwards, another horrendous wrenching hit the arena, almost knocking Olinthus from his knees. He heard a loud crack, and his eyes fastened on the locked door of his cell. He saw the door tremble violently, and watched in amazement as the wall around it shattered and the door fell to the earth.

With a prayer of thanksgiving on his lips, Olinthus sprang to his feet, knowing that God had given him one last opportunity. He ran down the corridor, avoiding whatever debris he could as he made for the small shaft of light that signaled his freedom. He raced up the steps and burst onto the field only a few seconds before the tunnel collapsed behind him.

Olinthus paused for a moment and looked around. When his eyes scanned the amphitheater, his breath caught in his chest. The entire center of the stands was collapsed in a screeching, groaning landslide of wood, stone, and human life.

Turning from the spectacle of death, Olinthus searched for a way out, ignoring the ashes that fell upon him and the burning specks that stuck to his clothing. But when he turned to race toward an opening in the wall, he heard the terrifying wail of the lions. Their cages had been torn apart and they were now roaming the field, not twenty feet from him.

He saw their large, fear-glazed eyes, and stood paralyzed as they charged toward him. Throwing his arms across his face, Olinthus once again prepared himself to meet his death. With a prayer forming on his lips, he felt the large beasts rush past him and toward the very spot he had hoped to use for his escape.

Turning again, Olinthus sprinted toward the stands. When he reached them, he climbed through the body-strewn rubble. He paused as he saw Julia and Clodius, embracing each other in death as they had never done in life.

Forcing his eyes from their lifeless bodies, Olinthus scampered across the remains of the amphitheater and was soon running along the fissure-torn streets of Pompeii.

Having seen his end coming, Arbaces plunged the knife into Clodius' stomach and then sped out of the arena, followed by two of his priests. He reached the street only seconds before the first violent tremor shook the city. Instantly a chasm opened before him, like the jaws of a jackal waiting to devour him.

But he was agile enough to jump across to safety and run onward to the temple of Isis itself. The amphitheater collapsed behind him. Explosion after explosion thundered in his ears as Vesuvius gave vent to its rage, spewing ash and burning stone upon the city which it had given birth to.

Buildings toppled everywhere he looked, crushing people all around him, but Arbaces cared only for himself. He ran quickly until he reached the very steps of the temple. Then he was inside, with the two priests still at his heels.

Arbaces called them to him when he entered the sacrarium and raced to the lower passage, ignoring the quivering of the floor beneath his feet. He stopped at the treasury, seeing that the door was broken inward. Stepping inside, he saw the mountains of golden jewelry, silver platters, and stores of coin that had been strewn across the floor, the coffers overturned by the frenzy of the volcano's eruption.

"Hurry, damn you!" he shouted to the priests, handing them leather sacks. The three began to stuff the sacks with gold, but before they were half full another more violent tremor shook the treasury room, knocking one of the priests to the ground.

The two neophytes looked at each other, their eyes rounded with terror. Then, together, they threw the bags to the floor and ran from the room, fleeing the death they saw falling upon them. "Fools!" Arbaces shouted, picking up two of the half-filled sacks and following the priests along the corridor. Arbaces froze at the entrance of the sacrarium when he heard voices he recognized. Slipping outside, he pressed his back to the wall just as Glaucus and Nydia turned a corner of the corridor, urgently calling out Ione's name.

He waited, his breath held tightly, until their voices faded, and only then did he leave the wall and walk carefully toward the open temple itself.

Glaucus, with a firm grasp on Nydia's hand, maneuvered her through the panicked, disorderly mob, and pulled her into an alleyway to wait out the worst of the quake. When the screaming, churning mob had thinned somewhat, he guided her to the temple of Isis and entered the sacrarium, arriving only a short while after Arbaces and the priests.

A tremor struck the temple and Glaucus pulled Nydia to him, sheltering her from the debris that fell around them. When the ground settled again, he started into the sacrarium.

"Where is she? Which cell?" he asked as he looked down the multidoored corridor.

"I don't know," Nydia cried. "Where is Chloe? She knows."

"Ione! Ione!" Glaucus shouted as he began to wrench open door after door. They ran down the corridor, calling out her name, but there was no answer. They turned back only a second after Arbaces had slipped out the exit.

Glaucus spotted the open door that led downward. Grasping Nydia's hand tightly, he went toward it, still calling Ione's name. At the bottom of the steps, he shouted once again.

"Ione," called Nydia, her voice hoarse now from the shouting.

"Wait," Glaucus whispered, his hand squeezing hers tightly. From the far distance came a barely audible sound. Then it was repeated.

"Ione," Nydia whispered, able to hear the woman's voice more sharply than Glaucus.

They walked forward slowly, their senses focused on the faint calls. When they passed the treasury room, Glaucus could finally make out the words. It was indeed Ione who called.

"Help me. . . . Help me. . . ."

Glaucus moved quickly. A moment later he stood before a locked door and stared at the spidering cracks radiating from its frame. Stepping back, he took a deep breath and charged forward, his shoulder slamming hard against the wood.

Chloe had been waiting for what seemed endless hours. She prowled the underground corridor, calling out Ione's name each time she reached the locked cell. There was no response. Then she went outside into the open temple to await the aid she prayed would soon arrive.

When the first earthquake struck, she was knocked against a column, striking her head at its base. Dazed, she sat on the floor until her strength returned and she could pull herself to her feet. Looking about her, she gasped when a towering flame shot skyward from the top of the mountain.

As another violent wave of tremors ripped through Pompeii, Chloe held onto the column with all her strength. When the ground stopped its mad shaking, she took several calming breaths in an effort to hold back the panic that welled within her.

Then came the sounds of people screaming and the horrendous groaning of the buildings that were falling apart all around the city. When she looked up again, she saw a black mass slowly descending from the sky, blanketing all of Pompeii. Small pieces of rock rained down from the sky, and with them glowing charcoals of lava that hit indiscriminately.

Across the way, one building in the forum erupted in flames, and soon Chloe herself was choking from the fumes of the volcano and the burning city.

But still she refused to run from the temple and leave Ione trapped within. Gathering her courage, she readied herself to return to the darkened depths of the sacrarium. Just as she was about to leave the protection of the column, she heard footsteps running toward her, and she shrank back.

She saw Arbaces run past her, followed by two priests. "Where are you?" she called to Medon and Nydia. "Glaucus, be alive," she prayed. Holding herself back, she waited for help to capture Arbaces and to free Ione. Suddenly another tremor struck, this one more violent than any before it. Again Chloe was thrown to the ground. While she lay there, covering her head against the debris that fell from the roof of the temple, Glaucus and Nydia ran past without seeing her. Nor did she see them.

After Chloe had thrown the rubble from her body, she rose unsteadily to her feet and leaned against the column again, to wait for help.

Hearing footsteps coming from the sacrarium, she slipped around to the back of the column, her hand dipping inside her robe to grasp the dagger hidden there. Two young priests burst from the building, their faces twisted into masks of fright. Without pausing, they ran into the streets where they were soon enveloped by the howling, maddened crowd.

Then Arbaces came out, moving slowly, stealthily forward. Chloe held her breath as she watched him, noticing the two heavy sacks in his hands. When he moved forward, Chloe slipped from the column and quickly hid behind another, stalking the man she now hated above all others.

Arbaces reached the statue of Isis and paused to look about him, just as another quake struck the city. The center of the forum split open, swallowing a mass of screaming people. The temple shook and more of the ceiling fell inward.

Arbaces stared at the statue of Isis, seeing it tremble. Its base cracked with the sound of striking lightning, and he whirled in terror from the death that was slowly toppling toward him.

He began to run, but stopped when he saw Chloe step from behind a column.

"You!" he cried, breathing easier with the recognition of the prostitute.

Chloe smiled at him as she lunged, sinking the dagger's blade deep into his chest.

"No!" he screamed as he stared at the dagger protruding from his chest.

Chloe watched the high priest, as the realization of his death spread across his features. He shook his head slowly and then staggered away from her, finally sinking to the floor.

"Why?" he whispered.

"For Petrus," she told him as his eyes closed for the last time.

Turning, Chloe saw Philos stagger into the temple, her son cradled in his arms, protected from the putrid air by a blanket.

"Chloe!" he cried, as another tremor shook the temple. Seeing the ceiling begin to crack, Philos rushed across the floor. He held the baby tight against him with one arm while he shoved Chloe out of the way just as a huge piece of stone fell. Then he grabbed her unsteady hand and jerked her after him. "We must get out of here!"

"Ione!" she argued.

"Now!" he ordered, dragging her from the temple. Behind them, Vesuvius exploded again, sending yet another heavy cloud of flaming lava toward Pompeii.

The door held against Glaucus' shoulder for only a second before the hinges cracked and the wood splintered. Stepping back again, he lowered his shoulder and hurled himself at the door. An instant later he crashed through, stumbling into the cell itself.

Spinning, he saw Ione rush toward him, tears pouring from eyes filled with love. Then they were together, holding each other tightly. Their lips met and they tasted the sweetness of each other.

"Oh, Glaucus," she cried when their mouths parted, "you're alive."

He gazed at her for a moment more, drinking in the radiance of her face before he pulled her closer again. "We must get out of the city," he said, leading her out of the cell.

With Ione and Nydia in his firm embrace, he swiftly fled the underground corridor of the sacrarium and reached the doorway only a minute after Vesuvius' last eruption had dissipated.

They raced across the temple floor, stopping when they saw Arbaces' body lying in their path. Glaucus and Ione stared at the dead man with revulsion, but for only a moment. Glaucus quickly galvanized his mind into action and led the women to the steps of the temple, where he and Ione guided Nydia down the rubble-filled steps.

The air was thick with ash and fumes. Fires burned everywhere, and Glaucus' eyes stung painfully. He wiped them, but it was useless. He could only see a few feet away. He turned to Ione and saw her clawing at her eyes desperately.

Fear gripped Glaucus as he realized that they could not penetrate the swarming masses. He stood for a moment, staring at the blurry figures of the people charging every which way. Three feet in front of him, a woman's hair exploded with flames when a small piece of flying lava lodged within her curls. She fell to the ground, and an instant later was trampled beneath a thousand feet.

"We can't get through," Glaucus stated. "I can't see."

Nydia knew exactly where they were and, for once in her life, felt no disadvantage. She knew her blindness at this moment was their only salvation.

Reaching out to Glaucus, she grasped his wrist. "This way," she ordered. "Come this way." When he hesitated, she stamped her foot impatiently. "I've made my way about Pompeii all my life in darkness. Come!"

Glaucus glanced at Ione and saw her nod her head. Sighing, Glaucus let Nydia guide him through the ever-thickening darkness.

Olinthus, free from the dungeon and the arena, fought his way through the mobs, pushing relentlessly forward toward the waterfront and his shop. He hoped that he would find there whatever members of his small band had survived and that he would find a way to save them from the doomed city.

Looking up, he saw the sky darkening further, as more and more ash filled the air. He knew the darkness would grow stronger, and he redoubled his effort to get through the panic-ridden streets.

Turning a corner, he tried to stop when he saw Catus floundering helplessly ten feet from him. "Catus!" he shouted impotently, while the frenzied mob continued to sweep him along. Seeing the young boy stumble and fall, Olinthus flailed his arms wildly at all in his way, until he cleared a path toward Catus.

Bending, he scooped the boy into his arms just before the crowd could trample him. Olinthus breathed deeply of the sulfurous air, unmindful of the burning in his lungs as he pressed the boy to his massive chest and began to work his way toward the waterfront.

He stopped again when he heard his name called frantically. Recognizing Chloe's voice, he searched everywhere, but the denseness of the falling ash did not allow him to see more than a few yards. He did not hear her voice again, as the crowd surged forward, dragging him along within its midst.

Vesuvius gave vent to yet another mighty explosion, sending more ashes into the heavens. Lava gushed from its peak and rushed downward toward the city at the same moment that Nydia led Glaucus and Ione onto the waterfront.

Glaucus stopped, his eyes wide with disbelief at the frenzied mass of people who shoved, pushed, and even killed to get onto one of the boats at the dock. Flames licked skyward from the wooden buildings along the waterfront, and the cries of the dying echoed horribly in the air.

No matter which way Glaucus turned, he saw death. Many people in their panic rushed to board a ship and slipped and fell into the frothing sea, whose waves were reaching higher and higher as the volcano made the ocean's bottom churn with quake after quake.

Still grasping Nydia and Ione's hands, Glaucus led them forward. Then he saw Olinthus, his bearded face covered with soot, emerge from Marine Street and head toward the docks.

Olinthus paused when he saw them. "Glaucus!" he shouted. "This way, over here!" He veered toward them, Catus still protected by his strong arms.

"Thank God!" Glaucus yelled as he pulled Nydia and Ione forward toward the sailmaker. So intent was he on reaching

Olinthus that he did not realize until too late that Nydia had slipped her hand from his.

Nydia hesitated for only a moment when her hand was free. She was not yet ready to flee. There was another thing for her to do, and she knew that unless she tried she would regret it for the rest of her life. Turning and shrinking back from the crowd, Nydia retraced the steps that she had just traveled.

"My ship! Get to my ship," Glaucus shouted to Olinthus. Turning, they looked at the docks and saw a ship burst into flames. People screamed madly, and the crowd surged backward, but Glaucus and Olinthus held firm until the crushing wave of humanity eased.

"Now!" Olinthus commanded, leading them to Glaucus' ship. Glaucus, suddenly aware that Nydia was not with them, glanced back but did not see her.

"Nydia," Ione cried, looking about also, her eyes large and frightened. "Glaucus! Where is Nydia? Nydia!" Ione screamed. She turned back into the crowd, trying to go after the blind girl, but Glaucus caught her and held her fast.

"We must get to the ship, Ione," he told her in a firm, unyielding voice.

Lydon staggered under the weight of his father, but refused to give up as he carried Medon on his back. He was sickened and disgusted by everything he had seen. The city was crumbling around him, dissolving within the ever-darkening cloud of ash. The people, rather than helping each other, trampled one another in their wild bid for freedom.

When he had worked his father free from the fallen beam, and then secured him to his back, Lydon had slowly made his way out of the amphitheater. As he staggered over the debris, he saw Marcus, lying half crushed beneath a column, plunge his own dagger into his heart. The man who was called the merchant of death then jonied the untold numbers of people he had dispatched before him.

Tightening his hold on the bindings that secured his father to him, Lydon entered the street and pushed through the crazed mob. But he stopped again when he saw Nydia flung against a wall by the rushing crowd.

Spinning, and staggering under his father's weight, he fought his way slowly toward her.

"I can't go on! Leave me," Medon gasped. "Help her."

"You must!" Lydon shouted. "We're almost there."

Nydia stiffened when she heard Lydon's voice. Turning slowly, she called out to him. "Lydon. . . . Please, Lydon, help me."

Lydon reached Nydia's side and, moving slowly, lowered his father until his back was against the wall.

"Lydon," Nydia cried, "I must find . . ."

Lying in a doorway three feet from Nydia, Chloe opened her eyes and saw her friend standing near her. "Nydia," she called in a strangled, weak voice.

"Who?" she asked, but quickly she realized it was Chloe who spoke.

"Nydia," Chloe whispered in a choked voice. "Nydia, please take my baby. Nydia," she gasped. "Save him."

Lydon saw that blood ran down Chloe's cheek from a deep wound in her scalp. Philos lay silently next to her, his neck twisted in an impossible position. The baby lay silently in Chloe's arms, his eyes wide and frightened as he looked all around him.

"Oh, Chloe, no," Nydia whispered, unable to stop her tears.

Lydon tore his eyes from Chloe's the instant he saw them glaze over in death. Turning, he went to Medon. "Father," he whispered as he knelt beside him.

Medon gazed at Lydon, smiling tenderly at his son's concern. "I love you, my son," he said in a low voice. Then he sighed, and closed his eyes for the last time.

"Father!" Lydon screamed, grasping Medon's shoulders and shaking him harshly. "Father!" Unable to stop his tears, Lydon pulled Medon to him and held him close. "Goodbye, Father," he cried. Then he heard a baby wail, and turned to see Nydia clutching Chloe's son to her breast and heading into the crowd.

"Nydia!" he shouted. Releasing his father, he rose to his feet. He saw her stop and turn at his call. He raced to her, embracing her and the baby tightly just as a wall near them gave way with a thundering crash.

The waterfront was ablaze with the flames of destruction. For blocks, buildings burned wildly. Sparks flew into the air, sails caught fire, and ships exploded with the cries and screams of death.

Olinthus, his body dripping with sweat, ignored the acrid fumes searing his lungs as he worked on the rigging of Glaucus' ship. Glaucus stood guard, making sure the ship would not be overrun by the fleeing citizens of Pompeii. Ione and Catus were in the center of the deck, their eyes desperately searching the dock for anyone they knew. Behind them sat a half-dozen Christians they had rescued.

When the last knot was tied, Olinthus jumped to the deck. "She's rigged and ready," he told Glaucus.

"No!" Ione cried, rushing to the two men. "We can't leave with Nydia!"

An explosion of flames erupted on Diomed's ship, not thirty yards from theirs. Glaucus and Olinthus looked at it before exchanging worried glances.

"We may have no choice now," Glaucus told Ione as sparks flew in the air toward them. He gazed deeply into her saddened eyes and saw tears roll down her cheeks. Closing his eyes against the pain, he turned toward the others. "Cast off!" he ordered.

A sudden rumbling filled the air of the waterfront. Every eye turned to watch the gate at the entrance to Marine Street burst apart under the assault of a thousand crazed people rushing toward freedom.

"Dear God," Ione whispered.

Glaucus motioned the others to continue to cast off, willing himself not to hear the sounds of the dying multitudes. But he froze when he heard Ione's voice call out.

"Nydia!" she yelled. "Nydia! Here!"

Whirling, Glaucus stared past Ione and saw Lydon charging toward them. He held a bundle above his head, out of harm's way from the crowd; Nydia stood next to him, her arm locked in his.

Glaucus jumped from the ship to the dock, knocking several people aside in his rush to get to Lydon. He caught Nydia and embraced her tightly before spinning her and handing her over to Olinthus, who helped her into the ship. He took the baby from Lydon and handed him to another set of eager hands.

Glaucus and Lydon stared at each other for a long, intense moment, until the emotion both felt at seeing each other alive filled their hearts, and they embraced.

In the ship, Ione and Nydia clung together, both crying tears mixed equally with despair and joy. The moment Glaucus and Lydon stepped aboard, Olinthus nodded to the men who manned the oars. The small ship broke free from the dock, leaving behind the dying city that was once proudly called Pompeii.

Epilogue

Throughout the long night that followed that day of death and horror, the survivors in the ships that had been able to escape floated far out in the harbor, watching the final destruction of their city.

Even through the massive cloud of ash, the glowing red bed of lava could be seen, moving inexorably onward, burying everything under its fiery depths. Buildings continued to collapse, and even a mile out at sea the death cries of those unable to escape floated in the air—as a grim reminder to those who lived.

It was after midnight when the coalescing waves of flaming lava reached Diomed's villa. It flowed slowly over his body and that of Lucretia. The couple had died when a shockwave had torn the stone ceiling from its mooring and sent it crashing down upon them. The jewelry and coins they had gathered had fallen from their hands, now only litter on the rubble-strewn floor.

Arbaces, too, was encased in a cocoon of lava, preserved forever next to the shattered statue of Isis, whom he had never worshiped in life but with whom he would share an eternity of death.

The molten mass crept slowly over Julia and Clodius, and sealed them together in death as they had never been in life.

Out in the sea, as the night began to change into a smoky gray dawn, many of the survivors slept on their ships, recovering from their close calls with death. Others stared numbly.

On Glaucus' ship, Ione slept with her head upon her

savior's chest, drawing comfort from his warmth, secure now beneath the gentle stroking of his hand on her hair.

Lydon sat next to Nydia, staring out at the dead city, mourning for his father. Chloe's son slept peacefully on the small blanket next to them. Nydia, understanding many things about herself for the first time, gently took Lydon's hand in hers.

"Lydon," she whispered.

Lydon turned to look at Nydia's young face, and suddenly he saw within it the very thing he had been hoping and praying for. A tear fell slowly from her eye, and Lydon, his throat tight with emotion, gently wiped it away. As he did, he left his hand on her cheek, caressing her soft skin.

"Lydon, I . . ."

"I know, I see it on your face," he said, a moment before he bent to kiss her.

A few feet away, on the prow of the small ship, Olinthus knelt, gazing at the now visible mountain. Smoke still rose from its shattered peak, and jagged red streaks were sown through the clouds of ash and dust. His eyes filled with tears and his voice was thick with emotion as he began to speak.

"Dear God, I thank you for this gift of life, for this new day which I had never thought to see. I had hoped for heaven, and do still; yet, now I understand you have more work for me."

As these words carried into the air, the sun rose over the horizon and illuminated his bearded face with a soft, gentle glow. "Let me do it well, God. Let me do it well."

Olinthus rose then, and saw that Glaucus and Ione were coming toward him, followed by Lydon and Nydia, who carried the baby in her arms.

"Let us look our last upon this place," he said to them, sweeping his arm toward the shore, "and then turn away, forever."

Their eyes rose to the top of Vesuvius, and to the dark, mushroom-shaped cloud that hung above it. Their eyes traveled along its blackened slopes until they were at last staring at the smoldering city itself, half buried in lava and ash.

"See the ashes of Pompeii, and in them read the future of the empire, which will one day die by its own evil hand. But it will not be an easy death, my children. We, and others like us, may have to spend the lives that God has spared us locked in battle against the Roman sword, his justice against its inhumanity, his love against its hate.

"But fight we will," Olinthus continued in a strong, powerful voice that rang out clearly over the ship. "And as we fight, we'll grow, until our legions swell beyond Rome's own, until at last our God brings order from the chaos man has made of his once perfect world."

Then a gust of wind whispered softly. The scarlet sails began to fill with wind, billowing out and stretching tautly. Moments later the ship began to sail away from the dead port city of Pompeii.

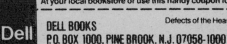

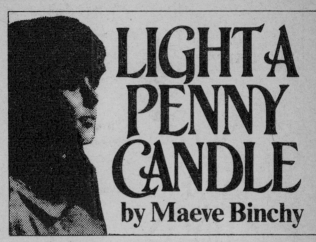